ALSO BY E.E. HOL

DAUGHTERS OF SEA AND STORM

THE VESPER COVEN
BOOK 1

E.E. HOLMES

FAIRHAVEN PRESS

Fairhaven Press

Townsend, MA

www.eeholmes.com

ISBN 978-1-956656-13-8 (Paperback edition)

ISBN 978-1-956656-12-1 (Barnes & Noble edition)

ISBN 978-1-956656-11-4 (Digital edition)

Publisher's note: This is a work of fiction. Names, characters, places and incidents are either the product of the author's imagination or are used fictitiously.

Cover design by James T. Egan of Bookfly Design LLC

Author photography by Cydney Scott Photography

For Susan, with all my love from one book-loving heart to another.

"A bird is safe in its nest—but that is not what its wings are made for."
    — **Amit Ray**

PROLOGUE

On stormy nights, I dream of the Gray Man.

  He holds my hand and walks with me through an ocean of swaying marsh grasses beneath a mass of rolling thunderclouds. The wind whips my hair around my face, and I can see the white caps on the roiling ocean in the distance.

  I call him the Gray Man because that is all I can see of him. In the gathered darkness, his features are blurred and dark, his figure solid and yet somehow not, a companion seemingly composed of shadow or smoke. I have to look up at him, and he down at me. My bare feet in the sand have the pudgy dimpled toes of early childhood.

  As we walk, he whispers to me.

  What he whispers, I can never remember when I wake up; when I try to recall the words, I hear only the susurration of the sea breeze through the dunes and the gentle rolling of distant thunder. But in the dream, I nod my head along to his murmurs as though he is speaking the very truths that nestle in my little heart.

  We stop at the edge of the dunes, where the long grasses give way to a stretch of sand bleached white in the storm-drenched darkness. I look out to the crashing waves beyond. I can hear them calling to me, an ancient song. The Gray Man bends low and whispers in my ear, and though I hear only the moan of the wind and the crackle of lightning, I understand him. I know what will happen next.

The Gray Man and I, hand in hand, will walk into the sea.

I feel no fear, no trepidation. I only know that disappearing into the raging waters with the Gray Man by my side will be the most natural thing in the world. My childish heart does not pound, but thrums peacefully, like the purring of a contented cat.

I am ready. I have always been ready.

The sand compresses beneath my feet. I leave a trail of sunken crescent moons behind me. He leaves no footprints at all. I look up at his face, the question in my eyes. The answer he murmurs to me satisfies my youthful curiosity and fades immediately from my memory.

At last the water licks at our toes, sending a delightful shiver up my spine. We pause only a moment before we walk forward, churning water swirling and bubbling up over my ankles, my calves, weighing down the hem of my white summer dress.

The wind howls my name, and the Gray Man's hand tightens around mine. I look up at him.

At the absence of him.

He is gone, and I am already forgetting what he looks like when I hear my name again. I'm suddenly cold and afraid. A frantic hand grips my shoulder. I turn.

And I wake up.

1

I had only a handful of memories of my grandmother, like glittering stones tucked away in a childhood pocket. Whenever I would take one out and turn it over in my palm to examine it like a secret treasure, I was always struck by how each one felt more like a dream than an actual memory, hazy around the edges and full of tiny details that I decided afterward certainly couldn't have been true.

But they were true. This I knew as well as I knew my own name.

My grandmother, Asteria Vesper, swept into my life once a year on my birthday, from my earliest memories until the day I turned ten years old. She arrived in a whirl of color and sparkle and barely tamed energy like a gift I couldn't wait to unwrap. And my mother opened the door to her every year with an expression of stony resignation, like she was doing it against her better judgment.

Because she was.

"Wren! Where's my little guiding star?" came that musical voice, and I would stumble forward into her arms, where I would be enveloped in a heady perfume of herbs and oils and florals that made me deliciously dizzy.

"I missed you, Asteria!" I would cry, for Asteria would have none of those matronly titles associated with grandmothers.

"I have a name and prefer to be called by it," she would say. "My name is my power and my song. Why would I want another?"

My mother rolled her eyes at this, but I would remember it for years afterward. Sometimes, I would whisper my own name into the silence as I lay in bed, listening for that music and power that Asteria claimed a name could contain. All I ever heard was my own uncertain voice curling up into a question mark in the darkness.

Asteria always brought a gift for me, but she never wrapped it. Instead, she made me hunt for it through the dozens of pockets and pouches of her flowing skirts and dresses, or else guess which of the bangles or rings or necklaces was for me among the jingling collection she always wore that made her sound like a human windchime. I would finger each bauble reverently, as though the right one would speak to me if I only knew its language. When I finally closed my shaking fingers around one, looking up at Asteria with the unspoken question in my eyes, the answer was always the same.

"You found it! However did you know?" Asteria cried, and plucked the item from her person at once to present to me. When I was very small, this would fill me with a kind of wonder at my own cleverness. By the time I was ten, logic had begun to creep in to spoil the magic of the little birthday ritual, and I began to suspect that my grandmother was simply allowing me to select my own gift, and that there never could be a wrong answer, whatever I chose.

It was this yearly ritual of choosing a gift that always seemed to wind my mother up into a tense coil. She would stand silently by, watching with her arms crossed tightly over her chest and her lips pressed together. When I held up my new treasure for her to see, her response was always the same.

"It's very nice, Wren. Say thank you to Asteria," she said, the words ground out through clenched teeth.

Although my mother would not admit it, I knew that my tenth birthday gift was the reason Asteria never came back again. The morning of my birthday that year had arrived wrapped in a warm, foggy drizzle. From the moment I woke up, I waited breathlessly for Asteria to appear out of that fog like a dream out of slumber. When she finally swept into our apartment that evening, there were tiny beads of moisture glittering in her hair and on her skin so that she looked half made up of starlight.

"I can hardly call you my Little Bird anymore! Look how tall and graceful you're growing to be!" Asteria had proclaimed, looking me over.

I mumbled my thanks, though I knew Asteria's words to be a lie. I'd shot up nearly three inches in only a few months, and I was all angles and knobbly knees with frizzy hair and a mouthful of braces. I'd never felt less graceful in my life, and if I resembled a bird at all, it was surely the drabbest, most awkward of flamingos.

I shuffled forward for my hug as usual, feeling unaccountably shy until I breathed in the familiar scent of her and felt my diffidence melt away. She pulled me back and took my face between her hands, staring down into my face with an inscrutable expression.

"A blessed tenth year to you, my darling," she whispered.

"You know, Mom, usually people just say, 'happy birthday,'" my mother suggested.

"When have I ever been interested in what other people usually do?" Asteria retorted with a jingling wave of her hand.

I must have been shooting a covetous look at the source of the jingling, for Asteria's face broke into a wide smile. "Ah, wondering already what the birthday gift will be, I see."

I had the good grace to flush as I shook my head vigorously. "No, I was just..."

"Ah, your tenth year is a special milestone. It requires a special gift, don't you think?" she interjected.

My heart performed a little flip inside my chest. "A special gift?"

"*Mom...*" my own mother's voice carried a sharp warning in it. I scented the danger at once, but Asteria chose to ignore it.

"That's right. A very special gift indeed, and it's not hanging around my neck or my wrist this time. Would you like to guess what it is?"

I stood there stupidly, my mouth opening and closing like a fish. The truth was that my mind could not conceive of what Asteria would consider a special gift. Everyone else I knew got gift cards or cash from their grandparents. Somehow, I knew there would be nothing of that sort tucked away in Asteria's sweeping collection of trailing skirts or dangling pouches. And so I just shrugged helplessly.

"No? Well, why don't you have a little peek in here, then, and see if you can figure it out," Asteria whispered conspiratorially.

I caught one glimpse of my mother's furious face before Asteria turned me from her and beckoned me to open a patchwork bag she carried on her hip. I tugged at the drawstring and pulled the mouth wide, peering down into it. At first, I didn't understand what I was looking at until Asteria reached down into the bag and pulled out a fluffy black ball that blinked bemusedly up at me from sleepy, grass-green eyes.

"No way!" I gasped as she deposited the kitten into my trembling hands. She was warm and thrumming with life, and the moment I scooped her to my chest, she began to purr contentedly.

"Mom, I need to talk to you. *Now.*"

Even Asteria couldn't ignore the storm now brewing in my mother's words. She looked up and smiled coolly. "Of course, Kerridwen. I'm always happy to talk to you; surely you know that."

"Do not call me Kerridwen."

"That's your name."

"And it's ridiculous, which is why I go by Kerri," my mother replied. She turned to me. "Wren, take that kitten to your room, please."

"Can I keep her?" I begged breathlessly, clutching the still purring kitten to my chest. "Please, Mom, I'll take such good care of her, you'll never have to—"

"We'll talk about it later. Do as I say, please, and take her to your room."

I did as I was bid, my heart pounding painfully already at the thought of being separated from this thrumming ball of life cradled against my chest. I felt as though she had become inextricably part of me the moment Asteria had placed her in my hands. What would I do if my mother made Asteria take her away again? A sob lodged itself in my throat and sat there stubbornly. I had to know. I wouldn't be able to breathe until I knew.

I walked all the way down the hallway, slapping my feet against the floor-boards louder than was necessary. Then I opened my bedroom door and shut it again before creeping halfway back down the hallway to listen. The argument had already begun.

"...know that I don't want to get her caught up in all of that, and you go and give her a... a..."

"It's a *kitten.* Lots of little girls have kittens, Kerridwen."

"It's *Kerri,* and don't talk to me like I'm an idiot! It's not just a kitten. I'm your daughter. You think I don't know when you're up to something?"

"Kerri, you can't keep her from this forever."

"Watch me."

"It's who she is."

"You don't know that yet."

"Fine, then, it's who *you* are!"

"Not anymore, Mom."

A heavy silence settled over the kitchen. I could imagine the two of them staring holes through each other through nearly matching sets of gray-green eyes. It was Asteria's voice that finally cleaved the silence, cutting through it like a sharp and broken thing.

"You truly think it's that simple, to just walk away?"

"It's not simple at all. But I'm doing it. I've done it," my mother replied quietly.

"I don't believe that."

"Believe what you like. You always have."

A beat, and then...

"I'd like to say goodbye to her before I go."

"Fine, but make it quick, and remember the rules. Not that you ever have before."

A swishing sound signaled Asteria's exit from the kitchen. I had only seconds before she swept into the hallway and saw me standing there, eavesdropping. I scuttled back to my bedroom door like a frightened mouse and slipped inside. When Asteria opened the door a few moments later, my kitten and I were huddled together on the bed, waiting for her.

Asteria sighed as she floated down to rest on the edge of the bed like a leaf on a breeze. "I'm afraid I have to go, my Little Bird."

"But you just got here," I argued. I could hear the note in my voice, that sound that was almost the whine of a younger version of myself, but I didn't care. I didn't want her to go.

"I must do as your mother wishes... for now," she said, and gave me a little wink.

"But why?"

"Because she loves you. And sometimes a love so big can be hard to see around. It crowds your vision; obscures it. But one day she'll see again. We must be patient."

I couldn't help it. My eyes filled with tears. I dropped my head so that my hair swung down over my face, hiding them.

Asteria let me have my moment to gather myself. She wasn't one of those grandmothers who smothered you with kisses. She gave a kid space to just be. Instead, she reached out and stroked the tiny kitten's forehead.

"You'll have to give her a name. Make sure it's a name that is worthy of what she can become—a name she can grow into, all right?"

I nodded, though I wasn't sure what she meant. At last, I had blinked the tears away and it felt safe to raise my head. When I did, it was to find Asteria looking at me, staring into my eyes as though hungering for something she didn't see there yet.

"You'll find your way back to who you're meant to be, Little Bird. I promise you that," she whispered.

She reached out to touch my cheek, just a gentle stroke of a fingertip, and then she was gone, sweeping from the room and leaving me to fill the absence of her as best I could.

It was the last time I would ever see her.

2

Six years later to the day, I woke up to a room full of streamers and balloons.

I sat up and rubbed the sleep from my eyes, blinking around at the decorations. My mom had even strung up a banner over my computer desk that read "Happy Sweet Sixteen!" in Barbie-pink letters on cardboard cupcakes. Pink wasn't really my thing, but I smiled up at it anyway.

The decorations weren't actually a surprise. For the past six years, my mother had crept into my room the night before my birthday and decorated in the dark while I slept. The problem was that she wasn't exactly quiet, and I was a light sleeper, and so every year I kept my eyes closed and tried not to laugh as I listened to her clamber around on my furniture and whisper strings of curse words as she struggled with tape and scissors and string. Still, I loved her for doing it—even if I knew she was trying to fill the hole of another, now defunct birthday tradition. As though to underscore the thought, my cat Freya leapt up onto the bed to demand scritches, which I happily supplied.

"Happy 'gotcha day', Freya," I whispered to her.

I rolled over and spotted the birthday card my mom had put on my bedside table. I read it—it was cheesy, but sweet. There was no present, because she'd already done what I'd begged her to do and transferred some money into my savings account, currently nicknamed "Wren's Car Fund." Tossing the card aside, I stumbled out of bed, maneuvered through the curtain of streamers, and made my way into the bathroom. I showered, got dressed, and packed up my backpack before heading out toward the kitchen. The tantalizing smell of chocolate chip pancakes and bacon wafted down the hallway, and I walked in to find my mom at the stove, already in her scrubs, with her wet hair hoisted up into a bun. She turned and smiled at me.

"There she is! Happy birthday, honey!"

"Thanks, Mom," I said as I flopped into one of the chairs. She plopped a plate of pancakes down in front of me and kissed me on the head.

"Do you want me to drive you this morning?" she asked as she sat down across from me, munching a piece of bacon. "I've got time if you—"

"No, no, that's okay," I said, looking out the window. "It looks nice. I'll take my bike today so that I can get home after rehearsal."

She frowned. "I'm so sorry I have to work. Are you sure you don't mind me missing the performance tonight? Maybe I could get someone to cover the last hour for me."

It took several seconds of chewing before I could answer. "Mom, stop. It's fine, seriously. I'm not even onstage."

"I know, but—"

I put up a hand. "Stop apologizing. It's my birthday. I command it."

My mom chuckled. "Okay, okay." She got up to make herself a plate of pancakes. "Did you turn in your creative writing paper?"

I nodded. "I just have to get through my chem final this morning and the performance tonight, and I'm done."

At that moment, my phone buzzed in my pocket and I pulled it out. A text from my best friend, Poe Reyes, blinked up at me, full of party horn and heart emojis.

Happy birthday, bestie! See you at rehearsal later! Good luck with chem!

Thanks, I texted back. *At least I can escape the embarrassing locker decorations and hallway singing this year.*

Don't be so sure about that, she replied with a string of winking emojis. Poe was one of those people who enjoyed other people's birthdays even more than her own.

I smiled. My birthday always coincided with the end of the school year, but this was the first time it had fallen on the actual last day of classes. I was really looking forward to celebrating the start of summer, as well as my first taste of adulthood. Sixteen was a milestone birthday, after all. I was old enough to get a summer job and old enough to drive. Suddenly, my world seemed full of possibilities, and I was so excited about all the things that would be happening that I almost forgot about the thing that wouldn't be happening.

No visit from Asteria. Again.

I tried not to let it bother me, but I couldn't help it. The silence was always loudest on this day. Six years without a visit, a card, a letter. It was hard not to resent my mother over it, but I'd given up asking her for an explanation. The answer was always the same.

"Wren, I need you to trust me. This is best for everyone. Life with Asteria in it is too... too complicated."

It wasn't an answer; in fact, it was the opposite of an answer. But this year, at least, I could see a light at the end of the answerless tunnel. In a few short months, I would have my license. I was planning to save every penny of the money I made this summer scooping ice cream to put toward my own car. And once I had that, I was free—free to drive right to the tiny coastal town where Asteria lived, knock on the door, and reintroduce myself. Whatever reasons my mother had for keeping us apart, they wouldn't matter anymore. I intended to see just how "complicated" life with Asteria could be, and there wasn't a damn thing my mom could do about it. I wasn't exactly a rebellious teenager, but this, I knew, would be one situation in which I intended to show her just how teenager-y I could be.

"What are you thinking about?" Mom asked, her brow furrowed, and I realized I'd been silent for too long. I mustered up a smile.

"Just finals today. But it'll be fine. I studied."

She looked at me hard, mouth half-open, like she wanted to say something. But then, a moment later, she closed it again, reached out, and mussed my hair.

"Of course it'll be fine. It's your birthday, after all."

Three hours later, I arrived at the theater, happily allowing my brain to forget all the chemistry formulas I'd unceremoniously crammed into it over the last twenty-four hours. I'd finished early, and my teacher had allowed me to turn in my paper and leave. It was relatively quiet now, but in a few minutes, students would be thronging the halls, some celebrating loudly and throwing binders into garbage cans, others shouting their goodbyes and wishes for a great summer. I slipped into the cool, dark haven of the theater, let the door close behind me, and left them all behind.

A single bare bulb, glowing and white like a skull, hung suspended in the darkness. The halo of light it cast was barely enough to cut through the gloom, but it was a gloom I knew well. Anyone else would have stumbled or fallen over something, but not me. I could maneuver this space with my eyes closed —and they may as well have been. The light flickered once, twice. The only sound in the cavernous space was the quiet buzzing of the charge coursing through the filament.

I sighed contentedly. In the barely controlled chaos of high school, this was home.

My footsteps echoed hollowly as I crossed the floor toward the light. The floorboards beneath my feet were painted black and dotted with bits of brightly colored tape, which helped me avoid obstacles as I closed the last of the distance between myself and the light. I stared into it for a moment, hypnotized by the elongated shadows it cast around the space. As I watched, my own shadow twisted oddly, almost like it was peeling itself away from the wall. I gazed at it, fascinated for a moment. Then I reached behind the curtain, mashed my hand against the bank of switches, and the theater was flooded with light.

Ahead of me, out of the darkness reared row upon row of seats upholstered in faded red velvet. Above my head, drops and flats were suspended in shadowy relief in the flies. And on the stage floor, the formerly threatening shapes looming up around me resumed their true forms: several wooden cubes, painted black, and a battered old kitchen table and chairs rescued from the aisles of the local Goodwill. As I reached down to unplug and put away the ghost light at the edge of the stage, I heard the bell and then a great rumbling, like an earthquake, erupting from every side.

Class dismissed.

"Let the chaos commence in three, two, one..." I muttered to myself.

Right on cue, the backstage door burst open and my best friend Poe came flying into the auditorium.

"Wren, how did you get here so fast?" Poe gasped. "My final was literally next door. Did you teleport or something?"

I smiled. "Ms. Kremer let me go early because I finished my test. And Mr. Pisani asked me to come get things set up for the rehearsal. He has his end of the year faculty meeting after school, so he's gonna be late."

"Ooh, good, that means you have time to run lines with me, but first... TA-DA!" She flashed her million-watt smile and pulled a birthday tiara and sash out of her backpack.

"Absolutely not," I protested, backing away from her, but she completely ignored me.

"Don't be difficult. You know I'm going to make you wear it anyway, so you might as well bow to the inevitable," she sang, kissing me on the cheek as she perched the tiara on my head.

Poe Reyes had been my best friend since we were the only two kids in Mrs. O'Connell's first-grade class to wear glasses. One look at each other's self-conscious little faces, and we were bonded for life. Of course, a few years later, Poe's parents got her contacts, whereas I was still pushing my tortoise-shell frames up the bridge of my nose every thirty seconds.

We had also bonded over our unusual first names. My mother said that when I was born, I was scrawny, all eyes, and that I threw my head back when I cried, just like a little baby bird—hence the name. I'd seen a lot of pictures of baby birds since then, and I was pretty sure I should be offended, but my mother swears she meant it "in a cute way," whatever that means. Poe's mother, meanwhile, had gone through this kind of rebellious goth phase in her early twenties that she hadn't quite gotten over when she had Poe, and decided to name her one and only daughter after the American master of Gothic fiction. Poe thought her mother probably regretted it, but also that she would basically rather die than admit it, especially in front of Poe's *lola*.

Poe was the kind of pretty you usually only saw in magazines—her olive skin was flawless and her long black hair shone like she was some tower-trapped princess who had nothing better to do but sigh with timeless longing while she brushed it a hundred times a day. At least seven boys at Portland High School were hopelessly in love with her—like, the kind of love that results in cringeworthy grand gestures in the middle of crowded cafeterias—but Poe could not have been less interested. She had her sights set on Broadway, and high school boyfriends were just one more distraction on her road to the Tony Awards.

I let her drape the sash over my shoulder with a long-suffering sigh.

"Are you happy now?"

"Delighted," she said, stepping back to admire my transformation into a mortified birthday princess. "So now that I've tortured you appropriately... lines?"

I pulled out one of the chairs onstage and plopped myself into it, flipping open Poe's script to her scene. She had every line highlighted, and there were several sticky tabs with notes on them stuck to every page. "Poe, why are we bothering? You've had this memorized for weeks."

Poe shrugged, settling into the chair across from me. "It's different when I'm just saying them to myself. It's better when someone else reads with me."

As I stumbled my way through Demetrius's lines opposite Poe's Helena, I could feel my cheeks burning, which was stupid, because Poe was the only other person in the room. But I couldn't help it. I knew the script as well as she did—better, even. As the stage manager, I was constantly on-book for everyone else, feeding them their lines from the house when they flubbed them—which in Poe's case was never, but in everyone else's was frequent. As a result, I could likely have jumped up on stage and played any one of their parts, word-perfect. Of course, that would mean overcoming my crippling stage fright, which was definitely not in the cards. That was how I'd fallen into stage management in the first place. Poe had dragged me along to auditions for the fall play our freshman year—I mean, *literally* dragged me; like, I'm pretty sure there were long scuff marks on the linoleum from my shoes. I managed to stand up in front of the director with the script in my hand without passing out, but not a sound would come out of my mouth. Mr. Pisani took one look at me, legs trembling, hyperventilating, and said, "You know, we're looking for an assistant stage manager."

And that had been it. Now I pulled the strings from dark corners of the wings and from the safety of the tech booth where no one could see me. I made magic invisibly, and I loved it.

The rest of the cast began trickling into the theater, and I tossed Poe her script back.

"Congratulations, you're still memorized," I told her.

Poe snatched at the script and buried herself in it as though determined to find a spot where she might have screwed up. She wouldn't find one.

"Mr. Pisani's notes from the last rehearsal are on the call board!" I called over the chatter of arriving actors, and there was a general groan as people pulled out their scripts and notebooks and congregated around the neatly typed pages pinned to the corkboard. Poe scrambled over to join them and our friend Charlie took her place at the table.

"Just a heads up, Roman is not happy about his costume for the Midsummer scene," Charlie announced in a weary sort of voice.

I groaned. "Of course he isn't. What happened?"

Charlie sighed, running a hand through their short blue hair. "Well, he stormed out of his fitting yesterday saying he was going to quit the show if he had to wear 'that girly ruffled blouse thing.'" Charlie made sure to add enthusiastic air quotes and imitated Roman's deep voice for good measure.

"It's not a girly blouse, it's a poet's shirt and it fits the time period!" I said.

"That's what I told him. I even showed him the book we were using for historical accuracy. Would you like to know his thoughtful and measured reply?"

"Probably not?"

Charlie pressed their mouth against their palm and made a long, loud fart noise that echoed across the theater and made several people giggle.

"That, of course, is an approximation," Charlie said, rolling their eyes.

"Oh, for God's sake," I groaned. "Fine, I will talk to him. But before I do, just... remind me why we put up with him?" I muttered.

"Because he's tall and not completely talentless and he reads straight, which, in the world of public high school theater, makes him practically a unicorn," Charlie replied evenly.

"I refuse to believe we're that desperate," I grumbled.

"Well, it doesn't matter now. The performance final is tonight and we're stuck with him," Charlie said resignedly. "Just... do what you can before I lose it completely and make him wear the bear costume."

Charlie was always threatening to make people wear the bear costume, even though no one had even touched the thing since probably the 1970s. It hung, dusty and drooping, in the rafters of the costume shop like a moth-eaten trophy a hunter had shot and then forgotten to stuff properly. I will never forget being sent up to the shop to fetch something during a stormy evening rehearsal freshman year and having the living daylights scared out of me when a flash of lightning illuminated the thing like a monster from a horror movie.

By now most people had scribbled down their notes and settled into the red-upholstered seats in little clustered groups. The chatter was louder than usual, as this rehearsal—and the night's performance—were the only things standing between us and the freedom of vacation. I squinted into the dark beyond the stage lights and picked out Roman's tall, lanky form toward the back of the house. I descended the steps and marched up the aisle. I could already feel my palms sweating, because I hated confrontation almost as much as I hated acting.

"Roman, can I talk to you for a second?" I said, coming to a stop beside him.

"I guess so," Roman said, digging noisily into a bag of chips.

"You aren't supposed to eat those in here," I said.

"I'm hungry. Finals are hard work."

I rolled my eyes but decided to pick my battle. "Whatever, just don't let Mr. Pisani see you, and try not to get crumbs everywhere. I need to talk to you about your costume."

"Good, so you think it's hideous, too?" Roman asked through a mouthful of chips.

"No, I came to say that you have to wear it. Everyone has to wear the costumes they are assigned. They fit the time period and Charlie worked very hard to design them."

"This is such bullshit. First, Mr. Pisani cuts the fight scene, and now I have to go onstage looking like a—"

"Like a *what*?" I asked, and there was a warning in my voice. *Go ahead and say it, so I have a reason to kick your ass right out of this production*, I thought to myself.

Unfortunately, even Roman knew where that line was, and he swallowed the rest of his sentence with an ugly grimace. "Whatever. Never mind. You know, I could just drop out of the show."

I wish, I said silently. Aloud, I said, "Well, sure, you could. But then you'd fail your final and you wouldn't have enough credits to graduate. Seems like a waste of a perfectly good swimming scholarship just because you don't like the shirt you have to wear for all of five minutes, but obviously, the choice is yours."

Roman glared at me, chewing loudly.

"Fine. I'll wear the costume. It's bad enough we have to perform Shakespeare and a bunch of dead Greek dudes..."

"Roman, it's a *classical* theater showcase," I ground out. "Did you read the description before signing up for the class, or did you just close your eyes and point randomly at the course catalog?"

"Couldn't we at least do it like that movie we watched in English class of Romeo and Juliet? The one with the car chases and the guns and the Hawaiian shirts? That was *sick*."

I pretended to write on my clipboard. "Car... chases... are... sick. Helpful feedback, thanks, Roman. I'll pass it along." Then I stalked back up the aisle and joined Poe, who had returned to studying her script. "One day. Just one last day and then school will be over and I won't have to deal with Roman Peterson in my theater ever again."

"Oh, so it's your theater now?" she asked, smirking.

"You know what I mean," I grumbled. "I'm the one who has to deal with his little diva fits."

"It could be worse," Poe said, looking up from her script to glare at me. "You could be the one who has to kiss him."

"Ew. Okay, you win," I said.

"Oh, I think we both know I lose."

At that moment the door at the back of the theater opened and Mr. Pisani, our director, swept down the aisle looking, as usual, like a slightly frantic former matinee idol—his thick salt-and-pepper hair swept back from his forehead and a harried expression on his face, like he'd only just escaped the clutches of the paparazzi outside the door; when in reality, all he'd escaped was a brief faculty meeting. He snatched the glasses hanging precariously from his black turtleneck and perched them on the end of his nose. Charlie and I hurried down to the edge of the stage and sat on the lip, waiting.

"I need everyone's attention please," Mr. Pisani called, his voice instantly filling the space with the kind of booming projection he could only rarely coax from his students. "We have a lot to get through if this show is going to be ready for an audience tonight. Wren, do you have the—"

But I was already holding the production clipboard out to him, and he took it with a nod of thanks before looking over the cover page. "Stage notes?" he asked.

"Everyone's taken them down," I confirmed.

"Final fittings?" he asked, looking at Charlie this time.

Charlie shot one last warning glare in Roman's direction, and Roman threw up his hands in silent surrender before Charlie replied, "All finished. Everyone's fully outfitted except for wigs because you said you wanted to—"

"Yes, yes, I'll handle the wigs," Mr. Pisani said. His single greatest horror in life was bad wigs. Well, that and faculty meetings during rehearsal time. "Props?"

"The tables are all set up and labeled. There are posters backstage so everyone can check which table their prop will be on and which table to return it to when they've finished," I confirmed.

"And if anyone touches the prop swords without permission?" Mr. Pisani asked the room at large.

"Slow and painful death," the cast chanted.

"Very good, thank you. Let's get started. Places for the top of the show!" He clapped his hands and the whole company sprang into action. I scuttled off to my place in the wings, donned my headset, and took a deep breath.

"Let's make some magic," I whispered.

3

A dispiriting three hours later, we were as far from magic as we could possibly get. The rehearsal had been a disaster from start to finish. Poe continued to be the only actor who didn't need to call for a line, the lighting board kept blacking out the stage lights, and no fewer than five people had been threatened with the aforementioned slow and painful death for dueling backstage with the prop swords they'd all promised not to touch. By the time the lights came up on the final scene, I was fighting a headache and glancing at the clock more often than I was glancing at the script. Above me, the stage lights flickered ominously again.

"Jayden, what is going on up there?" I whispered into the headset microphone hovering in front of my face.

"I don't know!" Jayden, the lighting designer, hissed back. "It's like the board's possessed today! Like, full-out haunted."

"Okay, well, I'm guessing that's probably not the actual problem, unless one of those idiots was a little too enthusiastic with the prop swords and we just haven't found the body yet," I said. "Besides, we don't have time for an exorcism. Did you check the cables? Last year someone used an audio cable by mistake and it screwed everything up."

"I'll have to wait until the rehearsal is over to get up in the—"

Jayden's answer was cut short as all the lights went out again. Mr. Pisani let out a string of curse words which were actually just the names of Broadway divas who sounded like swear words when spoken angrily.

"DAME JUDY DENCH, WILL SOMEONE PLEASE SORT OUT THAT LIGHTING BOARD!!!" he shouted.

"We're on it!" Jayden shouted from the booth. "Wren?"

"Yeah, I'm on my way up!" I replied, pulling the flashlight from the prompting table, and stomping my way over to the ladders. A swift climb later, and I was standing up in the catwalk, breathing in the familiar scent of sawdust, paint, and the warm tang of electricity buzzing all around me. I swung the flashlight around, illuminating the individual lamps and reading the chalk markings on them as I checked their connections. I was just about to call down to Jayden when a movement in my periphery distracted me. I turned my head, startled to find two glowing green eyes looking at me.

I shrieked and dropped my flashlight, scaring everyone below me.

"Wren? Are you okay?" Poe called.

The eyes hadn't so much as blinked. I cleared my throat. "Yeah, I'm fine," I managed to call out. I knelt down shakily, feeling around for the flashlight, unable to look away from those eyes.

Because they looked at me as though they knew me. And I knew them.

"Freya?" I whispered.

It was absurd to even consider it, because how on earth could my *cat* have gotten into the upper reaches of the fly space, let alone out of my apartment? The logical side of me knew it was impossible, and yet...

"Freya? Here, kitty!" I whispered even as I groped around for the flashlight which had rolled away from me. The eyes blinked and seemed to drift a bit closer.

"Wren? What's going on?" It was Jayden's voice that hollered up to me this time.

"I... I think there might be an animal up here!" I called back.

A number of reactions, from delight to disgust, rose from the company of students below me, but I ignored them. My fingers found the flashlight at last. I fumbled with the switch and swung the beam of light toward the eyes.

But there were no eyes. They were gone.

"Freya?" I whispered again, swinging the beam of the flashlight right and left across the scaffolding. There was an answering "meow" from behind me, and I wasn't quick enough to stifle the shriek that exploded out of me.

"Wren?! Oh my God, did you fall?" Poe's voice had gone up an octave in her hysteria.

"Of course I haven't fallen! Don't you think you'd notice my body hit the stage?" I called back. My terror had made me snippy. I spun on the spot, searching for any sign of Freya. There was a skittering sound, and a soft thump of landing paws. I spotted the glowing eyes again, this time nearly at the other end of the catwalk, a veritable forest of lamps and cords and railings between us. I shined the light toward her and illuminated what was, unmistakably, my cat.

"Freya, what are you—"

She hissed menacingly and I stepped back because I'd never heard her hiss before. It was then I realized her eyes were not fixed on me, but on something over my left shoulder. What happened next happened so fast that I couldn't even take it in.

I started to turn my head and was overwhelmed with a sudden whiff of salt air and petrichor. A strange whispering began in my ear, and my feet seemed to sink into the floor, like the metal grates had softened to sand. In the corner of my eye, a shape emerged from the shadows and yet, *was* the shadows...

"Wait, I think I've got it, let me just... yeah, I think this should do it!" I heard Jayden's triumphant cry from the booth as the lights hummed back to life, bathing the theater in a warm glow. The shape—if it had even been there in the first place—was gone. The familiar smells of sawdust and paint filled my nose as I sucked in a startled breath. I spun on the spot, but Freya was nowhere to be seen. I walked the full length and breadth of the catwalk whispering for her, but she was gone. I climbed down the ladder to the stage, my heart still pounding.

"Wren, are you okay? You look like you've seen a ghost. Wait, *did* you see a ghost? Is the theater haunted? Oh, God, it is, isn't it, I can tell from your face." Poe said all of this in one breathless jumble the moment my feet hit the stage floor.

"Calm down, Poe, I didn't see a ghost," I said with more conviction than I felt, because I wasn't at all sure what I'd seen. If it had really been Freya, how had she gotten there and where had she gone? And if it hadn't been Freya... well, "ghost" wasn't exactly the word I would use, but I'd definitely seen *something*. And then there was the figure in the shadows... but surely *that* hadn't been real. I pushed it firmly out of my mind as nothing more than the specter of a childhood nightmare.

"Everything all right up there?" Mr. Pisani asked, and I wondered what my own face must look like to cause so much concern in his. I took a deep breath and composed myself, even managing a smile.

"All fine. I think there might have been an animal up there... a bird maybe."

"Patti LUPONE, that's all we need, a pigeon trying to do a star turn in the middle of our performance. I'll speak with the custodian and ask him to check the vents up there before tonight," he said, removing his glasses and pinching the bridge of his nose, a classic sign that he was about to end rehearsal in a dramatic huff.

Five minutes later, huff over and done with, I was biking home as fast as my legs could pedal. Poe had begged to take me out for birthday coffee, but I made a hurried excuse as I climbed on my bike.

"But you need birthday treats!" she insisted.

"I'll see you tonight!" I called over my shoulder. "Bring me a cupcake or something!"

Our apartment was on the third floor of a renovated Victorian in downtown Portland, only about a ten-minute ride from my high school, but the ride home had never seemed longer. All along the way, while looking out for cars and pedestrians, I was also peering into every shadowy corner for a glimpse of a bottlebrush tail or a pair of green eyes. My heart was threatening to pound straight out of my chest, between the breakneck speed and my mounting fear. If Freya was gone... if she'd gotten out somehow...

Freya and I had been inseparable since the moment six years ago when Asteria had placed her into my hands, a mewling little ball of fluff. Even my mother, as angry as she'd been at Asteria for gifting me a live animal without her permission, had taken one look at the two of us cuddled up in my bed, and knew it was a lost cause. She trudged out to the pet store first thing in the morning and bought a litter box with only minimal grumbling. After some internet searching, I'd identified my kitten as a Norwegian forest cat, and because I was a huge nerd, I went down a Norse mythology rabbit hole to find her a name, settling on Freya, a goddess who traveled around in a chariot pulled by two gigantic cats.

I'd looked over at the snoozing fluffball on my bed and whispered, "Freya?"

She had lifted her head at once, looked straight at me with those glowing green eyes, and mewed her approval, officially claiming the name for herself.

The thought that she might not come slinking around the corner when I called for her made me feel like a great crushing fist had closed over my heart. I could hardly breathe as I skidded around the corner to our driveway. I abandoned my bicycle against the house and took the steps two at a time all the way to our door. I cursed my shaking hands as I fumbled awkwardly with my keys, but finally, the door swung inward and I practically fell inside.

"Freya! Where are you, sweet girl?" I called, tears thick in my throat.

She's gone, she's gone, she's...

A little mewling sound preceded the appearance of Freya from my bedroom, looking at me with an almost impatient expression as though to say, "Where have you *been*?"

I let out a sob of relief and dropped to my knees in the hallway, reaching for her. She trotted toward me and climbed at once into my lap. I scooped her into my arms and buried my face in her gloriously fluffy coat. She tolerated my emotional display for a minute or two, and then gave an impatient little huff as she tried to extricate herself.

"Sorry," I mumbled, releasing my too-tight grip and placing her back in my lap, where she was content to sit, staring solemnly up at me.

I stared back at her, wishing, as I always did, that she could speak.

"What were you doing at the theater?" I whispered.

She tilted her head and blinked, and then startled as I burst into laughter.

"I really must be losing it. First, I convince myself you're in the rafters of the theater when you've obviously never left the house, and now I'm interrogating you like you're going to open your mouth and answer me." I scratched Freya behind the ears. "Let's chalk it up to pre-show stress, okay? I promise I'm not crazy."

Freya yawned pointedly.

I scooped her up and carried her into the kitchen. Maybe my nerves were still frayed from the rehearsal because she wriggled impatiently, and I realized I was probably holding her too tightly.

"Sorry," I whispered to her as I put her down again. "I'm just really glad you're here."

I dropped my backpack on one of the kitchen chairs, opened the fridge, and started rummaging through the take-out containers and Tupperware of leftovers for something to eat. There were a few pancakes left, and though I was tempted, I decided I should probably eat something a little more substantial if I was going to make it through the show that night. I pulled the cover off a bowl to inspect the contents and then pulled back, retching slightly.

"Oh God, we really need to clean out this fridge," I coughed and turned to dump the contents in the trash, but I froze.

On top of the junk mail and eggshells and extra streamers was an envelope with my name handwritten on it. I tossed the Tupperware into the sink and bent down to snatch it up. Why the hell was my mom throwing out my mail? I flipped it over to see that the envelope had already been torn open. And reading it?

I pulled a letter out of the envelope and as I unfolded it, something small fell out of it. Instinctively, I reached a hand under it and caught it before it hit the floor. I stared down at it, bemused. It was a small pouch made of purple velvet strung on a fine golden chain. I tried to open it, but it was sewn shut with gold thread. I turned it over in my hand. It smelled of lavender and the ocean, as well as other scents I couldn't quite place.

"What the—?"

I looked down at the letter and began to read.

Dearest Wren,

Happy sixteenth birthday, my Little Bird, though I fear you are not so little anymore. I am sorry to have missed so much time with you, but now that you are a young woman, I hope you can accept this token of my affection and my apologies that I have not been able to see you. Please don't blame your mother. She only wants to protect you, and while I certainly don't want to be the means of driving a wedge between you, I can no longer be silent. There are things you must be told—truths that must be revealed to you, and I fear that your mother cannot see that. Come to me this summer as soon as you can, and until then, please promise me you will wear this charm. For protection. For guidance.

With all my love for a blessed year,

Asteria

I read the letter through three times, once in the numbness of shock, once more in the hopes of gleaning deeper meaning, and one final time as I allowed every feeling to bubble up to the surface. The first wave of emotion was anger. I couldn't believe my mother would simply throw this letter away—how could she do such a thing? And then I began to wonder how many other letters

Asteria may have written me, what other gifts she may have sent along tucked into envelopes that never found their way to me because of this bizarre paranoia of my mother, and the anger boiled over into fury.

I turned the little charm over and over between my fingers. I thought about Asteria's words: *"For protection. For guidance."* I couldn't really think of anything I needed protection against, except maybe arm muscle fatigue from an impending summer of ice cream scooping; but then, that was the kind of thing Asteria used to say all the time about the little trinkets she bestowed on me—I figured she was just a bit superstitious. There was something inside of the little pouch. I couldn't tell what it was simply by feeling it, but the herbal smell of it reminded me of those cherished birthday visits from Asteria, and so I put it on, feeling suddenly rebellious. Whatever Asteria's eccentricities, she was still my grandmother, and I was not going to be kept from her anymore. If my mother could lie to me, steal my mail, and throw away my birthday gifts, then she shouldn't be surprised when I abused her trust in return. I tucked the little pouch into my shirt and felt the comforting weight of it against my skin. It looked like the first place I'd be driving myself this summer was straight to Asteria's house for a long overdue visit, and there wasn't a damn thing my mother could do about it.

There are few places as superstitious as the theater, and one of those superstitions goes a little something like this: "A disastrous final dress rehearsal means a triumphant first performance." Was it just something theater folk told themselves to soothe frayed nerves and battered egos on the eve of opening night? Probably. But happily, on this particular night, it turned out to be true.

Well, okay, maybe "triumphant" was a bit of a reach. But as the curtain closed on final bows and the cast erupted into cheers, I tossed aside my headset with a satisfied sigh. The few flubbed lines had been well-covered by the better prepared actors. Everyone who was supposed to have a prop in their hand had managed to find it, and Jayden must have performed an exorcism on the light board because every cue worked like clockwork. Even Mr. Pisani looked smugly pleased as he swept backstage to congratulate everyone. And Roman Peterson could muster up nothing more offensive than pulling his poet's shirt over his head, dropping it to the stage floor and announcing that he never wanted to see it again.

Poe ran over to me and shifted her enormous bouquet of flowers to one arm so that she could hug me. "We did it!" she squealed.

"We did," I agreed. "And you were brilliant."

"Thanks," she said, and there was genuine relief in her voice. That was one of the great things about Poe; she was so talented that she probably could have gotten away with being an insufferable diva, but she wasn't. She treated every role like a challenge, not a crown that she got to flaunt at everyone else.

"I'm kind of shocked. I really didn't think it was going to come together," Poe admitted in a murmur.

"You're forgetting we say that about every show," Charlie said, sidling up to us and throwing an arm around each of us.

"Everyone looked great, too," I said.

Charlie inclined their head in acknowledgment. "Not bad, if I do say so myself. And I stitched a few extra ruffles onto Roman's shirt right before I gave it to him, just as a form of self-care."

"You're a legend," Poe declared.

"So, Franny's?" Charlie asked.

"Franny's," we both agreed.

Franny's was the local diner. It was like a 1950s time capsule, all silver chrome exterior, red leather booths, linoleum countertops and vintage Hollywood decor, but that wasn't why we frequented the place. The real appeal of Franny's was that it was within walking distance from the school with cheap food and late-night hours. It was sort of a theater kid tradition to flood the place after a show, everyone donning matching t-shirts and too much stage makeup. And luckily, Franny herself had a soft spot for us, having once performed in the ensemble of the original Broadway cast of "Applause." We tolerated her starry-eyed reminiscences of the New York theater scene in the 1970s, and in turn, she put up with the fact that we split our checks twenty ways and paid with crumpled piles of small bills and change.

My mom knew we would be at Franny's after the show, so I didn't bother texting her; she was at work anyway and probably wouldn't even be able to respond. Charlie already had their license, so it wasn't like I needed a ride home, and anyway, curfew was still a couple of hours away. So I was surprised to see my mom's number pop up on my phone before we'd even made a dent in our mountain of fries.

Wren, I need you to come home.

"What the hell?" I mumbled.

"What's wrong?" Poe asked, plucking another fry from the pile with greasy fingers.

"My mom just texted me to come home."

"What? Why? It's not even ten," Poe said, frowning.

I shrugged and then looked down at the text again, feeling resentful. No "How did it go?" or "Congratulations," just a demand to get home. My heart sank. Did she get home early and notice the letter from Asteria was no longer in the trash? Well, if she did, it wasn't as though I had anything to apologize for. After all, she was the one stealing other people's birthday gifts. All I did was take back what belonged to me in the first place.

We just started eating. Is it an emergency? I typed back.

I ate another fry as I watched the three little dots appear and then disappear as my mom evidently struggled with how to respond. Finally her reply popped up.

OK, just be quick and get home as soon as you can.

Everything okay?

Just be quick.

I put my phone away and tried to fall back into the post-show celebration routine, but my mind kept wandering back to the texts. It wasn't like my mom to be cryptic; in fact, she was usually embarrassingly blunt in that matter-of-fact way that nurses often had. I wanted to know what was going on, but a stubborn part of me refused to rush through our meal. I had earned this night out and so had my friends, and I resented that now I couldn't even enjoy it.

When Charlie dropped me off forty-five minutes later, I shut the door just a bit harder than was strictly necessary. The kitchen was empty, my mom's bag dumped unceremoniously on the table, her mostly empty water bottle beside it.

"Mom?" I called out. She didn't reply, but I thought I could hear her voice; it sounded like she was talking on the phone.

For some reason, this annoyed me. I slammed my bag down into the chair and started down the hallway toward the living room. As I got closer, I heard a snatch of the conversation and stopped, listening.

"...should have told me it was like that." A pause, and then, "Of course it would have mattered! How can you even say that?"

I couldn't imagine who my mother would be arguing with like that. I rounded the corner into the living room to see my mom sitting on the couch, her elbows on her knees and her head in her hand. I hesitated, hovering in the doorway.

"Of course we'll be there. Yes. Fine. Goodbye." My mother ended her call, lowered the phone to the table and pressed both hands over her face.

All of the anger and resentment drained out of me and I felt suddenly, terribly scared. "Mom?" The question in my voice made me sound like a child, and for a moment I felt like one, all knobbly knees and frizzy hair and a pounding heart.

My mom looked up, her eyes rimmed with red and glistening with tears.

"Mom, what is it? What's wrong?"

She reached a hand wordlessly out to me and I moved forward to take it. Only when her fingers were tightly closed around mine did she speak at last.

"We have to go to Sedgwick Cove, Wren. Your grandm—Asteria is dead."

4

My dreams that night were full of Asteria.

It had been almost six years since I'd seen her, and yet she appeared to me with a clarity that took my breath away. We didn't speak. She was simply there: now sitting on the end of my bed with Freya purring in her lap, now walking past me on a crowded street corner, now sitting in a chair across the room with a book in her hand. Each time I spotted her, she smiled at me and nodded her head, as though I'd done something to meet with her approval.

I lay in the dark when I woke up, staring up at the ceiling, half expecting her to appear there, still smiling enigmatically. If she had, I might have opened my mouth and whispered the shameful truth to her: that I didn't know how I was supposed to feel about the fact that she was gone. I wonder if she'd still be smiling then if she heard those words out loud.

Yes, she was gone. But she'd been gone for a long time.

I knew it wasn't Asteria's fault that I hadn't seen her since I was ten. It probably also wasn't her fault that I'd only seen her once a year before that. I'd sort of come to accept that Asteria was no longer a part of my life, and it had seemed like Asteria had accepted it, too. But the letter that had appeared for me yesterday had ripped that old wound open afresh. How many other letters had my mother intercepted? Had Asteria been writing to me for years, hoping for a reply that never came? The moment a relationship with my grandmother had once again become a possibility, it had been snatched away again in the most brutal way I could imagine. I felt like I had mental whiplash; my head spun, and I could hardly breathe. I wrapped my fingers around the charm that hung from my neck and squeezed it. It was now the last thing I'd ever receive from my grandmother.

And then there was my mom. I had absolutely no idea what to say to her. Every impulse to vent my anger about the letter shriveled into nothingness. How could I be mad at her when she'd just lost her own mother? I *was* mad, of course, but that anger didn't feel very important anymore. I'd lost the idea of Asteria, but my mom had lost the real thing. For all my mother had cut herself off from Asteria, it had never once occurred to me that she hated her. I sensed frustration and anger, but never, ever, hatred. Any time I summoned the courage to ask why we didn't see Asteria anymore, the answer was always the same; a deep sigh followed by the words, "Because my mother is impossible."

The words had made sense to me, but not in the way my mother meant them. Asteria had been impossible. Impossibly free. Impossibly unique. Impossibly like a dream. And now it was impossible that I would ever see her again. Impossible used to feel mysterious and intriguing. Now it felt like a door someone had slammed in my face just as I tried to step through it.

Morning came on the heels of broken and restless sleep, and I suddenly didn't have the time or the mental resources to dwell on it anymore. From the moment my mom dragged me out of bed, we were in a flurry of preparations. Bags had to be packed. Appointments had to be canceled. My mom was frantically trying to trade shifts with the other nurses in her unit to make sure she was covered.

"What about Freya?" I asked.

"We'll have to bring her. There's no time to find a pet sitter."

"She hates the car."

"Wren, we don't have a choice. Just get the crate ready and throw her food in the trunk."

Freya watched all of this chaos unfold with unbothered curiosity. Even the appearance of the dreaded pet carrier elicited little more than a disdainful glance.

I knew Poe wouldn't see my text until she woke up, and sure enough, a little after 10 a.m., my phone blew up.

OMG!!!!!! Oh Wren, I'm so sorry!!!!! What can I do??? Can I do anything????

I smiled down at the excessive punctuation. Poe was extremely close to her *lola*, so it was no surprise that she saw the situation as inherently traumatic. When your grandmother died, you were supposed to be inconsolable. Guilt burrowed into my guts like an animal, all claws and squirming warmth.

I'm okay, thanks. I'll be back in a few days. Sorry I won't be able to come to the beach tomorrow.

OMG why are you apologizing?! We can go to the beach anytime. Just let me know if you need anything.

I will. Love u.

Love u back.

I pocketed the phone again and looked over at Freya.

"Let's not make this any harder than it has to be, okay?" I murmured to her.

And, as if taking pity on me, she walked right into the carrier and settled herself down like a queen on a throne. Then she made a noise that sounded suspiciously like a sigh.

By ten thirty we were all packed up in my mom's old Subaru and on our way out of town. My mom was wearing her big sunglasses that obscured half her face and made me suspect she'd been crying again. We double parked outside our favorite cafe so she could run inside and grab our to-go order that was waiting for us on the counter. Lorelei, the owner, waved at me through the window, and I waved half-heartedly back.

We sipped on our lattes in silence as we drove out of the city, but it wasn't until we hit the long stretch of Route 1 North that would carry us most of the two-hour drive that I finally got up the courage to speak.

"Mom, what did Asteria die of?" I asked.

She hesitated for a moment before she said, "She died in her sleep. They think it was her heart."

"She had heart problems?"

"Not that I knew about."

I bit my lip. Of course my mother wouldn't have known if Asteria had heart problems. She hadn't seen or spoken to her in almost six years, as far as I knew. I wanted to ask her if she regretted that now, if she wished she'd changed her mind and reached out before it was too late, but I couldn't shake the words loose. Thankfully, my mom spared me from trying to figure out what to say next.

"I'm sorry you couldn't have had more of a relationship with your grandmother, Wren," she began, and there was a tremor in her voice I'd rarely heard there before. "I want you to understand that I would have liked it to be different. But among other things, your grandmother was a very stubborn woman. She demanded things be done her own way, or not at all. There was no compromise, no discussion. And in the end, I had to walk away, for both of our sakes."

I froze. My mom had just said more about Asteria in the last few minutes than she had in the last six years. Was I finally going to get some answers? "What was it she didn't want to compromise about?" I asked, hating the desperation in my voice.

Mom laughed a short bitter bark of a laugh. "Everything. Anything. But especially about Sedgwick Cove."

I held my breath. My mother never talked about Sedgwick Cove, the little mid-coastal Maine town where she grew up and where I spent the first few months of my life. The one time I'd asked her to visit the place, when I was maybe seven or eight, her refusal was so vehement that I never dared ask again.

"Our family has lived there for centuries," my mom went on, her eyes fixed unblinkingly on the road ahead. "And I'm the prodigal daughter because I was the one who didn't want to spend the rest of my life cooped up in the same tiny town I'd been born in."

"Lots of people grow up and move away from home, Mom," I said.

My mom shook her head. "Not the Vespers. We haunt the same old house and walk the same old streets and run the same old shop forever, or else we're a stain on the family legacy."

"That sounds kind of harsh," I said, frowning. "I mean, you only moved two hours away. And you became a nurse. Wouldn't most families be proud of that?"

"I have no idea. Our family isn't most families," she replied shortly. "Who needs a college degree or a steady income when you can putter around a dusty old shop, following your mother like a shadow for your entire life?"

I felt the stirrings of something like a memory, but it was hazy, a distant shape in the fog. "You've told me about that shop before," I said.

My mother looked at me sharply. "Did I?"

I frowned in concentration. I could almost see it, a tantalizing something dancing in my peripheral vision. "What was it called again?"

My mother hesitated. "The Shadowkeep."

I stared at her. "The *what?*"

My mother rolled her eyes. "I know. It's a little tourist trap down by the water. They sell candles and crystals and tarot cards, that kind of stuff."

"And that's why you and Asteria stopped speaking? Because you wouldn't help sell a bunch of gimmicky, new-age junk?" I asked.

My mother's mouth quirked into a crooked smile. "Something like that."

"But your sisters both work there?"

"Sure, as long as we're using a vague definition of the word 'work,'" my mother said dryly.

"And it's not a very big shop, is it?"

My mother shook her head. "Tiny."

"Well, then, why would Asteria care whether you worked there or not? It sounds like she had plenty of help."

My mother smiled at the indignation in my tone, reached out, and ruffled my hair. "I see your point, but Asteria wasn't exactly famous for her logic."

I tilted my head. "Was she famous for something else?"

There was that hesitation again. Then, "No. Your grandmother wasn't famous. At least, not outside our little town." She took her eyes from the road for a brief moment to smile at me. "Everyone knows everyone in Sedgwick Cove. You'll see what I mean."

She went silent again, and I turned to look out the window, my mind whirling. I'd learned more about my grandmother in the last few minutes than I had in my entire life up until today, and it was still all I could do to swallow back a steady stream of questions. I decided to be patient. We'd be in Sedgwick Cove soon, and then my mother would have to answer my questions. And even if she still tried to avoid them, there would be other people and places from which to get answers. I reached down and ran my fingers over the necklace from Asteria which I had tucked carefully down my shirt. I could wait.

The drive was mostly highway, and I could feel my eyelids getting heavy as I stared at the endless yellow lines rushing toward us. I rubbed the pad of my thumb back and forth over the little velvet pouch, stifling a yawn, and then another…

I turned my head to the left and gasped to see not my mother, but Asteria behind the wheel of the car. The window was down and the breeze whipped strands of her silvery hair around her face like dancing cobwebs.

"Where are we going?" I heard myself ask the question.

Asteria looked at me, gray-green eyes agleam. "On an adventure together at last!" she whispered.

I looked back out at the road ahead of us again, but it had gone, replaced by the crashing edge of the sea, battering itself against the low cliffs we now stood upon. The sun, too, had gone, and a full moon hung in her place, a pale imitation of her brighter counterpart. Asteria reached over and brushed a finger over the necklace that still dangled around my neck.

"Are you ready, Little Bird?" she whispered.

I started awake as Freya gave an indignant yowl. She'd been suspiciously well-behaved since we'd set out; normally she made her displeasure very evident in the loudest and most dramatic ways possible. Now she stared imperiously at me through the bars of the carrier as though to say, "Did you hear that? I could have been making that sound the entire time." I poked a couple of fingers through so that I could scratch her forehead.

"Sorry for the long ride," I told her. "We'll be there soon."

"Sooner than you think. Did you have a nice nap?" my mother asked.

"How long was I... oh!" I cried, for at that moment I realized we were no longer on the highway. A two-lane road wound lazily up the coast, the shimmer of the sea visible in the distance out of my window. We rounded a bend and a battered, faded wooden sign rose up to meet us. Several antique wooden buoys and a fishing net hung in nautical accent to the pale blue letters: *Welcome to Sedgwick Cove: A magical haven by the sea.*

I felt a shiver of anticipation as the hairs on the back of my neck rose to attention. We were here. Here, in the town where I was born—the town where my mother and her mother were born. I gazed hungrily out the window for something that would kindle a spark of recognition in me. It seemed impossible that I could be in this place and not recognize it as an intrinsic part of myself.

The road turned sharply around a copse of scraggly trees and the first houses came into view—a smattering of weather-beaten little capes crouching in blooming gardens behind picket fences. Then the houses began to crowd together more closely, and a battered ribbon of sidewalk appeared. Then we rounded a corner and the picturesque downtown of Sedgwick Cove came into view at last.

The road widened and spilled out into a quaint collection of shops, restaurants, and houses converted into bed and breakfasts, their tiny yards hemmed in by borders of crushed white sea shells. The buildings were painted in a rainbow of once-bright colors which had faded to pastels, as though the town had become an old photograph of itself. A bakery, pink like the inside of a conch shell, stood shoulder to shoulder with a lavender-hued art gallery and a minty-green antiques shop. A rambling blue Victorian with a wraparound porch had a sign swinging gently in the breeze that read, "The Bumblebriar Inn: Come Sit a Spell." All of it was basking in the constant tang of the salty air sweeping in off the water like seals sunning themselves on a pebbled shore.

Narrow side streets cut down between the buildings on either side, the ones on the left leading up into further clusters of houses and shops, and the ones on the right cutting down toward the cove itself, many too narrow even for a car to drive down them. As I peered down one of them, I spotted an old woman securing an old-fashioned bicycle to a crooked fence before vanishing through the gate. These little narrow streets wound down toward the beach, dissolving into crooked boardwalks that cut down through high marsh grasses to the sandy beach below. Beyond the roofs of the buildings, little boats bobbed on the glimmering waves that stretched to the neat division between ocean and cloudless sky.

It was all I could do not to press my nose to the window like a small child as we drove slowly through the town center, but it became clear that I was not the only curious one. People were openly pointing and staring at our car as it drove through down the main thoroughfare, which seemed odd. Surely they were used to tourists here? I could see groups of them here and there, peering in shop windows and strolling the boardwalks with ice cream cones in their hands. Why in the world would we be drawing so much attention in our nondescript car on a busy, brink-of-summer day?

I turned to ask my mother the question aloud, but the words shriveled up in my mouth. Everything about her had gone rigid and tense, as though crossing the border into Sedgwick Cove had turned her to stone. I felt my own budding excitement and curiosity crumble to dust as I remembered that for every memory I wished I had of this place, my mother had a hundred she was trying to forget. I tried to cast around for something practical to say.

"Are we staying in one of these hotels?" I asked.

Mom shook her head. "My sisters wouldn't hear of it. We're staying in the house I grew up in. And anyway, I'd been hoping to keep a low profile while we're here. If a Vesper checked into a hotel in Sedgwick Cove, every local would know about it before she even got her suitcase unpacked."

"Oh, come on, you're exaggerating," I half-laughed.

But there was no laugh in my mom's reply. "I promise you, I'm not."

I thought of the staring and pointing as we drove through the center of town and decided to take my mother at her word.

We were moving away from the bustle of downtown now. We turned off the main road and down one of the narrow side streets that dropped down behind a second row of houses and skirted the rocky shoreline. Tall beachgrass waved to our right, beckoning unwary wanderers toward the cliffs beyond. On our left, the houses gave way to more trees and low, dense shrubbery. The road turned from pavement to sandy gravel, climbing a small hill. When we reached the top of it, I gasped.

A lighthouse came into view, perched out on an outcropping of rock that sheared off into a craggy cliffside. The weathered wooden tower was white-washed, dotted with arched windows, and topped with a massive golden-green copper cupola and a weathervane. As it was daytime, no lights were shining from the top, but the sun glinted off the glimmering panes of glass that circled the top, and an open walkway encircled it, hemmed in by a metal railing.

"Wow," I managed to breathe.

"It is beautiful, isn't it?" my mother sighed, somewhat grudgingly.

"It's... that's not... are we staying there?" I asked, pointing to the lighthouse.

"No, no, no one lives in the lighthouse, not anymore. The house is down here, just around this... yes, you can see it now." And she stopped the car in the middle of the road as though steeling herself before she dared to venture any closer.

The house was a rambling little Victorian with a turret on one side and a wraparound porch with elaborate gingerbread trim. It had once been yellow, but the salt air had faded it, and creeping fingers of climbing roses and ivy had run riot over it, obscuring the cream and pink accents and the faded lavender door. The house had a garden—or maybe it was more accurate to say that the garden had the house, for it appeared to have grown up out of the surrounding splendor like another blossom. Flowers of every color and herbs of every variety grew in glorious chaos all around it, flourishing in flower beds, spilling out of pots, twining together around fenceposts, and tangling over the walkways. The air was full of twinkling discordant music from a dozen windchimes hung from the porch roof and a purplish smoke rose in curling tendrils from the slightly crooked chimney. A tall stone wall ran through the shade-wrapped yard behind it, obscuring what lay beyond.

"There it is," my mother murmured. "Lightkeep Cottage, home of the Vespers."

5

I couldn't make sense of it. I gazed down on the little house, which looked as though it had been plucked from the pages of a fairy tale. Was this really the home my mother had fled without looking back? Could this truly be the place she shuddered to return to?

I could almost hear the house calling out to me, reaching for me with welcoming arms and waiting to enfold me in an embrace that felt and smelled like a hundred thousand memories I'd forgotten. But judging by the look on my mom's face as we rumbled down the gravel road, her time here would be less of an embrace and more of a prison sentence.

The road didn't continue past the house but widened into a little circular turnaround in front of it. We parked there, and my mom sat in the car, frozen.

"Mom? Are you okay?" I asked tentatively.

"Sorry. I just need a minute," she said, her voice strained, her knuckles white on the steering wheel.

But the cottage wouldn't give us a minute. As I opened my mouth to say that we could wait as long as she needed, a shriek erupted from somewhere inside the house and an object came crashing through one of the first-story windows, breaking the glass and landing with a thud in a lilac bush.

I let out a little yelp, but my mother just closed her eyes as though praying for patience. When she opened them again, she looked at me resignedly.

"It appears my sisters are home. Come on. It's time to meet your aunts."

She said this the way someone else might say, "It's time to enter the fray," before storming off into the field of battle. My heart began to thump uncomfortably against my ribs, and I wondered if the house wasn't the trap that my mother feared after all.

We got out of the car. It was only when Freya yowled indignantly that I remembered her and opened the back door to retrieve her carrier. My mother walked around to the back of the car and popped the trunk, but then closed it again.

"If this goes badly, I don't want to have to repack the car," she said with a humorless smirk. Then she turned, lifted her chin, and marched to the garden gate. I scurried along in her wake, clutching Freya's carrier.

The gate opened with a creak that silenced the shouting still emanating from inside the house. We walked up the garden path, the ocean breeze making every bloom wave in greeting and sending an intoxicating perfume wafting over us. Up close, I could see that the paint on the house was peeling, but somehow that only added to its charm. My mother paused for a moment at the base of the stairs and then turned sharply, marching between the flowerbeds until she reached an azalea bush. Then she reached down and picked up something that was lying in the grass. She held it up so that I could see it; it was a geode. I stared down at the pinkish crystals inside it, like jagged teeth in a smiling mouth.

"Is... there a rock garden?" I asked in a weak attempt at a joke.

"No, this is what came through the window. If they're already throwing things, I should probably be armed."

I laughed weakly, but my mother wasn't smiling. "Wait, seriously?"

Instead of answering me, she crossed to the steps and ascended to the porch, past a trio of rocking chairs and a crooked porch swing. I followed her, tripping over my own feet as I tried to avoid spoiling the blossoms that surrounded me like a carpet. She waited until I stumbled to her side, and then my mother reached up a hand and knocked sharply on the peeling lavender door.

We waited a few tense seconds, then heard footsteps from inside. The door flew open, revealing a startlingly attractive woman with porcelain skin and rippling cascades of jet-black hair. She deigned to bestow one withering glare on us both before slamming the door promptly in our faces again.

My mother looked over at me, expression wry. "That was your Aunt Persephone. And that greeting was actually warmer than I was expecting."

Before I could shake off my surprise and muster a response, there was an outbreak of angry hisses and scuffling noises behind the door. It sounded for a moment like a fight had broken out between several angry cats. Then the sounds stopped and the door was pulled open again. I had just a moment to see that the woman who had opened it was not the same woman who had just slammed it before she flew at my mother and flung her arms around her, enveloping them both in a cloud of white dust.

"Kerridwen! You came! I knew you'd come! I told her you would and you did! Oh, Kerri!" The words were muffled against my mother's shoulder.

"Of course I came, Rhi. Get a hold of yourself!" my mother coughed.

"Right, sorry. Oh, you're all flour-y. Sorry, I'm so sorry," the woman said, and stepped back from my mother, trying to wave the rest of the flour out of the air and off of my mother's tank top. As the flour cleared like smoke, I could see her for the first time.

Rhiannon Vesper was average height, with a slight, boyish frame and a mess of honey-blonde curls which she had tied up off of her face with a flour-smudged scarf. The wide blue-gray eyes behind her glasses blinked bemusedly at me for a moment before her lightly freckled face broke into a wide grin that revealed a gap between her front teeth. I could see echoes of my mother in the shape of her narrow nose, the point of her chin, and the freckles that were sprinkled across the apples of her cheeks. Her clothes—a pair of patched jean overalls and a blouse patterned brightly with flowers—were covered in flour and smudges of chocolate.

"Wren, this is your Aunt Rhiannon. Rhi, you remember my daughter Wren," my mother said.

"Of course I do! Oh, Wren! You're... do you know, all this time, I was picturing a toddler running around, but that's just silly, isn't it?" she said with a trilling laugh that made her sound like a rodent with anxiety.

I had no idea how to respond without sounding rude, because of course it was silly. So I just smiled weakly instead.

"It's nice to... um... see you again," I mumbled. I'd almost said, "meet you," but I knew I must have met her before, and I didn't want to hurt her feelings by admitting I didn't remember her.

"Oh, let's not stand on ceremony, you're home now. Come here," Rhi said, and she pulled me into a hug. She smelled like a bakery, and my stomach rumbled loudly as I breathed in the sugary vanilla scent of her.

"Well, we can't just leave you standing on the doorstep! Do come in, both of you." Aunt Rhi stepped back to let us pass, but my mom hesitated.

"I think leaving me on the doorstep is exactly what Persi intended."

Rhi gave that manic squirrel laugh again. "Oh, she's just being Persi. Don't pay her any mind."

"Oh, I'd love to, but at this point I'd be afraid to turn my back. Is her aim as good as it used to be?" my mom asked, holding up the geode.

Rhi's face flushed and she smiled sheepishly. "Oh, that. I was hoping maybe you hadn't seen... well, you know Persi. She always could get a bit dramatic when she was stressed."

"Or angry. Or tired. Or hungry. Or bored..." my mother added. "You'll forgive me, but I am rather hoping to avoid actual armed combat today."

"No combat. Cross my heart. Now, won't you please come in?"

My mom handed the geode back to Rhi and stepped through the door into the house. I watched her whole body tense up like a coiled spring and then release again, like she'd expected lightning to strike her upon crossing the threshold.

If the garden outside was glorious chaos, it was nothing to the inside of the house. The entryway looked like a jungle as we maneuvered our way through it, crowded with plant stands and hanging plants in macrame hangers. Between the plants were strung twinkle lights and crystals and drying bunches of herbs and flowers. The overwhelming smell of it all hit me like a punch in the gut; Asteria had smelled just the same, the scents of her house clinging to her clothes and curls. My eyes began to sting with the salt of unshed tears.

Rhi led us through the entryway to a large sitting room full of mismatched furniture that all somehow blended perfectly together. A red velvet chaise squatted under a rainbow of cushions. A mustard-colored wingchair perched regally beside a sagging denim loveseat buried in knitted throws. An antique steamer truck plastered with faded travel stickers served as a coffee table, above which hung a ludicrous chandelier made of brightly hued crystals that threw little rainbows like confetti over everything. What little of the walls not covered in ornately framed prints and photographs was plastered with green striped Victorian-era wallpaper. Potted plants crowded the windowsills of windows so old and tall that their sills nearly brushed the floorboards, framed by lacy white curtains and heavy eggplant-colored drapes. A battered gold gramophone crackled away in the corner, adding a soprano's aria to the air.

But the focal point of the room was undoubtedly the massive stone fireplace. Driftwood and white pillar candles were stacked up in its mouth like mismatched teeth, and the enormous mantel was crowded with knickknacks, statues, books, and more candles. Above it hung a gilt-framed painting of a woman standing on a stormy beach, her hair whipped out in front of her like a flag, a light shining from the lighthouse in the distance. A strange feeling of déjà vu burrowed into my stomach as I stared at it, sure I could hear the ocean in the brushstrokes.

I'd stood where that woman stood. I'd felt that same wind in my hair.

"Won't you both sit down? I can make us some tea, and we can... can talk over some things," Rhi said, and there was still an audible tremor in her voice.

An indignant meow sounded from inside the carrier still clutched in my hand, and I cleared my throat. "Is it all right for me to let Freya out? She's had a long car ride."

Rhi cocked her head. "Freya?"

"My cat."

"Oh, of course! Is this... this must be the kitten that..." Rhi looked up at my mother, who nodded mutely. Rhi approached the carrier and bent down to peer inside.

"Hello, my lovely. And have you been a good little companion to our friend here? Have you been looking out for your charge? I'm sure you have, good kitty," she whispered, poking a finger through the bars to scratch Freya between the ears. Freya closed her eyes lazily and began to purr.

"Do you think she'll be all right, with all the plants?" I asked. My mother always insisted she couldn't keep a plastic succulent alive, and so we'd never had a single plant in the house; but I knew that lots of plants could be poisonous to cats.

"Oh, yes, my dear, just let her out to explore. We have a cat, Diana, and she's never had any trouble with the plants."

"Diana?!" My mother laughed as she sank down onto the loveseat. "There is no possible way that cat is still alive."

"Well, granted I haven't seen her yet this morning, but she was certainly alive last night when she chased that old gray tom out of the garden. You should have heard him yowl. She was quite pleased with herself when she came in," Rhi said absently, releasing the catch on Freya's carrier and pulling my cat up into her arms. She gave her an affectionate squeeze, kissing her between the ears before setting her down gently on the floor. Freya wound once around her legs before stretching luxuriously and then vanishing behind the drapes, tail twitching like an antenna as she began her explorations.

"Now, I'll get some tea started," Rhi said, brushing the cat hair from her hands. "Herbal all right? I make my own blends, you know."

My mother gave Rhi a pointed look, and Rhi rolled her eyes. "Yes, it's just tea, I promise," she said, sounding somewhat exasperated.

I looked back and forth between the two of them, but no one seemed inclined to explain the odd exchange, so I cleared my throat. "Could I use the bathroom?"

"Upstairs, second door on the left, honey," Rhi said, pointing to the staircase.

I mumbled my thanks and turned for the stairs. My mother jumped to her feet, an anxious look on her face.

"Do you want me to come with you?" she blurted out.

I raised an eyebrow. "To the bathroom?" I asked.

"I, uh... can show you where it is," she stammered.

I stared at her. "Second door on the left, Mom. I can handle it. I promise."

She continued to stand there, fists clenched, staring at me as I ascended the stairs. I shook my head. I'd never seen my mother like this. Like most nurses I knew, she was never one to make a fuss. She had always been a 'get up and dust yourself off, you're okay' kind of mom, and I'd learned how to take care of myself because of it. So the fact that she was now hovering over me, offering to escort me to the bathroom at the top of the stairs was... unsettling.

The stairs creaked and groaned comfortably as I ascended, staring at still more framed paintings and photographs crowded onto the wall along the staircase. Right at the top of the stairs, I paused in front of one photograph that caught my eye. From it, three little girls with gangly limbs and gap-toothed smiles grinned out at me, their arms thrown around each other and caught by the camera flash in mid-laugh. They were wearing an assortment of too-big clothes and wide brimmed hats, like they'd been raiding their mother's closet.

I leaned forward to peer closer. The photo was a bit blurry and faded, but I could tell that the girl on the left was my mother. I had never seen such joy on her face, and it brought a lump to my throat.

"Happier days."

I whirled in alarm to see the woman who had slammed the door in our faces upon our arrival, standing just a few feet away from me in the threshold of the first doorway at the top of the stairs.

"What are you doing up here?" she demanded in an accusatory tone.

"I... I was just coming up to use the bathroom. Aunt Rhi said it was upstairs."

"Oh." A bit of the fight seemed to go out of the woman's posture as she slumped against the door frame. "I thought perhaps... well, never mind, I suppose. I'm your Aunt Persephone," she added, her tone implying that the moniker "aunt" was a dubious one at best.

"I... it's nice to... I'm Wren," I managed to stammer out.

"I know," Persephone said, smirking. "And..." she sighed almost grudgingly. "Look, I'm sorry about the door, earlier. That wasn't really meant for you."

I had no idea how to answer that, so I just shifted my weight awkwardly and changed the subject. "I'm... I'm really sorry about Aster—um, about your mother."

Persephone sucked in her cheeks. "Well, I'm glad to hear that *someone* is. I rather expected Kerri to throw a party."

I scowled at her. "My mom was really upset when she got the news."

Persephone took a step toward me and leaned closer. "Good," she whispered. "I hope the guilt eats her alive."

And without another word, she stepped back into her room with a toss of her glossy black head and closed the door between us.

I stood frozen to the spot, my heart pounding for a moment. It was shocking to hear someone talk about my own mother with such venom. Every doubt I'd had about my mother's reluctance to come back here vanished on the spot. I was starting to feel antsy about staying under the same roof with Persephone, and I'd only just met her.

Feeling now like an unwelcome intruder on the second floor, I quickly used the bathroom, which was decorated from ceiling to floor with hand-painted vines, blossoms, and insects, washed my hands with a lump of rough-cut lavender soap, and hurried back downstairs before Persephone could accost me again. My mother gave me a piercing look as I joined her on the loveseat.

"Everything okay?"

"Fine."

She pressed her lips together but said nothing else.

A moment later, Rhiannon returned with a big silver tea tray, crowded with colorfully mismatched cups and saucers, a round-bellied blue teapot, and a plate heaped high with cookies. She poured out the tea and offered around a chipped purple bowl of sugar cubes. I wasn't exactly a tea drinker, but I took a cup anyway. The steam that wafted up into my face smelled of roses, and I inhaled it deeply as I watched my sugar cube melt away at the bottom of the cup among the scattering of tea leaves.

My mom took a long sip of the tea and closed her eyes with a sigh. Rhi's face was lit for a moment by a soft smile as she watched her.

"I imagine tea like this is hard to find in Portland," she said.

"Tea like this is hard to find anywhere," my mom said, and she managed a smile as well.

Rhi offered around the plate of cookies next, and I unstuck one from the tower, suddenly realizing how famished I was. I'd been so anxious that morning that I'd only picked at the muffin from the coffee shop, and that had been hours ago. The first bite—lemon and lavender with a drizzle of vanilla icing—was heaven, and I let slip a little groan of delight.

"You made these?" I asked as soon as I could swallow.

"My own recipe," Rhi confirmed, looking delighted. "I sell them in the shop sometimes, and they're always gone before lunch time."

"I can see why," I said, popping the rest of the cookie in my mouth and reaching for a second, "because it's literally the best thing I've ever eaten."

Rhi's freckled cheeks flushed with pleasure. "Well, help yourself. I've got more in the oven."

We sipped and munched in silence for a few minutes, and then finally, Mom put her cup down.

"I wish you'd told me she was sick," she said.

Rhi bit her lip. "I was in denial," she said. "If I couldn't admit it to myself, I could hardly have admitted it to you."

"Still, Rhi."

"I know. But she didn't want you to know. She didn't want anyone to know."

"But why?"

Rhi's smile was sad. "You know Asteria. Completely convinced of her own invincibility. When did she ever admit weakness?"

Mom gave a weak chuckle. "Not once in her whole damn life. Yeah. I get it."

"She hid it well, too. Even Persi and I didn't realize how sick she was until it was too late," Rhi said. She dropped her gaze to her cup, but not before I spotted the telltale sparkle of tears in her eyes.

"Speaking of Persi, do you think she'll deign to be in the same room with me while I'm here?" Mom asked.

Rhi's flushed cheeks darkened from pink to scarlet. "She's in a dark place right now. She'll come around."

I thought back to my encounter with her upstairs and wondered if that was really true.

"And anyway," Rhi said, cramming a cookie into her mouth, "she's not going to have a choice. We all have to be here for the reading of the will. Asteria left very specific instructions."

I looked up, surprised. My mother had told me that we had to go to Sedgwick Cove to "make arrangements", but I had just assumed that meant a wake and a funeral. The thought of a will had never even crossed my mind, probably because no one close to me had ever died before. I wondered for a moment if Asteria had thought to leave any little trinket to me, and then pushed the idea away. I raised a hand to the little bulge of the necklace under my shirt. It seemed to me, if Asteria knew she was sick, she had made sure to send me the one thing she really wanted to make sure I had.

"What time is it happening?" my mom asked.

"Lydian will be here at four o'clock. It shouldn't take long," Rhi said.

"Lydian?! Oh, dear God, *that's* who mom used to make her will?" my mom asked, dropping her head into her hands.

"Lydian's always handled all of mother's legal affairs," Rhi said, a note of defensiveness in her voice.

"And our grandmother's. And probably our great-grandmother's too, for all we know. The woman's about a thousand years old!"

"She's very lucid," Rhi hurried to say. "And we've never had any trouble. Well... nothing we couldn't sort out," she amended.

"Is she even still practicing? Are you allowed to just... be a lawyer in perpetuity, or can they take your accreditation away for the safety of the public, like a driver's license?" Mom asked.

"Oh, Kerri, stop fussing. She may be old, but she's perfectly capable. She still sees clients nearly every day, working out of that little office downtown," Rhi said.

My mom looked as though she wanted to protest, but pressed her lips together and snatched a cookie off the plate instead. It was clear she would have to pick her battles while she was here, and based on Persi's behavior, this one was the least of her problems. We all sipped our tea in silence for a minute, and then...

"Where is she now, Rhi?" my mom asked. Her voice was quiet and brittle.

Rhi put her cup down. "She's been moved to the summer house. The others will attend her there until we're ready for the final send off."

It took me a moment to realize they were talking about Asteria. Well, not Asteria, but her body, at least. I swallowed my bite of cookie with difficulty owing to the sudden appearance of a lump in my throat.

"What's the summer house?" I asked to break the silence.

"Oh it's just a... a little sort of greenhouse out in the garden," Rhi answered.

I frowned. "I didn't see a—"

"She means the walled garden behind the house," my mother explained.

"Oh," I said, remembering the moment I'd noticed the wall. "But... hang on, did you say Asteria is back there? Like, right now?"

"That's right," Rhi said, nodding her head.

"Isn't that... I mean... isn't she supposed to be at a... a funeral home or something?" I asked.

"That's not how our family does things," Rhi said, rather cryptically, I thought, and offered no further explanation. Along with my cookie, I swallowed back about a hundred other questions, most prominent among them, who in the world she meant by "the others."

"There must be other arrangements to make," my mother said.

"Yes. I'll need to persuade Persi to come down," Rhi said, looking terrified at the very prospect. I couldn't say I blamed her, not after my brief encounter with my Aunt Persephone.

My mom glanced at me and said, "Wren, we won't need you until the reading of the will. Do you maybe want to explore the garden for a little while? Or take a nap? I don't think either of us got much sleep last night."

I was tired, it was true, but I was also full to the brim with curiosity and I knew I'd never be able to shut my brain off sufficiently to actually fall asleep. I considered the garden for a moment but knowing that Asteria's body was out there somewhere made my stomach twist into anxious knots.

As though she could read every thought on my face like the words on a page, Rhi nodded and said, "Why don't you go for a walk downtown?"

My mom straightened up, looking wary. "Are you sure that's a good idea?"

"Of course! There are some cute little shops you can poke around in. It will keep you busy, and we can get on with our... more morbid pursuits," Rhi said with a shudder.

Mom chewed on her lip. "How will she—"

"She can take my bicycle. It's barely a mile back up the road to town. Can you ride a bicycle?" Rhi asked me politely.

I blinked. "Uh, yeah. I ride my bike to school every day."

"Lovely! That's all settled then," Rhi said, clapping her hands together.

"I'm still not sure—" my mother began.

"Unless of course you think she should be here while you and Persi have a proper reunion," Rhi said pointedly.

My mom sighed, defeated. "A ride into town sounds like a good idea," she said.

"Excellent. Wren, I'm going to give you a package to take to a friend of mine who lives in town. I made something for her. Would you mind dropping it off for me? It will save me a trip."

"Uh, sure, no problem. Can you tell me how to find—"

"Oh, you can't miss it. She and her family own a restaurant right on the main road. It's called Xiomara's Cuban Cafe."

My mom made a sound halfway between a groan and a laugh. "Oh, man, I almost forgot about Xiomara's. Is the food still as good as I remember?"

Rhi smiled. "Better. I'll write down the address for you, Wren." And with that she hopped up from the wingchair and hurried off to the kitchen.

"Mom, are you sure it's okay if I go?" I asked, reaching out to squeeze my mom's hand. "I can stay here and help with... whatever you need."

"No, no, Rhi is right. It's better if you're not here for this. You've seen what Persi's like, and that's on a good day. We don't need to shovel any more generational trauma on top of this trash heap of a situation. Go explore. Have fun."

"Are you sure?"

"Surely sure," my mom replied, a call-and-answer we'd come to claim as our own. "Just make sure you're back by four. Here, take some money and grab yourself some lunch at Xiomara's while you're at it." She fished a twenty out of her wallet and handed it to me.

"You want me to bring you anything?" I asked, pocketing the bill.

"No, I'll be good. Rhi probably has a seven-course feast planned, and I don't want to disappoint her. Feeding people is kind of her thing. She and Xiomara have that in common. You'll have to roll me out of here in a few days."

I leaned forward and hugged her around the neck, breathing in the familiar scent of toothpaste and coconut shampoo. As though propelled by jealousy for the snuggles in which she was not included, Freya appeared from around the corner, mewed loudly, and leaped up into my mother's lap.

"That's right, you keep an eye on her while I'm gone," I whispered into her fur. Freya answered with an imperious look as though to say, *As if you even had to ask.*

Rhi emerged from the kitchen carrying a small package wrapped in simple brown butcher paper, tied with a length of twine and a bundle of dried lavender. I followed her out the door and into the yard, where an old-fashioned bicycle was waiting for me propped up against the side of the house. It was light blue, with white tires, a wide wire basket attached to the handlebars, and a round little silver bell that trilled merrily when I tested it.

"I imagine your bicycle is a little more... modern," Rhi said, an apologetic note in her voice. "But it should do the trick to get you there and back. She's very reliable."

"It's adorable, actually," I said, and I meant it. A bike like mine would have looked like an anachronism in this wild tumbled wilderness of a garden; Rhi's fit right in.

"Just go straight back up the road you came and you'll find yourself downtown," she said. "Do you think you can..."

"I'll be fine, I promise," I told her. "And I've got my phone with me."

"Oh, yes, of course," Rhi said. "Well, then, just... just be back by 4 o'clock."

"Okay, then," I said, taking the handlebars from her and mounting the bike. "Thanks for loaning this to me."

"Of course. Anything here is..." Rhi cleared her throat. "We're family, whatever happens."

Something about the look in her eye made me feel like I might burst into tears, so I thanked her again and pushed off toward town. I could feel her eyes on me all the way down the road, until a bend swallowed the cottage up from view.

6

It took hardly any time at all to pedal back into the downtown area. The road mostly dipped downhill, and I could let my feet dangle to the sides as the bike coasted effortlessly beneath me, requiring only an occasional pedaling on my part to keep going. The sea stretched out to the horizon on my left; the waving marsh grasses provided tantalizing peeks of it whenever a particularly gusty breeze bent them low. I briefly considered just leaving the bike by the road and finding a path down to the water but decided against it. I'd told my mom I was going downtown, and I didn't want to upset her by wandering off somewhere else instead. And besides, I had Rhi's package to deliver, and I didn't want anything to happen to it, or the bike for that matter, if I left them unattended by the roadside. I resigned myself to the fact that I would have to save my walk on the sand for another day.

Downtown Sedgwick Cove was so charming, however, that I soon forgot all about the beach. It was the quintessential little tourist spot, each shop and restaurant more quaint than the last. I lived in Maine, of course, but this place was the Maine people imagined when they planned their vacations by the sea, and even I couldn't help but be charmed by it.

I dismounted Rhi's bike outside of a little gallery where there was a bike rack and carefully locked it up, though she had assured me it wasn't necessary "around here." The watercolors displayed in the windows were pretty, so I decided to poke around inside. Tucking Rhi's package carefully into my bag, I entered the shop, causing a bell to jingle merrily over the door. An older woman sat at a wide, low table toward the back, pausing in the framing of a watercolor print to greet me.

"Hello, there, and what can I—well, bless my soul!" The woman blinked owlishly at me from behind her glasses. "Well, if it isn't the Vesper girl! I'd know you anywhere!"

I felt my smile freeze on my face as I processed my confusion. I hadn't been back to this town since I was a few months old, and my resemblance to my mother was passing at best. But I swallowed and renewed the smile.

"That's right. I'm Wren. It's nice to meet you."

"Wren, that's right. I'm Phoebe Sterling. Why, I just can't believe that... oh." Her face fell as the realization hit. "Oh yes, of course. You must be here for Asteria's funeral. I'm sorry about your grandmother."

"Thank you. So, you knew my grandmother?" I asked.

Phoebe smiled. "Everyone knew your grandmother." She fingered a black ribbon tied around her right wrist as she spoke. "The Vespers have lived in Sedgwick Cove since its founding." She laughed. "But listen to me, telling you about your own family history! Don't you mind me, I never know when to stop talking!"

I just nodded, trying not to look surprised by this information. I knew our family had lived here a long time, but I didn't realize it had been that long.

Phoebe's lips pressed together as though she was trying to prevent herself from saying something, but after a few seconds her curiosity got the better of her, and the question burst forth. "And does that mean Kerridwen is back as well?"

It was so strange to hear people use my mother's full name, like a misplayed note in a familiar song. But I nodded.

"I never thought I'd live to see the day," Phoebe murmured, more to herself than to me, and then she turned an almost too-bright smile on me. "Well, welcome back, child," Phoebe said. "And feel free to have a look around. We're just putting the finishing touches on the exhibit: 'Sedgwick Cove: A Watercolor Journey.' Been two years in the making. And there's going to be some new artifacts on display next door at the Historical Society." She gestured to the wall near the front windows; the name of the exhibit had been hand-painted on a sea-smoothed piece of driftwood and affixed to the wall. Then she dropped her eyes to her work again and left me in quiet to experience the exhibit.

Having been invited, I began to wander through, lingering in front of each painting and examining it closely. I didn't have an ounce of artistic talent myself, but I'd always enjoyed museums. I thought I felt Phoebe's eyes on me as I browsed, but when I chanced a glance at her, she seemed to be deep in concentration over her work.

The paintings themselves were fascinating, tracing the history of the town. Many portrayed a place long gone: a busy fisherman's wharf with old-fashioned boats and horse-drawn carriages, a bustling general store with a dog drowsing on the porch, women in long petticoats dancing barefoot on the sand.

I turned the corner and saw a blank stretch of wall that had clearly been prepped for artwork, though none had been hung yet. A light shone down on a bare space of fresh paint along with a small brass frame carrying a description: "Untitled watercolor of Sedgwick Cove Beach, one of three. Bernadette Claire, local artist, 2010."

"I'm still waiting for that one to come in," Phoebe explained when she looked up and saw where I was. "The artist is a bit reclusive and is dragging her feet, so I—well, bless my soul, if this isn't her walking in this very minute!"

I turned in time to see two women walk in from the street. My first thought was that they must be twins—they had identical tall, willowy frames and long, straight curtains of white-blonde hair. As they entered and moved closer, however, I realized that they were more likely to be mother and daughter. The slightly shorter of the women, upon closer inspection, was significantly older, but carried herself with a regalness and upright bearing that belied her age. The younger woman, on the other hand, followed meekly in her wake, her shoulders slightly hunched and her eyes cast downward.

"Hello, Phoebe," the older woman said, her face breaking into a somewhat strained smile. "My apologies for the delay. We appreciate your patience."

She looked pointedly at the young woman behind who chimed in without looking up.

"Sorry," she mumbled.

"Oh, please don't apologize," Phoebe said, waving their words away. "I know it can be a difficult decision, to put one's work on display, especially after the theft."

"Theft?" I asked, unable to help myself.

"Yes, from the Historical Society. There was an old family heirloom on loan from the Claires that was stolen—a mirror, belonging to a very pivotal personage in our town history. The other volunteers and I were devastated to discover the break-in."

"As I've said before, no one blames you, Phoebe. And in any case, the Claires keep their word. Bernadette agreed to allow you to display her work. Such an agreement must be honored, and she must learn that."

She looked disapprovingly at the younger woman—Bernadette, I realized—the way an owner might look at a naughty puppy; and a wave of dislike for the older woman rippled through me.

As though she could hear what I was thinking, the older woman turned toward me and caught me looking at her. Rather than turning her rudeness on me, however, her face split into an expression of wide-eyed surprise and dawning recognition that I was starting to grow accustomed to in this town.

"Well, I never thought I'd live to see the day. This is the young Vesper, is it not?" she asked, addressing Phoebe as though I weren't standing right there, perfectly capable of introducing myself.

Phoebe stepped in, though, perhaps sensing my indignation. "Yes, I'm so sorry; where are my manners today? Wren Vesper, this is Ostara Claire and her niece, Bernadette Claire."

Ostara held out her hand rather like she thought I might kiss it, but as I took it, she shook it with surprising vigor. I noted with interest the same black ribbon tied around her wrist that Phoebe wore around hers. I turned to shake Bernadette's hand, but she made no motion at all to take mine as I held it out to her. She simply stood there, staring at me as though I'd just introduced myself as the Queen of England, or something equally intimidating.

"Nice to meet you," I prompted, trying to smile.

Still, Bernadette only stared, a deer caught in the headlights.

"Please excuse my niece. She considers shyness a perfectly reasonable excuse for a complete lack of social etiquette," Ostara said, shooting Bernadette a furious look.

I had absolutely no idea how to respond. I'd never heard an adult speak about another adult in such a condescending manner, as though she was a mere child. Bernadette may have been Ostara's niece, but she was a full-grown woman, probably around my mother's age. I ignored Ostara's comment and smiled at Bernadette again, trying to tell her without words that I didn't mind that she hadn't shaken my hand. Ostara, meanwhile, went on.

"Our sincerest condolences on the loss of your grandmother," she said. "I've known Asteria all my life. We grew up together as girls. Sedgwick Cove will not be the same without her."

"Thank you," I replied, my cheeks flaming. I had never felt so awkward in my life. It felt like I should be apologizing to Ostara for her loss, not the other way around. After all, she had clearly known Asteria much better than I did.

Ostara gave me one last piercing look, and then returned her attention to Bernadette, who was still gawking unabashedly at me. "Well, Bernadette, go on then. Give her the painting."

Bernadette looked down at the brown paper-wrapped package tucked under her arm as though she had quite forgotten it was there. "I... I'm not sure if I..."

"Bernadette, for heaven's sake, we did not bring it all the way down here for you to change your mind now," Ostara snapped.

Bernadette was still looking at me as she pulled the painting carefully from under her arm and took it into both hands, which were now shaking. Phoebe was looking uncomfortable now.

"Bernadette, if you're uncomfortable, the exhibition has plenty of pieces. We don't have to—"

"Yes, we do," Ostara said sharply. "We do have to. This is an exhibition of the art of Sedgwick Cove. Bernadette is a prominent artist from a founding family, and this show would be incomplete without her work. Bernadette, give her the painting. Now."

Ostara's tone was so commanding that Bernadette had no choice. Still looking at me with unmistakable fear in her eyes, she reached past me and handed the painting to Phoebe, who took it rather reluctantly, laid it on the work table, and began to carefully unwrap it. I couldn't help but lean forward as the paper was pulled away, and the painting revealed.

Like many of the other paintings, it was a rendering of the beach with the lighthouse in the distance, a storm gathering on the horizon beyond frothing waters. I stepped closer to it, transfixed, the hairs on my arms standing up.

A little girl in a white summer dress stood in the surf up to her knees, hair whipping around her face, which was hidden as it gazed out over the water.

One tiny hand was held out to the side, as though reaching for someone else's hand.

"Well, what do you think?" Ostara said, her sudden question startling me so that I jumped. "Isn't my niece a talented artist?"

"I... she... yes, she is," I stammered. It was true. The entire painting seemed to *breathe*, the waves a second away from crashing, the clouds from rumbling with thunder. But it wasn't Bernadette's obvious skill that had my heart leaping against my rib cage and my palms sweating. It was the fact that she had seemingly reached into my head and plucked my childhood nightmare from my subconscious.

The dream of the Gray Man.

And yet the place where the Gray Man ought to have stood was empty— the little girl reached out for a hand that was not there. I stared at it, as though expecting him to materialize beside her on the canvas, but of course that was absurd. Shaken, I tore my eyes from the image to look at Bernadette again. She was still staring at me with an almost fearful expression.

She knows, a voice in my head whispered. *She knows about the dream. About the Gray Man.*

"It is stunning," Phoebe's voice broke in, popping the moment like a soap bubble and startling me back to the present, where Ostara was nodding her approval.

"Yes, she truly does excellent work. All of her mentors have said so. And so, you see, this exhibit would be incomplete without her contribution. The Claires *are* Sedgwick Cove."

Her eyes flicked to me at these last words, almost defiantly, like she thought I might contradict her. When I didn't, she nodded, apparently satisfied.

"Very well, then. We'll let you get back to work. Thank you again for your patience, Phoebe. It was a pleasure to meet you, Wren," Ostara said, though her slightly cool tone suggested that the word "pleasure" might be a bit of an exaggeration.

"You, too," I managed before she turned and swept from the gallery. Bernadette hesitated only a moment before tearing her eyes from me and scurrying out after her aunt.

Phoebe was clucking her tongue in disapproval. "I wish she'd handle that girl with a bit more care. She's been through a lot, Bernadette has," she said as she carried the painting to its prepared place on the wall. She hung it carefully and stepped back to admire it with an almost misty expression.

Suddenly, I couldn't bear to be in the same room as that painting a second longer. I said a hasty thank you to Phoebe in what I hoped was a cheerful voice, but it wasn't until I stepped back outside into the sunshine that I felt like I could take a proper breath again.

Calm down. That painting could be of anyone. It's not you. It's some girl on a beach. Get a grip, Wren, I thought to myself, repeating it over and over again, each repetition expelling a bit more of the strange, almost sick feeling the painting had given me, until at last I was free of it. *You're tired, and the last twenty-four hours have been an emotional roller coaster. That's the only reason you're reacting like this. People can't just paint other people's dreams. It's a coincidence; stop being paranoid.* I took one last deep breath, shook my head to clear it, and then started off again down the sidewalk. I needed a distraction.

I wandered into an antique shop next. There were two women behind the counter drinking tea and chatting. I nodded in silent greeting to them as I passed, and one of them raised a hand in acknowledgment. I noticed a black ribbon tied around her wrist, just as Phoebe and Ostara had worn. A quick glance at her companion's wrist confirmed that she was wearing one as well.

It happened again and again, shop after shop: black ribbons tied around the wrists of the people behind the counters or manning the registers. I even spotted them on people in the street, including a woman who passed by walking her dog. I'd heard of people tying black bands around their arms as a sign of mourning; was it possible half this town was wearing these ribbons out of respect for Asteria? And not only that, but it seemed that many of these people recognized me somehow. Total strangers were waving solemnly at me. An elderly lady on a mobility scooter shouted, "Welcome home!" at me as she puttered past. I felt like I was living in an episode of Black Mirror and was just starting to think about heading back to Lightkeep Cottage when I looked up and saw a sign over a bright red door painted with colorful flowers. It read, "Xiomara's Cuban Cafe."

I blinked, remembering suddenly Aunt Rhi's package sitting in my bag, and realizing that this was the place I was meant to drop it off. Also, the smells coming from inside instantly made my mouth water, and I realized I was famished. I pushed the door open and walked inside.

The cafe was tiny. Wooden benches were built along two sides with small tables pushed up to them and a long counter across the back separating the kitchen from the dining area. I didn't imagine more than a dozen people could eat inside at once. The decor was a combination of sprawling potted plants, brightly framed prints of beautiful island beaches, and shelves crowded with candles in tall glass jars painted with brightly colored images of saints. Three kids about my age were hanging out at the counter, one leaning on it, one sitting on it, and one standing behind it, at the register. They all looked up and stared at me as I walked in. I noted with a sense of relief that none of them were wearing the black ribbons. The girl behind the counter shooed the other two away as I approached.

"Get off there, or my abuela will kill you," she muttered, shoving at the boy.

"Aw come on, your abuela loves me," he insisted.

"She loves me too, but she'd still flay me alive for parking my butt on that counter," the girl shot back.

The boy chuckled but hopped down, sliding into one of the benches instead.

Interloper vanquished, the girl turned to me, flashing straight white teeth in a winning smile. "Welcome to Xiomara's Cafe! What can I get for you?"

"Hi," I said. "Um, I have something for Xiomara, actually. My aunt asked me to bring it over."

The girl's smile flattened a little as she drew her eyebrows together in confusion. "Your aunt?"

"Yeah, Rhiannon Vesper? She asked me to—"

My voice trailed away as the mouths on all three faces dropped open in surprise.

"Rhiannon Vesper is your *aunt*?" the boy on the bench asked, his voice full of awe as though I'd just said my aunt was Taylor Swift or something. He pushed his dark hair out of his face and stared at me with renewed interest burning in his eyes, which were a startling shade of blue.

"Uh, yeah," I said. "Here." And I held the package out to the girl on the other side of the counter, who took it without looking at it. "She mentioned she and Xiomara were friends," I added in a desperate attempt to fill the silence. "Are you Xiomara?"

The girl blinked, and the spell seemed broken. She laughed a raucous laugh, the kind of laugh you couldn't hear without wanting to laugh yourself, even if you hadn't heard the joke. "No, Xiomara's my grandmother. She's in the back; I'll get her." The girl tossed her head over her shoulder and shouted, "*Abuela*! Someone to see you!"

"*Quien es?*" came a shouted reply.

Before the girl at the counter could answer, a wizened brown face appeared at the pass-through from the kitchen. Her dark eyes seemed to pierce right through me as she took me in. Her iron gray hair was twisted into a knot on top of her head, and she wore a hairnet over it.

"It's Rhiannon Vesper's niece," the girl said, the words weighted with significance I could hear but couldn't interpret. Why did this whole damn town seem to know who I was?

The narrowed eyes widened, and I heard the woman whisper what sounded like, "*Este no tiene nombre!*" Then Xiomara disappeared from the pass-through and appeared again about five seconds later barreling through the door. She hurried around the counter, wiping her hands on her apron as she went.

"Home at last then, child," she said, peering closely at me. Her dark eyes managed to be both sharp and warm at the same time, and she spoke with such surety that I had no choice but to nod my head.

"Yes," I managed hoarsely.

She nodded. "About time, and not too late, I hope," she said without further explanation, and then she looked me up and down appraisingly. "You're hungry," she announced. "I'll feed you and then you can show me what foolish nonsense your aunt has sent me this time."

"Oh, I..." I stammered, "that's... yes, I was going to order something, um..." I squinted over her shoulder at the menu, but she was already disappearing into the kitchen.

"I... doesn't she want to know what I'm going to order?" I asked her granddaughter, a little bewildered.

The girl laughed her infectious laugh again. "No, she said she wants to *feed* you. Trust me, whatever she puts down in front of you would be better than what you ordered, even if you know Cuban food." She cocked her head to one side. "*Do* you know Cuban food?"

I shook my head, reddening.

The girl chuckled. "You'll know it soon if you stick around. Feeding people is my grandmother's love language."

"Oh, it's so worth it," the boy added enthusiastically. "Just go with it, I'm telling you."

"Okay," I said, managing a smile at last. Frankly, whatever she was cooking back there already smelled like heaven.

"I'm Eva, by the way," Xiomara's granddaughter said. "Eva Marin. And this is Zale MacDowell, who you can mostly ignore." She flicked a careless hand over her shoulder to acknowledge the boy, "and this is Nova Claire."

I'd nearly forgotten the other girl, who had dropped back into the corner when I'd entered and hadn't yet said a word. Now she stepped forward, holding out a hand and staring at me as though trying to memorize every feature of my face.

"I'm Wren," I said, my voice cracking as I took her hand, which gripped mine firmly and then turned it over so that she could trace her fingers over my palm. I froze at the intimacy of the touch.

"The mysterious Vesper girl at last," Nova said. Her voice was as smooth and honeyed as her flaxen hair, which hung in two glossy curtains on either side of her pale, heart-shaped face. Her eyes were wide, and such a smoky shade of blue as to be almost lavender. Her full lips parted into an expression halfway between a smirk and a smile. "Well, well, well, I feel like I'm meeting a storybook character."

"Give it a rest, Nova, she just got here," Eva said. Was that a note of warning in her voice?

Nova heard it too, and dropped my hand, but continued to smirk. "Does anyone have a pen? I feel like we should ask for an autograph."

Eva rolled her eyes. "Don't mind Nova," she told me. "The Vespers are the only family who have been here longer than the Claires, and she's a little touchy about it."

Nova glared at Eva but said nothing, sliding back into her seat and pulling out her phone as though she was already bored with the proceedings.

"Wait, Claire?" I asked, the name finally clicking into place in my brain. "I think I just met some of your relatives over at the art gallery."

Nova's head snapped up again, looking startled. "Which relatives, specifically?"

"Um... Ostara and Bernadette?"

Nova rolled her eyes. "Excellent. So your first impressions of my family were my overbearing grandmother and my crazy cousin."

"They were dropping a painting off for the gallery. She's... your cousin is very talented," I offered.

Nova made a sour face. "Yeah, I'd probably be talented too if I locked myself in an art studio day and night and avoided the entire outside world." She looked down at her phone again, apparently bored with our conversation already.

"Anyway," Eva said pointedly, and I turned back to her. She was tucking a rogue braid into her hair wrap. "When did you get here?"

"Just today," I said. Eva's expression was open and friendly, and it allowed me to let my guard down just enough to ask the question that had been burning in me since we'd arrived. "I don't suppose you know why everyone already knows exactly who I am before I even open my mouth, do you?"

To my surprise, Eva and Zale both laughed. Even Nova gave a soft snort of amusement from her corner. "I expect you've felt like a tourist attraction ever since you drove into town," Zale offered.

I was so relieved to hear someone acknowledge that it wasn't all in my head that I genuinely laughed too, feeling the tension ease in my shoulders for the first time. "More like a carnival sideshow freak, actually. Step right up and see the mythical Vesper girl! Seriously, what's with this town, anyway?"

This time I was sure of it. Zale and Eva exchanged a fleeting look before they answered.

"It's a very small town. Everyone is always up in everyone else's business," Eva shrugged, a little too casually, I thought.

"It's more than that," I said, pressing them.

"Gossip is thick on the ground around here," Zale chimed in. "And your family is, like, a Sedgwick Cove institution. And with your grandmother dying —" Zale's face flushed. "Oh, uh, my condolences, by the way."

"Thanks," I said, because that's what you say, right?

"Anyway, it's all anyone is talking about, that Asteria Vesper died. And now you show up out of the blue—hence, all the staring. But don't sweat it. They'll get over it soon enough."

I knew that couldn't possibly be the whole story, but I let it go for the moment, as Xiomara suddenly appeared, backing into the room from the kitchen carrying a steaming plate of food.

"*Sientate!*" she ordered. I'd had enough high school Spanish to know to park my butt in the nearest seat. She plonked the plate down in front of me, along with a knife and fork wrapped in a napkin. Then she stood over me, hands on her hips, and stared expectantly at me.

"Thank you," I muttered, unrolling the silverware from the napkin, and taking up the fork. The plate was piled with shredded beef and vegetables in some kind of sauce, served over rice. I dug my fork into it and transferred a steaming bite to my mouth. It took a moment for my tastebuds to recover from the temperature, and then...

"Oh my GOD."

Eva grinned. "I know, right?"

Xiomara nodded her satisfaction as I dug my fork back in again.

Zale was leaning toward my plate, sniffing hopefully. "Is that *ropa vieja*?" he moaned.

"Yes, and I suppose you're going to be asking me for some now, too?" demanded Xiomara, hands on her ample hips.

"I mean, if... if it's not too much trouble," Zale said, sitting up straight like a soldier on inspection.

Xiomara scoffed but shuffled back into the kitchen. I couldn't be sure, but I thought I saw a hint of a smile on her face as she disappeared through the doors.

"This might be the best thing I've ever eaten," I said when I stopped stuffing my face long enough to speak.

"She was legendary back in Cuba," Eva said proudly. "If you'd come here on the weekend during the lunch rush, you would have found a line out the door and down the block."

"I believe it," I said.

Xiomara plunked another plate down on the pass-through, and Eva handed it to Zale, who dug in at once.

"You want one?" she shot at Nova.

"I just ate, thanks Xiomara," she replied. Then she turned to roll her eyes at Zale. "My God, control yourself. You're in public." To be honest, there were some borderline indecent sounds coming out of him.

"I can't, I'm having a religious experience," Zale moaned.

"Really? Because it sounds more like the kind of experience religion frowns upon," Nova snorted.

"How long will you be staying in Sedgwick Cove?" Eva asked me.

I forced an enormous swallow to answer. "I'm not really sure yet. A few days, anyway. My last day of finals was yesterday." I looked around, realizing that I was looking at three kids my age sitting in a cafe on a random Wednesday. "Have the schools here already started summer break?"

Eva looked like she wasn't sure how to answer, but Nova jumped in. "School's a bit different here. There aren't really enough kids for a traditional school, so it's sort of a... homeschool collective type situation."

"Oh. That's... um..."

"Weird," Zale finished for me, his mouth full.

"Yeah, kinda," I said, smiling sheepishly.

"Sedgwick Cove has always kind of done its own thing," Eva agreed. "But it works for us."

Just as I was in danger of seeing the bottom of my plate, Xiomara came out of the kitchen again, this time with a heaping plate of what looked like fried dough.

"*Buñuelos*," Xiomara said, putting it down in front of me. I could smell anise, cinnamon, and orange as I gingerly picked one up off the plate and took a bite. All three of the other kids descended on the plate, too. Nova actually threw an elbow at Zale so she could snatch one before he had a chance.

"I thought you already ate?" Eva reminded her, smirking.

But Nova was unabashed. "There is always room for *buñuelos*. Always," she said solemnly.

And a single bite later, I had to agree with her. Soon everyone was licking their sticky fingers and crowing over how delicious they were. Xiomara stood with her hands on her hips, watching the pile disappear with a satisfied expression, until there was nothing left but crumbs. There wouldn't even have been crumbs, but Eva slapped Zale on the back of the head when he tried to lick the plate.

"Seriously, boy, who raised you?" she snapped at him.

"A woman who boils the taste out of everything and who thinks salt and pepper are the pinnacle of seasonings," Zale muttered, rubbing his head ruefully.

"Well, now that I've fed the neighborhood," Xiomara said, "what did Rhiannon Vesper have the audacity to send to me this time?"

Wiping my fingers on a napkin, I reached into my bag and pulled out the package Aunt Rhi had given me. Xiomara yanked unceremoniously at the tape and unraveled the brown paper wrapping.

"Eva, get me my glasses," she barked as she squinted down at the contents.

"I mean, I could, but you can reach them easier, abuela. They're on your head," Eva said with a determinedly straight face.

Xiomara muttered a string of what I could only assume were expletives as she untangled the glasses from her hairnet and perched them onto the end of her nose. Then she lifted a sealed mason jar from the package and read the tag that Rhi had tied to it. A moment later, she snorted.

"And what does your aunt expect me to do with this useless muck, fertilize my garden with it?" she demanded, staring over her glasses at me.

"I, uh... I don't even know what it is," I confessed.

"I mentioned to her that I've been suffering from arthritis in my hands, and she insisted she had the perfect remedy for me." She snorted. "It's a miracle, she tells me, you'll be a new woman! As if I haven't tried ginger and chamomile. Wait here." She slammed the jar on the counter and hurried off into the kitchen again.

I stared after her before turning to Eva, eyebrows raised.

"Don't worry, they always do this," she said. "It's like a friendly rivalry they have, to see whose remedies are the best. Of course both of them would rather die than admit that the other's recipes were effective at all, so no one ever wins."

A moment later, Xiomara re-entered and shoved a big, crumpled paper bag into my hands. "You tell her that's a real remedy in there, and she's lucky to have it because I don't give that to just anyone. Not that she'll appreciate it, of course. She never does."

The bag was warm and smelled delicious.

"I packed up the rest of the food for you, too. If her remedies are any indication of what comes out of her kitchen, you're all going to need it," she insisted.

I doubted that assumption, based on the cookies I'd already eaten from Rhi's kitchen, but I didn't dare say so out loud. So instead I said, "How much for lunch?"

"Little Vesper, that's your homecoming meal. Don't you insult me by trying to pay for it!" Xiomara said, and then, for just a moment, her expression softened and there seemed to be a crack in her no-nonsense exterior. "Welcome home, child."

"Thanks," I said, surprised to feel the tightness of sudden emotion in my throat. There was something about the way Xiomara said "home." It was like a counterpoint to the feeling that had already begun to sprout in me at the sight of Lightkeep Cottage: the feeling that I belonged to this place, or maybe that it belonged to me, somehow.

"Well, I guess we'll see you around, Vesper," Zale said as I stood up.

"We'll all be at Asteria's funeral," Eva added.

"Really?" I blinked. "All of you?"

Nova gave a tight smile. "Oh, yes. All of Sedgwick Cove, in fact. It's the mourning event of the year."

Eva gave Nova a withering look before smiling brightly at me again. "Like my *abuela* said, welcome home."

"Thanks. Right. Well, see you then, I guess," I said. The words "looking forward to it" had nearly escaped my mouth, and I barely managed to swallow them before I humiliated myself. No normal person says they're looking forward to seeing someone at a damned funeral.

Then again, I thought to myself as I walked back out into the humid June afternoon, with every moment I spent in Sedgwick Cove, I was starting to feel more and more like there was very little about me—or this town, for that matter—that qualified as normal.

7

I took my time riding back to Lightkeep Cottage, anxiety swirling in the pit of my stomach like a tide pool on the beach below. My aunt Persephone would have no choice but to be in the same room as my mother for the reading of the will, and I was already sick with dread at the thought. I would rather the floor swallow me up than have to witness a confrontation between the estranged sisters. It would almost have been worth whatever trinket my grandmother had left me to simply get back on the bike and go eat more of Xiomara's delicious cooking—almost. I was propelling myself back to the house on the sheer force of curiosity.

I parked Rhi's bicycle where I'd first seen it, leaning up against the side of the house. As the handlebars turned to lean against the peeling paint, the little pouch swung forward and caught my eye. For reasons I really couldn't explain, I untied it and slipped it into my pocket. Asteria had said it was for luck. Well, I thought, as the pit of dread mounted in my stomach, I could use a little luck right about now. Then I stomped up the steps a little louder than was strictly necessary, just to forewarn them of my arrival. There was no car in the driveway other than ours, but there was a two-seater bicycle attached to a small purple rickshaw with a basket of flowers on the front, and a fringed white roof shading the cracked leather seat. I stared at it for a moment in wonder before pushing open the door.

"Hello?" I called tentatively, into what I could already sense was an uncomfortable silence. I nervously checked my watch, but I wasn't late.

"We're in the living room, honey," my mom called back.

I stepped out of my shoes, leaving them lined up neatly by the door alongside my mother's, and padded reluctantly toward the living room. Aunt Rhi met me in the hallway, wiping her hands on a dish towel she had tucked into her apron. She smelled of warm sugar.

"Were you able to deliver my package to Xiomara?" she asked.

"Yeah, and... um, she told me to give you a message."

Rhi raised her eyebrows expectantly. "Let's have it, then."

"Um, okay, but don't get mad, all right? I'm just the messenger." I took a deep breath. "She said, 'what does your aunt expect me to do with this useless muck, fertilize my garden with it?' and then told me to give you a 'real remedy.'" And I held out the paper bag to Rhi, watching her face anxiously.

Far from being offended, Rhi threw back her head and laughed hoarsely, and then plucked the bag from my hands. "Lovely," she said, and then sniffed. "She sent food as well?"

"Yeah, there's some *ropa vieja* in there, and *buñuelos*, too."

Rhi smacked her lips and then jerked her head over her shoulder. "I'll get this into the refrigerator. Go on into the living room, everyone's here."

"Everyone?" I asked, but she was already halfway down the back hallway, so I swallowed my question and walked toward the living room, stopping dead when I reached the threshold.

There, as I'd expected, were my mother and Aunt Persi, Persi standing as far from my mother as she could possibly have managed within the confines of the room. In front of the fireplace, however, were three women I had never seen before. I tried not to stare at them, but it was impossible because everything about them was practically screaming to be stared at.

The women on the right and the left were identical down to the last eyelash. I guessed they were in their early seventies. They had heads of wild gray curls, and bright, inquisitive blue eyes which they fixed unblinkingly on me the moment I entered the room. They sat like matched bookends on either side of undoubtedly the oldest woman I'd ever seen. Oh, who was I kidding— the oldest woman *anyone* had ever seen.

My mother gestured to the woman. "Wren, this is Lydian Larkspur. She's the executrix of your grandmother's will."

Before I could reply, Lydian barked out a command so suddenly that I jumped. "Well, don't just stand there gawking, girl! Come closer so I can get a good look at you. These eyes aren't what they once were." Her voice, which I'd expected to be as high and fluttery as a butterfly, was a powerful boom.

I shuffled awkwardly forward until I was standing only a few feet in front of her. She leaned forward and stared at me with milky blue eyes magnified by cat-eye glasses encrusted with multicolored jewels. She seemed to have shrunk inside her skin, so that it hung from her, crinkled and crepey. Wisps of fine white hair stuck out haphazardly from her bright, pink velvet turban, and she was draped in a loud floral caftan that clung to her bony shoulders and pooled around her feet, which were encased in white orthopedic sneakers. She reached out a gnarled, blue-veined hand and snatched at my wrist, yanking me forward so that I was almost bent double. She examined my fingers and the palm of my hand minutely before looking back up into my face and nodding once, sharply.

"You look like a Vesper," she proclaimed after this lengthy assessment was complete.

"Thanks," I muttered, gently pulling my hand out of her grip. "Um, it's nice to meet you."

"No, it's not," Lydian barked. "No one likes meeting old people, not even other old people, and I should know. I've been old longer than you've been alive, child. These are my granddaughters, Selene and Vesta." She waved a careless hand at the women on either side of her in turn, and each of them nodded solemnly.

"Nice to meet you," I repeated lamely, because I could think of nothing else to say as my brain struggled to take in this piece of information. These women were her *granddaughters*? They were easily close to seventy years old! How old was this woman?

Lydian clucked her tongue impatiently. "All right, we've dispensed with the niceties. Now find a seat, little Vesper, so that we can get on with this." She waved her hand vaguely across the room.

I spotted Freya curled up on a little cushioned footstool in the corner near my mom, so I crossed the room, scooped her up, and sat on the stool myself, replacing her on my lap. She grumbled a little at being disturbed, sniffed curiously at my clothes, and then resumed her napping in the nest of my crossed legs. My mom reached out a hand and squeezed my shoulder.

"How was downtown?" she asked, and though she was trying to sound casual, there was an edge to her voice, like she was afraid to hear the answer.

"It was nice," I told her, glad that I didn't have to lie. I had enjoyed my ride downtown... despite the rather odd reception I received from a few of the locals. And of course, that Twilight Zone moment with the painting... not that I was about to tell her that.

She gave me a searching look and then bit her lip and nodded, as though not sure she could trust my words. But there was no time to reassure her further, because Lydian cleared her throat and every eye in the room turned to her. Rhi had returned to the room during this exchange and had perched herself tensely on the corner of the sofa.

"As you all know, we are here to carry out the final wishes as laid out in the last will and testament of Asteria Vesper. I was her friend for many years, and I see it as my solemn duty to make sure that every last syllable is carried out to her specifications. It was her wish that all members of her immediate family be present in the same room here at Lightkeep Cottage for this to be carried out. You have all come. Let us proceed."

She leaned toward the table in front of her, and in perfect synchronicity, the two women on either side of her leaned forward also, their hands hovering anxiously on either side of Lydian as though expecting to have to support her at any moment. Lydian seemed not to notice, however, nor did she seem in need of them. Instead, she placed her hands on the box and slid it closer to her. Then she lifted the lid off of the box and set it aside.

Everyone leaned forward to get a better look, even Persi, who was still trying to act disinterested from her distant corner of the room.

The box contained a sheaf of paper, thick and creamy and more like parchment than the kind of paper you'd expect to see a legal document printed on. The bundle was tied with a wide purple satin ribbon, and I spotted a purple wax seal on the bottom of it. Lydian lifted the bundle out of the box, revealing a second something underneath it wrapped in rich, dark blue velvet with strange symbols burned into the cloth. I leaned forward to try to examine this second object, but Lydian replaced the cover on the box, shielding it from my view. She began muttering something under her breath as her arthritic fingers fumbled with the bow on the papers now sitting in her lap. Then, the ribbon fell away, and she cleared her throat, ready to read. The air was thick with tension—I could practically taste it on my tongue. Over in her corner, Persi had pulled a rose-gold hip flask from her cleavage and was taking a generous swig.

"I, Asteria Artemis Vesper, being of sound mind and memory, do hereby make, publish, and declare the following instrument as my last will and testament," Lydian began in her quavering voice, "and I revoke all other wills and codicils previously made by me. I direct that any debts incurred by me during my life, secured and unsecured, be paid and settled as soon as is possible after my death."

Here, Lydian raised her head and looked at my mother and her sisters each in turn. "I have a list for you. She has requested that you handle them together and has left instructions for you."

"I don't understand. Did Mom have a lot of debts?" my mom asked, her brow furrowed.

"Not of the kind you're implying," Lydian said pointedly.

"But... oh." My mom obviously understood something in those words that went right over my head, but I didn't want to interrupt by asking her what that "oh" meant. After all, it wasn't really any of my business. I looked from my mom to her sisters. Now that the reading had begun, all three sisters' faces were solemn, their eyes wide, their complexions pale and drawn. As different as they all were, they suddenly looked, for the first time, unmistakably like sisters. Lydian cleared her throat to continue.

"I direct that my executrix and beneficiaries abide by the following written list directing the disposition of tangible personal property and assets as follows."

Lydian sniffed and shoved her glasses up her long, crooked nose, so that the gold chain they hung on swung wildly on both sides of her face. They reminded me of the reins on a horse, and I suddenly had to fight down a mad, inappropriate desire to laugh out loud. I pressed my lips together and waited desperately for the moment to pass.

"To my daughters Persephone and Rhiannon, I leave Shadowkeep and all of its contents, with the hope that they will carry on the family business with pride and perseverance."

Rhi sniffed quietly and fumbled in her pocket for a bandana, which she used as a handkerchief. Persi's face was set and white, and though she did not cry, her lips were trembling.

"To my daughter Kerridwen, I leave my collection of books currently residing in my library, in the pages of which she can find her way back home, if she so chooses."

Here, Lydian's head snapped up and she eyed my mother beadily from behind her glittering glasses. My mom pressed a shaking hand over her eyes and did not speak. I reached a hand out toward her, but then let it fall in my lap. Whatever she was going through in that moment, it felt too private to interrupt with my awkward attempts at comfort.

"To my granddaughter Wren," Lydian went on, and my heart immediately began to thunder in my chest. She *had* remembered me in some way. A multitude of random objects crossed my mind—everything from one of her jingling bracelets to pouches of gemstones, even one of her gauzy scarfs she used to tie around her hair. I wondered if it would smell like her, and if it would help me remember her face more clearly...

"...I leave Lightkeep Cottage and all associated property and contents."

I blinked. "Wait. What?" I whispered.

"WHAT?!" My quiet exclamation was echoed from all corners of the room as Persi, Rhi, and my mother all reacted identically.

"That can't be right," Persi said.

"Can you... what does that mean?" Rhi stammered, her hands fluttering anxiously like startled butterflies.

"It means exactly what it says," Lydian answered.

"But—"

"NO! Absolutely not!" my mother cried.

"Read it again!" Persi demanded, "You've read it wrong, old woman! You've made a mistake!"

"Read it yourself, Persi, if you don't believe me," Lydian said coolly, holding the paper out to her.

Persi shot forward and snatched the paper from Lydian's claw like hand. I watched breathlessly as she scanned the text for herself, her mouth moving silently. Her eyes widened as the truth settled over her. "Impossible."

"Improbable, perhaps, but clearly not impossible," Lydian said, her lips quirking into the slightest of smirks. "I was surprised myself, but it wasn't my place to question Asteria's final wishes, and she was very clear about them. And before you make one of your dramatic gestures, Persephone, you should know that I have multiple copies of this document. Ripping it up or tossing it on the fire will change absolutely nothing."

Persi growled and shoved the paper back at Lydian, who took it and settled it neatly back on the stack in her lap. My aunt then shot such a vicious glare at me that I shrank away from her in terror.

"She can't do this!" my mom said, standing up, Diana dropping from her lap to the floor with a loud, resentful hiss before stalking away.

"She can and she did," Lydian replied.

"Wren is a minor! She can't inherit property!"

"I assure you, Asteria was aware of the age restrictions, which is why she arranged to have it all put into a trust to be overseen by myself and you, Kerridwen, until Wren turns eighteen," Lydian said.

"Oh, perfect, so now Kerri can just toss us out on our ear, I suppose, when she hasn't so much as visited this place in years?" Persi snarled.

My mother fired up as well. "I would never do that!"

"Yeah, well, you also said you'd never come back here, so you'll excuse me if I don't put total faith in your sweeping declarations," Persi shot back.

"Don't be absurd, Persephone," Lydian snapped, and Persi turned her glare on her. "She can do nothing of the sort. Her only role is to carry out Wren's requests."

"But this is our home," Rhi whispered, more to herself than to anyone else. She was looking imploringly at the sodden handkerchief in her hands as though it was going to explain everything to her.

"Okay fine, then, so the kid gets to kick us out and Kerri has the privilege of slamming the door?" Persi ground out between tightly clenched teeth. I half-expected her to crush the flask in her hand like a soda can.

But at last I managed to find my voice, hoarse and trembling though it was.

"I don't want it!" I cried. "I... I don't want to..." I looked from my mother's ashen face, to Rhi's tearful one, to Persi's thundercloud of an expression. "Can't I just give it back?"

"Give it back?" Lydian asked, peering at me.

"I'm in high school! I don't even live here!" I said, my voice rising hysterically with every word. "Can't I just... just give it back to my aunts?"

"The trust is binding until you turn eighteen, at which point, you may presume to do what you want with it," Lydian said. "But until that time, Lightkeep Cottage legally belongs to you."

"You said 'associated properties,'" my mother said, her voice muffled behind her hands. "Does that mean..."

"Yes. Sedgwick Cove Lighthouse also belongs to Wren."

My mother swore. Persi walked right across the room, opened the front door, and slammed it behind her, the colorful glass panes rattling. Rhi blew her nose into her handkerchief and gave me a weak attempt at a smile.

"It's not your fault, Wren, honey. No one blames you," she said.

"Of course it's not her fault! It's Mom's fault, just like the rest of this god-awful mess!" my mother shouted. "Leave it to Asteria to cause more trouble dead than alive."

"That's not fair!" Rhi cried out, her voice thick with tears.

"You're right! None of this is fair! Or sane! This is absolute lunacy and I won't stay here to listen to another minute of it. Wren, grab your things, we're leaving."

She marched straight for the door without looking at me. Something inside of me snapped and I jumped to my feet, Freya held tightly in my arms.

"No!"

My mother froze as she was about to open the door and turned. "Excuse me?"

"I said, no! We can't just leave! It's not going to solve anything!"

My mother took a deep breath, her knuckles white on the brass doorknob. "Wren, we can't stay here. This is..."

"I know," I said quietly. "It's a mess. But if we leave it will still be a mess. We have to... to sort it all out."

My mother looked for a moment like she might shout at me, and I held my breath. But then suddenly her shoulders sagged and she dropped her head with a sigh that seemed to expel every ounce of fight left in her.

"Okay. You're right. We... we have to figure this out. But once we do—"

"We go home," I finished for her, nodding.

My mother deigned to come back into the room, but she didn't seem able to sit, choosing instead to pace back and forth behind the sofa while we listened to the rest of the reading. The words washed over me, full of complicated legal terminology I didn't understand. Then, when it was all over, Lydian pushed the box across the table toward Rhi.

"The final bequest is in that box, and your mother has left it to her three daughters," she said. "And she wanted to make sure I put it into your hands at the reading, just in case."

Rhi looked down at the box in bewilderment. "In case of what?" she asked.

"In case you need to use it," Lydian clarified.

Frowning, Rhi lifted the cover of the box and shifted aside the blue velvet fabric. I couldn't see what she was looking at. Her eyes widened, and she turned to look over her shoulder at my mother, who paused in her pacing and stepped forward to look into the box as well. I watched my mother's expression harden until she resembled a statue of herself, carved from stone. She clenched her hands, and then loosened them again before nodding once, curtly.

"Very well. You've given it to us. Is there anything else?" Rhi asked. She sounded exhausted.

"I'll need to see Wren and Kerri at my office over the next few days to go over some paperwork; but for today, there's just this." Lydian reached into the voluminous depths of her caftan and produced a small manila envelope. She held it out to me. "Go on, then, child," she barked when I just sat there staring at it.

I forced my hand out toward her and she deposited the envelope into my grasp. It was heavier than I expected and made a strange clanking sound. I unwound the string that held the top of the envelope closed and tipped it upside down onto my palm. A large ring of mismatched keys fell out.

"What's this?" I asked blankly.

Lydian rolled her eyes. "The keys to your new property, of course."

I looked down at them, suddenly wishing I could give them back. I didn't want the keys. I didn't want the cottage. I didn't want to be the one responsible for tearing my mother and her sisters even further apart than they'd already managed to run from each other. But I couldn't say any of that, not into the loaded, sorrowful silence of the room. And so instead, I slid the keys back into the envelope and tied it up with the string again.

"Thank you," I muttered.

"Well, I ought to be getting along, then," Lydian said, and I yelped in surprise as her two granddaughters jumped to their feet. They'd been so motionless and silent that I'd literally forgotten they were still sitting there. Now they fussed over Lydian, offering hands to help her up, and arms for her to lean on as she crossed the room to the door. She batted them away like irksome flies, although she did allow them to hold the door open for her as she shuffled across the threshold. Persi was standing just outside on the porch, smoking a clove cigarette.

"I'm sorry this has been such an ordeal for you girls," Lydian said. "But I had to discharge my duty."

"It's not your fault, Lydian," Rhi said.

"We're sorry you had to be in the middle of all of this," my mother added.

Persi, however, was still looking to cast blame. "Why the hell didn't you talk her out of it, for goddess's sake?" she muttered. Maybe she thought Lydian wouldn't catch her words, for she started in alarm when Lydian turned to glare at her.

"Persephone Vesper, no one ever talked your mother out of anything once she'd made up her mind, and you damn well know it," she said. Then she looked at me. "My office, this week, you hear me, young Vesper?"

I nodded.

Lydian gave a satisfied grunt and tottered her way toward the stairs, her granddaughters hovering like anxious insects on either side of her. I watched her climb with surprising nimbleness into the little rickshaw. Selene and Vesta hoisted themselves onto the two bicycle seats in front of her and began to pedal her away like a pair of matched ponies. Lydian turned before she reached the end of the drive to give a regal wave over her shoulder.

And then she was gone, leaving a heavy silence in her wake, and unanswered questions burning on all of our tongues.

8

Lydian may have been gone, but the emotions she'd unleashed in the room loomed over everything like a sentient being.

My mother sat staring into the fireplace. Persi continued to smoke out on the porch, lighting a second cigarette off the first. I was afraid to open my mouth, feeling quite suddenly like a villain in a story I didn't fully understand. Finally, it was Rhi who broke the silence.

"Well," she said, stuffing her damp bandana back into her overall pocket, "I suppose I'd better get supper started."

"Don't go to any trouble, Rhi. I'm not hungry," mom muttered.

"It's no trouble, and anyway, I've got to stay occupied. I can't just sit here anymore, it's too..." She swallowed hard. "Anyway. I'll be in the kitchen."

"Can I help?" I asked. I was just trying to be polite, but there was a note of desperation in my voice, and I knew I wasn't really talking about dinner.

Rhi smiled at me in a way that made me feel like she could read my thoughts on my face. "No, Wren. You relax, sweetheart. You've had a long day today." And she hurried off through the hallway to the back of the house.

The back of my house, a tiny voice whispered in the back of my head. This was nuts. I felt like the walls were closing in on me. I had to get out of here, get some fresh air, or this house that was suddenly mine would swallow me whole.

I didn't dare go back out the front door; the thought of facing Persi's wrath was more than I could handle. My eyes found the French doors at the back of the living room, and I crossed to them, peering out. They led to a flagstone patio surrounded by a wooden trellis, up which a riot of flowering vines raced each other toward the sun. I took the brass handle in my hand.

"I'm going outside for a few minutes," I told my mom. She made a sound like "Mm-hmm," which I took as acknowledgment, and slipped out into the garden before she could protest.

The smells of the garden were cloying at first in the early-summer humidity. There was a constant underscore of buzzing bees and the steady trickle of water from somewhere. A fountain, maybe? I couldn't see one from where I was standing. To my left the lawn sloped away from the gardens into a little sunken orchard of fruit trees, and in the midst of them stood a greenhouse and another small building rather like a large garden shed. Rhi had said that Asteria was in the summer house—was that the place she was talking about? I shuddered at the thought and turned my back on that part of the yard, choosing instead a path that wound through a collection of rose bushes in the opposite direction. The air was so heavy with moisture that I could taste it on my tongue, and it clung to my hair, weighing it down in bedraggled tendrils against my neck. My glasses seemed in imminent danger of fogging up and made near-constant attempts to escape down the bridge of my nose.

I followed the path through some low flowering trees and beds of herbs, past a birdbath and a low, stone bench, finally arriving abruptly at the stone wall I'd seen when we'd first arrived. I turned and walked along it, running my hands over the mossy stones, and following it to an arched door so overgrown with ivy and clusters of morning glories and Carolina jessamine that I wouldn't have seen it at all, but for the peeling remains of lavender paint. The door had an old-fashioned keyhole and a simple iron ring for a handle. My fingers itched to pull it, to open the door to whatever lay beyond, but I didn't even try. The rustiness of the hardware and the greenery creeping over the bottom of the doorframe meant it probably hadn't been opened in years. And so instead, I walked past the door, trailing my fingers over it wistfully before turning around a massive azalea bush, and stopping dead in my tracks.

Persi was sitting on a swing that hung from the branch of an ancient-looking tree. One arm was wrapped around the rope, the other holding her flask.

"Oh. Um... hi," I said stupidly. I took a deep breath and tried again. "Sorry, I didn't mean to bother you. I didn't know anyone was out here."

"Bother me? Haven't you heard? This is your garden now. I'm the interloper, not you."

My cheeks burned as I struggled to respond.

"I suppose you want to case the place, decide what to chop down and replace. Here, would you like the clothes off my back? I'm pretty sure I stole this from Asteria's closet, so it's probably yours now anyway."

"No!" I gasped, for she showed every indication of pulling her blouse over her head.

She smirked at me, letting her shirt fall back in place. Then she reached out and waved her flask under my nose.

"Fancy a little nip? It takes the edge off."

"I'm only sixteen," I told her.

She smiled and winked conspiratorially. "Never stopped me," she said. When I hesitated, she narrowed her eyes. "You're not one of those girls who follows all the rules, are you? How dull."

Actually, I was. I had never been remotely susceptible to peer pressure, not that anyone tried to put any on me. I'd never attracted enough notice from any of the popular kids to warrant an invitation to the kind of party where drinking happened, and I wouldn't have accepted even if someone had thought to ask me. But something inside me seemed to ignite at Persi's words. I didn't want to be the girl she thought I was. I wanted to do something to show her that I wasn't the devious interloper she'd clearly pegged me as. I wanted to impress her. And so I did the only thing I could think to do in the moment: I took the flask from her hands, put it to my lips and took a swallow.

My regret was instant and all encompassing. The liquor—whatever it was —was like fire down my throat, and I coughed and choked as I tried to force it down.

Persi laughed at me, but there was a glint of something like approval in her gaze when I caught her eye between coughing fits, and I managed a smile. I collapsed onto an overturned bucket beside her, trying to catch my breath.

"I distilled that myself," Persi said, taking the flask back from me and taking a long, smooth draught. She smacked her lips. "Can you taste the juniper and the orange peel?"

I nodded, suppressing another cough. It was a lie. All I could taste was burning. When she offered it to me again, I only pretended to take a sip, letting only the tiniest trickle pass my lips. This time I managed to swallow it without humiliating myself.

"I don't want this house," I blurted out. "I don't want any of it. If I could just... just give it to you—"

"I know that," Persi said, if somewhat grudgingly. "This isn't your fault, and I shouldn't be treating you like it is."

I blinked. I hadn't expected an apology.

Persi laughed at my expression. "Never dreamed I could be so reasonable, did you? Sorry about that. I've always been the dramatic one of the Vesper sisters—shouting first and thinking afterward. It's gotten me into a fair bit of trouble, but I'm no better at controlling my temper now than I was when I was a toddler, so I don't expect I ever will be. I'm sure your mother's probably told you all kinds of stories about me."

I shook my head. "I hardly know anything about her life before me. She doesn't like to talk about it, so eventually I stopped asking."

Persi let out a low whistle. "My, my. I'd been prepared for demonizing, but not complete erasure. I thought I was the only one in this family who could hold a grudge like that. I can see now that I underestimated my little sister in that regard. She's turned us into complete strangers, hasn't she?"

I nodded. "I'm sorry. I don't really understand why."

"She's trying to protect you," Persi replied evenly, staring out over the garden, the swing creaking comfortably. "She's wrong, of course, but that's what she's trying to do."

"Protect me from what?" I asked. "I still don't—"

"It's not my place to tell you," Persi said. "I might be the resident trouble-maker, but I've made enough trouble for one day. You're going to have to talk to your mother."

I joined her in a moment of quiet contemplation. Just a few minutes ago, I'd thought talking to Persi would be the most challenging conversation I'd have to have here. Now I knew I'd rather face Persi's temper a hundred times over than ask my mother to break open the defenses she'd so carefully constructed over all these years.

Except now I knew that they weren't defenses at all. They were walls, and they were around me, not her. And I didn't want to be walled in.

I wanted to be free. I wanted the truth.

But not now. Now my head ached, and I felt dizzy and sort of floaty from the gin. The truth could wait until tomorrow, when we'd all had a bit of time to process what had happened. My mother always used to tell me, when I was a little girl grappling with big questions at bedtime, that things would look clearer in the morning, and she was usually right. Granted, this was a much bigger conundrum than any I'd whispered to her from the stuffy-mountain of my childhood bed, but still. I thought we'd all be more reasonable after some sleep and a morning cup of coffee.

"Thanks for the gin," I said awkwardly.

Persi smiled a tight smile. "I'd appreciate it if you wouldn't tell your mother I tried to get you drunk. She's angry enough with me as it is."

"*Were* you trying to get me drunk? I thought you were just testing me."

The smile widened, and I saw how arrestingly beautiful Persephone Vesper could be when she let her guard down. "Well played."

"And?"

Confusion swept her features. "And what?"

"Did I pass, or what?"

The smile returned. "Yeah. Yeah, you passed."

I smiled back. "I won't tell my mom."

I made my way back inside and trudged up the stairs. It was barely dinner time, but my legs felt like they'd been encased in cement, and I couldn't stop yawning. It was as though my conversation with Persi had unwound a bit of the tension that was keeping me alert, and now I couldn't wait to crawl into my bed. I stopped at the first door on the right, which was hanging ajar. My mother had opened her suitcase on the bed and was digging through it for a pair of pajamas.

"I think I'm going to turn in," I told her. "It's been a long day."

"You haven't even had dinner yet. Rhi is—"

"I'm not hungry. I ate a late lunch downtown, remember?"

"Oh, that's right. Well, if you're sure..." She sank onto the bed as though the exhaustion had just that moment hit her, like a slap in the face. She patted the quilt and I crossed the room to sit next to her. "Wren, I know I have a lot of explaining to do—"

She faltered and I looked at her face, so pale, with deep blue circles under her eyes. I wanted answers so badly, but even more than that, I wanted her not to have to give them to me. Not tonight.

"It's okay, Mom. We can talk tomorrow."

Her face crumpled with relief. "Are you sure?"

"Surely sure. We can do it while we pick out paint colors for my new house."

Her face slackened with shock.

"I'm just kidding!" I said quickly, throwing my hands up in mock surrender. "Sorry, I should have realized you were too tired for sarcasm."

She allowed herself a weak chuckle as she reached out to muss my hair. "Tomorrow. I promise."

I bent forward so she could plant a kiss on the top of my head, and then got up. "Where am I sleeping?"

"The door right at the end of the hall. I already put your suitcase in there."

"Okay. I love you."

"I love you too, kiddo."

I opened the door into a sweet little room in the back corner of the house, which overlooked the gardens. I pulled aside the lacy white curtain and peered below me. Persi had abandoned the swing and vanished. The blossoms took on more vibrant colors in the lengthening shadows, and I watched them for a moment, waving hypnotically in the salty ocean air. If I turned my head and craned my neck, I could make out the cliffs and the top of the lighthouse... *my* lighthouse, I thought with an incredulous half-laugh.

I turned from the window and inspected the room a little more closely. It had the kind of old, uneven, wide-plank wooden floors that people in the city would pay a fortune for, with a cream-colored braided rug in the middle of it. The walls were painted a pale minty green. One wall was covered with framed watercolors that looked as though they'd been torn from a nature journal, each one featuring a different botanical or bird. A wrought iron bedframe was pushed into the corner beneath these and was spread with another colorful patchwork quilt and a mountain of mismatched pillows that nonetheless seemed to belong together—a little found family of cushions. Against the opposite wall was an old-fashioned wingback chair and above that, a set of open shelves covered in a hodgepodge of items: porcelain tea cups, bird nests, bits of driftwood, seashells and sea glass, and chipped mason jars full of dried flowers and feathers. Beside these was another window, with a little white-washed writing table and chair pushed under it. I crossed to this second window and opened it. Now that the air had cooled, I let the soft breeze play over my face and listened to it tinkle the music from the windchimes down on the porch—their tunes a gentle counterpoint to the distant crashing of the waves. I pulled out the drawer in the desk and found a dusty pile of drawing paper and a scattering of colored pencils rolling around inside.

I knew in that moment that I loved this room—that it was *mine* in a way that even my bedroom back in Portland could never be. I knew I wasn't supposed to want this house, and I didn't—at least, I didn't want to take it from anyone. But I was finding with each new room I explored and trinket I examined, that I didn't just want to spend the night here or stay for a visit; I wanted to *belong* to this place.

Even though I didn't know how long we were staying, I decided to empty the contents of my suitcase into the little whitewashed dresser beside the door. I looked at my reflection staring back at me in the mirror over the dresser, and experienced a memory so sharp and clear that I thought for a moment I was seeing the ghost of my younger self behind me twirling and twirling on the rug in a white summer dress. It was so real that I gasped and spun on the spot, expecting to stare into my own eyes. But the room was empty, apart from Freya, who had nudged through the door. I caught just a glimpse of her tail as she disappeared to explore the uncharted wilds beneath the bed.

I pulled up the edge of the quilt and peered beneath it. Freya blinked her green eyes back at me.

"What do you think of this place?" I asked her.

She meowed softly and slunk out from the shadows to pounce upon the bed and curl up on the pillows, as if she owned them.

"I like it, too," I admitted to her.

I curled up next to her and she wound herself into a fluffy little knot in the crook of my legs. I stroked her fur and listened to the hypnotic rhythm of her purring. Maybe I'll just close my eyes for a minute, I thought.

Just for a minute...

I woke suddenly in darkness and blinked around in confusion. The clock informed me that it was after nine o'clock. Had I really slept the whole evening away? It seemed so, though I still felt exhausted. I turned on the overhead light, as well as the one on the bedside table, which had a stained-glass shade that threw little colorful geometric patterns onto the wall behind it and revealed a plate heaped with food on the bedside table, long gone cold. Someone—probably Rhi—hadn't wanted me to miss dinner, but I was too tired to eat. I peeled myself out of bed stumbled into some pajamas, slid my feet into my slippers, and padded down the hallway to brush my teeth at the little porcelain sink in the bathroom. As I walked by my mom's room, I saw that she wasn't there. I strained my ears and heard the quiet mumble of voices downstairs—maybe she and her sisters were trying to talk things through. I hoped so, though I suspected that if Persi were also a part of the conversation, there'd be a lot more yelling.

Back in my room, I snuggled down under the quilt; Freya was already snoring softly as I turned out the overhead light. I half-expected to lie awake after such a prolonged nap, but instead my eyelids grew heavy again almost at once, as sleep washed over me like the incoming tide.

Tide.

Waves.

Ocean.

~

I dreamed of the Gray Man again, but for the first time, we were not walking along the beach. Instead, we stood side by side on the cliff top, looking out past the lighthouse to the sea beyond. My hair whipped around my face; my bare toes curled over the damp, slippery rock. There were stars out above us, but a dark and forbidding bank of clouds was rolling in off the water. I could see the flashing glow of lightning deep in its rounded belly.

"There's a storm coming," I said.

The Gray Man nodded, his face a shadowy blur.

I stretched out my arms on either side of me and tilted my face to the sky. "I wish I could fly right into it."

The Gray Man pointed to the clouds with his specter of a hand. His strange, whispered words coiled into my ear like smoke, and I heard them like a snatch of song on the wind.

"Then fly, Little Bird. Fly into the storm."

I closed my eyes, bent my knees, and flung myself off the edge into nothingness.

~

I hit my bed with a thump and woke with a gasp of terror. The room was dark, and Freya blinked sleepily at me, annoyed at having been woken up.

"Sorry," I told her. "Just a dream."

Just a dream, I repeated to myself, though the sweat still glistening on my body had the salty tang of the sea, and the shadows in the unfamiliar room were gathered in strange places. I rubbed my eyes and let them adjust, my heart pounding, until the dark shapes resolved into furniture and a suitcase splayed open on a chair. The battered gold alarm clock on the bedside table told me it was just after midnight. Strange. I could have sworn I'd only just fallen asleep a few minutes ago.

The fear that had flooded me upon waking receded now, leaving my limbs feeling like water and my mouth parched. I slipped out of bed to get a drink of water from the bathroom but stopped before I reached the bathroom door. Raised voices from downstairs caught my attention, and I strained to listen.

"...to please keep it down. I don't want to wake up Wren."

It was my mother's voice. I crept forward down the hallway, holding my breath at every tiny creak of a floorboard, until I reached the top of the stair-case and squatted down, holding onto the banisters for support while I eaves-dropped.

No, *listened,* I corrected myself. This conversation concerned me as much as it did them, and if they weren't going to include me in it, then I had every right to insert myself into it. Besides, how would I ever find out the truth if they clammed up every time I was with them?

"I knew she was sick, Rhi, but I didn't know she'd lost her damned mind!" my mother cried.

"Well, at least we're in agreement on one thing," Persi replied.

"Don't say that! It's not true!" Rhi's voice rose an octave in her distress, making it even higher and squeakier than usual.

"Look, I know how much you loved her—how much we all loved her—" Persi snorted loudly at this, but my mother plowed on, ignoring her, "but this isn't the kind of decision a sane person makes," my mother went on. "You can't just leave a house to a child."

"A child, moreover, whom you could pass in the street and not look at twice because you haven't seen her for the better part of a decade," Persi added.

"It wasn't mother's fault she couldn't see Wren! That was Kerri's decision," Rhi interjected.

"Oh good, I thought we might wait until later to heap all the blame on me," Mom said. "Go on, then, let's have it. This is all my fault, right?"

Rhi sighed. "I didn't say that, I—"

"You didn't have to!"

"I'll say it, if we're taking volunteers," Persi offered.

"I swore to her face that I would never come back to this house, and now she has actually saddled me with it!"

"She didn't—"

"Wren is only sixteen! She's not even legally allowed to own this house, which means it's my responsibility! If she wanted me to have the house, why didn't she just leave it to me?"

"Because she knew you'd sell it out from under us at the first opportunity?" Persi suggested. "Either that or burn it to the ground and dance around the flames."

"I wouldn't do either of those things and you know it," Mom snapped. "I would have signed it over to the two of you and that would have been the end of it! But of course I can't do that now, can I? Because it's not mine, it's Wren's, and I can't just make that decision for her! This is just an underhanded way to keep me here and tie me to this place the way she couldn't thirteen years ago."

I frowned. Thirteen years ago? But Mom and I had left this place when I was only a few months old. So what had happened thirteen years ago?

But Auntie Rhi had finally found her voice.

"Mom knew exactly what she was doing, I know she did, and it certainly wasn't to spite you, Kerri!" Rhi said. "You want to call it madness, fine, but there was a method to it, I know it. We just have to figure out—"

"It's not a riddle, Rhi, it's a will, and it's supposed to make sense!" Mom cried. "How are we supposed to figure anything out when she's dead? She didn't leave us an explanation!"

"I can't believe you two are being so obtuse!" Rhi shouted. "If you could see past your own indignation for a second, you'd realize she left us a way to get an explanation!"

"What are you—"

A silence descended so suddenly and completely that I dug my finger into my ear, convinced for one wild, sleep-addled moment that I'd lost my hearing. But then the silence was broken.

"No."

"But—"

"Absolutely not."

"How else are we supposed to—"

"I'm not doing that, and I can't believe you're even suggesting it." My mom's voice was shaking now.

"My God, what happened to you? You used to be fun," Persi said.

"Fun?! This is your idea of fun?" Mom cried out.

"Okay, maybe fun is the wrong word. You used to have a goddamn *spine*."

"Persi, shut up," Rhi snapped.

"Oh, great, so you're taking her side, now? I knew you would," Persi snarled.

"I'm not taking anyone's side. I just don't think you're being fair. This isn't about fun or what we want to do. It's about a duty to understand and carry out Mom's wishes."

"Oh, but I *do* want to do it. I have a few choice words I'd like to say, and this is the only chance I'm going to get to say them," Persi said. "They aren't exactly fit for the eulogy."

"We need clarity, not revenge."

"Says you."

"So, you want to do this, too?" Mom asked, her voice quietly dark now as she turned to Rhi.

"Honestly, no. But I don't see how else we're going to solve this. She left this for us for a reason. It was the only other thing in that box. We can't just ignore it. If we want to understand why she did what she did, we're going to have to use it."

A realization fell heavily into my brain like someone had dropped it there, and I finally understood what they were talking about. There had been another... *something* inside the box Lydian had brought with her, an object wrapped in blue velvet fabric. I struggled to remember what Lydian had said about it.

Your mother wanted to make sure I put it into your hands at the reading, just in case.

In case of what? Rhi had asked.

In case you need to use it, Lydian had answered.

This didn't make any more sense to me than it had during the will reading, but I was sure, at least, that this was the object they were arguing about using.

But what the hell was it? I wished I could creep further down the stairs to try to get a glimpse of it, but I knew I couldn't risk getting caught spying on them. Then my mom spoke again.

"This is... I can't believe this is... I knew coming back here was a mistake."

"Oh, believe me, we all knew that," Persi grumbled.

"Fine. Fine." I heard a creak followed by footsteps and I knew my mother was pacing the living room now. "Well, we'll have to wait for the full moon—"

"It's the full moon tonight," Rhi said quietly.

"Seriously?"

"You don't even follow the cycles of the moon anymore?" Persi asked, clearly disgusted. "My goddess, who are you?"

My mother didn't reply. Instead she said, "Do you have what we need?"

"Of course," Rhi said.

"Well, then let's get it over with."

"Communication will be clearest at three o'clock," Rhi said tentatively.

"Fine! Three o'clock. Where should we—"

"In the garden," Persi answered. "Under the elder tree, like we used to."

"I'll bring everything with me. Just... just come, okay?" Rhi implored.

My mother didn't reply out loud, but suddenly there was a creaking of floorboards and the shutting of a door, and I realized I had about five seconds to sneak back to my room or get caught at the top of the stairs. I scrambled to my feet and dashed on tiptoe back to my room, closing the door behind me and darting for the bed. I'd only just managed to pull the quilt up over me when the door opened again, and a golden shaft of light stretched across the floor and over the foot of the bed. I held very still, eyes screwed shut, breathing slowly and evenly. I heard my mother sigh, then pad across the floor until she stood beside my bed. She bent down and kissed me on the top of my head. My anxiety screamed that she would know I was awake, but if she did, she said nothing. Then I heard a strange, quiet clanking noise, almost like the wind-chimes out on the porch, but less musical. Before I could identify it, silence fell again. I heard my mother cross the room, and darkness descended as she eased the door shut again.

I sat up, blinking. The room seemed undisturbed. I turned to stare out the window at the moon bright patch of garden, my mind spinning. My mother was going to meet her sisters in the garden at three in the morning to "get answers," but how? And from whom? It almost sounded like... I put the idea out of my mind. Asteria was dead. There was no speaking to her. The more I thought about the conversation, the more confused I became. The elder tree? The moon? None of it made sense, and there was no way in hell I was just going to let it go. I had questions, and no one was bothering to answer them—in fact, no one even seemed to think I was entitled to answers. And so my decision was made.

I just hoped I'd be able to stay awake until three o'clock.

9

I don't think I could have slept even if I'd tried. For the next few hours, my thoughts writhed in my head like serpents, coiling and intertwining and slithering away before I could get a hold on them. I tried to distract myself scrolling through my phone and reading a book, but it was useless, and I tossed them both aside in frustration. Desperately, I tried to make sense of the last twenty-four hours.

My grandmother had died. No one seemed bothered to explain exactly how. My mother and I returned to a town where everyone knew us and stared at us in the street like a bigfoot sighting. Now, a few sentences in Asteria's will seemed to have tied me to this place forever, this house that felt strange and yet familiar, a song to which I could feel the tune deep in my bones; and yet, I'd forgotten the words. As hard as my mother had tried to cut ties with this place, here she was, more tangled up in it than ever, and now here I was, climbing out of bed and into a pair of jeans to sneak out into the garden and spy on...whatever the hell it was my mother and her sisters were overcoming their estrangement to do together. Freya watched me dubiously from the bed as though to say, "Better you than me, human."

I stopped in front of my mother's bedroom door, heart pounding, and eased it open the tiniest crack I could manage. The bed was rumpled and empty, and I expelled a held breath. She was already outside, then.

The house was silent—a heavy quiet that pressed down on my skin like humid air. I considered which way I had best enter the garden. Persi had mentioned their meeting spot as "the elder tree," but as a city girl, I was useless at identifying different types of trees; and so my earlier walk through the garden had left me no closer to knowing what tree she might be talking about. I decided, therefore, to enter the garden from the front of the house and work my way around the outer edge of Lightkeep Cottage's extensive garden, pressing myself into the added shadows of the fence and border hedges for a little more cover, in case I rounded a corner and came upon them suddenly. Eventually, however, I had to venture further toward the center, thinking perhaps I just couldn't glimpse them from the perimeter; but even these explorations turned up nothing but Diana prowling for unsuspecting mice. I began to panic. Had I gotten the time wrong? Was there another part of the garden I hadn't noticed? I wound along a path that ended in the stone wall I'd discovered earlier; a dead end, I thought, and had nearly turned back when I noticed the door.

In the brightness of day, the door with its lavender paint had been locked tight, half-hidden in a curtain of creeping vines and blossoms. Now, however, there were crushed petals scattered on the ground in front of it, and the door had been pushed inward. I bent to see a key, ornate and rusted with age, sticking out of the lock, and the sight of it unlocked something else: the realization of what I had heard in my room, the strange clanking sound when my mother had lingered by my bed. If I went back up there and examined the key ring on my bedside table, the one that Lydian had given me only earlier this afternoon, I knew I would find the largest, oldest key was missing, swiped in the night by my mother, who needed it to open this door.

The door had been shoved open far enough for me to slip through it easily, and so I made no sound as I entered the walled part of the garden. The moment I crossed beyond the boundary of the wall, there was a shift in the very air around me. It was as though a veil had fallen over the garden, one that separated this inner sanctum of the garden from the outside world. Here, the distant crash of the ocean waves could not reach my ears, and the persistent breeze that ruffled the leaves and shook the blossoms had been tamed, like a wild creature into purring submission. Above my head, stars were blooming between scuttling, purple-tipped clouds, and the moon shone round and full. I felt the pulsing of my anxiety calm as I looked up at it and found myself suddenly glad of its face shining down on me, watching. I felt braver under its gaze, less afraid of what I might encounter here.

The inner garden was as lush with bloom as the outer garden as I entered it, but there was something more exotic about the foliage here. I was quite sure that some of these plants shouldn't be growing on the coast of Maine. There was a hothouse heaviness to the air as I breathed it in, ripe with dizzying perfumes. I kept to the shadows of larger bushes and shrubs, listening over the insistent pounding of my own heart. I heard nothing to guide me to where they sat; but then, a seductive scent reached my nostrils and, at the same moment, a swirl of gray smoke rose from the center of the garden.

I crept forward, using a massive hydrangea bush for concealment, and spotted them at last. They sat, all three, under the branches of a squat tree with a rough, furrowed trunk and an impressive canopy of thick green leaves. Among the leaves were clusters of deep purple berries—elderberries, I realized. This was the elder tree, then. I'd found it. The three sisters sat cross-legged in a triangle facing each other, their faces pale and drawn in the colorless cast of the moonlight. As I watched, Rhi lifted her arm, gently waving a smoking bundle of sage over her head. She circled it once, twice, three times, and then passed it to Persi, who did the same. Then Persi thrust it toward my mother, who hesitated, and then took it, imitating her sisters' motions before handing it back to Rhi again, who placed it in a wide, shallow basin, still sending tendrils of curling smoke up into the sky.

"Ready?" Rhi asked, looking at each sister in turn. Both nodded, though my mother's was more of an unwilling jerk of the head. Rhi took a deep breath, closed her eyes, and held out her arms as though welcoming an embrace. "We come to this place of our roots, to be rooted, grounded in our purpose to find answers. We imagine ourselves planted here, reaching downward, downward, deeper, deeper, finding purchase, claiming home in the soil that sings to our power. As our mothers and grandmothers did before us, we connect ourselves to this place, and to our sacred purpose."

Goosebumps began to creep up my arms and the back of my neck. My breathing, calmed at first by the tranquility of this place, had begun to pick up again as I tried to make sense of what I was seeing: some sort of ritual? I wiped a trickle of sweat from behind my glasses and inched forward, the better to hear their next words.

Rhi next lifted a large wooden spoon from a bag on the ground. It was rounded and smooth, with scorch marks along its edges. She kissed it once and handed it to Persi, who took it into her hands with the kind of reverence a mere spoon could never conjure up. She stood up and then turned to face the east, with a far-reaching gaze that seemed to reach the cliffs and the ocean beyond the garden wall. She raised the spoon like a conductor's baton and pointed as though to conduct the music of the waves themselves.

"Element of air, I call on you," she commanded in a clear voice. As though in answer, the tranquility of the inner garden was disturbed by a sudden gust of wind that whipped Persi's hair around her face before settling again.

Air, announcing its presence. I could scarcely breathe.

Persi turned in a clockwise direction, dragging the spoon against the dirt as she did so, so that she drew a quarter circle in the earth. Now she was facing the south and, I realized with sudden panic, me in my hiding place. I froze like a small animal scenting a predator, but if Persi knew I was there, she didn't let on. She raised her chin, lifted the spoon and said, "Element of fire, I call on you." A searing heat flashed past me along with a crack and a brightness that rent the night in two. From nowhere, lightning and the electric tang of static in the air. I threw my hand up over my mouth to contain the scream that had coiled there, waiting to escape.

Next she turned away from me to the west, dragging the spoon in the earth again to create a half-circle. "Element of water, I call on you."

At once, a fine mist was cooling my face, as though the earth itself had given up the water in the ground, in the air, in the plants, to answer the call. Persi turned her face up, enjoying the feel of it on her skin before turning one last time to face her sisters and the north, still drawing with the spoon.

"Element of earth, I call on you."

In a single movement like stretching toward the sun, the foliage around me shifted, reached, orienting itself as close to the sisters as it could without uprooting itself. The very bush in which I was hiding bent forward as though it had suddenly become alive in a new way. If it had been the first strange thing to happen, I would surely not have been able to control myself. But luckily, the sudden manifestation of the other elements had somewhat prepared me that something would happen, and therefore I did not run shrieking in terror out of the garden. Instead, I flung a second hand over my mouth and forced myself to sit impossibly still until the moment had passed and the garden had settled itself comfortably around me again.

While I barely avoided giving myself away, Persi drew the final quarter circle, so that all three sisters now sat within its borders. Then she stepped to the center, lifted her face and her arms to the sky and said, "With these elements together under spirit, I cast a circle of protection above, below, and within."

Around them, a humming of insects began, and the circle Persi had dug into the ground with her spoon glowed momentarily white. Then it settled again, the humming faded to nothing, and the three women sat once again facing each other, not one of them seeming in the least surprised by anything that had happened since Persi had begun. I crouched in my hiding place waiting, sweat dripping down the back of my neck, my hands shaking, and my heart beating like it desired nothing more than to escape my body. I was both eager for what would come next, and terrified, not least because they had just cast a circle of protection and I was decidedly outside its borders.

Persi handed the spoon back to Rhi, who put it back in her bag and now pulled out a set of the windchimes I recognized from the porch, and a tall silver thermos. I watched in confusion as she hung the wind chimes from one of the branches over her head, and then opened the thermos. She placed three teacups in the grass, poured a bit of steaming liquid into each of them, and handed one to each of her sisters before taking up the third herself. Was this just some sort of bizarre picnic?

Rhi raised her cup. "To Asteria."

"To Asteria," the other two repeated, and together they drained their cups. Mom pulled a disgusted face.

"Goddess, I hate mugwort tea."

"I put some honey in to help sweeten it," Rhi said.

"It doesn't help," Mom retorted, handing the cup back to her.

"Want a chaser?" Persi offered, holding out her flask.

"Persi, we want a clear head, remember? Put that away," Rhi scolded as she wrapped the teacups in fabric and placed them back in the bag. "All right. Close your eyes. Center yourselves. Open yourselves up to communication, to connection, to understanding."

They sat in silent contemplation for maybe a minute, and then Rhi produced the stumps of three candles stuck into glass jelly jars. She lit them with a cigarette lighter from her pocket, placing one down in front of each of them. Then she reached into the bag one last time and pulled out the object

I'd been curious about since I'd seen it yesterday: the object that had lain inside the box Lydian had brought, the one she said the sisters could use if they "needed answers." It was still wrapped in the blue velvet covering, and I couldn't help but lean forward, risking my balance to get a better look as Rhi carefully unwrapped it and pulled it out.

It was fairly flat and rectangular, about the size of a cookie sheet, but made of wood and stained and finished in a honey-colored hue that showed every whorl and knot in the wood. The edges were worn and rounded, too, as if by age and frequent use. Rhi placed it down in the grass between them, and by rising up onto my knees and craning my neck, I could just make out a collection of letters, numbers, and symbols painted onto the board in an ornate hand, black curling characters with lots of decorative flourishes. Then Rhi produced a large, triangular piece of green sea glass with a hole bored right through the middle and set it down on the board. All three sisters reached forward and placed a finger lightly on the glass, and suddenly I understood what was happening. The surprise and the relief hit me with such force that I came dangerously close to laughing out loud.

It was an antique version of a Ouija board—a spirit board, I'd heard them called. My mother and her sisters were about to do what every sugared-up eleven-year-old girl has tried at least once at a Halloween sleepover; they were going to try to speak to Asteria through a Ouija board. Despite everything I'd experienced in the garden so far, skepticism flooded my thoughts, calming me down from the heightened fear of watching them cast the circle. I'd played with a Ouija board maybe half a dozen times, usually because Poe had forced me into it. She was convinced that they worked, but all we'd ever managed to do was get mad at each other, because we were convinced the other was moving the planchette on purpose; or else overcome with a fit of giggles so strong that we abandoned it altogether to roll on the floor with streaming eyes instead. Not once, in all the times we'd tried it, had anything even remotely like ghostly communication come to pass; and so it was hard for me to feel anything but disappointment that this was the answer to the mystery of what the sisters were doing in the garden at three o'clock in the morning.

I also couldn't help but feel a little disappointed in my mother. She was buying into this crap? My logical, strait-laced mom, who lived in scrubs and listened to science podcasts while she shopped at Target? I was shocked she hadn't gotten up and stormed out of the garden already. I wondered if it was worth my staying and had half-resolved to sneak back up to my bed for some much-needed sleep when the sounds started.

At first, it just seemed as though the wind had picked up, but after a moment or two I realized that I could feel nothing—no cooling breeze over my sweaty skin, no rustling of leaves in the foliage that surrounded me. The sound wasn't air at all, but a whispering of voices that seemed to come from nowhere and everywhere all at once, enveloping the entire garden in a susurration that sent cold shivers skittering up my spine, and reignited the fear which had been nearly extinguished at the sight of the Ouija board. The temperature in the garden plummeted in an instant, and with a gathering horror, I realized I could see my terrified breath puffing out in front of me. I stared at my mother and her sisters, expecting to see some of my own panic mirrored back to me on their faces, but there was nothing of the kind. All three of them were sitting with their eyes closed, their hair whipping gently around their serene faces. My eyes fell to the board between them. The piece of sea glass was vibrating about six inches above the wood, as though the sisters' fingers were the only things stopping it from shooting up into the canopy of the elder tree above.

My mother's voice rang out, clear and powerful, "We call on the spirit of our mother, so recently departed. We call on her to give us the answers we seek, to the questions in our hearts. Speak to us, Asteria Artemis Vesper. Help us to understand the legacy you left behind, and how to move forward. Vesper witches who have gone before, watch over us in this moment of connection, and protect us from harm. We seek the light—shadow is not welcome here."

The whispering rose and fell, almost like the tide I could no longer hear. I watched in terrified fascination as the sea glass floated around above the board. Rhi's eyes were closed, and yet her hand, which held a pencil, was moving across a pad of paper that I hadn't noticed lying in the grass by her knee. Could she possibly be writing down the message the spirit board was revealing when she wasn't even looking at it?

Suddenly the whispering rose, and the sea glass shuddered violently beneath their fingers, causing all three sisters to open their eyes. My mother glanced around her, looking nervous for the first time. "Persi will this circle hold?" she hissed.

"Of course it will hold," Persi snapped. "You watched me cast it. The elements were strong."

"I can feel a presence trying to interfere. Can you feel that?" my mother asked.

"No, I think you're just being a... hang on," Persi cut herself off. She was silent a moment, and when she went on, her voice had a tremor in it. "Yes, I can feel it, too."

I began to panic. Were they talking about me? Could they feel that there was another person in the garden, spying on them? I started to wonder if I should back my way slowly out of the garden and go back to bed. I tried to envision how I would do that without being seen, and realized it was likely impossible. They were on the alert now; I'd have to stay where I was, even if I was interfering.

"The circle will hold," Persi said, sounding like she was trying to convince herself as much as the others, "but she won't be able to come through if we aren't concentrating."

Rhi's voice sounded out, a little sharp, but forceful, nonetheless. "Persi's right. We have to focus our energies and trust to the circle to protect us."

My mom looked like she wanted to argue, but swallowed her objections and closed her eyes again, doing her best to concentrate. The sea glass under their fingers steadied and began to swing around the board again. Rhi continued her documenting with the pencil.

This, I realized, might be my only chance to escape unnoticed. I put my hands down on the ground in front of me and began a kind of reverse crawl, placing each knee and hand carefully behind me, trying to avoid twigs or fallen leaves that might crackle under my weight and give me away. I'd only gone a few feet, though, when I stopped, heart in my throat.

Someone or something was behind me.

I didn't know how I knew it, only that I had the undeniable feeling of being watched closely. A deep, vicious cold had concentrated in the air at my back, like I was crouching with my back to a deep freezer. My ears were filled with a strange humming buzz, as though a million insects were speaking with a single voice. Beneath my fingers, beetles and ants emerged from the earth. I stifled a cry and snatched my hands back from the ground as they skittered toward the sound, which grew louder and more insistent behind me.

Don't turn around. Dear God, whatever you do, do NOT turn around, I told myself over and over again; and yet, the urge to do just that was growing stronger by the second.

The cold deepened, drew closer, until what I felt was no longer a blanket of cold, but a cold that moved. A cold that ventured closer, that poked and prodded, that reached out a long icy finger and ran it along the back of my neck. And all the while, the buzzing, humming, whispering voice grew louder. I could no longer see my mother and her sisters, obscured now on the far side of the shrub, but I could hear their strained whispers, and I knew things were not going as planned within their circle.

It wasn't me that was interfering with their seance at all. It was the thing that hovered behind me, so close now that the cold had resolved into a steady breathing, in and out against the back of my neck. I couldn't move. I couldn't think. The horror of it petrified me, leaving me paralyzed and helpless. It would reach out and touch me, I knew it. Any moment, that icy breath would become an icy touch, and I would be powerless to stop it. Then the whispering, skittering sound congealed into a voice unlike any living voice—a voice made of the buzz of insect wings, and the scratching of their legs, and the darkness of their eyes; a symphony of horror that spoke four words:

"Welcome home, Little Bird."

My eyes fluttered closed. I smelled the sea. I felt the lapping of waves around my ankles, and I was falling...

Falling...

10

"Expand the circle!"

My eyes, which had been drifting closed almost without my realizing it, snapped open again. Rhi had suddenly realized something was wrong. As I watched, frozen, the strange voice still echoing in my ears, she glanced down at the paper under her fingers and gasped, jumping to her feet. "Expand the circle! Do it now, Persi, now!"

"What do you—?"

"It's a warning from Asteria! Protect the garden! All of the garden, do it now!"

I forced my eyes open again, pulling away from the call of the voice that wasn't a voice, and watched in a haze as my mother and her sisters jumped to their feet and joined their hands. They were chanting something, but I couldn't hear it over the voice, which threatened at every moment to drag me back into the darkness with it...

And then two things happened in quick succession. First, the necklace that Asteria had sent to me, the one still hanging around my neck, began to grow warm, and then hot against my cold and clammy skin. I fumbled for it with my fingers before gripping it tightly in my fist, and as I touched it, I felt the dark cold energy around me retract slightly, like a startled animal.

And then, before the coldness could reassert itself, a wave of power crested and broke over the garden, flooding every corner, washing away the cold and the voice and the darkness. I felt it go, felt it try to take me with it like a riptide, but I clasped one hand around my necklace, and dug the other into the soil of my family's garden, squeezing my eyes shut against the pull. Rhi's words echoed in my head, and I whispered them over and over again:

We imagine ourselves planted here, reaching downward, downward, deeper, deeper, finding purchase, claiming home in the soil that sings to our power.

At last the sentient cold released its hold on me. Warm balmy summer night air swirled around me once more. I gasped, and then called out the only word I could think of, because it was the only person I wanted.

"Mom!"

"Wren! Oh my God!" My mother's voice was strident with fear, and I heard her crashing through the flower beds toward the sound of my voice. Carefully, I got to my feet, wobbling a bit on shaky legs, but trying to pull myself together so that she wouldn't know how scared I'd been—how close to succumbing to whatever that thing was that had found me; and, perhaps most disturbing of all, how familiar it had seemed.

She found me as I rose, and crashed into me, nearly knocking me flat again as she hugged me. "Wren, are you all right?"

"I'm fine," I said, and though the response was automatic, I realized it wasn't a lie. Second by second, the ill effects of the experience were fading away, leaving me feeling more and more like myself—confused as hell, but definitely myself. I was already starting to doubt everything I'd just experienced, and yet I felt a nagging disappointment that I hadn't turned around to see who—or what—had been behind me. A tiny part of me was shouting that if I hadn't been such a coward, I'd understand everything.

My mother had her hands on either side of my face, staring into my eyes as though afraid she was going to see someone other than me staring back out at her. But having ascertained that I was, indeed, fine, her anger kicked in. "What in the world are you doing out here?"

There was a scolding edge to her voice that ignited my own temper. I pulled my face out of her grip. "Are you kidding me? What the hell are *you* doing out here?!" I asked, gesturing over to the elder tree, where both of my aunts were still standing, pale and wide-eyed, with the same fear that had infected both of us.

My mother blinked at me as though that was the last question she was expecting instead of the first. "I... we... it was a private... you shouldn't have followed me!" she blustered, but there was no way she was getting away with that kind of amateur deflection, not this time.

"I followed you because you were acting sketchy and you won't tell me anything! I'm not a kid anymore, and I need some answers!"

She was shaking her head violently. "This is between me and my sisters. It was just something we needed to work out."

I barked out a laugh. "You can't seriously just expect me to believe that this was normal sisterly bonding stuff! I realize I don't have sisters, but I'm not an idiot, Mom! You have to tell me what's going on!"

My mother was staring at me, chewing on the inside of her cheek, opening and closing her fists at her sides, and looking like she might break into a sprint and run from me at any moment.

"Kerri, it's time. You've run from this for thirteen years. Enough running."

It was Persi who said it, in a voice that sounded bone tired. I looked over at her, and her eyes were fixed on my mother's rigid form, her expression sad, almost defeated.

"I'm not running," my mother ground out through a mouth that didn't seem to want to open.

"But you're still hiding. Enough hiding. Tell the girl. She has a right to know."

"She's only sixteen."

"And it's a miracle that something hasn't happened already to make her suspect the truth," Rhi chimed in. Her voice shook with the tears welling in her eyes. "You've run out of road, Kerri. I know you don't want to hear it, but it's the truth. And now Wren deserves the truth, too."

I watched as my mother's resolve crumbled. She seemed to diminish in an instant, all the air and fight and anger whooshing out of her. She dropped her head into her hands. I held my breath, unwilling to push her now that it seemed she might finally give in. When she raised her head again, her face looked more tired and defeated than I'd ever seen it. It scared me, but the fear was pale and feeble compared to the burning curiosity that eclipsed it.

"Mom?" The word was an invitation that she finally accepted.

"Wren, our family—the Vespers—we're witches."

The words hung in the air between us, echoing in my brain, which refused to make sense of them.

"Witches," I repeated weakly.

"That's right." She sighed and sat down on a nearby bench, resigned at last to letting it all come out. "For centuries, for as far back as our family history has been documented. When the Vespers settled in Sedgwick Cove, they did so because they were guided here, to a place where they could practice their craft safely."

"But it wasn't only that," Rhi added, crossing over to us and coming to stand behind the bench. "Sedgwick Cove itself is a very special place, a place where natural energies surge and come together, where the veil between worlds is very thin. Practicing our craft here enhanced our abilities and strengthened our spells. Here we were more powerful. Here we could truly test the boundaries of our own capabilities."

The words had a learned-by-heart sound to them, as though Asteria had whispered these very words into their ears as they lay their childish heads upon their pillows—a bedtime story that was at once legend, and truth.

And now Persi added her voice to the recitation. "And then others came, drawn by the same promise of power. Some came with good intentions, and others with dark. Ever since then, we have stayed here, to expand the light, and to banish the dark."

"Witches?" I said again, because my brain couldn't seem to process any other word but that one. "What... exactly does that mean?"

My mother looked too dejected to answer. Luckily, Rhi was there to help. "There are nearly as many traditions and ways to engage with witchcraft as there are witches in the world, so that's not exactly an easy question to answer. Anyone can decide to take up a form of witchcraft, just as someone might decide to take up a hobby or convert to a new religion."

"You make it sound like a fad," I said.

"That's because some people treat it like one," Persi said disdainfully. "Anyone can cast a circle or complete a charm. But whether it will hold any power for them is an entirely different matter. Abilities and affinities matter, as does commitment to learning and growing. A witch may find herself to be powerful without a family history of magic, but it's very unlikely. Mostly she'll just wear dark eyeliner and start a TikTok for attention."

"That's not the kind of witchcraft you're talking about in our family, though," I said. "Nothing about what just happened here tonight was a social media trend. There's no hashtag for that shit."

Persi threw her head back and laughed. "Exactly. In our family, witchcraft means powerful hereditary magical abilities. The kind of abilities that will surface, whether you seek to develop them or not."

"Wait so... does that mean that I have them, too?" I asked. I'd hoped to sound excited, but it came out a bit dubious.

"Undoubtedly," Persi said.

"Probably," Rhi added cautiously.

"Well, which one is it?" I asked. "Undoubtedly or probably?"

"Do we really need to get into all of this at three o'clock in the morning?" my mother mumbled into her hands.

"Of course we do! I just found out I might have, like, magical abilities! Do you really expect me to—"

But Rhi held up a hand, and there was a warning in her eyes even I couldn't ignore in my excitement. "This will be a more fruitful conversation if we can have it in the morning, after everyone has gotten some rest and a little time to think," she said. I wanted to argue with her, to say that no sane person could actually sleep after finding out something like this, but she threw me a look that was so pleading and earnest that my next question died on my tongue.

"I just... okay. Yeah, this can wait for the morning," I said, more grudgingly perhaps than I'd ever uttered a sentence in my life. "But... I do have one last question."

"Okay..." my mother said warily, with an expression on her face as though she expected me to strike her, instead of simply ask a question. I noted the expression, and tried to soften the question as much as I could, while still asking it.

"You said that Asteria sent a message—that you had to expand the protection to cover the whole garden. What did you need to protect us from?"

I didn't imagine it. All three sisters traded a swift but significant look that communicated more than most people could have expressed out loud. It was Rhi who finally answered.

"You remember we told you that Sedgwick Cove is a special place—one in which magic has the potential to be more powerful?"

"Yeah."

"Witches aren't the only beings who want to take advantage of that. And so, we have to work our magic carefully, and protect ourselves. Creating a circle is like creating a door—anyone can walk through it if you aren't vigilant."

I felt my expression twist sourly. "You know that doesn't really answer my question, right?"

"It's as close to an answer as we can give you," Rhi replied firmly. "Asteria's warning was cryptic. It only said that our circle had attracted darkness, and that we had to protect the garden."

"Did you see or feel anything, Wren?" my mother asked, her fingers twisted together into an anxious knot.

I swallowed. Later, in my bedroom, I couldn't retrace the logic that led me to keep the details of what happened to me in the garden to myself. It seemed silly to think they wouldn't believe me—in fact, they probably would have understood more about my experience than I did. And yet, some small resentful part of me wanted to keep a secret, too. I still wasn't getting all the answers I wanted—why should they? So when given the chance to explain, all I said was, "It... got really cold."

The sisters looked at each other again, a bit mystified, perhaps, but no one was looking particularly alarmed by what I'd said, which I was glad about; because I couldn't bear to make my mother look more distraught than she already looked. I'd never have even the slightest chance of learning more about our family, and witchcraft in general, if she thought I'd been traumatized the very first time she dared dabble in spellcasting again.

"You were really talking to Asteria?" I asked, even though I'd promised no more questions until the morning.

"Yes," Rhi said.

"And did you find out what you wanted to know?" I asked, knowing I was pressing my luck.

"We... have a better idea," Rhi hedged. Whether consciously or unconsciously, she shifted the hand that held the paper, so that the words she had written now faced away from me. "We can discuss it in the morning, over breakfast, all right?"

I couldn't imagine sleeping after everything that had just happened, but I also recognized a lost cause when I saw it. I would get no more answers tonight. Better to preserve what goodwill I could and try for answers in the morning.

"Okay," I said.

Rhi, Mom, and I began trudging slowly back toward the house. As I turned to shut the French doors behind me, though, I saw Persi was still standing in the garden, peering into shadows. Then she suddenly bent down and scooped Diana up from under a bench and whispered in her ear.

My last nonsensical thought as I closed the door, was wondering what Diana had whispered in reply.

11

Miraculously, I slept.

The strange encounter in the garden had taken more out of me than I'd realized, and just when I was sure that I'd be staring at my ceiling all night, burning with unanswered questions, I drifted irresistibly into sleep almost as soon as my head hit the pillow. I had just enough time to wonder if my mom or aunts could possibly have slipped me a witchy sleep potion or something before I surrendered to it. If I dreamed, my memory refused to conjure the images to my waking mind when my phone buzzed at not quite 7 a.m.

Are you okay? I've barely heard from you! How is it going?

I stared down at the text from Poe with bleary eyes. I considered, just for a moment, telling her the actual truth.

Well, I caught my mother and her sisters communicating with the ghost of my dead grandmother out in the garden and SURPRISE! We're all actually witches and they summoned something dark and terrifying into the garden that seems to know me. Oh, and also I'm now a homeowner.

Just imagining the look on Poe's face caused hysterical laughter to bubble up in my throat, and I had to swallow it back down with half a sob as the reality of the words hit me again.

Witches. We were witches. Well, *they* were—my mother and her sisters and my grandmother. I was nowhere near convinced that I possessed any of the alleged powerful generational magic that the women of my family were supposed to be born with. Maybe this kind of thing skipped generations.

Thinking back to my memories of Asteria, and what I knew of Persi and Rhi so far, I guess it wasn't all that hard to believe, but my *mom*? The practical, no-nonsense nurse, the woman who didn't even read fiction or burn candles or have houseplants? In all the years I'd grown up, never once had she shown even the slightest hint of anything approaching magic or witchcraft of any kind; and yet, if her sisters were to be believed, she'd been born and raised a powerful, practicing witch. How was it possible that there was never a hint, never the slightest sign of where she had come from, or what she could do?

Because she rejected it, I reminded myself. Not only that, I suddenly realized, but she over-corrected. She went to the exact opposite extreme, the way that rebellious young people often do, just to spite their families and defy their expectations. She didn't want her life to be planned out for her. She didn't want us to be trapped here.

And after everything she did to get away, here we were. Trapped. Only...

Only it didn't *feel* like being trapped—not to me, at least. I knew my mother was angry and bitter about it, but there was no trace of that feeling in me as I stared up at the ceiling of the little back bedroom by the sea. I didn't feel like something had been taken from me. Quite the opposite. I felt as though I had been given something—a kind of gift. What the hell I was supposed to *do* with that gift was an entirely different story. I felt a little like a kid who'd been handed a professional painter's palate, a blank canvas, and a beautiful set of brushes and told to make art... with no paint.

And it wasn't just me. If Aunt Persi was to be believed, Sedgwick Cove was full of witches, and had been since its founding; generation after generation of powerful magical families, their roots running under every square inch of this town. I thought of all the people I'd seen wearing the black ribbons yesterday —were they all witches? What about Xiomara and Eva and Nova and Zale? Xiomara and Rhi were trading herbal family remedies back and forth. Eva had mentioned that Nova's family, the Claires, had been in Sedgwick Cove almost as long as the Vespers. And all of them said they would be at Asteria's funeral today. Would I be walking into a funeral home packed with broomsticks and black hats? The absurdity of it all made me want to pinch myself to see if I'd actually woken at all last night, or if the events in the garden were just a bizarre dream from which I still hadn't roused. Then Freya stretched and caught me in the forearm with one of her claws.

Ouch. Nope. Definitely awake.

In the midst of this tangle of the incomprehensible, at least one single aspect of my past had finally become clear: now I finally understood why my mother was in full-fledged panic every time Asteria came to see me on my birthday. She was terrified that Asteria would let something slip, say, or do something that would give it all away. I thought back to the way my mother hovered nervously on the periphery of every interaction I'd ever had with my grandmother. The way her voice always carried a warning note in it, the way she seemed to count the seconds until it was all over, and she could breathe again. And what had been the moment that had brought her to her breaking point? What else but a witch bestowing a literal black cat on her granddaughter. No wonder she panicked.

I didn't know how to feel. How to deal with your family's hidden magical history isn't the kind of shit they cover in high school—or even therapy. There was definitely one feeling I could parse out, though... one that I wasn't at all sure was fair to my mom, but which I was feeling just the same: anger. I was angry at her for keeping this from me. Angry that, if I hadn't snuck out into that garden last night and spied on her, I'd still probably be in the dark—wandering like the village idiot through a town full of strangers who knew more about my own life and family than I did. And the worst part was that they all seemed to know that I didn't know. Everyone handled me with kid gloves, talking to me in vague riddles and trading looks I couldn't interpret. I thought back to Eva's warning words to Nova in the cafe: *Take it easy. She just got here.* My face burned with shame at the memory, and suddenly I couldn't lay there for another second. I needed distraction and, I suddenly realized as my stomach grumbled at me, I needed food.

I slid my feet into my slippers and an oversized cardigan over my pajamas, wondering if *buñuelos* could possibly be as delicious cold out of the fridge as they were hot out of Xiomara's kitchen. I tried to coax Freya to follow me, but she was entirely too comfortable, so I ventured out into the hallway myself. My eyes felt like sandpaper as I rubbed them behind my glasses and blinked around. It was early—the light outside was bright and golden. At the top of the stairs, I laid my ear against my mother's closed bedroom door. I could hear the soft, even breathing that meant she was still asleep. That was probably a good thing. I wasn't ready for a confrontation on an empty stomach, and anyway, she probably needed the sleep even more badly than I did. As unreasonable as I wanted to be, I knew that this whole situation was probably harder on her.

The sitting room was deserted except for Diana, who glared suspiciously at me from her one eye, tail flicking lazily. I snorted. Even this cat knew I was an imposter. I put out a hand for her to sniff before giving her a good scratch behind the ears.

"So, you're a witch's cat, eh?" I murmured to her. She leaned her head into my hand, enjoying the attention. "You'll have to show Freya the ropes. Wait, are you actually a cat, or did one of my aunts just turn you into one when she got annoyed?"

Diana gave me a look that made me thankful cats couldn't deliver devastating replies. Then she lifted her nose into the air and sniffed. A moment later, I caught the scent as well—someone had just started frying bacon. I left Diana to her lounging and went down the hallway to the kitchen.

Though I'd been at Lightkeep Cottage since the previous day, I still hadn't seen any of the downstairs of the house other than the living room. I passed down a narrow hallway encased in white-painted wood paneling and decorated with twinkle lights and a series of black-and-white photographs in gold frames, each showing a different view of the cove and the lighthouse. I lingered over them for only a few moments, long enough to feel relieved that none of them depicted a little girl walking into the sea.

I passed two doors on the right, one leading into a formal dining room, and another into a cozy library lined floor to ceiling with overcrowded bookshelves. On the left only one door led off the hallway, opening into a beautiful solarium full of morning sunlight. It seemed to be part sitting room, part greenhouse, for it was also full of a variety of brightly blooming plants hanging from the rafters and tucked into the corners. I'd never tried to grow anything in my life except a chia pet, and that thing had barely survived a week. The thought of having responsibility for all this lush greenness made anxiety twist in the pit of my stomach. I kept walking toward the doorway at the end, from which the smells of breakfast were wafting tantalizingly. I reached the threshold and froze.

My very first thought was that if I'd seen the kitchen yesterday, I'd already have known I was in a house full of witches. My Aunt Rhi stood in the center, bent over a massive stove, a bulbous cream-colored antiquity that looked to be at least a hundred years old, squatting comfortably on claw-footed legs in a bricked alcove that looked like it might once have been a massive fireplace. Bundles of dried herbs, bunches of feathers, baskets, and corked bottles of every color hung from the rafters overhead. The counters were crammed with antique tins and glass jars of every shape and size imaginable, each labeled in a spidery, faded hand. The sink under the window was a massive double farmhouse sink of cracked white porcelain and was currently full of armloads of blooms. A pair of pruning shears lay abandoned on the sideboard. The refrigerator, tucked into a corner, looked nearly as old as the stove. There was no sign of any modern-day convenience, such as a dishwasher or a stand mixer or even a toaster, but there was a huge mortar and pestle on the sideboard. Rhi was humming to herself, and I recognized Joni Mitchell crackling away on a turntable in the corner.

Rhi looked up and spotted me as she transferred the first batch of bacon to a wire rack.

"Wren! I wasn't expecting to see you so early. I thought teenagers like to sleep in late," she said, wiping her hands on her apron and smiling at me. She was still in her pajamas, feet bare and pale on the wooden floor.

"I usually do, but... well, there was a lot to think about," I said.

Her smile drooped a bit as a sadness crept into her eyes. "My goodness, you said it. I couldn't sleep either. Come sit down, honey. You want some coffee?"

"Yes please," I said, and watched, fascinated, as she heated the kettle and pulled out two glazed pottery mugs. She covered each with a cheesecloth filter in a wooden frame, and then ground the beans by hand with a little silver hand-crank grinder. Then she scooped the freshly ground coffee into a little heap on each filter and slowly poured the hot water over each cup.

"I've never seen anyone make coffee like that before," I admitted.

Rhi smiled. "Your grandmother always said it was the only way to drink coffee." She pushed my cup across to me, along with a little tray that contained a sugar bowl and a little pitcher of cream. She sipped hers black while I added cream and sugar to mine. "Personally, I think there are probably lots of ways to drink it, but your grandmother had a hard time breaking with tradition."

"Our family has a lot of traditions, I'm guessing," I said.

Rhi's smile slipped. "Yes. But you'll learn them easily enough. If you want to, that is."

"If I want to?" I asked. "I sort of got the feeling after last night that I might not have a choice."

"There's always a choice," Rhi said. "Just because you have an affinity for witchcraft doesn't mean you have to practice it."

I just sipped the coffee, letting my silence express my doubts.

"Persi said last night that I would definitely have magic, but you said, 'probably.'"

Rhi looked a little wary. "I did."

"So which is it?"

Rhi took a long sip of her coffee. "There is always the possibility that someone in a family of hereditary witches could simply... not inherit the same abilities. It's by no means common, but it does happen."

"Has it ever happened in our family?"

"Not that I've ever heard of."

"Great. I'll probably be the first genetic dud of the lot."

Rhi's laugh burst from her in a high-pitched giggle. "Why in the world would you think that?"

"I don't know. I'm just so... ordinary. There's nothing particularly unique or special about me."

"I'm sure that's not true," Rhi tutted. "Everyone is unique."

I snorted. "Just wait till you get to know me. I'm pretty underwhelming."

"That's nonsense," Rhi scoffed. "You just haven't discovered your thing yet."

"My thing?"

"Of course. Everyone has their thing," Rhi went on, as though this was common knowledge. "Some folks are fortunate—they figure out their thing when they're five years old and get to spend their entire life doing it. Other people take longer—after all there are a lot of things out there—it can take a bit of luck to stumble onto yours."

"What's your thing?" I asked, although I thought the answer was very obvious.

"Cooking, of course," Rhi said. "Specifically, baking. And I didn't figure that out until I was nearly twenty years old. Isn't there anything you enjoy?"

"Sure, but enjoying something and being good at it aren't always the same thing," I pointed out.

Rhi smiled. "Just answer the question."

I hesitated. "Well... I like stage managing."

Rhi narrowed her eyes. "I... don't know what that is."

I laughed. "It's part of theater. I sort of... run the whole backstage."

Rhi looked fascinated. "Go on."

"Well, I wear this headset that connects me to the actors and the lighting designer and the other crew members. And I keep track of everything that's supposed to happen during the show—the entrances, the exits, the lines, the set changes, the lighting cues, the sound cues—and make sure it all runs smoothly."

Rhi looked impressed now. "Well, that sounds very complicated!"

"It is," I admitted. "But it doesn't take any kind of talent. In fact, I fell into it because I wasn't talented enough to be in the show." This wasn't strictly true. It was possible I was a brilliant actress, but I'd never find out thanks to my crippling stage fright, so it might as well be true.

"See, that's where you're wrong," Rhi said between sips of coffee. "That's a job that requires a very organized mind, much like baking. You can't let your attention wander. You have to multi-task. You need to know everyone else's job and keep track of it. Just because it's not flashy doesn't mean it's not a talent."

I wasn't sure what to say, and so I didn't say anything. I'd never thought of it that way before.

"The same is true of magic, Wren. You'll likely have to explore it for a while before you find the medium that channels your power best. For some witches, it's obvious. Flashy, like I said. For others, it can be subtler; it takes time and study and exploration. But don't be fooled into thinking that subtle means less powerful. In fact, the opposite is often true."

Something about the way she said this... with a hint of pride... made me think that her magic might be considered of the more subtle (and therefore more powerful) variety. I tucked this information away for when I knew her better and had the courage to ask what seemed to me like a personal question. So I decided to ask another question—one to which I thought I might be entitled to an answer.

"You really spoke to Asteria last night?"

Rhi's face fell, and I almost regretted the change of subject—almost. "Yes, we did."

"Did you... get the answers you needed?"

Rhi furrowed her brow. "In a way. It's not... completely clear. But she did try to answer us before she... got distracted."

I felt the blood rush to my cheeks. It was me. I was the distraction who had prevented Asteria from telling her daughters what they needed to know. But I didn't let that stop me from asking the next question.

"Did she... am I allowed to know what she said?"

Rhi bit her lip. "I think that's up to your mother. She's the one who... oh damn!" She dropped her coffee cup and hurried to the stove to remove the bacon from the smoking pan. "Sorry, I got distracted. I'm just going to finish this up, all right?"

"Sure," I told her, though I felt a sinking feeling of disappointment that I'd have to wait for more answers. "Can I help at all?"

"There are some potholders right there, if you wouldn't mind getting the Dutch Baby out of the oven for me."

"Get the... I'm sorry, I thought you just said 'baby.'"

Rhi laughed. "I did. A Dutch Baby is a kind of big pancake you bake in the oven."

"Oh, right. Sorry," I said, blushing as I reached for the potholders.

"We're not those kind of witches," Rhi said.

"What kind?"

"The kind that cook babies in their ovens."

I blushed even deeper.

A few minutes later and I wouldn't have cared if the Dutch Baby had, in fact, been made with real babies, because it was one of the most delicious things I'd ever eaten, with cinnamon baked apples and powdered sugar spooned over the top. And that was only part of the feast Rhi had whipped up. My plate was loaded with bacon and fried eggs, and hot buttered toast as well. Having my mouth full meant less talking and more gazing around the kitchen. Rhi watched my eyes roving over her little kingdom for a while before she swallowed and spoke again.

"I'm what's known as a kitchen witch in witchcraft circles," Rhi said, gesturing around her with a contented sigh. "Like I was saying before, every witch finds the most natural ways to channel and harness her magic—mine always came most readily when I was here, working with food and experimenting with remedies."

I leaned forward eagerly. "Please tell me you have a cauldron."

Rhi laughed. "Oh sure, I keep it in the closet next to my broomstick."

"Well, if the witchcraft thing doesn't work out, you could definitely be a chef," I told her through mouthfuls of breakfast.

Her hollowed cheeks flushed with pleasure. "I do sell some of my baking around town, in Shadowkeep and at my friend Petra's coffee shop right down by the water."

"Are they, like... *normal* baked goods?" I asked.

"I'd like to think they're exceptional, but—"

"You know what I mean!"

Rhi raised an eyebrow. "Are you asking if I put spells on my scones?"

I grinned. "I guess?"

"Well, let's just say that they're all made with *intention*," Rhi said cryptically. I was still too overwhelmed by it all to ask her to clarify, so I decided to change the subject.

"Do you think Persi will come down to eat with us?" I asked.

Rhi rolled her eyes. "Persi's been coping with mom's death in other ways that don't involve baking everything in the house. I don't think she's home this morning."

"Oh," I said, and I couldn't help feeling relieved. Persi still intimidated me, even though I knew she didn't blame me about the will. "She's still pretty mad, huh?"

"Persi's always mad about something. She'll get over it. Or at least, she'll find something new to get mad about," Rhi said, with such certainty that I felt a little better.

"This is all... it's a lot," I said, sopping up a bit of egg with a corner of my toast.

"It'll be okay, Wren," Rhi said. "If you choose to learn, we'll teach you. If not, we're still family. Okay?"

I smiled. That felt manageable. "Okay." I pushed my plate away, sighing. "I can't eat another bite. Would you mind if I took some up to my mom?"

"That's a great idea. I'll help you make a tray. And after she's eaten... she has Asteria's messages from the spirit board. Ask her to help you understand. I think, after last night, she might finally be ready."

12

Together we piled a plate with eggs, bacon, toast, and a big slice of Dutch Baby. Rhi made another pour-over coffee while I found a jam jar and filled it with orange juice from a pitcher in the fridge. Then I carried the tray carefully up the stairs and knocked on my mom's door with my elbow.

"Breakfast delivery," I called.

"You're an angel," came the reply.

There was a precarious moment as I tried to balance the tray against my hip and open the door; but in the end, the whole tray of food made it to my mom's lap without a disaster.

"This looks amazing," she said, stifling a yawn.

"Oh it is, trust me," I said, curling up next to her.

Mom had a sip of coffee and then said, "Well, this is a good sign."

"A good sign?"

"You're talking to me. And bringing me food. Does this mean you aren't mad at me?"

I put my head on her shoulder. "Oh, I'm definitely mad at you. But I can't yell at you before you've had your breakfast. It wouldn't be fair."

Mom rested her head on mine. I couldn't see her face, but I could tell from the sniffing that she was working through some tears. So I just sat quietly and let her get a grip on herself, stealing a bit of cinnamon apple from her plate. Then I let her eat in silence until her plate was nearly empty.

"Better?" I asked when she had drained the last of her coffee.

"Better," she sighed, and turned to me. "All right, then. Let me have it."

But I couldn't yell. She looked so tired, so defeated. Besides, I'd done all my yelling last night. "I just... I wish you would have told me."

"I meant to," Mom said. "But I kept putting it off. At first, I told myself it was because you were still too young. But then as time went on, I got too comfortable. With each passing year, I told myself, well, I've gotten away with it this long. What's one more year? By the time you were ten, I was in full-panic mode. I knew at that point that I had run out of excuses. But when your grandmother showed up with Freya, well... I freaked out. Just as I was deciding you might be ready for the truth—or at least part of it—Asteria swept in like a tornado and whipped up every fear I had. Instead of inching the door open wider, I slammed it shut. It wasn't right, and I'm sorry. All I can say is that I was scared."

"Okay, fair enough, but I don't understand what it was you were afraid of," I said.

My mom was silent for a long moment. "Witchcraft is a complex thing. It can be beautiful and powerful. It can be healing and exhilarating and joyous and scary. It can be deep tradition, and it can be wild experimentation, and it can be all these things at once—so that you don't know who or what you are without it. But being a witch is also like walking on a knife's edge. It would be so easy to fall to darker intentions if you aren't vigilant."

"What do you mean, darker intentions?" I asked, a shiver coiled in my spine.

"I mean that wielding any kind of power can be dangerous. There is always the chance that you will slip, that it will control you rather than the other way around. Witchcraft has a dark and constant shadow, and the temptation is always there, to walk in the shadow rather than in the light."

My exhausted brain dragged up the words I'd heard last night: *And then others came, drawn by the same promise of power. Some came with good intentions, and others with dark.* At the time, I'd barely absorbed them, and now as I tried to interpret them, the best I could do was drag up a line from one of my favorite childhood movies: *Are you a good witch, or a bad witch?*

"So... you were worried that if you told me about our family, that I might turn out to be an evil witch, or something?"

"No!" My mother's voice was sharp, but she softened the word at once by wrapping her arm around me. "No, that's not what I mean at all. It's just... Sedgwick Cove has attracted witches of many traditions and backgrounds. It's been a haven for us, a place where we knew we were safe and, later, where we were, if not always safe, at least understood. But there is much power here, and not everyone walks in the light all the time. Not everyone is good at avoiding the temptation and excitement that hides in the darkness. So, that makes Sedgwick Cove a bit more dangerous than your typical small town. That's why we left. I couldn't bear the thought that I'd put you in danger simply by being who I was. So I decided to leave myself behind and become someone new, someone who could keep you safe. I should have realized I couldn't run from it forever, but at the time, I was willing to try."

"But it wasn't when I was a baby, like you told me," I said. "It was later, wasn't it?"

What little color her breakfast had put into her face drained out at once. "How do you—?"

"People keep saying it; 'thirteen years ago.' And I... I think I might even have a few memories of this house. It feels familiar to me. I wasn't three months old when we left Sedgwick Cove. I was three years old, wasn't I?"

She took a breath to steady herself, but the breath itself was so weak and fluttery that it seemed hardly to help. "Yes."

"What happened?"

She pressed her lips together. "I don't know."

"Mom—"

"Truly, I don't. This isn't me trying to protect you again. One night, soon after you turned three years old, your grandmother was watching you while I met some friends for dinner. When I came back, she had you in your own protective circle. You were wet and sandy and smelled of the sea, and you were sound asleep. She wouldn't tell me what happened, only that you were safe now. But I looked at her and I looked at you and I knew you weren't safe. I packed our things and we left that night."

"And Asteria never told you what happened?" I asked.

"No. She refused. She didn't want to scare me, I think, but her refusal to tell me the truth scared me even more. She let us go, Wren, rather than explain to me what happened that night."

She smiled sadly, and I felt the cold lump of my anger melt away. How could I stay mad at her for wanting to protect me? How could I blame her for loving me too much?

"But we're here now," I said, my voice a gentle nudge. "And thanks to Asteria's will it seems like we need to stay—at least a little while."

"It... it's not just Asteria's will anymore. After last night, it's more than that."

My heart began to pound. "What do you mean?"

My mom didn't answer right away. Instead, she reached past me toward the little bedside table. She pulled open the drawer and extracted a folded piece of paper. Then she put her nearly empty plate on the table and smoothed the paper out on the breakfast tray in front of us."

"Is that—"

She nodded. "These are the messages that came through from Asteria last night, the ones that Rhi wrote down."

I couldn't believe she'd taken them out without my even asking her to. "Am... I allowed to read them?"

"Yes. I think I owe you that, at least, although I'll admit to you right now that I don't fully understand them all. But I'll explain what I can," Mom said. "You probably saw us burning little bits of paper?"

I blushed a little at the allusion to my eavesdropping but nodded.

"We were feeding our intentions to the flames—the papers had our questions written on them. As each question burned, Asteria would answer them as best she could."

"And you're sure it was really her?"

"Yes." Her expression was so strange—fragile in its emotions, but strong in her conviction. I may not have seen or heard Asteria for myself, but I didn't doubt my mother that she had been there, somehow.

"I didn't think you believed in any of that stuff," I said, and it was hard to keep the accusation out of my voice.

My mom's smile was sad. "Just because you turn your back on something doesn't make it go away. I've learned that the hard way. Anyway, would you like to see what she said?"

I looked down at the first question and felt a welling of guilt bubble up inside me.

How the hell could you just leave her the house?

I looked up to see my mom smiling apologetically. "Sorry. The first question was Persi's and she was still in a temper from the will reading."

I examined the answer written under it: *There are answers in the house for her.*

I stared at the words. "Answers for me?"

"That's what I thought it meant," my mom agreed.

"Answers to what?"

"I wish I knew."

We sat silently contemplating the words for a few moments before moving on to the next question.

Why did you drag me back here?

I threw my mom a sidelong look and she smiled sheepishly. "I was also still in a temper," she admitted.

My eyes returned to the paper, to read the answer beneath it: *You need to be here. There must be three.*

I read the words several times, but they didn't make any more sense than the first time. "What does that mean, 'there must be three?'" I asked.

"None of us knew," Mom said, "which is why we asked follow up questions." She pointed down the paper at the next question. The printing was messy and it took me a moment to figure out what it said.

What do you mean? There must be three what?

And beneath that, Asteria's answer:

Three Vesper witches in Sedgwick Cove.

I looked up at my mom again. She was frowning right back at me.

"We tried to ask what that meant, but that's when everything went sideways," she said quietly.

I looked back at the paper. There were no more questions. Just a haphazard scrawling of messages from Asteria.

Something dark followed me.

Protect the garden. Expand the circle.

It has been waiting so long.

You must renew the Covenant of the Three. Protect each other.

"Well, that's creepy," I announced finally.

My mother managed a small laugh. "It was certainly frightening at the time. Now it's just..."

"Confusing?"

"Exactly."

"Do you have any idea at all what it might mean?"

"Well, the first part makes more sense than the last part," my mom said, plucking a last lonely bit of bacon off her plate and chewing it thoughtfully. "When you open up communication like that, it's sort of like lighting a candle in a room full of moths. The one you're trying to communicate with won't be the only one attracted to the light. Most of the moths are like Asteria—spirits we are connected with, probably mostly ancestors, who want to speak to us. But some are..." She hesitated.

"Evil moths?" I suggested.

Mom laughed again. "Evil might be a strong word. But yes. There might be spirits or... or other beings with darker intentions."

"And one of those spirits or other beings was in the garden last night?" I asked, trying to sound as though I merely wanted clarification, and not like I was scared out of my wits.

"Asteria seemed to think so," Mom said, and she was looking closely at me now. "We were already inside the circle, and so we didn't feel anything amiss. But you were out there."

She was asking the question without asking it, and yet again, I couldn't bring myself to tell her the whole truth. I couldn't explain why, except that it still felt like something that belonged to me, that I didn't want to share.

"I told you last night, it... it got cold. And I guess... there was that feeling you get, you know? When someone's watching you? But that's it, really," I said with what I hoped was a casual shrug.

I could tell by the way she put her arm around me that she wasn't buying it. "I'm sorry I didn't tell you what we were doing. It was my fault that you were out in the garden unprotected. If I'd just told you the truth—"

"Mom, don't beat yourself up over this," I told her. "I'm fine. Was I a little freaked out? Sure. But nothing bad happened to me. I'm just sorry that I screwed up your chance to speak to Asteria."

"You didn't screw up anything, Wren. Like I said, it was my fault for not telling you. In fact, I'm pretty sure all of this—this whole mess of a situation—is my fault."

"That doesn't really sound fair. A situation this complicated has to be more than one person's fault," I said.

Mom smirked. "Are you giving me permission to be mad at my mom?"

I shrugged. "You gave me permission to be mad at mine. It's only fair."

She still had her arm draped over my shoulder, and she hugged me with it once more before letting me go. Then she sighed again as she looked back at the paper. "I just wish I understood these answers better. Part of me—the part that's still trying to rebel against my mother—thinks it's just another manipulation tactic to get me to stay here and carry on the family traditions. But another part—"

"Thinks that communicating from the spirit world is a lot of trouble to go to just to manipulate your kid?" I suggested.

Mom frowned. "Exactly. Asteria was stubborn and devoted to our traditions, but that seems extreme, even for her. We need to find out more about this Covenant of the Three. Last night was the first I'd ever heard of it."

"Did either of your sisters know?"

"If they did, they didn't show it," she replied. "We're going to have to work together to unravel this, I think. I don't know how long it will take."

So... does that mean we're staying?" I asked, not quite able to keep the note of hope out of my voice.

She looked at me and smiled, though the smile did not quite reach her eyes. "How would you feel about giving it the summer?"

I perked up. "Really?"

She nodded. "I know you had a summer job lined up, but I'm sure Rhi would let you work at Shadowkeep, if you wanted to. And I know you'll miss your friends..."

"Poe and Charlie can come visit," I said hastily. "It's not that long of a drive from Portland, and Charlie has their own car now. Or I could take the train down for the weekend."

"That's true." She looked at me more closely. "You *want* to stay, don't you?"

"I want to know more about this place," I hedged. "And I want to get to know our family. Even Persi."

At this my mom threw her head back and laughed. "Oh, my brave girl. Okay, then. We have a lot of arrangements to make. I've got to figure out work, and—"

"That can all wait until tomorrow, Mom," I said, reaching out to squeeze her hand. "Let's just get through the funeral, okay?"

She squeezed back. "Good idea." She looked down at the paper one more time and then folded it up again, placing it back in her bedside table. "I suppose this can wait until after the funeral, too. Oh, and one last thing." She opened the drawer in the bedside table again and pulled out the key to the inner garden. "I'm sorry, I stole this from you last night. It's the only key to that door," she admitted sheepishly.

I held out my hand and she dropped the key into my palm. I looked down at it, and remembered Asteria's words regarding me and the house that was now mine: *It holds answers for her.*

It looked like I might actually get the time to discover them after all.

I knew enough about my family now to know that Asteria's funeral would be unlike any funeral I'd ever been to—not that I'd been to many. But my first hint at just how different it would be came an hour later, when I saw the trucks driving past the cottage up the winding sandy road to the cliffs. I watched them pass from the front porch, where Freya and I were amusing ourselves with a ball of yarn swiped from Rhi's knitting basket. At the same moment, Persi appeared at the front gate, wearing the same dress she'd been wearing at last night's seance, her stiletto heels dangling from a single careless finger.

"What's with all the trucks?" I said aloud, not really expecting her to answer; but she paused to chirp at Freya, who trotted forward for attention, and replied as she scratched my cat behind the ears.

"Funeral pyres don't build themselves. They take a lot of wood, you know."

"F-funeral pyre?" I gasped, watching the trucks with mounting horror. Their flatbeds were piled high with logs. "Like... like Vikings?"

Persi scooped Freya into her arms, cooing softly at her. "I suppose, though I don't think there's a direct connection between the traditions. It's ironic, isn't it, that we'd choose to burn ourselves, given how frequently and historically our enemies got in line for the privilege?"

"Oh, God." I instantly regretted my huge breakfast as my stomach began to churn in horror."

"I went to my first Sedgwick Cove funeral when I was five," Persi went on, scratching absently at Freya's chin as she watched the trucks make their slow winding progress past the dunes. "It's really quite magnificent, once you get past the smell."

"The what?!"

Persi glanced down and spotted the look on my face. "Just a little joke, Wren. Head between your legs, darling." She deposited Freya on the ground and placed a cool hand on the back of my neck, pushing gently on my head until it hung down between my knees.

"Is this supposed to help?" I asked.

"Personally I prefer a swig of gin, but I don't think it's your thing."

"Anything else I should be warned about?" I asked, and I could hear the hysteria creeping into my voice as it got progressively higher. "Animal sacrifice? Brooms flying in formation? Dancing naked under the full moon?"

"Not at funerals," Persi replied lightly. I lifted my head to find her smirking at me. "It'll be okay—beautiful even. The other Sedgwick covens will be there. There will be music and feasting and words of power spoken to the night. It will be magical—just the kind of celebration Asteria deserves." She just managed to hide the hitch in her voice. "We don't believe in somber or sullen send-offs. Our spirits burn bright, and so do our goodbyes."

I felt like I should say something—anything—to help ease a little of the pain in her eyes. It was strange to think that Persi could be anything like vulnerable, and certainly not in front of me, the stranger niece who swooped in and ruined her life. But what could I say? I didn't know her. I didn't know this place. I was starting to wonder if I knew anything at all. And so when I opened my mouth, what came out was, "I wish I'd known her better."

Persi stood up and smoothed her dress. I noticed a smear of blush lipstick on the neckline—a very different shade than the vibrant red on her lips. "Well, if you stay here, you'll soon have more Vesper knowledge than you'll know what to do with, I promise you that. She gestured to my outfit. "Please tell me that's not what you're wearing."

I frowned down at the simple black dress and cardigan. "It was the only appropriate thing in my closet."

"Appropriate for funeral homes and standing under umbrellas by freshly dug graves, perhaps." She pointed out to the garden. "You see any black out there?"

I looked all around me and then shook my head.

"Well, you won't see any at the funeral either," she said firmly. "So, go back upstairs and find whatever you've got that would help you blend in out in the garden."

"I don't think I've got anything else. This is all I brought that isn't jeans or t-shirts," I said despairingly. The last thing I needed was to advertise my ignorance of our family traditions to the whole population of Sedgwick Cove.

Persi rolled her eyes. "Oh for goddess's sake. Come with me."

I followed Persi into the house and up the stairs. My mom was sitting at the desk in the living room, her cell phone pressed between her shoulder and her ear as she spoke to someone at work. Her eyes widened in alarm when she saw us ascending together, but I gave her what a hoped was a reassuring smile. "It's fine," I mouthed. She nodded, though she didn't look convinced, and returned to her conversation.

Persi pushed open the door to her bedroom. My first thought was that it looked like a rebellious teenager lived here, rather than a grown woman. She had clothes strewn over all the furniture, as though she'd recently tried on half her closet at once; and yet the closet itself, the doors of which were flung wide, was stuffed to overflowing. The vanity table, topped with three tall, angled mirrors, was cluttered with makeup and perfume bottles and hair products and jewelry boxes. I ran my fingers over a silver-backed hairbrush and a string of pearls.

Persi turned from her closet to stare at me appraisingly, her eyes raking me from head to toe so that I blushed with mortification, arms crossed protectively over my midsection.

"You're just a little slip of a thing, aren't you?" she murmured, and she twirled her red-taloned finger in a little circle that meant I was supposed to turn around, which I did grudgingly. "You're built like Rhi. Most anything of mine will hang off you."

Well, that much was obvious. Persi had curves for days, and she chose her clothes to accentuate them to their most glorious fullness, making me feel like a twelve-year-old boy by comparison. I wanted to cry when I thought about what her plunging necklines and body-hugging silhouettes would look like on my angular frame. Persi, however, didn't seem to share my hopeless view of the situation.

"Hmmm," she said, eyes narrowed, lips pursed, then she clapped her hands together. "Okay. I've got some ideas." And with that she fairly dove into the closet and started flinging out things behind her, heedless of where they landed or what they might knock over in the process. I only just managed to save her lamp from a wayward leopard print pump. At last she turned around, surveyed her newly compounded sartorial chaos with satisfaction, and smiled mischievously at me.

"Right, then. Let's get started."

What she did next was very nearly witchcraft—in fact, I wouldn't have been surprised to find out there was actual magic involved. She unearthed a basket full of sewing supplies and started flinging dresses and scarves and tops over my head, cocking her head to each side as she examined each one. I didn't dare profess an opinion—I just stood there like a mannequin and let her get on with it. I didn't even protest when she started literally ripping garments apart at the seams—she appeared to be doing it on purpose and enjoying herself in the process. Soon she was demanding I hold my arms out like a scarecrow in a field while she pinned and tucked and draped and folded. Finally, she pulled all of it off me and tossed me a kimono-style robe to wrap myself in while I sat on the edge of her bed and waited for her to unearth and use an antique sewing machine, singing to herself as she did so. At last, she snipped the thread and flourished her creation with a grin.

"It's done! Try it on!"

She looked so hopeful that I didn't bother to inform her that the reason I always wore t-shirts and jeans is because I looked so frumpy in girly clothes. Seriously. It was like when people dress their pets up in human clothes; it just didn't look right. But as I slid the confection over my head, something happened that had never happened to me in a department store changing room. The skirt dropped down around me and I got the urge to twirl—this impulse was one I felt sure I'd been born without, and yet here it was, practically forcing me to spin in a circle. The colors and patterns were riotous, and yet they all seemed to belong to one another as seamlessly as though they were a single piece of fabric. The sleeves flared out from my arms like bells. The bodice hugged me without making me feel restricted. And best of all, when I turned and looked in the full-length mirror propped in the corner of Persi's room, I barely recognized the girl staring back at me.

"Oh!" I said, blinking in confusion.

"Oh? That's it? That's all you have to say?" Persi asked, frowning in consternation.

"It's... I barely recognize myself!" I murmured.

"That's more like it," Persi said, smiling with satisfaction. I tried to ignore the implied insult. "Now, how about that hair?"

Twenty minutes later, I was officially a stranger in the mirror. Persi had attacked me with a straightening iron, and then a curling iron, working like a mad scientist in a misty haze of aerosol hair products. Then she filed and painted my nails and dug out a little pair of beautiful beaded slippers for me to wear. While nothing else in her closet would fit me without serious alterations, we were at least a similar shoe size. She tried to get me to ditch my glasses, but as I would literally walk into walls without them, she removed them only briefly to use my face like a canvas for her endless supply of makeup. Finally, when I put them back on and looked at myself, I could do nothing but gape.

"See? And to think that lovely creature was in there all along!" Persi sang as she cleaned a makeup brush.

"She wasn't in here," I murmured. "You just put her on me, like a costume."

"Well, you wear her well," Persi said, giving me a sharp look that said she would not tolerate any self-deprecating remarks after she'd worked so hard. But even if I'd wanted to, I couldn't have found anything to criticize about the girl standing in front of me. All I could wonder was who she was and how long she'd stay before I woke up with one shoe and a broken heart, like Cinderella, minus the singing mice.

"Thank you. You really didn't have to do all this," I said, gesturing broadly to myself.

"Yes, I did," Persi said bluntly, rolling her eyes. "Did you seriously think I was going to let you represent the Vesper Coven in front of the whole town in that shapeless black clearance rack monstrosity? Ew. Now, shoo. I need to change."

And just like that, I was dismissed. It looked like it would take more than submitting to a make-over before Aunt Persi and I would really be friends. Well, it was a step in the right direction anyway, I thought, as I closed her door behind me.

13

I almost lost my nerve when I saw my mother's reaction to Persi's handiwork. She looked for a moment like she might actually burst into tears at the sight of me.

"Is it really that bad? I thought it was... I can go change..." I mumbled, turning on my heel and making to sprint up the stairs in humiliation; but my mom reached out and caught my arm.

"No! I'm sorry, honey, it's just... my goodness, you look like your grand-mother," my mom choked out.

"Is that... bad?" I asked, squirming under the emotion in her gaze.

"No. It's... it's perfect," my mom said, and planted a kiss on my cheek. "You're beautiful, Wren."

I felt the color rise to my cheeks and I smothered a smile. I didn't think she was lying to me or anything, but it was hard to feel good about a compliment that couldn't be delivered without tears. Nevertheless, when it was time to go and my mom came downstairs, she too had abandoned the black dress I'd seen in her bag for a long, purple skirt and a blousy white top, her usually pony-tailed hair falling in loose waves over her shoulders. She caught Rhi smiling at her and pointed an accusatory finger.

"Don't. I just don't want to deal with Persi's comments," she insisted.

"I didn't say anything," Rhi insisted, but a smile played on her lips for the next few minutes.

That liminal space of twilight seemed, to me, the right time to hold a funeral. There was something wrong about standing around a coffin at ten o'clock in the morning, and then having to just... continue with your day. Eat lunch. Run errands. Twilight felt more fitting somehow—saying goodbye as the day says goodbye, and letting the stars rise over a quiet night of reflection. If you simply wanted to tumble into bed and cry yourself to sleep, you could; and no one would expect you to make conversation or politely pick at a plate of buffet pasta. Still, as the sun reddened the horizon and we walked quietly up the road together, it was hard to feel anything but dread and sadness.

The four of us walked side by side in the sand. Rhi had given us each a small lantern with a candle burning inside, and we carried them swinging from our hands up the winding path to the clifftop. As we got nearer the top of the path, more lanterns began to appear, shining like stars in the gathering darkness. They came from the direction of the woods, from the beach, from the road behind us; and as they drew closer, I could make out the people carrying them.

A few of the faces were familiar from the time I'd spent downtown. Lydian rolled past us in her rickshaw, lanterns hanging from the corners. The woman from the gallery, whose name I'd already forgotten—Penelope? No, Phoebe—smiled gently at me as she passed. The lanterns all began to converge on a point ahead, moving into an evenly spaced formation as people filed into rows of benches that had been arranged on either side at the top of the path; it was like watching fireflies suddenly fly into formation. I spotted Eva Marin sitting between Xiomara and another woman, who looked so much like Eva, she could only be her mother.

Eva smiled at me, gave me an exaggerated once over with her eyes, and then winked, mouthing the words, "Looking good!"

I rolled my eyes and smiled back as though to reply, "It wasn't my idea."

But I had to admit, I fit in much better than I would have in my shapeless black dress. All around me were flowing skirts, fluttering scarves, and clinking jewelry. No fewer than a dozen people had brought pets, and one woman was absently feeding sunflower seeds to a bird that was perched on her shoulder. Even those among the guests who wore black did so with pops of other bright colors, and I spotted at least half a dozen flower crowns on people's heads.

Even the men—though there weren't as many of them—had dispensed with the traditional button-down shirts and suits they usually had to stuff themselves into at these kinds of things and joined the crowd in soft linens and bare feet. I returned a wave from Zale, who smiled at me over the ruffly collar of the same kind of shirt Roman Peterson had thrown a tantrum over having to wear. On Zale, it looked perfectly natural, somehow.

As we approached the back row of benches, a group of women stepped forward to greet us; and I realized I already knew several faces amongst them, including Nova, who hung back a little from the others, like she'd rather not have been associated with them. She gave me a quick quirk of a smile before dropping her face to watch her own toes drawing circles in the sand. All of the women in the group had hair so blonde it was practically white, and when the eldest of the group cleared her throat to address us, I knew her at once.

"From the heart of our coven to yours, our sincerest condolences on the loss of your matriarch," Ostara Claire said in a solemn voice. She had loosely braided her long hair and it lay draped over her shoulder with several blossoms tucked into the plait.

Rhi seemed to be waiting for someone else to speak, and then realized, with a start of surprise, that she was now the eldest member of the coven—in essence, the new matriarch. Her voice shook as she answered, "We thank you for your words of comfort."

I spotted Bernadette at the back of the group, recognizing her despite the fact that she seemed to be trying to hide behind the curtains of her hair. As I looked at her, she ventured a glance up and caught my eye. I tried to smile at her, but her eyes went wide and she dropped them again to her feet at once, murmuring something under her breath that I couldn't hear. Nova threw a warning glance at her, and she lapsed into silence again.

The Claires floated off to their seats in the front row, and we continued our slow walk up the center aisle. As we walked, hands reached out to grasp ours, and murmured condolences created a soft, solemn soundtrack to our progress. The sense of community took my breath away—I'd never experienced it before.

Finally, we took our seats in the front row, across the aisle from the Claires, and I finally lifted my eyes to the sight I'd been trying not to look at since we'd arrived on the clifftop: the funeral pyre. It loomed before us, much taller than I'd expected it to be. Atop it was Asteria's body, the outline of which was just visible beneath a fluttering white gauzy shroud strewn with flowers. It was only the suggestion of her, like a ghost, and yet I felt like I could recognize her: the sharp point of her chin, the slender lines of her form. Beside me, my mom was shaking. I reached over to grasp her hand and felt her gentle squeeze in return.

In that moment, music began. I couldn't see where it was coming from, but someone nearby was playing a flute of some kind. The music had a soothing sweetness to it, carried over the gathered mourners by the ocean breeze. As I glanced around in search of the source of the music, I realized that many of the other mourners were involved in their own rituals. Candles were being lit, herbs were being burned or else bundled or tied with ribbons. Soft incantations were being spoken. One woman walked in a complete circle around the entire assembled group, circling a great bundle of burning sage over her head, cleansing the whole area, and offering comfort to those gathered there. When she had finished, she called over the assembled mourners in a clear, calm voice that nevertheless carried.

"The mourners are invited to come forward to send our sister off on the next part of her journey."

People began, in ones and twos, to leave their seats and approach the pyre. They left things in the sand around the base of the logs: candles with guttering flames, sealed jars full of herbs and liquids, bundles of dried flowers, charms on strings, crystals and gemstones scattered on the ground or else tied up in pouches. Some of them were silent, others were speaking or singing softly. One woman scattered a pouch of what looked like ashes as she sang in a language I didn't know. Another was working studiously over what looked like a voodoo doll. Through it all, people came up to us and dropped other things into a basket that had been placed at our feet. Sometimes, the object was simply left without a word. Other times, the person who offered it explained what it was.

"A tincture for grief and mourning."

"A charm for connection."

"An oil for healing of rifts and separations."

No one seemed to expect us to say anything, and so we didn't, merely nodding our thanks as the basket at our feet filled with a community's potluck of magical offerings. Xiomara appeared before us with several small, stoppered bottles and a huge baking dish covered in tinfoil.

"*Perfumes espirituales* for you, *pobrecitas*. And dinner, because you need to eat."

Rhi sniffled and reached out a hand. Xiomara took it and squeezed it tightly in her own, before shuffling back to her seat. I smiled softly to myself. It seemed even witches brought casseroles to neighbors when someone was grieving a loss, and something about that made me feel unexpectedly comforted.

Finally, the last of the mourners had left their offerings, both for Asteria and for us—the ones she had left behind. The music flowed to a natural conclusion, and then Aunt Rhi stood up, pulling a crumpled piece of paper from somewhere in her flowing skirts. She walked to the base of the pyre, and then turned to look at the crowd. Beside me, Persi made a sound like a dry, stifled sob; but when I chanced a glance at her, she had composed her face into an expressionless mask.

"I thank you all, on behalf of the First Daughters of Sedgwick Cove, for those that have gone before us, and of those who still tread this sacred ground. I know that my mother Asteria would be overwhelmed by the number of you who have come this evening to wish her well on her journey."

It was so hard for me to think of death as the start of a journey, rather than the end of one. Perhaps it was both. There was something comforting in that thought, and I tried to cling to it while I listened to Rhi talk about Asteria.

Even an hour later, I'm not sure I could have recalled many of the details of that speech. I listened to it in a haze of emotions that made it very difficult to concentrate. She named many people I'd never met and told anecdotes that held no memory for me. She mentioned Asteria's stubbornness, which got an appreciative chuckle out of nearly everyone listening, including my mom. But what I would remember most of those moments, listening to my aunt talk about my grandmother, was a terrible sense of disconnection and grief.

I was saying goodbye to someone I'd barely known, and yet my grief felt bottomless because, I realized, I was grieving for all my lost chances. I always thought, one day, Asteria and I would find each other and gather up the thread of our relationship. I would get to know her, and she would get to know me—maybe even help me get to know myself, which I'd felt like I'd only just begun to do. Surely a woman so in tune with herself, so comfortable in her own skin, and living life on her own terms, could help her awkward granddaughter learn to do the same?

But now she never would. And none of the magic heaped in the basket at my feet could fix that.

I suddenly realized that Rhi had stopped talking. I refocused on her and saw that she was placing her own little charm on the pyre, tucking it between two of the logs, and whispering softly to herself. Then she sat down again, placing both of her hands on her knees. As I watched, Persi and my mom both reached out and placed a hand on top of Rhi's. A lump came into my throat and wouldn't go away no matter how hard I swallowed against it.

Music began again, and now four women appeared in long white dresses, two on either side of the pyre, bearing torches. With measured steps in perfect synchronicity to the music, they walked to the front of the great structure, and set their torches to the very base of it. The wood caught quickly, the flames licking up the logs and sending grayish-white tendrils of smoke up into the sky, to be swirled and buffeted by the wind. The flames reached the shroud, catching at its edges, and I suddenly felt that I couldn't stand to be there another second. I turned to my mom, panic thick in my throat, but she was looking at me as well.

"Are you ready to go?" she asked me.

I blinked. "I... don't we have to stay?"

She shook her head. "The volunteers from the Conclave will watch over her. Others have set up a farewell feast in the garden at the cottage. Everyone else is just waiting for us to lead the way down there."

I looked at the women in white, standing sentinel at the four corners of the pyre, and felt something like reassurance. I nodded to my mom, and we stood, Persi and Rhi taking their cue from us, and rising at the same moment. Together, the four of us turned our backs on the pyre.

It felt like the closing of a door.

Back at Lightkeep Cottage, our neighbors had been hard at work. Mismatched tables and chairs stood all over the gardens, draped in table cloths and adorned with candles and jars of flowers. Lanterns hung in the trees. Several women were swaying softly to the music coming from a pair of musicians playing a fiddle and a lute. The guests milled about, carrying platters and serving bowls and pitchers and casks. My mom and her sisters stood at the center of it all, looking worn but grateful, receiving guest after guest, having more charms and gifts pressed upon them. They were distracted enough by all of this that I could slip away from them to find a quiet spot in the garden. Perhaps it was because I was as much of an outsider as I felt, but no one went in search of me, and those who did spot me left me to my solitude.

All except one person.

"Hey, there. Does she belong to you?"

I looked up to see Eva standing on the path, Freya clasped in her arms.

"Oh, hey! Yeah, that's my cat Freya," I told her.

"I thought she might be," Eva said, transferring her to my outstretched arms. "Do you mind if I sit down?"

I hadn't thought I wanted company, but Eva's friendly smile set me at ease. I nodded, and she plopped down on the bench beside me.

"I wish I had a familiar," she said, reaching out to stroke Freya's head.

"Sorry?"

Eva laughed a little incredulously. "A familiar."

"I... don't know what that is," I admitted.

"A familiar is like a spirit in the form of an animal that is tied to you, one that protects and helps you in your magic."

"I... wait, what?" I asked. I looked down at Freya, who looked up at me, purring contentedly.

Eva laughed her throaty laugh. "Did you just think you had a regular old cat all this time?"

I blinked. "Uh... yes?"

"Where did you find her? Or I should say, where did she find you?"

"I didn't find her at all. Asteria gave her to me," I said.

"Ah. Well, she must have felt drawn to you, or she wouldn't have stayed," Eva said, nodding sagely. "Your grandmother must have sensed the affinity."

"I... I think you might be mistaken," I said.

"Really?" Eva looked surprised. "Hasn't she ever done anything to help or protect you?"

I opened my mouth to say no, and then stopped. My mind cast back to the day Asteria died, when I was in the catwalk of the theater. It had seemed impossible that Freya was there, and yet I'd seen her. And... and there'd been something else too, something dark and shadowy that brought with it the sounds and smells of the sea...

I looked down at Freya. She had leapt between me and the... whatever it was. And when it disappeared, so had she...

I looked back up at Eva and she laughed at the expression on my face.

"See? A familiar if ever I saw one."

I just shook my head, trying to absorb the idea.

"Look, this is going to go on for a while," Eva said, gesturing around the garden. "But all the younger generation will likely head out soon. It's a kind of tradition to host a bonfire on celebration nights."

"Celebration nights?" I asked, incredulous.

"I know, I'm sorry," Eva said, cringing apologetically. "I realize it doesn't feel like much of a celebration to you, but that's how Sedgwick Cove has always treated funerals—a celebration of someone's life rather than a marking of the end of it. Anyway, it's going to be on the clifftop tonight at midnight."

"The clifftop?" I swallowed hard. "You mean where the—"

"No! On the far side of the lighthouse, nowhere near the pyre; and anyway, that will be all cleared away by then. It's a chance for the younger people to let off a little steam."

"Oh. Right."

"So anyway, you should come!" Eva said.

"I... thanks Eva, but I'm not sure if I—"

But Eva put up a hand and I fell silent. "You don't have to make a decision now. The invitation is open. Come, if you want to. No one will pressure you either way."

I mustered a smile. "Thanks. I... I'll think about it."

Eva stood up and winked at me. "Okay, but don't think too hard. Thinking too much is how we talk ourselves out of stuff."

I watched her walk away, and then looked down at Freya.

"So, you're a familiar, huh? How come you didn't tell me? Any other big revelations you're hiding from me?"

Freya merely threw me some side-eye as she groomed herself, as though to say, "Wouldn't you like to know."

14

Asteria's celebration continued for hours, contracting and expanding like a living, breathing thing. The music caused spontaneous bursts of singing and dancing. The food was passed around from table to table, and someone had tapped a huge wooden barrel of homemade mead, which I learned was a kind of spirit made from honey—and which soon had many of the adults in a pleasant haze of nostalgia, and celebration, as the potent spirit took its effects. I watched it all unfold in a kind of mystified wonder, but as the moon rose and the stories turned to the years before I was born, my mind began to wander over to the clifftop, and the other celebration that had already begun there.

"Mom?"

My mom looked up from the table where she was sitting deep in conversation with Rhi and several other women who looked to be of Asteria's generation. One of them was smoking a pipe and sporting an eyepatch.

"Wren!" My mom looked at me in surprise, like she'd forgotten I was even there in the garden. "I'm so sorry, sweetheart, I've been neglecting you. You must be so... did you eat? Do you need—"

"I'm fine, Mom, don't worry about me. I was actually wondering if you'd mind if I went over to the bonfire."

My mom blinked confusedly at me for a moment. "The... the bonfire?"

"Yeah, over on the cliffs? Eva invited me, and I thought I might... but if you don't want me to..." I was already regretting asking her.

"No, no! It's not... sorry, I just didn't realize they still did that around here," my mom said, and she looked over at Rhi, who nodded.

"Oh, yes. That particular youthful tradition is alive and well, Kerri," she confirmed.

"Oh. Well... yes, I guess that's all right. If you think you really want to," my mom hedged, looking like she hoped I might change my mind.

"I won't stay for long. And I'll bring my phone. I just... I thought it might be nice to meet some of the other kids, especially since we'll be staying for a bit."

My mom's anxious expression relaxed a little. "Of course. Yes, you should go meet some new friends."

"I won't be too late," I promised.

"Have fun, sweetheart," my mom said, pulling me close to her in a one-armed hug. Then she whispered to me, "If those bonfires are anything like they used to be, you'll need to make some safe choices, okay? Just... be careful, okay?"

I smiled at her. "I could say the same thing to you about the mead."

My mom grinned. "Touché. I'll pace myself."

I kissed the top of her head and headed for the garden gate, where I found Persi on her phone. As I passed her, I overheard part of her conversation.

"... didn't end well for us. I don't know why you'd want to see me again."

I waved to her, and she flicked a hand absently in acknowledgment as she listened to whatever the person on the other end of the call was saying to her.

"Well, then come over. You know where to find me..." Persi said, turning from me to head back into the garden.

I watched her go, and then turned onto the path that would take me up to the cliffs.

~

"You came!" Eva called.

"I said I'd think about it," I reminded her.

"Which is usually universal code for 'not a chance in hell,'" Eva replied, waving my words away impatiently. "But whatever, I'm so glad you changed your mind. Can I get you a drink?"

She gestured over her shoulder where several coolers had been plonked down in the sand near an impressively roaring bonfire.

"Sure... just like a Coke or something, if you've got any."

"Of course," Eva said, and dug through the ice, tossing me the freezing cold can, which I only just managed not to drop.

I couldn't help but notice the way the other kids were staring at me— mostly because none of them were even attempting to hide it. When I caught their eyes, they didn't look away, but stared boldly back. Awesome. I'd been here for all of thirty seconds and I was already regretting my decision to come. Luckily, Eva chose that moment to take control of the situation.

"Everyone, this is Wren Vesper," she announced, as though there was the slightest chance that was new information to anyone, given that almost every single one of them had spent the earlier part of the evening at my grandmother's funeral. Then, she pointed to each teenager in turn and introduced them. I smiled and waved awkwardly at each of them, sure that I would forget every single one of their names the instant I heard them. I didn't disappoint myself; a few moments later, when a tall willowy girl with black hair and purple lipstick sauntered up to me, I had absolutely no idea who she was.

"We weren't sure if you'd come," the girl said eagerly, for all the world like I was some kind of celebrity. "You know, because of your mom."

Eva rolled her eyes. "Subtle, Kaia."

"My mom?" I asked.

"Yeah," the girl named Kaia said, her eyes widening. "You know, because of how she, like... ran away, and stuff."

I just stared at her for a moment. "Can grown adults run away, or do they just... move?" I asked her.

She looked startled, as though she'd never considered the possibility of an adult having free will, and then just sort of shrugged. "People don't usually move away from Sedgwick Cove," she said.

"Okay, well, we did, but now we're back, okay?" I said, barely staving off a flare of anger at this girl and the way she presumed to know anything at all about me... and an even stronger flare of anger that she probably knew more than I did.

But then she smiled, a totally guileless and friendly expression. "Well, anyway, welcome back," she said.

I felt something akin to mental whiplash as I tried to adjust to her change of manner. "Uh... thanks."

"Sure thing," she replied, and though she didn't say anything else, she continued to stare avidly at me, as though expecting me to start doing tricks.

"Sorry, but as you've probably noticed, it's been kind of a big deal that you're back," Eva said, taking me by the arm and steering me away from Kaia's goggling. She brought me over to a long driftwood log that they were using as a sort of bench and sat down on it, patting the place beside her. I sat, trying to ignore the continued stares and whispers.

"How are you holding up?" Eva asked, and I was relieved to see genuine empathy in her eyes, rather than morbid curiosity.

"I'm okay," I said. "I didn't know my grandmother that well. I haven't seen her since my tenth birthday, so it's not as though we were very close."

"That's really sad," Eva said, her lips pressed into a thin, pitying smile. "I can't imagine what it would be like not to see my *abuela* for that long."

"Are you really close with her?" I asked.

Eva nodded and chuckled. "Some days it feels a little *too* close. I've lived in the same house with her since I was born. And I work at the cafe. She can drive me nuts sometimes, but I'd be lost without her."

I couldn't decide if I was relieved that I'd escaped that kind of pain in losing Asteria or jealous of it. "I'm just sad we won't get a chance to get to know each other," I finally said.

"But I heard you were staying," Eva said, eyebrows raised in surprise.

"How did you hear that?" I asked.

Eva smiled. "I know you're not used to it yet, but everyone kind of knows everything about everyone in Sedgwick Cove. Word gets around, almost like magic." She winked.

"Right." I sipped my drink, then narrowed my eyes at her. "Almost like magic, or like... actual magic?"

She chuckled. "A little of both, probably. But my point is, what better way to get to know your grandmother than by spending time here? Sedgwick Cove and the name Vesper are practically synonymous. Nothing will bring you closer to your grandmother than hanging around this place, as long as you can cope with a bit of staring and unwanted attention, and that will pass."

"I guess I wouldn't mind so much that people knew all about me if I knew literally anything about anyone here."

Eva sat up straight, looking eager. "Okay, so ask me some questions, then."

I nearly choked. "Wait, really? I...didn't mean I want to interrogate you!"

"I know that. Ask me anyway."

"I... I don't know what to ask," I spluttered, noticing that Zale and Nova were walking towards us.

Zale dropped into the sand at our feet, exhausted and damp from dancing to the music blasting from a nearby bluetooth speaker. Nova perched herself on the driftwood log on my other side, hair and makeup somehow flawless despite the wind and the heat. At least it was some consolation to tell myself it was probably a result of magic rather than personal perfection on her part.

"Looks like Nova owes me money!" Zale crowed. "Pay up, princess! I bet her ten bucks you'd show tonight," he added for my benefit.

Nova sighed, barely looking up from her phone. "Zale, I don't know how else to explain this to you, but just announcing that you bet someone money doesn't mean they have to pay you. For example," she turned and looked at me. "I bet you $20 that you're drinking soda because you're a goody-two-shoes who doesn't drink alcohol." Then she held out her hand expectantly.

"Uh..."

Nova dropped her hand and turned to smile at Zale. "See? Just because you're right doesn't mean other people have to pay you for it."

"Whatever, you're just a sore loser. I'll put it on your tab," Zale said.

"Sure, babe, you do that," Nova replied.

"So, come on, girls, what are we gossiping about?" Zale asked, putting his elbows on his knees and cupping his face in his hands.

"You sucking face with Penny Willis. What's that about?" Eva said, waggling her eyebrows.

Zale's mouth dropped open in mock horror. "Excuse me, that is a lie. Everyone knows I only suck face with girls when I am very, very drunk."

"And are you?"

"Am I what?"

"Very, very drunk."

Zale promptly jumped up and began reciting the alphabet backwards while walking the driftwood log like a tightrope. He finished with a flourishy bow and hopped back down again. "Does that answer your question? Now what were you really gossiping about?"

"I just told Wren to ask me some questions. You know, to help her get acclimated," Eva explained.

"No parameters? Just... open interrogation?" Nova asked skeptically.

I tensed, but Eva rolled her eyes. "Oh, please, Nova. She's a Vesper, for goodness' sake! Do you really think there's anything we can tell her that she can't find out for herself? And besides, she just told me that she's staying—at least for the summer."

Nova sat up a little straighter. "Really? Your mother, too?"

"Yeah. My grandmother's will left some stuff that needs to get... sorted out. So, we'll be here the whole summer at least," I confirmed.

"And what about you?" Zale asked.

"What about me?"

"Are you... y'know... gonna become a real Vesper?"

I looked at his eager expression and faltered. I wanted to shout that I already was a real Vesper, but I knew that wasn't actually true. I might have carried the Vesper name, but that was the only thing I seemed to have in common with my family. Luckily, Eva broke in and rescued me from the embarrassment of having to admit such a thing to a knot of eagerly listening strangers.

"Hey, she's asking the questions, not us," Eva scolded.

"Oh, right. Sorry, Wren," Zale said, grinning sheepishly.

I smiled back. "It's okay."

"So, what do you want to know?" Eva asked.

Have any of you ever heard of the Covenant of the Three? was the question I really wanted to ask, but I swallowed it back down. If my own aunts were unsure of Asteria's mysterious last message, I couldn't imagine a bunch of teenagers being able to interpret it. And besides, what if it was some deep dark family secret no one else was supposed to know about? So, instead I said, "My aunts told me that most everyone in Sedgwick Cove has a family connection to... to witchcraft?"

Eva, Zale, and Nova all looked at each other, barely smothering their smirks. Nova scowled theatrically at me. "Are you calling us witches?"

"I... guess I was wondering if that's what you'd call yourselves?" I stammered.

Eva laughed. It was a warm sound, deep and throaty. "Yeah, we're all bona fide Sedgwick Cove witches. My family's been here for four generations now, and Zale's has been here for five. Nova's family's like yours... here so long they've probably lost track."

Nova looked smugly satisfied by this assessment, but added peevishly, "Goddess, I wish they'd lose track. Instead, I'm just subjected to volume after volume of family history; I could cheerfully fling myself off the cliff right into the sea."

"History none of the rest of us could even relate to," Eva pointed out. "Sedgwick Cove has its own traditions and customs and whatnot, but when it comes to individual families, we all have our own practices and traditions."

"Yeah, my aunt Rhi said something like that—that there are almost as many ways to be a witch as there are witches in the world."

"And each of them thinks their way of being a witch is the best," Eva laughed. "It makes for some pretty lively get-togethers, let me tell you."

"Potlucks usually end in violence," Zale added, his expression deadpan.

"And everyone in your families just... stays here?" I asked, fascinated.

Zale shrugged. "Not everyone, and not always. People get restless and pack up, but it's never for long. Everyone always seems to find their way back here eventually." He leaned forward and put on a spooky voice. "It's the Cove, Vesper. It ensnares us. It calls us back."

I couldn't repress the shiver that shuddered up my spine. Zale saw it and laughed, delighted at his own prowess in creeping me out, but Eva frowned.

"Don't be a dick, Zale," she muttered.

"He literally can't help it," Nova said, rolling her eyes. "It's his true form."

"No it's okay," I said quickly. "I... my aunts told me a little something about it... about Sedgwick Cove being a powerful place that witches are drawn to, or something like that."

Zale perked up at once. "She needs the origin story."

15

"Yeah she does!" Eva agreed.

"Yawn," Nova said pointedly.

"Oh, come on! It's nighttime! There's a fire! It's the full moon, and there's a Vesper who hasn't heard the origin story!" Zale cried out. A few of the other teens nearby heard him because they began to egg him on.

"Tell it, Zale!"

"Wait, don't start yet, I need another drink!"

"If I wanted to listen to more love letters to Sedgwick Cove, I could have just stayed home," Nova grumbled, but she settled in comfortably against the log, evidently resigned to the fact that she would hear one anyway.

"This is great, you'll love this," Eva told me, nudging me with her elbow and smiling broadly. "It's like, the official bedtime story of Sedgwick Cove kids."

I smiled back, wondering if I'd heard it before when I was very young. Sure enough, as Zale cleared his throat and raised his arms for silence, I felt a strange twist of déjà vu in my stomach; and I could swear, without being able to recall ever hearing it before, that this story ran like blood in my veins.

"Before the witches came there was only the Darkness," Zale began, and he dropped his voice melodramatically. I had just enough time to note that we seriously could have used his talent in our drama club before I got lost, along with the rest of the listeners, caught up in the web of words that he wove.

"The Darkness gathered in this place. It found much to strengthen it, to sustain it. Here, the veil between worlds was thin, and that closeness with the powers of the beyond fed and nurtured its power. The Darkness grew stronger, spreading its roots under the sand and between the rocks, claiming the Cove as its own."

Someone nearby giggled nervously. I gave in to the illogical urge to tuck my feet up under me rather than leave them in the sand, as though one of those roots of Darkness might even now be slithering under the sand, like a serpent waiting to coil itself around my ankles.

"Who knows how many years the Darkness slept here, growing and feeding, a hibernating beast, until..." Zale threw back his head and raised his arms, waiting...

"UNTIL THE WITCHES CAME!" The response rose up all around me like a battle cry, followed by snorting, laughing, and general merriment. Someone flung a beer bottle into the flames, causing them to leap higher. Eva whooped. I couldn't help but laugh, and just a bit of the tension was broken.

"Until the witches came," Zale repeated, nodding his head approvingly. "They came by the sea, their power both blessing and curse. Whether they were drawn here by that same lure of power, or came upon the place by accident, none living can tell us; but step into the sands of the Cove they did, and they knew at once that they were home. They did not know what slumbered here, only that this place fed their magic and nurtured their power. They grew here, and thrived here, until, at last... they woke the Darkness."

No laughter broke the tension now. Zale muttered under his breath, and I saw him reach into his pocket and extract something pinched between his fingers. He threw it over his shoulder into the flames and an unnatural hush fell over the group, like someone had thrown a muffling hand over the beach itself. It took me several seconds and a confirming nod from Eva to realize that Zale had performed a spell. I watched him eagerly now, more caught up in his tale than ever.

"At first, the witches did not know the true nature of what they had awakened. They knew it was of the Darkness, but they also knew that darkness and light must exist together, entwined in an endless dance. They were willing to share this place with the Darkness, each taking only what they needed to nurture their own existence. But the Darkness was greedy. It was not content to exist alongside the witches. It was hungry for them. It could see that their power was great, and the Darkness wanted that power for its own. It had grown too swollen, too greedy. It wanted to turn them, to consume them."

My imagination conjured a great beast emerging from its hibernation, something fierce and violent and hungry. Instinctively, I scooted closer to Eva on the log, and she pressed her side against mine, evidently just as happy as I was to have someone beside her while Zale spun his tale. Her eyes shone beneath the glorious halo of her natural curls, which had long ago sprung free of her headscarf.

"It was only after the witches lost one of their own to the Darkness that they understood they could not coexist in this place. But nor could they leave the Darkness to grow and spread unchecked. They had to find a way to bind it, to protect both their home and their magic from the Darkness that would seek to usurp them both. And so they called upon their sister witches and their deepest magic. They gathered upon the cliffs and summoned the elements..."

"Earth! Fire! Air! Water! Spirit!" came the sudden cry from all around the campfire, causing me to yelp in surprise, and drop my soda into the sand. Luckily, no one seemed to notice, as they shouted out the familiar refrain from the story they all knew as well as they knew their own names.

"And so it was, that the witches of Sedgwick Cove called up their deepest magic and bound the Darkness, so that it could not spread, and could not grow. And all these years later, the witches of Sedgwick Cove stand sentinel, guardians of the deep powers of this place, and bringers of the light. As stand the witches, so stands the Cove."

The chorus rose up again around the fire in a raucous reply, "So it has been, and so shall it be still!" And then the circle broke into a barrage of clapping and whooping and laughing, while Zale gave a deep bow, and batted away the various objects now being lobbed at him in a combination of appreciation and hijinks.

I turned to Eva. "That's what bedtime stories are like around here?"

"Yup."

"And I'm assuming you're all in therapy for your chronic nightmares, or is there just a potion you can take for that?"

She waved her hand impatiently. "Oh please. Have you ever read a fairy tale? All traditional children's stories are basically nightmare fuel. At least ours is true!"

"Is it, though?" I asked, unable to repress the question before I blurted it out.

She cocked her head to one side. "Of course, it's true. Can't you feel it?"

She said it so matter-of-factly, and it gave me pause. I'd been so busy doubting everything I'd been told, so sure that I had to push back against it, to question everything, that I hadn't given much thought to how I felt. Feelings were unreliable. They made it impossible to be objective, and in my mind, objectivity was as close as we could come to truth. But as I sat there under the stars, the salt breeze in my hair and the sand between my toes, I realized that the story *felt* true in a way no fairy tale ever could—a truth I could feel running in my veins and tingling in my fingertips. I might not be ready to acknowledge the possibility of my own power, but there was no denying the deep power of this place.

I looked at Eva and nodded. "Yes. I think I can."

"Well, what did you think? Your family history, courtesy of Zale MacDowell Productions," Zale said, plopping back down into the sand again and gesturing around him, as though the entire beach was nothing more than a prop of his own creation.

"It was awesome," I said with a golf-clap.

"It was tolerable," Nova corrected me.

"I wasn't talking to you," Zale shot back, sticking out his tongue at her.

"You should have been more specific. After all, it was my family history, too," Nova retorted, some sulkiness in her voice, despite her continued feigned disinterest.

"The Claires are the only other family besides the Vespers who can trace their roots all the way back to the binding of the Darkness. The Second Daughters of the Cove," Eva said.

Nova glared pointedly at me, as though she expected me to refute this for some reason. I merely nodded and said, "That's cool."

"Not as cool as being a First Daughter, as every Vesper since the beginning of time has been sure to remind us, but yeah. I guess it's cool," she said, pursing her mouth as though she could taste the bitterness I heard in her tone.

I didn't know what to say, so I didn't say anything. I remembered the odd tension when the Claire Coven spoke to us at Asteria's funeral, but I couldn't understand it. We were allies, weren't we, the First Daughters and the Second Daughters? We'd worked together to bind the Darkness, or so the story went. Did Nova really think I was here to one-up her?

Some music started up again and Nova got up to go join in the dancing. Someone began passing out marshmallows speared on long sticks, and I took one, watching as my marshmallow browned slowly in the flames.

"This is honestly not what I expected," I said.

"Really? What were you expecting?" Eva asked.

"At a bonfire hosted by witches? I don't know. Not smores," I said, laughing.

"We try not to mix too much magic with alcohol, as a rule, so it's probably not much different from other teenage bonfires," Eva said. "But then again, if someone does decide to make some poor life choices by showing off, the fallout is usually more entertaining." She leaned in closer to me and dropped her voice. "Keep an eye on Kaia. She'll likely start trying a little glamour to get Sergei's attention—he's the lanky blonde one. She's been lusting after him for like two years. And Justin and James Sloane—those two over there, next to the cooler, they'll likely light some shit on fire, or cause a minor explosion to show off."

"I was surprised to find out there were male witches," I admitted sheepishly.

"It's definitely more common in the female lines," Eva agreed, nodding. "And it's not every man who can get over his damn self and connect with the divine feminine; or accept a lesser place in a matriarchal hierarchy, which most witchcraft traditions have. The female witches tend to be the more powerful, as a general rule."

"Hence the history of demonizing witches?" I suggested.

Eva snorted. "You said it. Men intimidated by powerful, independent women. Tale as old as time, honey." She plucked her marshmallow from the end of the stick and popped it in her mouth. "You want another drink?" she asked me when she'd swallowed it.

"No, I'm good," I said.

She smiled and set off around the other side of the fire in search of the cooler, which someone had moved and was now using as a seat. Nova had gone off to join the dancing and Zale was over on the other side of the fire, trying to see how many marshmallows he could roast on a stick at one time. I stood up, my legs stiff from sitting for so long, and stepped away from the glow of the fire into the darkness gathered on the edges. It wasn't that I wasn't having fun—I was, and I was grateful to Eva for inviting me, but I still felt like an outsider—a feeling that grew as the night wore on, and people started breaking off into their little cliques and telling stories. It was like hearing a joke and being the only person who didn't laugh uproariously at the punchline. Someone could explain the joke to me, but by then, the moment to enjoy it along with everyone else would have passed.

The scattering of clouds had all but cleared away, and the moon hung, swollen, in the sky, casting a long, glittering path from the beach out into the water. I imagined having the kind of magic that would let me walk along it like a road to the horizon. Was that a thing witches could do?

There, closer to the edge of the cliffs, the wind muffled the sounds of the merriment at the bonfire, so that it suddenly sounded very far away from me. The wind also carried the sounds of the waves, whipping them around me until, if I closed my eyes, I could imagine I was standing right at the water's edge, instead of a hundred feet above it. I let my eyelids flutter closed and took a deep breath, trying to imagine what it would feel like to know there was magic running in your veins, to really, truly believe it. Every single one of the kids at the bonfire behind me believed it—knew it, the way they knew their own names.

Maybe I would have known it too, if it had really been there. Maybe there was no magic in me after all.

I opened my eyes to look back at the beach.

The beach looked back.

I blinked. It wasn't the water at all, but someone was staring right back at me from the shoreline; a small, slight figure, no bigger than a child. I took another step toward the cliff's edge. It was a child, a boy, I thought, surely no older than three or four. His lean little body was naked, his fair hair tousled in the wind.

"Hey, there's a kid down there," I said, first to myself and then to the group over my shoulder. "A kid! There's a little kid down on the beach!"

If anyone heard me, they didn't respond. Someone had lit some sparklers off the bonfire and people were laughing and drawing dizzying circles of sparks in the air.

I turned to look at the child again, and panicked when I didn't see him right away. But my relief at spotting him lasted only a split-second because the reason I hadn't spotted him right away was that he was now up to his waist in the water. I frantically scanned the beach for another figure—perhaps the child had merely wandered a few feet away from a parent—but there was no one down there at all except the pale little figure walking into the surf.

"Stop! Hey!" I shouted stupidly, the wind sucking the words right out of my mouth and carrying them in the opposite direction. I turned and shouted again to the other kids, but no one heard me. I was the only one who could help.

I looked to my left where I knew the cliff's steep face softened to a sloping path. It was by no means an easy climb down, especially in the dark, but it was either that or watch helplessly from the clifftop. Waves were breaking over his chest now as he moved steadily forward—not at all like a child playing in the waves, but like a sleepwalker, insensate to the cold and the dark and the tug of water.

I fumbled my phone out of my pocket as I ran, turning on the flashlight with shaking fingers, just in time to begin the treacherous descent. Sand and small rocks slid out from under my feet as I fought for purchase, the light from my phone strobing wildly off waving grass and craggy rock face, and my own frantic legs. With a cry of frustration, I clamped the phone between my teeth, so that at least I had use of both of my hands to steady myself. A larger stone came away under my right foot, and I sat down hard and began to slide downward. I flexed my feet and dug them into the ground in front of me, while reaching out on both sides to grasp wildly at clumps of grass and protruding roots—anything I might be able to use to help slow my descent. At last I slid to the soft sand of the beach, landing hard, and sending my phone flying as my teeth slammed together. I fell forward onto my knees and scrambled for the phone, but the light had gone out; and anyway, the moonlight was bright enough that I could see across the beach.

"Hey! Come out of the water, it's not safe!" I shouted toward the little boy. I could only see the gleam of his silvery blonde hair now—the water lapped up right to his neck. I sprinted across the beach, my breath burning in my lungs, losing both of my flip-flops along the way, the sand slipping out from under my feet as though the world itself was falling away. I swallowed a sob of panic. What if I couldn't reach him in time? Why didn't he turn? He must hear me by now!

I splashed out into the water, heedless of the biting cold, and flung myself forward into the oncoming waves. Even as I spluttered and shouted, I watched in horror as a sizable wave surged forward and crashed right over the motionless child's head. I plunged toward him, reaching out my hands to pluck him backward.

As my fingers closed over the little arm, the child's entire form dissolved in my grasp. I felt him melt away like a dream at dawn and looked down to see a handful of wet sand sliding through my fingers and taken by the sea. Another wave battered against me, sending me tumbling backward, still flailing and feeling for a small being that had vanished into nothing at all. I sucked in a desperate breath just in time as the wave tumbled me like a stone. I slammed into the sandy bottom before being rolled and buffeted until I was dizzy. I couldn't tell which way to swim; the world was a cold, rough tug-of-war and I was the rope, moments from snapping. My lungs burned for air, and my eyes burned with salt as I opened them in desperation, trying to see my way to the surface, but seeing nothing but murky blackness. The last of my air bubbled out in a scream as something closed tightly around my wrist.

I had one last thought, a thought that felt as though it had been whispered in my ear.

And now the sea shall take you as it was always meant to do...

My head broke the surface into the night air, and I rasped out a gasping breath, tears and saltwater stinging my eyes.

"Are you crazy? What the hell are you doing?" came a breathless, agitated cry.

I tried to answer, but all I could manage was a wet cough that brought up about a gallon of sea water into the damp sand, where I was now slumped after being dragged to the water's edge. I squinted through stinging eyes and saw Zale in the sand beside me, dripping wet and drawing ragged breaths as he glared at me.

"I... there was..."

"You chose a hell of a time for a nighttime swim. Hasn't anyone told you about the undertow at this beach?" he gasped.

"I... didn't..."

"Damn it, Wren, I thought you drowned!" A second voice joined in now, and I looked up to see Eva throwing a towel around my shoulders.

"Should we call an ambulance or something?" Nova stood a few feet away with a handful of other gawking kids, shifting her feet nervously in the sand, her phone halfway out of her pocket already.

"Don't be an idiot, Nova," Zale snapped. "She's talking and breathing, why the hell would she need an ambulance?"

"I dunno, Zale, maybe for a psych eval?" Nova snapped right back. "Because you'd have to be bat-shit crazy to do something like that?"

I tried to sit up, but my arms were shaking badly. Eva helped me into a sitting position, rubbing my back while I continued to cough and blink the salt out of my eyes. Within a few minutes, the other kids drifted away up the beach, evidently deciding I was no longer interesting enough to gawk at now that it was clear I wasn't going to die.

"I thought I saw a little boy in the water," I said, the words grating out like sandpaper in my throat.

"What?! Oh my God, I didn't see—" Zale was stumbling back toward the water again in a panic, but I reached out and caught the hem of his shirt.

"It wasn't... it wasn't real."

He turned to look at me again, bewilderment all over his face. "What do you mean it wasn't real?"

I opened my mouth to tell him: the way the child had been eerily silent, the way he had never turned no matter how loudly or desperately I called after him, the way he marched inexorably forward into the water, like his only purpose was to lead me there...

"I... I made a mistake," I finished lamely.

Zale bit his lip. "Are you sure?"

I nodded even as I struggled to swallow a sob. Now that the shock was wearing off, I was starting to tremble and my heart to pound. I turned away from Zale's incredulous expression to find Eva looking intently at me, like she was trying to read something reflected in my eyes.

"You made a mistake like it was a plastic bag or a log or something?" she asked, the words snapping out, each one pointed and edged with anxiety.

I met her eye. "No."

She nodded once, grimly. "A vision, then?"

I shrugged, stifling another cough. "I don't... maybe?"

"Have you ever had one before?"

"No, I..." but I paused, considering. What had the presence in the garden been? Or the figure in the catwalk at the theater? Surely they hadn't been real, and yet I'd experienced them seen and felt them as if they had been.

Eva interpreted my hesitation. "You're not sure?"

I shook my head.

"So, is the psych eval still on the table?" Nova asked, her tone snarky but her eyes wide.

Eva and Zale both ignored her. Zale was still gazing out over the waves with a searching look, as though he thought a small hand might still pop out of the water at any moment. Eva, however, was still looking at me with that same intensity.

"Some witches do have visions, you know," she said.

"I'm not a witch!" I cried, the words bursting from me in my confusion and burning my throat all the way up. "I mean... I don't even know if I... I've never..."

"Come on," Eva said, trying to haul me to my feet. Zale saw what she was doing and caught me under my other arm to help. My legs were shaking, but they managed to hold me up. I pulled the towel more tightly around my shoulders as a violent shiver rocked through me. "Let's get you back up to the fire. You'll feel better when you're warm again. I grabbed your phone, you dropped it over at the base of the cliff. Nova, can you get her shoes?"

Nova rolled her eyes but walked over to retrieve my discarded flip-flops. Out of the corner of my eye, I saw her bend over and pick something up out of the sand and stare at it. But by the time I had turned my head, she was walking toward us, expression neutral, and nothing in her hand except my flip-flops.

I took one last look at the waves crashing in on the shore, and shivered. There was no other way to explain it: someone—or something—had lured me into the water and had not intended to let me escape.

16

As I walked down the path from the beach, I could see a few figures still milling around the garden, folding up tablecloths and stacking dishes. I knew the polite thing to do would be to offer my help, but I couldn't afford awkward questions about why I was dripping from head to toe, so I made for the house instead.

My mom was inside in the sitting room with Rhi. I stayed in the darkened hallway, far enough from the light of the room that I didn't think she'd be able to tell I was wet.

"Wren! I was starting to..." She stopped herself. "Did you have a good time, honey?"

"Yeah, it was great," I lied. "The other kids were really nice."

She frowned a little and squinted at me. "Is your hair wet?"

I forced a laugh. "Oh, yeah. There may have been a bit of a water fight when all the ice in the coolers melted." I rolled my eyes, praying she would buy it.

Whether my acting skills were improving, or she'd had a little too much mead, I wasn't sure; but she laughed, too. "I'm so glad you had fun."

"Yeah, but I'm exhausted," I told her. "See you in the morning!"

I was careful not to overdo the cheerfulness in my voice—I didn't want her to get suspicious and start interrogating me. I waved, pretended to stifle a yawn, and trudged up the stairs to my room, closing the door behind me with a sigh of relief.

I stripped off my wet clothes, too sore and tired to shower. I examined myself in the mirror on the wall. Several impressive bruises were blooming on my legs and torso from when I'd half-tumbled down the cliff face in my race to the beach. I slipped on a pair of pajamas from my drawer, and then sat down on the bed, where I began working a brush through my salt-tangled hair, thinking hard.

I refused to believe I had imagined it all. It would have been one thing if I'd gone all the way down to the beach, only to discover that what I'd seen had been an animal, or a drifting piece of trash. But I'd seen the boy clearly, the outline of his limbs, his bright hair. I'd watched him walk toward the water, and I'd watched him disappear into it slowly. And then, when I'd finally reached him, I'd felt the solidness of him for one, brief moment, before he crumbled to sand in my grip—actual sand.

Eva had suggested a vision, but that didn't fit. You couldn't touch a vision. Or maybe you could if you were a witch? My head was starting to ache.

I decided to stop trying to understand what I'd seen, and instead ponder why I might have seen it. Why would someone have a vision if they weren't crazy; because I refused to believe I'd suddenly lost my grip on reality. If it had been a vision, could it have been a premonition? A warning of some kind, and if so, of what? It seemed so implausible. I'd never had an experience like it before, and...

Actually, no. That wasn't true.

I thought back to the night in the theater. There was no way Freya could have been there in the catwalk, and yet I'd definitely seen her. And there had been something else—a dark, menacing figure. Had I simply imagined them? And then in the garden, during the seance. I hadn't seen anything strange, but I had felt it and heard it, too. My mind had conjured both of those memories in the moments after Zale rescued me. There was something almost indefinable about all three experiences—a sort of thread running through them, connecting them together in my mind. They'd been very different experiences and yet, in some strange inexplicable way, they were the same.

I laughed darkly. Yeah, they'd all been the same because they'd all scared the shit out of me, I thought.

I didn't want to tell my mom about any of it. I knew she would want to help, but I also knew that she had only just barely agreed for us to stay in Sedgwick Cove for the summer; and if she thought I was being haunted or something like that, she'd pack our bags before I could even argue. I considered maybe asking Rhi or Persi, but I barely knew either of them, and there seemed a pretty good chance they'd just turn around and tell my mom anyway.

I thought of Eva, of the way she had looked at me, intently. Like she *believed* me.

I decided I would go see her the next day. I'd only known her a short time, but there was something about her that I trusted. My gut told me that if I confided in her, she would find a way to help me.

I laid down, staring up at the ceiling. Just making the decision to talk to Eva had loosened a small bit of the tension now coiled inside me. I closed my eyes and tried to clear my mind. Tomorrow, I'd get help. Tomorrow, I'd find answers.

As if it had been waiting for me on the other side of consciousness, and perhaps triggered by the events on the beach, my childhood dream was waiting for me. I dreamed once again of the Gray Man walking me to the sea, the same dream I'd always had. I clung to just a thread of lucidity as the dream unfolded, enough to remember, dimly, that I had never been afraid of the Gray Man in all the years I had dreamed of him. But though the dream was the same as it had always been, one detail had changed.

Tonight I was afraid.

My adventure into the ocean must have exhausted me more than I'd realized, because by the time I peeled my eyes open the next day; it was quarter of eleven. I cursed myself for sleeping so late, and then cursed myself again for the previous night's exploits. The areas I'd bruised sliding down the cliff face were now turning all kinds of bright and interesting colors. I took a long shower, letting the hot water run over me, loosening my muscles, which had worked themselves into tense knots during a night of unsettled dreaming. When I had steamed up the bathroom and wrinkled the skin on my fingertips, I finally felt ready to face whatever this day had in store for me—and I had never been more unsure of what that might be than I was today. Perhaps that was part of life in Sedgwick Cove, something I would have to get used to if I wanted to stay here.

I descended the steps to find the house quiet and the front room empty. I made my way back toward the kitchen to scrounge up some breakfast—well, lunch, at this point—when I passed the library, and found all three of Asteria's daughters sitting on the floor, surrounded by piles of books.

"Hey," I said. "What are you all doing?"

"Well, well, well, look who finally decided to rise from the dead!" my mom laughed. "I was starting to wonder if I'd have to wake you up for dinner."

"Sorry," I said, smiling. "I probably shouldn't have stayed out so late."

"Nonsense," Persi snapped from the corner, her face half hidden behind a massive leatherbound volume. "Staying out late is always the right choice. You can sleep when you're old, Wren."

"Thanks for that terrible life advice, Pers. Aunt of the year, seriously," my mom muttered drily. "Want to give her a primer on underage drinking while you're at it?"

Persi caught my eye, and I looked away quickly before either of us gave into the smiles we were both trying to smother.

"What are you doing?" I asked again, bringing the conversation back to my original question, which I was only just realizing my mother might have been trying to avoid answering.

As if in confirmation of my suspicions, she sighed reluctantly as she answered me. "It's what Asteria said about the Covenant of the Three. We're trying to find an explanation."

"Oh," I said, looking around the room at what I was only just realizing was a very old-looking collection of books. This wasn't a library full of novels and biographies, like most people's bookshelves were stacked with. This was a library full of unique treasures—books with a history. I suddenly felt torn. Part of me was aching to know what the Covenant of the Three was, while the other was screaming at me to go find Eva already. Nevertheless, I asked, "Do you want some help?"

My mother made the decision for me. "No," she said, almost a little too quickly. "I realize you know our family's history now, but this particular selection of books would be a pretty intense introduction to who we are. I'd rather... can we just ease you in, a bit?"

"I guess so, but this covenant thing sounds important," I said.

"If we need your help, Wren, I promise we'll ask for it," my mom said. "But most of this would be indecipherable to you without a background in witchcraft. That's my fault, not yours," she added quickly—perhaps my face had betrayed a hint of aggravation. "But the result is still the same, which is that there isn't much here for you to do. I promise, if I think of a way you could be helpful, I'll let you know right away, okay?"

"And if she doesn't, I will," Persi added, giving my mother a challenging look.

"Fine," I said, making sure to sound a bit sulkier than I felt. "I guess I'll just take a walk downtown if that's okay? Maybe stop by Xiomara's again."

My mom looked relieved as she smiled. "Of course. Yeah, go have some fun. You need it, after yesterday. Just... text me, okay? Let me know where you wind up?"

"Of course," I told her.

"There's a plate of my lemon lavender scones on the counter in the kitchen, if you're hungry." Rhi added. "And maybe later I can take you over to see Shadowkeep? I have some stuff I need to do over there if we're going to open back up tomorrow."

"Yeah, I'd like that a lot," I said eagerly. I'd been curious about Shadowkeep, my family's shop downtown, ever since I'd learned of its existence. "Okay, well, good luck. I'll text you."

"Bye, honey," mom said, her eyes already roving the bookshelves again.

Once out on the porch, I pulled out my phone. Eva had put her number in it the night before, and so I pulled her up in my contacts and sent my first ever text to her.

Hey, it's Wren. Are you around? I was hoping we could talk about last night.

The three little bouncing dots appeared almost instantly.

Yes! I'm glad you texted. Do you want me to come over?

No, I don't want my mom to know anything's up. Can I come to you?

Come over to Nova's. We're all here. Zale, too.

I hesitated for a moment. I'd decided to talk to Eva about what was going on, but I hadn't yet considered telling the others. Zale seemed cool enough—not to mention the fact that he'd actually jumped into the ocean to save me; but Nova had a bit of an edge to her. She didn't seem particularly happy about the fact that I'd shown up in Sedgwick Cove, but I thought that might not have anything to do with me and more to do with the chip she carried on her shoulder about being a Second Daughter. I still wasn't quite sure what all the fuss was about. Did it really matter if the Vespers got here first? There was more than enough room for two covens in Sedgwick Cove. In fact, there seemed to be room for hundreds. Besides, all Nova would have to do is spend a little time with me to realize I wasn't going to steal her witchy crown. I could deal with a bit of her attitude, if it meant figuring out what the hell had happened to me last night.

Sounds good. What's the address?

I followed Eva's directions to the Claire house, known to the locals simply as "the Manor." As Nova would later inform me, the Manor marked the southernmost point of the Cove, while the Vesper Lighthouse marked the most northern point. The beach and the town lay cradled between them, guarded on each end by a bastion of generational magic.

The Manor was a stunning old house made of stone, so that it looked almost like a castle. A great wide porch wrapped all the way around it, looking out over the sea below. A turret jutted up on one corner, and connected to a widow's walk that ran the length and width of the mansard style roof. As I took it all in, a flash of silvery blonde hair caught my eye in the turret window, but when I turned to look, only the shadowy blankness of the window stared back.

I left Rhi's bike leaning against the Manor's stone wall and made my way up the walkway. The front of the house was flanked by rows of massive hydrangea bushes the size of small trees. I passed between them, surrounded by the constant droning hum of bumblebees bouncing around between the creamy white bunches of flowers.

The front door had no doorbell, only a large brass knocker in the shape of a mermaid. I cringed a little at the deep, booming sound it made, and waited. After a few moments, Nova came to the door. She opened it, looking like she stepped out of the pages of a fashion magazine in a gauzy, white ruffled skirt, and a crocheted crop top that dangled carelessly off one shoulder over a bikini top.

"Glad to see you came to the front door instead of flinging yourself off the cliff again," she said with a wry smirk.

"Yeah, I only do that at parties," I replied, in what I hoped was as coolly sarcastic a tone. Her smile widened a bit, and she stepped back to gesture me inside.

The Manor had none of the cluttered witchy vibe that burst from every corner of Lightkeep Cottage, but the whole place had a light, airy beach vibe with high ceilings, pale furniture, and lots of accessories made from shells and driftwood, including a magnificent driftwood chandelier that hung over the front entry hall as we walked in. Nova didn't bother with a tour, leading me instead directly up the wide staircase and down a long, wood-paneled hallway to her bedroom. She pushed the door open and said, "Welcome. And just so you know, we've been talking about you."

Eva looked up from the fluffy white rug where she was sitting. "Nova, do you have to be such a bitch?"

Nova scoffed as she shut the door behind us. "Oh, so telling the truth is bitchy now? Good to know."

Zale smiled a little sheepishly. "Okay, well, we have been talking about you, but not in, like, a mean way. We were discussing what happened last night."

I put my bag down on a chair in the corner and came over to sit with everyone else, settling onto the rug next to Eva while Nova draped herself across a cream-colored chaise lounge.

"What happened last night? You mean with you and Sergei? Kaia's going to hex you at the first available opportunity, by the way," Nova said, not looking up from her phone.

"Excuse me, that is an unsubstantiated rumor, and I will not dignify it with a response," Zale said loftily, raising his chin.

Eva rolled her eyes. "Obviously, we were talking about what happened down on the beach." She gave me a searching look. "How are you this morning?"

"A little sore," I admitted, "but otherwise fine, unless you count being really freaked out."

"I think we were all a little freaked out," Zale agreed, nodding fervently.

"Do you think you could walk us through it all again?" Eva asked.

I looked at their eagerly listening faces. Even Nova had deigned to look up from her phone. I took a deep breath and explained how I'd seen the boy from the cliff, how he'd been on the beach one moment, then wading out into the water the next. But when I got to the moment I reached for him, I hesitated.

"This part is going to sound really weird," I said.

Eva rolled her eyes. "Oh, honey, remember who you're talking to." She gestured between the three of them. "Three witches, remember? I know all this magic stuff is new to you, but we have seen some shit."

Zale nodded eagerly. "Go ahead. We'll believe you."

I gathered the courage I needed from their open expressions. "Well, the thing is, I don't think it was a vision at all, because when I reached for his arm, I could actually feel him. And then he... well, he crumbled into sand."

Zale's eyes went wide. "Wait, seriously? He was made of sand?"

"Yeah," I said with a shiver. "Like, I had a handful of him in my hand before that wave took me out."

They all traded a significant look that made my heart begin to pound.

"What does that... is that bad?" I asked when no one spoke.

"Well, it's... it's not good," Zale hedged.

"That kind of magic... well..." Eva seemed to be trying to choose her words carefully. "Do you remember the origin story Zale told last night? The part about light and dark having to be in balance?"

"Yeah."

"Well, that kind of magic... it's the dark kind," Eva said.

"The dark arts, to be exact," Nova said, and even she was having a hard time looking casually disinterested.

"So it was a spell? Someone put a spell on me?" I asked, my voice rising hysterically.

"Not on you, no," Eva said quickly. "But it does seem like they used the spell to lure you down to the beach."

"But why would someone do that?" I asked. "And who?"

"I'm not sure if we can help with the 'who' or the 'why,' but we might be able to figure out how," Eva said thoughtfully. She turned so quickly on Nova that Nova jumped a little in fright. "We need the library."

"What? No! My mom will kill me!" Nova said.

"Oh, come on, Nova, when did you start caring what your mom thinks?" Eva snorted.

"Right around when she promised to take my car away before she's even bought me one," Nova snapped back. "Seriously, I am on thin ice already after this winter. If I get caught in the library—"

"But we won't get caught!" Eva said. "And besides, isn't your mom away on a vacation in Indonesia or something?"

"A retreat," Nova corrected her, rolling her eyes. "She's off to 'find herself' again." She used exaggerated air quotes.

"And she thinks she left herself in Bali?" Zale asked.

"Apparently," Nova muttered.

"Well, while she's looking, we can use the library," Eva said, getting to her feet. "Come on. We'll be quick. Is anyone else even home?"

"I don't think so," Nova said. "Bernadette might be in her studio, but she's not even on this plane of reality, so we don't need to worry about her."

"Bernadette? She's the artist, right?" I asked.

"Yeah, the walking stereotype of the mad genius," Nova said sulkily. When I looked confused, she added. "She's an oracle. Apparently it messes with your sense of reality."

"An oracle?"

"Yeah. It's what we call witches who have, like, premonitions and stuff," Nova said. "But the predictions shift and change; it's an unreliable gift, and most of the witches with it wind up a little not right in the head."

"That sounds awful," I said.

Nova shrugged. "Whatever. She's harmless. And she almost never comes out of her studio anyway."

"And Ostara?" Zale asked.

"At the Historical Society meeting," Nova said.

"Great! So there's nothing stopping us," Eva declared. "Unless, of course, Nova Claire is now a rule follower."

Evidently, there was no greater insult that a person could hurl at Nova. She stood up with a long-suffering sigh and marched toward the bedroom door. "Fine. But if we get caught, it was your idea, and I tried to stop you. That is the story we will be sticking to."

Eva gave a military salute. Zale and I scrambled to our feet and followed them back downstairs.

Nova led us through several large and tastefully decorated rooms before arriving at a set of French doors, which she carefully pried open just enough to peek inside. "Okay, the coast is clear. Everything goes back exactly where you found it, or Ostara will know someone's been in here."

We all nodded in agreement, and she tugged the doors open further to let us in, closing them carefully behind us.

I could tell at first glance that the Claire family's library was full of the same kinds of books as the library at Lightkeep Cottage. Rows and rows of worn leather tomes lined the shelves. Glass-topped cases had even older books on display, books that looked like mere contact with a human hand would cause them to disintegrate. There was a long wooden table under the windows, with a long bench pulled up to it. It was to this table Nova led us, perching herself upon it, and glaring at us.

"So? What are we looking for?" she demanded.

"Where's your dark arts section?" Zale joked. Nova narrowed her eyes at him, and his grin slipped off his face. "What? You're telling me you don't have one?"

Nova rolled her eyes but slid off the table again and walked over to the far corner of the room, where an ornately carved glass-fronted cabinet stood against the wall. A skeleton key dangled from a hook beside it. Nova swiped it off the wall, and carefully unlocked the cabinet.

"Here it is—all the magic we're not supposed to learn," she said, and even she couldn't keep the note of awe out of her voice. We all stood silently for a moment, contemplating the rows of spines.

"So I guess we just... pick one and start looking?" Eva suggested, a slight tremor in her voice.

We all nodded grimly and got to work. Nova took the first four books off the top shelf and handed one to each of us. Eva abandoned hers quickly for another, because the first one was in antiquated French. Zale turned through the pages of his with the very tips of his fingers, as though worried it might infect him if he touched it too much. Eva settled onto the bench and started going through two books at once, while I sat down on the floor in front of the cabinet and started looking through the one she'd handed to me.

A variety of sigils and crude animal shapes had been burned into the leather of the cover as though with a branding iron. Inside, the pages were handwritten and barely legible, being water-stained and smudged. The words I could read were in very old English, and the person who had written them either didn't care or didn't know how to spell properly. I struggled through the first few sentences before realizing it was some sort of introduction. I flipped ahead and was grateful to find a listing of the spells included within the pages. I read through the descriptions with a creeping feeling.

"A charme to summon the dead"

"A potion to inflikt grav fever on thy enemy"

"A hex for terrible dreems to plague sleepers"

It was all fascinating and, loathe as I was to put it down, I closed the book. There were a great many awful spells in those pages, but nothing that sounded like what I'd experienced on the beach. I carefully replaced the book on its shelf and reached for another.

The minutes ticked by, punctuated occasionally by a noise of disgust when someone came across a truly gruesome piece of magic. At first, I couldn't seem to wrap my brain around the idea that any of these spells could actually do what they claimed to do; but the others treated it all with such horror, that I soon felt that doubt slipping away. Instead, I began to wonder why anyone would keep such books in the first place. If you didn't mean to actually use them, why not destroy them, so that no one could ever work such terrible magic again?

"I think I found something!" Zale shouted suddenly. Nova whirled around and shushed him, and he continued in a whisper as we all gathered around him. "Sorry. Look at this: 'A magick spell to raise a living effigy.' Isn't an effigy basically a likeness of someone?"

"Yeah, that sounds right," Eva said, nodding. "What else does it say?"

"It's mad complicated," Zale said, poring over the page. "It requires a full moon and a crazy list of ingredients, including an object that belongs to the person you are making the effigy of."

"Wait, so that means that the boy I saw... he's a real person?" I gasped.

"Or was," Zale pointed out. "It doesn't say anything about the person having to still be alive."

"That's a really big assumption to make," Nova said, her voice a little higher than usual. "We don't know that someone used this exact spell."

But no one replied. We were all too engrossed in Zale's discovery.

"What did you say he looked like, Wren? The little kid?" Eva asked eagerly.

"No more than five or six, unless he was really small for his age. Skinny and very blonde. That's all I could see from the top of the cliff, and by the time I got to the beach he had turned from me, and was mostly submerged," I said. "I never got a good look at his face."

"It... it says you can use "sande, mud, or clay" to construct the effigy, and you mold the form around the object. Then you complete the rest of this ritual; and the effigy comes to life," Zale announced, still bent over the page.

"This has to be it! You said he was made of sand!" Eva said.

I sat back on my heels, my heart pounding. "But none of this makes sense," I said. "Why would someone want to lure me down to the beach? And how did they know that I'd be the one to see it, and not someone else?"

"I think this spell answers that, too," Zale said. "There are further instructions to 'haunt thine enemy with the living effigy.' If I'm reading this correctly, you can literally target someone, if you have something of theirs as well; 'A lock of hair or else an objekt of deerest posession.'"

My throat had gone dry. Everyone was staring at me now.

"Did... did you give anyone a lock of hair recently?" Eva asked, with a nervous laugh.

"Yeah, because she's a lovestruck heroine in a Jane Austen novel," Nova snapped. "Of course she hasn't."

I shook my head.

"Have you lost anything since you got here?" Zale asked, undeterred.

"I... I don't know. I don't think so, but..." I couldn't think of anything I'd misplaced, but then I owned the entirety of Lightkeep Cottage now. I didn't even know what half my possessions *were*, let alone if I was missing any of them.

"Look, I think we can safely say that even if it wasn't this exact spell, it was something like it," Eva said. "I've heard of effigies and bringing inanimate objects to life in lots of different magical cultures."

"Me too," Zale said, eyebrows raised. "My grandmother likes to tell the story of a witch in the Scottish village where she grew up who enchanted a scarecrow to follow her lover around, and throw things at him in the street, because he'd cheated on her. I was terrified of scarecrows for like five years after that."

"Okay, but we're overlooking something kind of important here," I said, more loudly than I'd intended, so that everyone jumped. "If we're right and it was a spell to lure me down to the beach, that means someone basically tried to drown me on purpose."

No one spoke. The silence hung heavy.

"I don't understand. No one here even knows me. Why would someone want to kill me?" I nearly choked on the last two words.

"Maybe... maybe that's not what they *meant* to do," Nova said, her voice shaky.

We all looked at each other. Not a single one of us believed that.

"The thing is, Wren..." Eva hesitated, squirming uncomfortably, "when a family is as famous as yours—I mean famous here in the Cove, obviously, not *literally* famous—well, it can stir up some complicated feelings. There's competition between covens, and sometimes there's bad blood."

She shot a lightning quick glance at Nova, who fired up at once. "Oh, sure, let's just come right out and say it. The Claires and the Vespers lowkey hate each other. That doesn't make us murderers, Eva!"

"I never said—"

"Hey, hey, everyone calm down!" Zale cried, jumping up and putting himself between the others. "Nova, that's not what she said and you know it. Stop putting words in her mouth."

"She didn't have to say it! We found the spell in my library! Our families are in some stupid epic feud for the ages. Why don't you all just ask what you want to and get it over with!" Nova snapped, her eyes glimmering now with unshed tears. No one seemed able to say anything for a moment.

"Nova, you were up on the cliff with us," Zale said softly. "You came running down to the beach to help. You're helping now, even though your grandmother would flay you alive for messing around with these books. No one's accusing you."

Nova chanced a glance at me and I nodded fervently. "I'm not interested in some stupid feud. I don't even know if I'm a real witch, for heaven's sake! I'd... I'd rather just be friends," I told her.

Eva looked like she wanted to say something else but decided against it. She nodded too, like she was making a decision. "I wasn't just talking about the Claires. This whole town is a hot mess of egos and coven pride and has been for generations."

"So, what you're really saying is that someone might want to get rid of me just because I'm a Vesper?" I asked, my voice hollow, defeated. Just when I'd thought I might find the place where I belonged...

"What are you doing?"

We all shrieked and turned to see Bernadette standing in the doorway, staring at us with round, inquisitive eyes.

"Bernadette! You scared the shit out of us!" Nova gasped.

"What are you doing?" Bernadette repeated, casting her wide-eyed glance down at the pile of books we'd accumulated on the floor.

"We're just... uh, doing a little research," Nova said, and she hastily began to pick up books and thrust them back on the shelf. We all hurried to help her.

"You aren't supposed to use the books in that cabinet. That magic is very dark," Bernadette said, and she scowled, shaking a finger at us like we were naughty toddlers.

"We know that," Nova snapped. "And we aren't trying to use it. We were just looking for information."

As though Nova hadn't even spoken, Bernadette turned to stare at me. "You're the Vesper girl. I met you in the gallery at the Historical Society."

"I... yeah, I remember. How are you, Bernadette?" I stammered as I picked up another book.

"I did not expect to see you," she said blankly.

I had no idea how to respond. "I, uh... I liked your painting."

Bernadette tilted her head. "Did you? I got the impression that you found it upsetting."

I felt the color rise to my cheeks. Had I been that obvious? "Oh, no, not at all. Just... just surprised. It reminded me of... of something, that's all."

Bernadette stepped further into the room, her eyes fixed on me. "Perhaps it gave you a sense of déjà vu," she suggested. "Or else, the feeling of something yet to come. My art has that effect on people, you know."

"Yeah, she knows, Bernadette," Nova huffed impatiently. "I've already told her about your gift."

Bernadette's face twisted oddly. "Gift is not the word I would use."

I couldn't speak. She was staring at me as though she knew exactly what I was thinking... as though she knew that she had painted the very dream I'd had for as long as I could remember. A single question burned on my lips: *Do you know about the Gray Man?*

But I couldn't bring myself to ask it.

A slamming sound in the front hall made us all jump, followed by the low murmur of several voices.

"Shit!" Nova whispered. "The books, get the books!"

We all scrambled to gather up the books we'd taken out and arranged them back on the shelves while Bernadette stood and watched us with a mildly amused expression. Nova locked the cabinet with shaking fingers and replaced the key, but by the time she'd finished, the voices were growing louder. Some of the words were becoming distinguishable, now.

"...ought to have met before this, but..."

"Ostara!" Nova hissed, her eyes alight with terror.

"In here, quickly," Bernadette said, suddenly starting forward.

Without waiting for any of us to respond, she started shoving us toward the righthand wall of shelves. She tugged on the spine of a brown leatherbound book that looked no different than the dozen books on either side of it, except for the fact that this particular book caused the entire set of shelves to swing inward, revealing a hidden door. I had just enough time to think that I'd always wanted to enter a secret passage behind a bookcase before she pushed us all through it and closed the door behind us.

17

The door closed behind us, not a moment too soon. We heard the French doors into the library open once again, followed by several sets of footsteps.

"...think we'll all be much more comfortable in here. Please, take a seat." Ostara's voice rang with authority.

There was a minute or so of general mumbling and shuffling and swishing, as whoever she'd brought with her settled into the library. I took advantage of the moment to look around at the room we now found ourselves in. It was small and square, containing more bookshelves, a writing desk, a leather wingback chair, and a single arched window set high into the wall. A small chandelier had blazed to life the moment the door had opened, casting a golden glow over the four of us as we crowded together, panting and trembling from nearly being caught.

"Who is—" Zale whispered, but Nova put a frantic finger to her lips and he pressed his mouth closed at once. Bernadette then whispered two words that caused the others to go still and cold as statues.

"The Conclave."

I wanted to ask what the Conclave was, but I didn't dare make a sound, so I just listened along with the others.

"As the acting High Mistress of the Conclave, I'd like first to thank our members for making themselves available to meet on such short notice. And secondly, I'd like to welcome our guests. Rhiannon, Persephone, Kerridwen Vesper, the Conclave welcomes you with open arms and open hearts."

Everyone turned to look at me. I thought my heart would pound right out of my chest. What the hell were my mother and her sisters doing here? They were supposed to be back at the cottage, researching Asteria's cryptic seance messages.

"I know we have all expressed it to you in our own ways, but on behalf of the Conclave and all it represents to the covens of Sedgwick Cove, I would like to offer our deepest condolences on the loss of your mother Asteria, the Conclave's former High Mistress and a dear friend to us all."

I heard some faint muttering that might have been my mom and the others saying thank you, but the bookcase door muffled the sound. Eva, Nova, Zale, and I crowded forward, pressing our ears to the door. Nova shoved Zale out of her way, so that he was forced to crouch on the floor to find room. Bernadette hung back, her expression calm, almost disinterested.

"...know that her friendships here meant a great deal to her," came Rhi's voice, high and tight with emotion.

"Just so," Ostara said, and then cleared her throat. When she spoke again, she had taken on a more businesslike tone. "We've brought you here today to discuss a matter of grave importance to our safety and security in Sedgwick Cove."

There was a loud sigh, and then Persi spoke. "Look, Ostara, if this is about the High Mistress position, none of us want to challenge you for it, okay? Your crown is safe. This whole meeting could have been an email. Can we go now?"

Ostara's tone was decidedly frosty as she answered, "While I appreciate your vote of confidence, Persephone, this has nothing to do with the leadership positions within the Conclave. This is a much graver matter, a matter that will affect every witch in the Cove if we do not address it."

There were a few seconds of silence before Rhi finally broke it. "Please, proceed."

"Get on with it, Ostara. The girls have been through enough, we don't need a dramatic recitation," snapped a familiar voice, and I felt Eva shaking with the effort of suppressing a laugh at Xiomara's impatience.

I could only imagine the look on Ostara's face as she said, "Very well. Zadia, would you please give us the account from the Records?"

There was some shuffling around, and I distinctly heard a large volume being removed from a shelf with a grunt of effort. Eva put her mouth directly to my ear and barely breathed an explanation.

"The Records are usually kept at the Historical Society, but they had a break-in recently, so they moved them to the Manor. Only Conclave members are allowed access to them."

I'd heard something about the break-in; Ostara and Phoebe had spoken of it that first day in Sedgwick Cove, when I visited the Historical Society. They'd mentioned an artifact that had gone missing, but I couldn't recall the details. Someone cleared their throat out in the main library, and I refocused my attention.

"I won't waste anyone's time by recounting the whole of the history, for we all know the story well enough. The First and Second Daughters settled here and began to practice their magic, drawing on the unique power of the Cove itself. They roused the Darkness with their craft."

I recognized the origin story Zale had told the other night, though this droning recitation was nothing like the dramatic performance he'd given of the same tale. Though we all knew it, we stayed glued to the door listening— all except for Bernadette, who was now wandering the little room examining the books, as though what was happening outside was barely worth her notice. She even began to hum softly, until Nova flapped her arms hysterically to quiet her.

"The Darkness rose and found a servant in one of the Second Daughters," the woman named Zadia continued, "and the remaining witches banded together to banish the Darkness and bind it from accessing the deep magic of this place, the magic it had been feeding on for centuries before their arrival. What is less widely known is that the binding could not last forever."

Utter silence greeted these words. Beside me, Nova's body was trembling. Even Bernadette had come to stop behind us.

"The Binding will only hold as long as three of the blood of the First Daughters make their home in Sedgwick Cove. Otherwise, the spell is broken, and the Darkness will be free once more." Zadia's voice had a ringing quality to it, and I felt a deep shiver of fear judder up my spine. Below me, Zale swore under his breath.

"I'm sorry, what... what exactly does that mean?" Rhi asked, sounding breathless.

"It means," Ostara's voice cut in sharply, "that three Vesper witches must make the choice to stay in Sedgwick Cove—must renew the Covenant in each new generation, if we want the Darkness to be held at bay."

There was a sharp dragging noise. Someone had pushed their chair back violently, and I knew who it was before she even spoke.

"No. There's no way this is true. Asteria would never have kept this from us. She couldn't have known about this, or she would have told us." My mom's voice was low but tremulous.

"But of course she knew about it," Ostara replied, a hint of amusement in her voice that made my fists clench at my sides. "She had to renew it herself, when the last of her mother's generation passed."

"I don't understand," Rhi said. "She never said a word. How could she not have said a word about something so important?"

"It has long been tradition to pass along the burden when the next genera-tion is ready to carry it. But you weren't ready. She didn't want to force you to stay here." It was Xiomara who spoke now. "She wanted you to find your own way to Sedgwick Cove, to stay here because you wanted to, not because you were obligated."

"We did try to persuade her otherwise," Ostara added. "Especially when you moved away, Kerridwen. We tried to impress upon her the importance of the Covenant, that knowing of its existence would surely bring you back. But she refused."

"This is not happening, this is really not happening," my mother was muttering. Her voice had a muffled sound, and I thought she must have dropped her face into her hands.

"You must see, Kerri," Xiomara said, and I appreciated her use of my moth-er's preferred nickname, "that she wanted to give you time—time to miss Sedg-wick Cove, time to realize that you could not outrun who you were, and that perhaps you didn't even want to."

"And she knew you wanted to protect Wren," Zadia added. "She knew you would never return if you had the threat of the Covenant hanging over Wren's head as well."

"I can't believe this!" my mom shouted. "It was just more lies, more covering up! Are you telling me that all this time, our control over our futures was always measured by how much longer Asteria was going to live? That when I thought I was making a choice to live my life and to let Wren live hers, there was really never any choice at all?"

"Of course, there is a choice," Ostara said, not unkindly. "The Conclave does not intend to force you to stay here, any more than Asteria wanted to. We are simply giving you the truth. You may do with it what you will."

"Bullshit!" Mom cried. "I can't leave now, and you know it. Not if this Covenant is real! How could I possibly leave, when the entire magical fate of this town apparently depends on my staying?"

"It is not certain that it does. We can search for other members of the Vesper family, distant relations with magical blood," Xiomara said.

"And if they don't exist?" Persi asked, breaking her long silence. "Or if they don't feel like uprooting their whole lives to save a town they've never heard of?"

Xiomara did not answer.

Rhi spoke up now, her voice choked with tears. "Who else knows about this?"

"It has only ever been the Conclave who kept this secret," Ostara said. "It was too dangerous for the rest of the town to know. If knowledge of the Covenant fell into the wrong hands, your family could be targeted by those who would see the Darkness rise again. We had to keep it as secret as we could, even from those it would one day include. The lure of the deep magic of this place, as well as the ties of home and tradition, have always been enough to hold the descendants of the First Daughters here. Until... until recently."

"Until I screwed it all up, you mean," my mom muttered bitterly.

"The world is changing. It is getting smaller. People do not cling to their roots as they once did, and the lure of the world beyond our borders has grown, become more tempting. It is only natural," Xiomara said. "The Covenant was never meant to last forever."

"Exactly!" All of us jumped as Ostara slammed her hand down on some surface or other. "And in light of that fact, I would like to point out that there is another choice. I suggested it once, to Asteria. She was not in favor of it, but it is an option nonetheless."

Someone snorted—Xiomara, I thought. Ostara was unperturbed, however.

"We could allow the Covenant to lapse," she said. "We could stop relying on the blood of a single coven to protect this place and find a new way to bind the Darkness; one that does not place the burden so squarely on so few shoulders."

"Well, that doesn't sound dangerous or complicated at all," Persi drawled. "I'm sure there are just heaps and heaps of spells that would work just as effectively. And I'm sure the Darkness will be happy to sit by while we try them all out."

"Ostara, we have discussed this before. We have voted on it," another voice said, this one with a Scottish brogue. "The will of the Conclave was clear: maintain the integrity of the Covenant if at all possible. We have three Vesper witches in front of us. Therefore, it is possible."

"Possible, yes, but not our choice to make, Davina," Xiomara said. "That choice belongs to the Vesper sisters, and we must allow them some time to make it."

"But there is no time!" Rhi cried. "Asteria is dead! The Covenant of the Three has lapsed, hasn't it?"

"Your mother took steps to ensure it would not," Xiomara said.

"What steps could she poss—oh." My mom's voice rang with sudden understanding. "The will. The house. She left it to Wren."

"It was a contingency plan," Xiomara explained. "She did not intend to die before telling all of this to you. She planned to come see you, to explain everything. But her illness had other plans."

"She called me," my mom said, her voice low, tremulous. "She called me several times. I wouldn't return her call."

My throat tightened. I hadn't known that. Add it to the long list of things my mother hadn't told me. I thought of Asteria's letter to me, cast into the garbage, and saw it for what it actually was—a desperate last resort. The words made so much more sense now, in light of everything I was hearing:

There are things you must be told—truths that must be revealed to you, and I fear that your mother cannot see that. Come to me this summer, as soon as you can, and until then, please promise me you will wear this charm. For protection. For guidance.

My hand flew to the charm I still wore around my neck, the one she had enclosed in the letter. Had Asteria known the kind of danger I would find myself in when we came here? Was I wearing a spell that was meant to ward off that danger?

"The will isn't just binding legally, it's enchanted as well," said a quavery voice, and I realized that Lydian was also there in the room. It was the first time she had spoken. "You have seven days, from the time of the reading, to renew the Covenant. Otherwise, it will lapse, and the Darkness will be free once more."

"Unless we find another way to bind it," Ostara added, sounding frustrated.

"Oh, Ostara give it a rest, won't you?" Lydian snapped.

Nova could barely suppress a gasp; evidently people did not generally dare to talk to Ostara in such a tone, as a rule. But from what little I knew of Lydian, she ran such rules over in the street in her rickshaw and didn't give a damn.

Lydian continued, "I don't deny that it would be preferable to use a binding that does not rely on a single coven's blood. I think we all agree that your point is a good one, Ostara. But we are hemmed in by powerful magical boundaries that we oughtn't to test. Once the Covenant is renewed, we will be free to explore other ways to defend our safety."

"We've had centuries," Ostara ground out. "And we've done nothing."

"The Covenant has never been in such a precarious state before, nor has it ever failed us," Davina said. "Why should we have searched for a solution when no problem had yet presented itself?"

"Yes but—"

"We must allow the Vesper Coven time to come to their decision," Zadia's voice cut through. "We cannot move forward without it."

There was a general flurry of arguing.

"We'll need time, if they refuse, to discover how—"

"There may be no other way! It's lunacy to gamble with—"

"You said we have seven days," Rhi said.

"Seven days from the reading of the will. That was two days ago," Persi pointed out.

"Fine, five days, then," Rhi said. "That's hardly enough time to..."

"We don't need five days." It was my mother who spoke now, and her voice, though quiet, cut through the room and silenced everyone. "I'll stay. I'll renew the Covenant."

I was holding my breath. The hand that grasped Asteria's necklace was trembling violently. I could hardly believe my ears. And neither, it seemed, could Rhi or Persi.

"Kerri, you should take a little time to—" Rhi began.

"Why? What other conclusion could I possibly come to in an hour or a day or a week?" my mom asked. "We all know that I'm the loose cannon here. Oh, you're all making a fine show of pretending that any of us might refuse, but I'd appreciate if we could end that pretense now. There was never any doubt that Rhi and Persi would renew the Covenant, even if they had no idea it existed. I'm the one everybody's worried about, the prodigal daughter who's destined to screw everything up, and land the entire town in danger. So, let me put everyone's minds at ease now. I'll stay."

A moment of silence, and then, "Is that truly your choice?" Xiomara asked.

My mom laughed bitterly. "There was never a choice. Let's all stop pretending that there ever was. Some of you may have come to the opinion over the last few years I've been gone that I'm heartless and selfish—an ungrateful daughter of the Cove. I'm not. I only ever wanted to protect my kid, and I don't regret it. But now it sounds like the only way to protect her—and the rest of us—is to stay, so yes. I agree. The Covenant of the Three will be renewed and the binding of the Darkness will remain unbroken. But on one condition."

"And that condition is...?" Ostara asked, her tone guarded.

"I refuse to do the same to Wren that Asteria has done to me. We are the last generation to be bound by this Covenant. It ends with us. My sisters and I will renew it, and then the Conclave will find a new way to protect this town—one that doesn't require my daughter to sacrifice her future."

There was silence as these words settled for a few seconds before Ostara spoke. When she did, there was a badly-suppressed note of triumph in her voice.

"Very well. I would like to make a motion for the Conclave to vote on Kerridwen's proposal."

A moment, and then, "Seconded," came Davina's voice.

"All in favor?" Ostara asked.

We could not see the hands that were raised in the air, but I did hear the relieved expulsion of breath from my mother, and therefore knew the result before Ostara spoke it.

"The motion carries. The Covenant of the Three will be renewed one last time. Conclave will seek to find a new way to bind the Darkness."

Then Xiomara cleared her throat and spoke with something less than her usual sharpness.

"Thank you, Vesper Coven, and particularly you, Kerridwen. On behalf of the Conclave and every coven in Sedgwick Cove, we are grateful for your sacrifice."

Ostara snorted softly, clearly taking offense to the term "sacrifice."

"Are we finished here?" my mom asked bluntly. "If I'm going to uproot my entire life, I have a few phone calls to make. And I need to speak to my daughter."

It was Ostara who answered stiffly, "Of course. We can conclude with—"

There was a resounding crash from behind us, and we all whipped around to see Bernadette on the ground, a stack of books scattered around her, and both hands clutched to her head as she cried out.

"What the—!" Zale said before slapping a hand over his mouth in horror.

Voices flew into a frenzy on the other side of the wall.

"What in the world was that?"

"Is there someone in the library?"

"Ostara, could someone be here?

Bernadette was already staggering to her feet.

"What the hell, Bernadette?!" Nova hissed. "We are so dead!"

"It's all right," Bernadette muttered. "I'm... I'm all right."

"No you're not all right! None of us are! Ostara's about to kill us all!" Nova snapped, barely mouthing the words.

At that moment, Ostara's voice could be heard, "There's a secret reading room. It's possible—"

"Go!" Bernadette hissed, and she pointed at the solitary window in the tiny room, the one set high into the wall above the desk. "Get out! I'll... I'll go out there. I'll tell her it was just me."

"That's never going to w—"

"Just go!" Bernadette whispered. She shoved us into the corner of the room that would be hidden from view when the door opened. "Wait for me to close the door behind me, and then go out the window!"

Before we could argue, Bernadette had flung herself forward and, still clutching at her head with one hand, she flung out the other and lifted the latch on the door. She then pulled the door toward us, shielding us from the view of the astonished group on the other side, before stumbling out to meet them.

"Bernadette! What in heaven's name...?" Ostara's voice was shrill with fury, a shrillness that was instantly muffled as Bernadette pulled the door closed behind her.

"What do we do?" Eva whispered.

"Exactly what she said to do!" Nova hissed back and tiptoed across the room to the desk. She climbed carefully onto it and, with slightly shaking fingers, released the catch on the window, and lifted the sash. She looked back at us where we stood, still frozen. "Stay if you want to, but I'm bailing, and I will deny to my dying day any knowledge of how the three of you got in here. So unless you want to get charged with breaking and entering…"

We didn't need any further persuading. One by one we climbed up behind Nova, who was already hoisting her slim frame through the window. Outside in the main library, Bernadette was explaining her presence. I could hear snatches of her tremulous voice.

"…only wanted some privacy while I researched a new painting. I must have dozed off, and a dream startled me awake…"

Nova landed cat-like in the mulch behind the hydrangea bush below and gestured frantically for us to follow. Zale went next, landing slightly less gracefully, but still managing to stay on his feet. Eva turned to me.

"Do you—"

"Just go!"

She slid through the window and, with a muttered oath, dropped to the ground. Zale and Nova reached out to steady her, and then all three looked up at me. I got through the window okay, but as I tried to jump, the cuff on my jeans snagged on a creeping vine, and I tumbled forward, arms flailing, not a chance in hell of landing on my feet.

"Oh shit!" Zale muttered, and all three of them hurried forward to help break my fall. I twisted around at the last moment and managed to take the brunt of the fall on my tailbone. Zale and Eva both caught my arms and held them, which helped prevent me from hitting too hard. Still, as they helped me to my feet, I was wincing.

"Are you okay? That looked—" Zale hesitated.

"Clumsy? Uncoordinated?" Nova suggested.

Zale shrugged. "I was gonna say 'painful,' but…"

"Can we stop wasting time and get out of here before we get caught? Just because we made it out the window doesn't mean they won't still spot us!"

We hid ourselves more completely in the hydrangea bush and waited.

After what felt like forever but was probably only a minute or two, the front door to the house opened, and we watched as Persi stormed out and down the steps. A moment later, Bernadette flew out after her.

"Persephone, wait!"

Persi rounded on her. "Did you know about this? This Covenant thing?"

Bernadette hesitated a moment, then nodded. "I've heard the Conclave speak of it before."

"And you didn't think that might be information I was entitled to?" Persi asked.

Bernadette lowered her head, abashed.

"Look, Bernadette, I just don't think we should start this all up again."

Bernadette looked up suddenly. "All what?"

"This! Us!" Persi cried, gesturing back and forth between the two of them. "It didn't end well last time, or the time before that... or any damn time! And I... I never should have invited you over. I was messed up about my mom, and drunk if I'm being totally honest, and I... I should have remembered how quickly this gets complicated."

All the blood drained from Bernadette's face. "No! You can't—" She swallowed the rest of her sentence and tried to compose herself. Then she stepped toward Persi, reached out, and took her hand. "You've had a very stressful week. Don't make any rash decisions, okay?"

Persi sighed. "B, you are a rash decision. One rash decision after another."

Bernadette lifted Persi's hand to her face. "I mean, a rash decision to end things. You've liked having me around the past few days, don't you?"

"That's not the point. We always—"

"It's been a nice distraction, hasn't it?"

"I don't... yeah, sure, but..."

"Then don't overthink it, Persephone," Bernadette whispered. Then she leaned in and planted a soft kiss on Persi's cheek. "I'll find you later," she added, and walked back toward the house.

Persi stood there for a moment, her expression slightly dazed. She seemed to shake it off just as Rhi and my mom walked out of the house together.

I turned to the others, but no one seemed the least bit surprised that Persi and Bernadette were in a relationship together. Nova caught the expression on my face and whispered, "You didn't know?"

"Of course, she didn't know!" Eva hissed back. "She's been here for like two days!"

"Bernadette and Persi have been on and off again for years," Nova explained, rolling her eyes. "They've never been good for each other, but they just keep getting back together, like a bad habit."

I opened my mouth to respond, but Rhi's voice caught my attention, and I turned back to the driveway.

"I... I suppose we'd better get home," Rhi said. She gestured toward the car. "Shall... shall I drive?"

Persi shrugged without answering and walked to the car, sliding into the passenger seat and slamming the door.

"No, I think I'm going to walk," Mom said. "I need to clear my head."

"Are you sure?" Rhi was bouncing anxiously from foot to foot, twisting her hands together. "It's a long way to—"

"Yes, I'm sure. Thanks, Rhi."

I watched as my mom stood at the end of the driveway. She waved after the car, watching it all the way to the bend in the road, where it disappeared from sight. Then she pulled out her phone and started typing something.

"No offense to your mom, who's clearly going through some shit, but I don't want to stay in this bush all day," Eva whispered.

"I know, I'm sorry," I murmured. "Maybe we can sneak around the—"

My phone started going off. Loudly.

"Shit, shit, shit!" I gasped, pulling it from my pocket. My mother was calling me, because of course she was. I'd told her I would text her to let her know where I ended up, and I'd completely forgotten. I silenced the ringer, but the damage was done. My mom was staring, bewildered, at the hydrangea bush.

"Wren?" she called uncertainly.

I considered just staying quiet, but then I realized my geo-locator was on, and all it would take was one click for my mom to know for sure that I was crouching like a criminal in the bushes. I sighed and walked out where she could see me, my friends following sheepishly behind me.

"Wren, what in the world are you—" my mom's voice faded as she glanced up and saw the open window and put two and two together as only a mom could.

"How much did you hear?" she finally asked.

I swallowed hard. "Everything."

I could feel my friends braced behind me for an onslaught of berating and shouting, but my mom just sighed, her shoulders slumping.

"That's really not how I would have wanted you to find out," she said.

"I really didn't mean to. We... we just happened to be in the library, and Nova panicked, and... I'm sorry. Are you okay?"

"I'll be fine. But the rest of you won't be if Ostara finds out you overheard that meeting," my mom said, looking at the others. "You should probably get out of sight before she spots you out here."

"We can pretend we were just walking back from town, unless..." Nova bit her lip and looked at my mom.

"Unless?"

"Unless you're planning on ratting us out."

My mom actually managed a smile. "Nova, you may not know this, but I used to be friends with your mom. We got into our fair share of mischief back then, and we didn't always get away with it. I still have stress dreams about getting caught by Ostara. Your secret is safe with me, as long as *our* secret is safe with you, because Ostara's right. The Covenant can't become common knowledge. I need you all to promise me that it won't."

My friends readily agreed, with palpable relief that they weren't getting busted.

"Good. Now, you three stay out of trouble. Wren and I are going to head home," Mom said.

I waved goodbye to my friends. Eva pointed to her phone and mouthed, *Text me.*

I nodded, and then followed my mom home.

Because that's what it was now, I realized, whether we wanted it or not: home.

18

The four Vespers sat around the living room back at Lightkeep Cottage, each of us at a loss for words. The events of the past few hours had rocked each of us to our foundation and now, though we had more to talk about than ever, no one seemed to know how to begin.

Asteria would have known what to say, I felt sure. But she was gone, and here we were, trying to sort it all out without her. I knew she hadn't planned it that way, but I couldn't help but feel frustrated at her regardless.

And I knew I wasn't the only one.

"Damn it all, Asteria," Persi muttered, staring into the fireplace where Rhi had lit some candles.

Rhi didn't answer, except to sigh and plop another piece of pie onto Persi's plate. No one had been hungry enough for dinner when Rhi had offered it; and yet somehow, we'd now eaten almost the entirety of one of her blueberry pies that she'd had cooling on the counter, along with an entire gallon of vanilla bean ice cream. Because, as Rhi declared while slicing it, "When you get a bomb like that dropped on you, you get to eat as much pie and ice cream as you want. That's the rule."

And generally, I am a rule follower. At least when it comes to pie.

"I still can't believe neither of you ever knew about this," my mom said, rubbing her temples the way she always did when she felt a stress headache coming on. "Like, seriously, not a hint, not even toward the end?"

Rhi shook her head, digging some melted remnants from the bottom of the ice cream container. "She talked a lot about family the past few months, about our heritage, our roots, and, of course, about reconciling with you. But no. The tiny detail of the centuries-old blood covenant seemed to have slipped her mind."

For once, my mother wasn't alone in her frustration at Asteria. All three sisters had found common ground in their collective shock.

"Well, Ostara will be happy, at least," Mom sighed.

"Ostara, happy?" Persi snorted. "There's an oxymoron if ever I heard one."

"I just mean, there's always been such a weird power struggle between our covens. At least now it makes sense. When the Covenant was formed, the Second Daughters weren't a part of it. That's likely rankled her ever since," Mom said.

"Why weren't they included?" I asked. "They must have wanted to bind the Darkness as much as we did."

"Sure, but only to save face," Persi said, licking her spoon. "You've heard the origin story by now, right? You know about the lost Second Daughter?"

I frowned, trying to remember. "Yeah, one of them served the Darkness, right? Like, she turned villain, or whatever?"

"Yes, but not because she was a rebel or a misfit or anything. The Claires have always dabbled a bit in darker magic than they should. They've got a reputation for it; a reputation Ostara's spent her life trying to clean up."

"Wait, so you think the Vespers didn't trust the Claires enough to make the Covenant together?" I asked.

"Ding, ding, ding!" Persi replied, pointing her spoon at me. "The Lost Second Daughter—"

"Sarah," Rhi told her. "Her name was Sarah Claire."

"Right, Sarah. Well, she might have been a weak link, but she couldn't have fallen to the Darkness without a thorough grounding in the dark arts. The Claires opened that door in their practice, and of course, one of them would eventually walk through it."

"Yeah, I thought it was weird they had all those books on dark magic," I said.

My mom looked down at me, frowning. "What books?"

"Oh, uh..." I almost choked on my last bite of pie. "In their library. Nova showed us. There was a whole locked cabinet full of books she wasn't allowed to even look at."

My mom and I had decided it was best to come clean to Rhi and Persi, and admit I'd overheard the conversation about the Covenant. But I still hadn't told them—or my mom, for that matter—that we'd actually been searching those books, or why. I wasn't entirely sure what was holding me back—except that my mom's decision to stay in Sedgwick Cove still felt too precarious. If I told her someone had used dark magic to try to kill me, she'd pack up the car, Covenant or no Covenant. And also, I told myself, the danger would be passed as soon as the Covenant was renewed.

Because that was what I had realized on our long, silent walk back to Lightkeep Cottage. Whoever had worked that wicked spell down on the beach must have known about the Covenant. I didn't believe for a second that the Conclave were the only ones to know about it. After all, five of us had learned about it by accident just today. Over the years, there surely must have been others. And getting rid of a Vesper probably seemed like a good way to prevent it from being renewed. My attacker probably thought my mother was a lost cause and saw me as the potential third Vesper witch who might be convinced to stay and renew the Covenant. Of course, if they'd just taken a little time to get to know me, I think they would have realized I was no threat at all. Not a bit of magical training, and not a scrap of obvious magical ability; I was hardly worth even bothering to get rid of.

But now my mother had surprised everyone. The Covenant would be renewed. I just had to stay out of trouble until that happened. When it was over, I could come clean about what happened on the beach. My mom would be pissed at me, of course, but it would be too late by then. We'd be tied to Sedgwick Cove in ways even she couldn't sever.

I wondered if I was supposed to feel upset. I was moving away from my friends. I was getting pulled out of high school in a thriving city and being forced to make a new home in a tiny town. I wouldn't have a choice in any of it. Any normal kid would have been throwing the mother of all rebellious teenage tantrums.

I was quietly celebrating instead.

Yes, I would miss my friends, especially Poe and Charlie, but we had social media and the train to keep in touch; and thankfully, I seemed to be making new friends already—friends who had helped me in pretty significant ways. And it was hard to be upset about being pulled from Portland High when my new education was going to require learning literal magic. And then there was this house, this town... I belonged to it in a way I could never belong anywhere else.

It was already home. We were just making it official.

"Did Ostara say anything about *how* you renew the Covenant?" I asked, after a few minutes of silence.

"We'll meet with the Conclave again tomorrow night, and they'll walk us through the ritual," Rhi answered. "Once it's completed we can... can move on. Figure out what's next, for all of us."

She looked at my mom as she said this and smiled gently. I was glad to see that Mom could return the smile, even if it was a little strained. Maybe she was more reconciled to all of this than I thought.

A buzzing sound startled us all. Persi swore and pulled her phone from her pocket, glancing down at it for a moment, looking thoughtful. "I should take this," she said, jumping up from the couch and heading out into the gardens through the French doors.

"Is that who I think it was?" Mom asked, raising an eyebrow.

"Probably, and don't get me started," Rhi said tartly. "I still haven't recovered from the last time I had to nurse her through a broken heart over that one."

I'd seen enough from the hydrangea bushes to know they were probably talking about Bernadette. I didn't feel like it was my place to ask for more details, curious as I was about such an odd coupling; but at least I was comforted by the fact that, from now on, I'd be privy to all the Sedgwick Cove gossip as it unfolded.

I tried to hide a yawn, but my mom spotted it.

"Bed sounds like a good idea, don't you think?" she asked.

"Oh, I'm glad you said it first. I wanted to be with you all, but I could happily have gone to sleep an hour ago," Rhi said, sighing with relief.

I glanced at the clock. It was a little after nine o'clock, but it felt like midnight. I guessed discovering that the safety of an entire town depended on your family left you a bit worn out.

I hugged my mom—the kind of hug that lasts a long time and says a lot without saying a lot—and headed up the stairs. As I passed the front door, I saw Persi out on the porch, still talking animatedly on the phone. I wasn't sure if I hoped things worked out for her and Bernadette, or not. I'd spent just enough time with Bernadette to understand that, while she was definitely beautiful, she didn't seem particularly stable. I knew that was a result of her harrowing magical gift, but still—it didn't seem like a great basis for a lasting relationship.

I looked around for Freya in my room, but a quick glance out the window confirmed that she and Diana were patrolling the garden chasing fireflies, so I went to bed without her. My last thought, as I fell asleep, was that it seemed like everything might finally work out okay.

My dreams had other ideas.

It began as my familiar childhood nightmare, standing upon the shore with the Gray Man beside me. But I was no longer the child I had been. I did not hold his hand. I did not feel safe. For the first time, I looked at him with true fear thrumming through my body. He reached for me. I turned and ran. Sand slipped under my feet as I stumbled my way across the beach, away from the water. When I reached the gate of Lightkeep Cottage, I turned to look behind me to see if he followed, but he stood where I had left him, staring after me with that strangely featureless face. I turned back to the gate to let myself into the garden.

He stood in the garden, waiting for me.

I screamed and ran, hopping the fence with an agility I could never manage while awake, and flew up the porch, slamming the door behind me, not stopping until I reached my bedroom. From there, I looked down into the garden. There he still stood, staring up at me.

A creeping feeling began in my bones. I looked down at my hands clenched on the windowsill and saw ants and beetles and spiders forcing their way through the cracks around the window frame, scuttling across my fingers. I screamed again, stumbling back from the window, and turned to face my room.

To face him. Because of course he was there. I'd known it before I turned around.

His form shifted strangely, as though it was harder to appear human when in motion. His limbs elongated, his neck stretched grotesquely as he leaned toward me.

"I have waited for you, Little Bird."

The words materialized in my head, though the sound was one of skittering legs and whirring wings. Every hair on my body stood at attention. I wanted to run, but my body wouldn't obey me. Without knowing why my hand drifted to the necklace Asteria had given me. It felt warm, like a warning.

The Gray Man reached for me, his arm lengthening, stretching, winding through the space between us.

I opened my mouth to scream, but a hiss sounded through the room instead.

Freya had appeared out of nowhere at my feet, hackles raised, bottlebrush tail at attention, mouth open in a ferocious yowl. The Gray Man withdrew his hand, took a single step back into the shadows...

I woke instantly, sitting up before I'd even opened my eyes. Heart pounding, cold sweat beading up all over me, I turned at once to the place the Gray Man had stood. Was it my terror still receding, or did the shadows in the corner of my room shift strangely?

I yelped at a violent hissing sound. I looked down at the floor to see Freya, just as I had seen her in the dream—arched defensively, glaring into the very corner where the Gray Man had just vanished in my dream. Without taking my eyes off her, I reached over to my side table and fumbled for the light switch.

There was nothing there, but Freya continued to glare into the empty corner. At last, after what felt like an eternity, but was probably only a few seconds, Freya relaxed. She seemed almost to shrink before my eyes before turning her glowing green eyes on me.

A wave of nausea rolled over me as the realization hit. It had been a dream, and yet, it hadn't. Freya had sensed him, too. I dropped my face into my shaking hands, feeling the beads of sweat that had broken out on my forehead. I shivered in the breeze that drifted in the open window. Everything was cold, shaking... except...

My hand went to the only warmth I could find—the necklace, with its little velvet pouch, as warm against my skin as though it had been laying in the summer sun all day. I pulled the chain over my head and looked down at the pouch. Not for the first time, I wondered what was inside it. But now, it wasn't an idle curiosity. It was a burning question that had to be answered, no less tantalizing because the gold thread that had been used to sew it up was slightly unraveled at one end, begging to be pulled.

I pulled it. The gold thread slipped effortlessly through the fabric, and the pouch opened. With violently shaking fingers, I reached inside and pulled out the contents.

It was a piece of paper, folded many times over, and tied with a piece of violet ribbon. I undid the ribbon and unfolded the paper, careful not to rip it. I smoothed it on my bed and stared down at it.

It was a child's drawing, a collection of crayon scribbles that were nevertheless unmistakable in their portrayal of the very figure who haunted my dreams. It was the Gray Man. And I remembered drawing him.

It was as though the memory had been beating down the walls I'd constructed around it, and finally burst through at that very moment. It flooded back with such clarity, it was like a mental slap in the face.

I was in the water. The Gray Man stood beside me. The water lapped around me, swirling with foam, soaking the hem of my dress. And then a hand reached out and grabbed my arm, just as a familiar voice called my name.

"Wren!" Asteria turned me to face her, and I felt nothing so much as aggravation at seeing her there, her face alive with terror. She wasn't supposed to be there. She was ruining the game.

"Wren, darling, what are you doing?!" Asteria gasped.

I turned to look at the place where the Gray Man had stood, but he had vanished. I felt the scowl form on my face.

"I was going with the Gray Man," I explained.

I watched, mildly fascinated, as all color drained from Asteria's face. She followed my gaze, staring at the emptiness as though it could reach out and snatch me from her. Then she gathered me up in her arms and ran.

We flew across the beach, over the road, across the garden, and into the cottage, as though Asteria's terror had given her wings. We didn't stop until we reached my room, where Asteria sat me down at the little desk, and put a piece of paper and a tin can full of crayons in front of me.

"Draw him," she demanded. I scowled at her again and she closed her eyes, taking a steadying breath. When she opened them again, her expression was cheerful, her tone gentle and placating. "Couldn't you please draw the Gray Man for me, darling? I'd so like to see what he looks like, and you draw such lovely pictures."

"You should have looked at him on the beach," I said, but her compliments had placated me, and I dug for a gray crayon before setting to work. Asteria watched in silence as I worked, until at last I threw down the crayon, and announced that I had finished. I flourished the paper and handed it to her, ready to be praised again.

"That's the Gray Man. He found me in the garden. We will go into the sea together," I said.

Asteria stared and stared.

"Don't you like it, Asteria?" I demanded when my toddler-sized well of patience ran dry.

She blinked. "Oh, my darling, it's wonderful. I love it. Come sit on the floor with Asteria, and we can draw some more lovely pictures together."

I colored away happily with a plate of cookies in the middle of the floor, scolding Asteria for drawing on the floor—because crayons were for paper, that's what Mommy always said, and demanding to know if she would hang my picture on the "fridgelator."

"Oh no, dearest," Asteria said, as she folded the paper up as small as she could. "I have much more special plans for your picture. And she wound the ribbon around it, muttering words I could not hear.

I surfaced from the memory, full of a fear so overwhelming, I thought I might pass out. I threw my legs over the edge of my bed, dropping my head between my legs, and forcing myself to take long, deep breaths, as Freya wound herself sinuously around my ankles.

All the pieces fell into place to make the most terrifying of pictures. It was real. It was all real. My dream wasn't a dream at all. It was a memory. The Gray Man was real, and he had once tried to take me into the sea with him. Asteria had rescued me, then tried to protect me. She'd been trying to protect me all these years. Every year, she brought me a trinket—I bet every one of them had some kind of protective charm on it. Then she brought me Freya—not just a pet, but a familiar, one who would help to protect me. And hadn't she done just that?

My mind flashed back to the afternoon Freya had appeared on the catwalk of the theater—the figure in the shadows... it had been the Gray Man. He had found me, the very day my grandmother had died, as though some protective spell had died with her, and Freya had chased him away. And then again, in the garden the night of the seance; that had been the Gray Man as well, come for me once again, a whisper away from me in the darkness, until Asteria's warning expanded the protection of the circle to the entire garden. And finally down on the beach, the night of the bonfire—hadn't I heard his voice calling to me out in the water as the phantom boy crumbled to sand in my hands?

He had come for me then. And he came for me now. And he would keep coming. But who or what was he, and what did he want?

It was agony waiting until morning. I refused to wake my mother up, no matter how scared I was. I sat up in my bed, Freya in my lap, my window closed tightly and my windowsill lined haphazardly with every single trinket Asteria had ever given me—my pathetic attempt at cobbling together some magical protection until the sun came up. The ribbon and drawing I'd tucked back inside the pouch around my neck where it hung, heavy with realizations, against my chest. I dozed off sometime around dawn and woke a couple of hours later sore and stiff from falling asleep sitting up, with nothing but the wall for a pillow. I looked down at Freya, who was watching me intently.

"What about you, did you get any sleep?" I asked her.

She yawned pointedly in response. I took that for a no.

I had to tell my mom, Covenant or no Covenant. I thought I could wait until that evening's renewal, but I knew now that I couldn't wait. Whatever protection Asteria had been able to provide for me all these years, it was gone now. I didn't know enough about magic to protect myself. I needed her help, even if it scared us both.

The door to my mom's bedroom was closed as I walked past. It was only eight o'clock, I reasoned. She would be up soon. I walked through the living room on my way to the kitchen, and spotted Persi out in the garden. Her black hair streamed down her back like dark water, and she gazed out over the fruit trees, a cigarette dangling from her fingers, barefoot and clad only in an ivory-colored slip.

"She's been out there since I woke up at six." I jumped and whipped around to see Rhi standing behind me, wrapped in a fuzzy purple bathrobe and plaid slippers. She held two cups of coffee in her hands. "I was going to take this out to her, but I kept losing my nerve. Would you like to drink it before it goes cold? She takes it the same way you do."

I reached for the coffee gratefully, and followed Rhi back out to the kitchen, where we sat sipping in silence.

"Have you seen my mom yet?" I asked. "She doesn't usually sleep this late."

Rhi shook her head. "No, but let her sleep. It's been a fairly traumatizing few days. She probably needs it."

I tapped my fingers on the tabletop, full of nervous energy despite how tired I was. I felt like a kid who'd skipped their nap and eaten a bag of pixie sticks instead. I didn't think I could wait another minute for my mom to wake up. I decided to see if I could at least get a general question answered.

"Rhi, what do you know about protective magic?"

Rhi raised her eyebrows in surprise. "Oh, a fair bit. Why do you ask?"

"I was wondering, if someone took a picture of... of someone, and wrapped it up with a ribbon... could that be part of a protective spell?"

"Hmm. That sounds like a binding. Yes, it's a protective spell. How do you—"

"A binding?" I jumped on the word at once. "What does that mean?"

"Well, like I said, it's a protective spell. There's a bit to it, but basically, you use an image of the person—it can be a photo, a drawing, a doll meant to represent them—and you wrap the ribbon or string around it to bind that person from doing harm to—"

"Wait, is that how the Covenant works? Wasn't it used to bind the Darkness?" I interrupted. "Everyone keeps using that word, 'bind.'"

"Oh, no, that is much more powerful magic. The kind of binding you're referring to is a much simpler spell," Rhi said.

"And if the witch who performed that binding... if she were to die... would the binding still work?" I asked.

"No, the spell would break." Rhi frowned, setting down her coffee cup. "Wren, where are these questions coming from? Where did you see—?"

I was saved from answering by the sound of the front door opening and closing, and a few moments later, Persi slunk into the kitchen. "Who does a woman need to murder to get a cup of that coffee?" she grumbled.

Rhi got up from the table. "I'll make you one. No homicide required," she said dryly.

"Any idea when your mom will be back?" Persi asked as she slumped into the chair beside me.

"Back?"

"Yeah. Her car's gone," Persi replied. "Where the hell did she go, anyway?"

A shiver of fear rocked through me, and I got up from the table. By the time I reached the front door, I was running. I pulled open the door, and stared out at the empty space in the driveway where her car should have been. My mouth went dry. I turned and sprinted up the stairs two at a time and skidded to a halt in front of my mom's bedroom door. I knocked once, twice, and then just shoved it open. Her bedclothes were rumpled, but the bed was empty. A glance under the bed revealed her suitcase was gone, too.

I ran down the stairs to find Rhi waiting for me at the bottom. I answered her unspoken question.

"Persi's right. She's gone."

19

"Wren, don't panic."

I knew Rhi meant well, but I had never ignored advice so thoroughly. I was pacing the living room, phone in my hand. I'd sent three texts and made three calls, all of which had gone straight to voicemail, and ended in me leaving three successive and increasingly hysterical messages.

"Don't panic? Rhi, she's missing!" I cried.

"Well, hold on, now, we don't know that yet," Rhi said, though her own voice trembled. "She... she might have gone for a drive to clear her head or... or gone downtown for a coffee."

"And she needed her suitcase for that?" I asked.

Rhi bit her lip. "I still think it's too soon to panic."

"Why should anyone panic? Isn't it obvious what's happened?" Persi snapped. She'd thrown a satin dressing gown on over her slip and traded the coffee for another cigarette. "She freaked out, changed her mind, and bailed!"

"No, she didn't!" Rhi cried.

"Oh, what, like she hasn't done it before? We practically had to drag her back here. Is it any wonder she left? I can't believe you're this naive, Rhi."

"Last time was different. She left to protect Wren," Rhi said.

"So?" Persi spat.

"So, I'm still here!" I said, feeling the anger boiling up inside of me. "She wouldn't leave me here, she wouldn't just leave without telling me!"

"Why not? She did it to her own mother. Once a coward, always a c—"

I couldn't take another word. Before I could even think, I had crossed the room and stood right in front of Persi, our faces inches apart. "Never call my mother a coward again, do you hear me? *Never.*"

For a moment I thought she might slap me, but then Persi dropped her eyes to the floor, abashed. I backed away from her, trying to calm myself down.

"When did you notice her car was gone?" I asked, and there was no venom in Persi's voice when she answered.

"A couple of hours ago, when B—when I got up," Persi said evasively.

"When what?" Rhi asked sharply.

Persi rolled her eyes, aggravated with herself for the slip-up. "When Bernadette left, okay? She... you know how she gets. I woke up, and she was getting dressed, saying she *had* to go paint; and so I got up to walk her down to the door, and that's when I noticed Kerri's car was gone."

"What time was that?" Rhi asked.

Persi shrugged. "Around 6? 6:30?"

"And you didn't think that was strange? Why didn't you tell anyone?" I cried.

"Your mother's a grown woman, Wren! She can go where she wants. I'm not her babysitter!"

"We have to go look for her. Something is very, very wrong," I said, pacing now.

Rhi held up her hands in a placating gesture. "Wren, why don't we just wait a little while and see if she—"

"We can't wait! Don't you get it! This is about the Covenant! Someone tried to stop me from renewing it, and now someone's trying to stop her!"

Rhi's eyes went wide. "What do you mean someone tried to stop you from—"

"Do you even have police in this town? Who do you call when there's an emergency?" I demanded. "Who can help us?"

"I... we... we should alert the Conclave," Rhi said, standing up. "I'll call Xiomara."

Persi looked at the two of us, and a tiny bit of the panic we were feeling finally sparked in her eyes. "I'll call Bernadette and tell her to send Ostara over here," she said, pulling out her phone. "And I'll ask her if she saw or heard anything last night."

"Thank you," I said, and though I was still so tightly wound with anxiety that I felt like a rubber band about to snap, I was grateful that they were finally taking this seriously. Because whatever doubts my aunts may have had, I had none.

Wherever my mother had gone, she hadn't gone there willingly.

An hour later, the entire Conclave was sitting in the living room of Lightkeep Cottage, squawking over each other like a flock of overexcited birds.

"...have to consider the possibility that she left of her own accord, or—"

"But she already agreed to renew the Covenant!"

"She changed her mind, then! What's so—"

"And left the child behind, knowing the dangers? Unthinkable!"

"It was unthinkable to leave in the first place! Imagine a Vesper leaving Sedgwick Cove!"

I'd been biting my tongue since they descended on us, but I was running out of patience. Perhaps Rhi could see it on my face because she raised her voice over the squabbling.

"I don't think this speculation is getting us anywhere!" she shouted, and the others fell silent. "Whether she left of her own accord or not isn't really the issue. We need to find her or we can't renew the Covenant."

"What do you propose then, Rhiannon?" Ostara asked.

"We can start by trying to trace her car. She might have GPS tracking or something like that," Rhi said, before turning to me. "Wren do you—?"

I shook my head. "I don't know. Maybe." I'd tried on her phone, but as it was turned off, I couldn't get a signal.

"And we can gather together some volunteers to spread around town. Someone must have seen something," Rhi said.

There was much disconcerted murmuring over this suggestion, and more useless, cyclical discussion. I wanted to scream. We were wasting time. I turned from the group to try to compose myself and happened to glance out the window into the garden, where a movement caught my eye.

It was Eva, standing among the flowerbeds, waving her arms frantically to get my attention. I gave a small wave back, just so she knew that I'd seen her, and turned back to Rhi.

"I'm going out to the garden for a minute. I need some air," I murmured to her.

She smiled wanly. "I don't blame you."

I slipped out and ran for the far side of an enormous Rose of Sharon bush. There I found not just Eva, but also Zale and Nova waiting for me.

"What are you all doing here? How did you—"

"My *abuela*, of course," Eva said. "And they both live with Conclave members, too."

I frowned at Zale. "Wait, you too?"

He nodded. "Davina's my granny. And since she'd rather fling herself off the cliff than admit she needs hearing aids, she hasn't successfully kept a secret since the mid-90s."

"I... I'm really glad you're all... thank you for..." I couldn't finish the sentence. I burst into tears instead.

"Aw, Wren, it's okay," Eva said, throwing her arm around me and letting me cry into her shoulder. Zale joined in the hug on the other side, and even Nova gave me an awkward pat on the back.

"It's not okay. Everything's a mess. They can't stop arguing about what to do, and no one seems to realize this is an emergency. My mom would never take off like this. Well, okay, she did once, but that was to protect me. She wouldn't leave me here, not with the Covenant hanging in the balance."

"We know," Zale said.

"We all heard her at that Conclave meeting yesterday," Eva said, nodding fervently. "She was serious when she promised to renew the Covenant."

"So you believe me, then?" I gulped, tears still streaming.

"Of course, we do," Eva said.

"And we also know the Conclave takes a year or so to come to a decision about literally anything, so we're here to help, because goddess knows they're useless," Nova said, gesturing back toward the house.

"Good because... because it's not just my mom. I think... I think I'm in danger."

"Well, sure, without the Covenant, we're all in danger," Zale said.

"No, I mean... ugh, this is complicated," I moaned, covering my face with my hands.

"It's okay," Eva said. "Just take a deep breath and start at the beginning."

And I did. We sat down right there in the shade of the Rose of Sharon and its lush white blossoms, and I started talking. The more I talked, the easier it became. They listened intently and, aside from the occasional exclamation or muttered curse word, without interruption, as I told them about every interaction I'd ever had with the Gray Man.

"And of course, I don't actually know what to call him, or who or what he is, and so I've always just called him the same thing I called him when I was three years old: the Gray Man," I said. "But he's connected to all of this, and I don't exactly understand how, but I think if we can find out, it might help find my mom," I finished, a sob hitching in my throat.

Three blank faces stared back at me, evidently stunned into silence.

"Uh, hello?" I said, waving my hands in front of their faces. "Anyone want to chime in here?"

Eva recovered first. "Sorry, uh... it's just... I don't know what I was expecting, but it sure as hell wasn't *that*."

"Seriously," Nova murmured.

"So... have any of you ever heard of anything like the Gray Man before? Is this some sort of witch thing, like familiars and cauldrons and stuff?" I asked impatiently.

"Not a normal witch thing, no," Zale said, shaking his head.

"It sounds like it could be more dark magic," Eva said, "like that spell we found in Nova's library."

Nova fired up at once. "We don't know if that was actually the—"

"Okay, okay, damn," Eva exclaimed. "The spell from the beach, then. But whatever the Gray Man is, it's not good."

Zale looked thoughtful. "What if we checked the Archives?"

I perked up at once. "The Archives? What's that?"

"They're in the basement of the Historical Society. It's where they keep the historical records and documentation of all the dark stuff that goes on in this town."

"Dark stuff? Like... you mean like the Darkness?" I asked, my fear peaking again.

"No. Well, I mean yes, that too," Zale said quickly, "but the Darkness itself isn't the only evil thing to take root here. The deep magic has drawn lots of evil things here, and it takes lots of forms. We should see if we can find anything out about this Gray Man."

"Why don't we just ask the Conclave?" I suggested. "Wouldn't they know?"

Nova snorted. "Please. You've seen what they're like. They'd have to hold three meetings and seven votes before they agreed to tell us anything, even if they did know what you were talking about."

"The Archives are restricted, though," Eva pointed out. "How are we going to get access to them?"

"Oh, that won't be a problem," Nova said, tossing her hair. "I'll just tell Phoebe I want to show you the Claire collection. She can't say no, it belongs to my family. And once we're down in the basement, we'll just... wander a little."

"I don't know..." Eva said, hesitating.

"What's the matter? Unless, of course, Eva Marin is now a rule follower?" Nova said with a smirk.

Eva recognized her own words thrown back at her and put up her hands in surrender. "Okay, okay! You win! We'll go to the Archives."

～

It wasn't easy to get away. The Conclave was still there an hour later, asking me a million questions, like I was being interrogated for a crime. All I wanted to do was scream, "Someone took her! She's not safe! What are you all sitting around asking me stupid pointless questions for?!" My face must have been giving away these silent thoughts, because Rhi swooped in and came to my rescue, taking me by the arm and steering me off the couch and into the kitchen with a cheerful call over her shoulder of, "I'm sure Wren has told you everything she can, and this is all very stressful, so she's just going to take a little break for a cup of tea, okay?"

She plopped me right into a chair, and then sat down across from me.

"You looked like you needed to get out of there," she said, with a sympathetic squeeze of my hand.

"They aren't taking this seriously!" I whispered furiously. "They're acting like she's some teenager who threw a tantrum and ran away to blow off steam!"

"Probably that's how they still see her," Rhi said, smiling sadly. "Your mom caused quite a local scandal when she left the first time, and none of them have forgotten it."

"But this isn't the same thing!"

"Of course, it's not, but..." she trailed off, letting her helpless shrug complete the thought for her.

"I can't just sit here anymore. I have to go... go look for her or something," I said, running a frantic hand through my hair, which I was sure had frizzed up to gargantuan proportions in my stress.

"Then why don't you go do that," Rhi said. "Persi and I are going to call around and see if anyone's seen her car or heard from her. She's got enough local connections here that she could have—"

"Rhi, she did not leave by choice, I know it!"

"I know, sweetie," she said, in a placating voice that told me she was only humoring me. It was obvious she didn't believe my mom was in danger, not yet. And by the time everyone else finally came to that conclusion, it would be too late.

"I'm going downtown to start asking around," I said. "If I sit here another moment, I'm going to flip out."

"Go ahead, but please stay in touch, okay?" Rhi said. "And we'll call you as soon as we hear something, okay?"

I nodded, but I knew I wouldn't hear from them. Mom wasn't just going to show up in the driveway with a box of pastries, looking bemused at all the bother, and apologizing that her phone had died.

I hurried past the room where the Conclave were still gathered and headed for the front door. I thought I'd managed to escape their notice when a voice called out from behind me.

"Wren!"

I turned. Xiomara was standing there, hands on her hips, eyes narrowed.

"And where are you off to?" she demanded.

"I... have to do what I can to find her, Xiomara," I said. "If I stay here, listening to more indecisive squabbling, I'm going to go insane."

The words were out of my mouth before I could stop them, but Xiomara only laughed.

"We're a useless bunch of old biddies, aren't we?" she said, shaking her head. "Here. You take this with you."

And she extracted a small bottle from her apron pocket and dropped it into my hand.

"What is this?" I asked.

"It's my elixir of rue," Xiomara said. "There are covens who would sacrifice one of their own to get their hands on that recipe. That's powerful magic in that bottle, *mijita*. Before you do anything too dangerous, you drink that right down."

"W-what will it do?" I asked, as I pocketed it.

Xiomara moved a step closer and cupped my face in her wrinkled palm. "It will protect you from those who would do you harm."

"You believe she's in danger, don't you?" I breathed.

"I do. And I believe you are, too. So tread carefully."

20

I texted the others that I was on my way, and we met in front of the Historical Society. The day was already half gone, and I felt like a sentient live wire, buzzing with dangerous energy, as we ascended the steps.

"Just let me do the talking," Nova said, just before opening the door. She smoothed her hair, plastered on a smile that belonged in a toothpaste ad, and pushed the door open.

Phoebe was there, bent over a very old book, and wearing a pair of rubber gloves as she did a repair to the binding. She looked up over the tops of her glasses and smiled kindly at us.

"Well, hello, there! Is there a field trip I wasn't aware of?" she asked with a chuckle.

"Hi, Phoebe," Nova said, in a voice that betrayed no hint of her usual sarcasm or general malaise of boredom. "No, we just thought we'd bring Wren by to catch up on some local history."

"Oh, well, that's very nice of you. Wren, I'm glad to see you've found some friends to take you under their wing and show you the sights!" Phoebe said, with grandmotherly warmth.

I forced a broad smile that I hoped looked happy, instead of manic. "Me too," I said.

"She *really* wants to see the Claire collection, so I think we're going to start downstairs," Nova said. "So, we'll just need the key."

Phoebe's smile slipped just a little. "Oh. I... I haven't given out the key since... that is..."

Nova nodded, her expression almost beatific. "Since the artifact of the Lost Second Daughter was stolen? That was shocking, wasn't it? I'd be very careful as well if I were you. But of course, you can trust us. I would never let anything happen to my own family heirlooms, obviously."

The girl was a genius. If it had been a cartoon, a halo would have appeared spontaneously over her head. I watched as Phoebe's anxious face relaxed.

"Of... of course. Here you are, dear. Please make sure you lock it behind you when you come back up, all right?" She plucked the keys from where they hung on the wall and dropped them into Nova's hand.

"Thanks so much, Phoebe. You're a peach," Nova said, blowing her a kiss before turning and strolling confidently to the basement door, the rest of us scuttling along behind her, trying not to look too guilty.

"That was diabolical," Zale said, once we had safely reached the other side of the door.

"Thanks," Nova said, with a flip of her hair. "Although, I don't really think she would have said no, regardless. People don't really say no to the Claires, as a rule."

She didn't sound boastful; more like she was stating a fact of life. And as neither of the others contradicted her, I took her at her word.

The basement wasn't what I expected. I'd been picturing stacks of boxes, but in reality, it was simply an extension of the museum-like atmosphere above. One wall was lined with paintings, another with glass-topped display cases full of a random assortment of artifacts—although I noticed one major difference. The displays upstairs had a much more tourist-friendly theme. Down here was where they kept the *really* witchy stuff. I drifted toward the back corner, where a sign affixed to the wall said, "This Collection on Loan from the Claire Family, settled in Sedgwick Cove circa 1720." Beside it, several tall display cases contained a wide assortment of items: a silver-backed hair-brush, several journals, a collection of silverware, a set of decorative statues, and the like. Most of it would look at home in a normal local history museum, except for a small iron cauldron, a set of candlesticks engraved with sigils, and a collection of spell books. On any other day, I would have found it all fascinating. Today, however, I barely glanced at it.

"The Archive is back here!" Nova called, and I followed her to the other side of the room, where she was unlocking a second door. She hesitated only a moment before pushing open the door and flicking the light switch.

Fluorescent lights flickered and buzzed to life, casting the kind of light that sucked all the color from the room. I think I'd been expecting something like the Manor's library—a massive dusty collection of books—but the Archive was much smaller. A single wall of shelves contained two rows of books, identical except for the volume numbers stamped on their leather spines, in peeling gold leaf. They looked like a set of encyclopedias, except that the volumes clearly got older the further down the shelves you looked.

"Here it is! A detailed history of all the dark magic recorded in Sedgwick Cove," Nova said, gesturing grandly. "When we enter into more advanced magical study, we can ask for access to these, but only by special petition to the Conclave. They have to approve all requests. And every five years, they elect a new town secretary whose job it is to update and maintain the collection."

"Why is it so secret?" I asked. "I thought knowledge was power."

"Well, around here, knowledge can be hell-raising, coven-crushing power," Zale said. I stared at him and he added, "They think we'll get in less trouble if we don't have, like, a centuries-old instruction manual on how to do it."

I just nodded. "So where do we start?" I asked.

"How about at the beginning?" Eva suggested, pointing to the very bottom of the shelves, where the oldest volumes sat covered in dust.

I thought it would help me to have a task, something to do, to distract me; but the longer we spent in that windowless basement, the more it felt like being buried alive. I was distracted and jumpy. I checked my phone every few minutes, desperate for news. I flipped through musty page after musty page with hardly a clue as to what I was looking for. My heart leapt at words like "shadow" or "man", only to read more closely and realize it was another dead end. We'd been at it an hour or so when my phone started to buzz. I didn't recognize the number, but I picked it up anyway, nearly dropping the phone in my haste.

"Hello? Mom?"

I heard a disjointed syllable or two and looked down to see I only had one measly bar of cell service. I jumped up from the chair I'd been sitting in, and ran to the door, flinging it open and running out into the main basement room again.

"Mom? Is that you? Can you hear me? Where are you?" The questions tumbled over each other in my desperation, but the voice that answered wasn't the one I needed to hear.

"Wren, it's Rhi. Where are you, honey?"

"I'm... I'm with my friends, they're helping me," I said, which technically wasn't a lie. "What's going on, did you find her? Did she call, or—"

"Not... not exactly."

My heart felt like a throbbing fist in my throat. "What does that mean? Tell me!"

"We... found her car."

The words hung for a moment, as I tried to take them in.

"And she wasn't in it?"

"No. It was pulled over on the shoulder of the road about a mile outside of town. The keys were gone, but her phone was in the cupholder, and her suitcase was still in the trunk."

I felt the air leave my lungs. I'd forgotten how to breathe, to think. My brain was just a blank buzzing of panic.

"Wren?"

I forced a breath. "I'm here."

"Honey, let's not jump to any conclusions, okay? We still don't—"

"I have to go," I squeaked, and ended the call.

I could feel three sets of eyes on me and turned to see all three of my friends standing in the doorway of the Archive, staring at me with expressions ranging from curiosity to pity. I sucked in another ragged breath, fending off the howl of a sob that was trying to force its way up from my chest.

"They... found her car. She wasn't in it."

I swayed, my vision dimming, and all three of them shot forward to grab me before I hit the floor.

"Breathe, Wren, honey, you've got to breathe," Eva said in a soothing voice, rubbing my back in a slow, circular motion.

Zale rubbed my back and pulled a water bottle from his bag. "Here, drink some of this."

"Something's happened to her. Someone's done something to her, I know it!" I gasped. I was having a full-on panic attack and I knew it, but there was nothing I could do to stop it. Zale moved the water bottle to the back of my neck.

"She needs air," Zale said.

"I'll see if I can open the window," Nova said, dragging a stool over to the only window, set high in the wall.

"It'll be okay, Wren," Eva said. "We'll... we'll find something!"

"Of course we will!" Zale chimed in. "We're still looking, there's got to be —Nova?"

The confusion in his voice cut through my panic. I glanced up to see that Nova was standing on the stool, one hand frozen in midair near the window latch, and her eyes fixed on a painting on the wall.

"Nova? What is it, what's wrong?" Eva called, her voice strained even as she continued to rub my back.

"I... I think I found something."

I jumped up so fast that Eva yelped and almost fell over. Still trying to get control of my breathing, I flew across the room to where Nova still stood on the stool.

"What? What is it?"

Wordlessly, she pointed to the painting on the wall.

It was a rendering of the beach looking north to where the lighthouse stood. The light shone out of the top of the lighthouse into the gloom of an oncoming storm, the ocean roiling in the shadows below it. And there, on the beach, staring out over the water—

The Gray Man.

There was no mistaking him. His form had the same abnormally stretched proportions, his features blurred out. One of his arms was raised, reaching out, as though waiting for someone to come and take his hand...

"Oh my God," I whispered. "It's him. It's the Gray Man."

Eva and Zale came running over, jostling in next to me so they could get a glimpse of him, too.

"Holy shit," Zale whispered.

"What is this?" Eva gasped. "Who—?"

But I knew who. I knew the answer even before my eyes found the signature down in the corner. Knew it, because I'd already seen an almost identical painting, in which a little girl in a white dress had reached into the emptiness beside her to grasp the very hand the Gray Man now offered. If they'd been superimposed over each other, they would have been hand in hand.

"Bernadette," I murmured.

Her name in my mouth was like a shot of adrenaline. I staggered back from the painting, all manic energy again.

"We need to find Bernadette, right now!" I cried.

Nova jumped down from the stool, her face aghast. "You don't think Bernadette did something to your mom, do you?! She's... she's harmless!"

"She obviously knows something, Nova, look at that!" I yelled, gesturing to the painting. "We have to find her!"

"Do you know where she is?" Eva asked eagerly.

Nova hesitated, biting her lip.

"Nova, come on! You must know—" I began, but Zale's tremulous voice cut me off.

"Um, I don't want to freak anyone out more than they already are, but did y'all see the title of this painting?"

I followed his finger to read the typed caption that had been affixed to the wall beside the painting, which included its title.

"The Darkness Waits on the Beach."

I turned to Nova, whose eyes had gone saucer-round.

"Nova. Please."

Nova swallowed convulsively, then said, "She's probably at home. In her studio."

Rhi texted me several times as we practically sprinted across town to the Manor, but I ignored them. I didn't want to read her empty platitudes about how it would all be okay. I'd just found out that the thing stalking me in my nightmares since I was a child was the Darkness itself. Nothing she could say would make me feel any better.

"They say the Darkness could take many forms," Zale gasped as we ran.

"How can the Darkness take any forms if it's bound by the Covenant?" Eva huffed.

No one answered because no one knew.

It had grown much darker since we'd entered the Historical Society—the late afternoon sun had been swallowed by a mass of iron-gray clouds, swollen with a promise of torrential rain. Even as the Manor came into sight, a few fat raindrops began to fall here and there.

We tore up the driveway, Nova in the lead, and burst through the front door and up the stairs before we knew if anyone else was even home, though Ostara's car wasn't in the driveway, which meant she was still probably at Lightkeep Cottage with the rest of the Conclave. When she reached the second-floor landing, Nova took off down a long hallway, and turned the corner down a second, shorter hall that ended in a door. She pulled it open, revealing a stone spiral staircase that led upward into the tower. I had just enough room in my brain to acknowledge that I would have found it all charming, if I wasn't in such a panic. We climbed the stairs, which ended in a trap door. Nova shoved it open, and the top half of her body disappeared into the opening while we waited, breathless.

"Bernadette? Bernadette are you up—holy *shit*," Nova gasped.

"What? What is it?" Eva cried.

I didn't wait for an answer, shoving my way up the last few stairs so that Nova had to climb the rest of the way through to make room for me. As my head and shoulders emerged into the tower studio and I gazed around me, my heart seemed to stop in my chest.

The Gray Man stared, eyeless, down at me over and over again from hundreds of charcoal renderings, each one affixed to the stone walls, overlapping each other, fluttering in the rain-scented breeze that drifted in the window.

"What the actual *fuck*?" Zale murmured, as he and Eva emerged behind me.

"I didn't know," Nova was muttering hysterically. "I didn't... she never lets anyone up here."

My eyes scanned the room for any sign of Bernadette, but it was clear she wasn't there. More half-finished sketches of the Gray Man were spread haphazardly over the work table. I picked one up, then another, revealing dozens more beneath. I slammed my hands down on the tabletop in frustration and heard something clatter to the floor near my feet.

I gazed down at the source of the sound: a set of keys. I dropped to my knees, snatching them up into my shaking fingers. My mom's keys.

"Mom," I whispered. Then I called out to the others. "These are my mom's keys!"

Eva dropped to her knees beside me. "Oh my God," she gasped. "Are you s—"

"Of course I'm sure! I know what her keys look like! I gave her this keychain!" I staggered to my feet, holding the keys like a talisman. "Nova, we have to find Bernadette. She knows where my mom is!"

But Nova didn't answer. She was still standing on the other side of the room, looking down at something in her hand.

"Nova? What is it?" Zale asked.

Nova looked up at us, her expression one of devastated bewilderment.

"I... I have to tell you something," she whispered.

"What is it?" I asked, taking a numb step toward her. She had dropped her gaze again, back to the object she was lifting from a nearby table. It was a wooden box with a glass cover—a shadowbox. The glass had been shattered. Little shards of it still glittered around the edges of the opening.

"Bernadette had a little brother. His name was Jacob... Jake, they used to call him. He was hit by a car just before his fifth birthday. The whole family was devastated. This memorial shadowbox is usually downstairs on one of the mantels. It's got Jacob's baby blanket, and a teddy bear, and... and a pair of shoes."

I shook my head, bewildered. "O-okay."

"I found this on the beach, the night of the bonfire," Nova said, her voice blank, almost mechanical. "I... thought I recognized it, but I wasn't sure."

Nova reached into the box and pulled out a tiny shoe with shaking fingers and placed it on the table in front of us. "The spell we found in the library, the one that creates a living effigy? It needed a personal object to bring it to life. You said you saw a little boy, right?"

The figure of the boy flashed into my head. White-blonde hair, like every Claire I'd met since I'd arrived here...

"Yeah..." I said, still not comprehending.

Nova's voice was a tremulous whisper. "This... this washed up on the sand right after Zale dragged you out of the water."

And she reached into her purse and pulled something out, placing it on the table.

The matching shoe, water-stained but unmistakable.

"You knew this whole time?" I asked blankly.

"I didn't want to believe it!" Nova cried, and there was a plea in her voice. "I thought there must be some kind of mistake! Bernadette has always been so gentle, so... I thought there must be a different explanation!"

"Nova, we've been trying to figure this out for days!" Eva cried, firing up. "That spell almost got Wren killed!"

"I know, but... I just... I didn't want it to be another Claire!" Nova cried, tears streaming down her cheeks now. "It's like a family curse, don't you get it? The Lost Second Daughter, she was a Claire! And you see the way Ostara keeps those old books under lock and key, because even she doesn't trust our family to stay out of trouble! She thinks we're all going to turn evil and disgrace her if we get even a glimpse of the dark arts!"

"You've been lying to us this whole time!" Zale said, shaking his head with disgust.

"I know, I'm sorry! But I just didn't believe that Bernadette would hurt someone on purpose! I swear I never meant to—"

"I don't care what you meant!" I shouted. "My mom is missing, and Bernadette took her!"

"We don't know that for—"

"Of course we do!" Eva snapped, snatching the keys from my hand, and holding them up in front of Nova, jingling them loudly, so that Nova flinched away from them. "How else would these keys have gotten here?"

"There still might be an innocent explana—"

"I don't care what the explanation is!" I shouted. "Bernadette has my mom, and now they could be anywhere, and if we don't find them—"

"Uh, Wren?"

"What?!" I shrieked, rounding on Zale, who was standing on the other side of the room staring at a canvas on an easel.

"I think I know where your mom is."

"What do you—"

"Come look at this."

Nova, Eva, and I abandoned our shouting match and dashed to the far side of the room to where Zale stood, transfixed.

The painting on the easel was half completed, the brush strokes appearing more manic and undisciplined than any of Bernadette's other works. It portrayed the lighthouse again, but the perspective was warped, almost twisted, like I was seeing it through an old window pane. There were three figures standing at the base of the lighthouse:

The Gray Man, his arms raised over his head in a triumphant gesture.

Bernadette, her long blonde hair streaming behind her, surrounded by a strange, blurred shadow.

And between them, her expression calm, almost peaceful: my mother.

21

"You don't even have a license!"

"I have a permit, okay? Just get in the goddamn car already!"

We piled into the little silver sports car, what Nova's mom apparently called her "weekend car," as Nova slid into the driver's seat.

Zale fumbled to get his seatbelt buckled. "I don't think this is a good—"

"It's going to take forever to get to the lighthouse on foot, even if we run the whole way!"

"What if you get pulled over?" Eva asked.

"Then they can arrest me!" Nova shouted. "Now buckle up!"

I didn't argue. I knew Nova was trying to make up for lying to us, and I was going to let her, if it got me to my mom any faster. Nova pulled onto the road and started driving, and I pressed my lips together to prevent myself from screaming at her to floor it.

We made it through downtown without getting arrested, and the road began to wind toward Lightkeep.

"We should stop at the cottage and get your aunts, and the Conclave, too, if they're still there," Eva said, as the cottage came into sight.

"Yeah, stop at the cottage," I said, letting out a steadying breath. My aunts would know what to do.

Ostara's car was gone, as was Lydian's rickshaw. I jumped out of the car before Nova even had it in park, bolted up the porch steps, and burst in the front door.

"Persi! Rhi! I know where mom is!" I shouted.

Only silence answered me.

I flew through the house, heart pounding, calling both of my aunts' names, but no one was there. I dug my phone out of my pocket and checked my texts, the ones I'd only just remembered that I'd ignored. They were both from Rhi.

We're going to identify the car and see if we can find any clues as to where your mom went.

Be back soon. Will keep you posted.

"Shit!" I muttered, and rapid-texted a reply.

Bernadette took Mom to the lighthouse. Meet me there ASAP!

I sprinted back to the car and threw myself through the still-open door.

"Nobody's here, let's go!" I gasped.

"Shouldn't... shouldn't we wait for—" Eva began.

"No! We've lost enough time as it is! I texted them to meet us there. Just drive, Nova, please!"

Nova didn't argue but threw the car into drive and peeled out into the road again. The gravel crunched under the tires, and the rain began to pick up, battering against the windshield as the lighthouse came into view.

I'd half-expected to see the painting come to life, with Mom, Bernadette, and the Gray Man standing on the rocks at the base of the lighthouse; but of course, they weren't there. The only signs of life, as Nova slammed on the brakes and threw the car into park, was a flickering golden light from the windows—someone had lit the lamps.

I leapt out of the car, and was halfway to the lighthouse's door, when I stopped suddenly, and turned.

"You... you don't have to come in with me. I don't know what's—"

"Obviously we're coming!" Zale said.

"Yeah, we didn't come all this way to abandon you!" Eva said, sounding almost offended.

I looked at Nova, who lifted her chin, marched right past me, and shoved open the lighthouse door in reply.

We all gaped around at the intricacies of the circle, of the sigils and markings that had been scrawled all over the inner walls of the lighthouse.

"This is some seriously dark shit," Eva muttered, and I could hear a tremor in her voice. She caught my eye, and I saw the fear reflected there. "We shouldn't be here."

Even as she said it, I could feel it: a low hum of energy that sent goosebumps skittering up my arms and made my palms clammy with sweat. She was right; we shouldn't be here, and yet, here we were. Everything we'd found, everything we'd done, had led us here—for better or for worse, and there was no turning back now, at least not for me.

"I can't leave, Eva," I said, hardly knowing how true the words were until they fell from my lips, so heavy with intent that I could not take them back again. "You guys go if you want to. I dragged you into this, there's no need for you to—"

"Hey, wait just a damned minute!" Zale snapped, looking frankly offended. "None of us got dragged here, we chose to be here!"

"That's right!" Eva said, firing up as well. "You think we're just gonna leave you here to face...whatever the hell all this is? You must be out of your mind."

"Look, no offense, seriously," Nova added quietly, "but you have no idea what you're doing. You've never properly worked magic before. You need us. And besides," she added, taking a deep breath, "this is partly my fault. I knew Bernadette was up to something, and I let my own complex about the Second Daughters cloud my judgment. I could have stopped this, and I didn't. If anyone should stay, it's me."

"Why are we even still talking about this?" Eva hissed, exasperated. "We're sticking together, okay? None of us is going to leave now, not after what we've seen."

"My thoughts exactly," said a quiet, cracked voice behind us.

We whirled around. While we'd been arguing, someone had been slowly and silently pulling the door shut behind us. As we turned, it slammed into place, making all of us jump and cluster together like frightened animals. The speaker was still somewhat obscured in the shadows of the doorway, but then she stepped forward, white-blonde hair wild and wind-tangled about her face—

"Oh, Bernadette," Nova murmured beside me, and I stole a glance at her heartbroken expression before turning back again to Bernadette, who was gazing at us with the strangest look on her face—one in which grief and triumph were at open war on her features.

"You found me. I knew you would. I knew..." she made a strange sound, half-gasp, half-giggle. Then her wide eyes filled slowly with tears. "You shouldn't have come here. It's very dangerous, you know."

"You left us no choice," I said, fighting to keep the tremor out of my voice.

"There's always a choice," she said, the words snapping out fiercely, almost defiantly, and I flinched back from her. Then she started, as if the words had surprised her, and more tears welled up into her eyes. "It's true, you know. I did have a choice. Part of me had to decide."

"Decide what?" I asked. "What are you talking about?"

She skittered forward on bare, bleeding toes, until she stood mere inches from us. I could have raised a hand and brushed the spray-dampened tendrils of hair from her face.

"I had to decide to serve him. To serve the Darkness."

A wave slammed into the rocky skirt of the island, and the whole tower seemed to groan in protest. Nova shrieked. Zale let loose a string of expletives. Grit and dust were shaken loose from the wooden boards high above our heads, raining down like a storm.

"He is waiting," she said, shuddering with something that might have been a thrill, and might have been fear. She gestured, and we turned to see the staircase leading into the upper chambers of the lighthouse. Zale let out a slightly hysterical bark of laughter.

"Lady, if you think we're just gonna trot on upstairs when you just told us the Darkness is waiting, you must be even crazier than we thought."

"Oh, you could try to run, of course, but I really wouldn't recommend it," Bernadette said seriously, and stepped back from us a step or two, sweeping the folds of her cloak back so we could see what she held in her hand. It was a knife, a small one, no bigger than a letter opener, but with a glint that promised it was wickedly sharp. She'd been holding it the whole time, and not one of us had noticed.

"There are four of us," Eva said, with as much bravado as she could muster. "You think we couldn't wrestle that out of your hands, four against one?"

"Perhaps, but certainly not without getting cut a few times." She held the blade up so that we could see it better, and even she couldn't take her eyes off of it. Her pupils were enormous, like great black tunnels in her face. "This blade has been dipped in Siren's Tongue, the deadliest poison in the pages of the Claire Coven grimoire. If I draw even a drop of blood, no magic or medicine on this earth can save you. Would you care to risk it?"

Eva seemed to shrink beside me. Nova threw me a sharp glance, which I understood to mean that she had heard of Siren's Tongue and we were, under no circumstances, to risk it. Zale didn't miss the look, and so replied, meekly, "Right, so up the stairs it is, then. After you, ladies."

I didn't miss that he was purposely putting himself at the back of the group, closest to the danger, and I could have cried and hugged him for it, if this had been any sort of moment for such a thing. Instead, I linked my arm through his as we walked, snaking my fingers down to find his and squeezing them. He squeezed mine back.

We ascended the winding stone steps, moving very slowly and carefully in the crackling, uneven light from the torches, which had been lit and hung in the old, rusted brackets that still protruded from the walls, even as the gas-powered lanterns hung dark, like shuddered windows, beside them. I had one wild, fanciful thought fly through my head—that I was a child again, dreaming of fairytale princesses in towers, and how this was likely as close as I was ever going to get to being the damsel in distress of my childhood fantasies. It had always seemed like it would be fun and exciting. Now I knew, too late, that it was only cold terror and the burn of uncertainty, fire and ice chasing each other through your veins as your mind buzzed with panic. I had a fleeting urge to reach back in time, snatch up every one of those princess stories, and rip them to shreds. We had to rescue ourselves or not at all, and it would be a fight all the way. Those stories were nothing but lies to keep us helpless.

Princesses abdicated their power. Witches claimed it.

Because, of course, they *had* power. How could I claim what I wasn't even sure I had inside me?

That was all the time I had to ponder my own inconveniently timed existential crisis, because at that moment, when my self-doubt was causing me to panic, we arrived at the top of the stairs. Eva was leading the group, another gesture of bravery in honor of our barely formed friendship, and she hesitated uncertainly in front of the closed door we found facing us.

"Go on then," said Bernadette from behind us. "Go on and open it. It's perfectly safe, I assure you."

Eva snorted her disbelief, but pushed the door open anyway, because what choice did we have? The poisoned dagger was still pointed at our backs. The door swung wide, and as we stepped through it and faced what lay beyond it, I had to slap my hand over my own mouth to keep from screaming.

The room was narrower than the one below, and also perfectly round. The only permanent structure in the room was a great ladder that projected through the trapdoor in the ceiling above, through which I could see the great light apparatus that signaled danger to ships when the fog rolled in. But I couldn't take even a moment to wonder about the workings of the lighthouse's light tower above—I couldn't take my eyes off the ladder.

My mother was tied to it.

Her head lolled to one side, her form kept in a crudely upright position solely by the rope wound round and round her body, like a violent cocoon. A wound bled freely on her arm, and for a moment, I couldn't breathe, thinking of Bernadette's knife. But then my mother let out a soft groan, and though the sound was one of distress, I rejoiced at it. She was alive. It wasn't over yet.

That tiny, kindled spark of hope nearly extinguished again as I let my eyes take in the rest of the room. My mother had been placed in some kind of circle—there were sigils and symbols around it that I didn't recognize from my extremely rudimentary introduction to magic. The expressions on my friends' faces confirmed that whatever we were looking at, it was a long, long way from the magic they practiced. Candles in closed lanterns had been placed at the four points of the compass around the circle, and it all hummed with a dark, powerful energy that fairly screamed at us to turn and run from it—a warning I completely ignored as I reached for my mother.

"What the hell have you done to her?" I cried, and it was only Eva's quick reflexes that kept me from stepping right into the circle. As it was, a strange sizzling sound began as I reached forward; and as Eva yanked me backward, I pulled my hand to my chest, the fingertips throbbing and red from momentary contact with whatever intention that circle had been formed with.

Bernadette locked the door behind her with a key—a key that was just one of many on a ring that I recognized with a sinking heart.

"Where did you get those?" I asked, the words squeaking their way out through my tightly clenched teeth.

Bernadette cocked her head to one side and smiled a little at me, as though the answer ought to have been obvious. "I found them in your bedside table."

"You broke into my house?" I shouted, though it seemed the least of the evils I'd already known her to have committed.

"Certainly not," she said, sounding almost offended even as she passed the unconscious form of the woman she had kidnapped. "I was invited in."

"But who—oh."

Of course. She'd been with Persephone. It would have been the easiest thing in the world to slip her something to make her sleep, and then steal the keys when she kidnapped my mom.

"Poor Persephone," Bernadette whispered. "She was in need of comfort, and I'm sorry to say she has always looked for it in the most dangerous of places."

I'd learned by now that Persi had a reputation for breaking hearts—but this time, it seemed, she had been the one whose vulnerability had been taken advantage of.

Bernadette slipped the ring of keys into a pocket in the inside of her cloak. I felt all of our eyes on it as it disappeared into the deep purple folds of velvet. We all knew that we would somehow have to get our hands on those keys if we were going to get out of here. Beside me, I heard Eva grind her teeth in frustration.

I looked back at my mother and felt my anger rise again, the sharp tongues of it licking at the heels of my fear. "What have you done to her?"

"I have done no more than I needed to do to bring her here," Bernadette replied.

"She's bleeding!"

"That was an accident. She's quite heavy, you know." She said this so matter-of-factly that I wanted to reach out and strangle her. Instead, I watched as she walked the perimeter of the room to a small mirror that had been affixed to the wall, with a blue ribbon tied around a rusty old hook. It was terribly old, with a tarnished silver frame and its reflective surface mottled with the black spots and cloudy complexion of desilvering. Bernadette stared into it as though entranced, even as she continued to answer my question. "She is only sleeping... sleeping in the arms of a simple charm. She will have only pleasant dreams until she wakes. Only... only pleasant dreams..." Her voice trailed away, and her eyebrows furrowed as she looked more closely at her own reflection. Then, as if answering herself, she said, "What does it matter how I've done it? It's done, isn't it? I'm sorry if you'd prefer crueler methods."

Eva, Zale, and I traded looks, each of us equally baffled, but Nova was staring at the mirror with realization dawning in her eyes. "Bernadette, where did you get that mirror?"

Bernadette started and jumped back from it, suddenly looking like a child who had been caught in wrongdoing. "I found it," she said evasively.

"But where did you find it?" Nova pressed.

A pause. "At the Historical Society." She drew herself up and glared at Nova defensively. "It belongs to our family. It was only on loan. I took it back."

But Nova's face was contorting with panic now. "But it was hers, Bernadette. You must know it was hers. It was kept under lock and key, under protective spells."

"None of that matters," Bernadette said, almost helplessly. "I had to take it. It called to me. There could be no protection from that call."

"Please, Bernadette, you have to explain," Nova said. "Start at the beginning. Wren has a right to understand."

"But this is the beginning," Bernadette said, eyes widening. "This was always the beginning."

She looked at each of us imploringly, as though one of us must surely understand what she was saying. When we all just stared—or glared—blankly back at her, she sighed and said, "Very well. I will tell you what I can, but there is not much time. When the candle burns out, his will shall be done." She pointed to the melted stub of a candle that flickered feebly mere inches from my mother's feet. It was already nearly a puddle of wax. But I could think of nothing to do but keep her talking, anything to give us more time to think, to examine the room, to figure out how the hell we would get out of this.

Bernadette sighed. "It's all jumbled. You'll understand best if I start with Sarah." She whispered the name, her voice thick with fear, and yet her eyes alight with reverence. "You all know of Sarah."

And just like that she had all of my attention. "Sarah Claire? The Second Daughter who was lost?"

"That's right," Bernadette said. "You have heard her story already, I see, though you have been here only a few days. But I heard her story many times, over and over, from my childhood."

"So did all the Claires," Nova said. "A cautionary tale, meant to scare us into obedience. It worked pretty damn well, for the most part."

"Yes, everyone was scared," Bernadette agreed. "But I was also curious. You see, I knew what it was like, to glimpse the future, just like Sarah had been able to do. I may be the first in our family since her to do it. It is a gift we share. I felt... tied to her. You see, people do not understand me—the gift, it frightens and confuses them. I thought... I thought perhaps people had misunderstood Sarah as well."

"She gave herself over to the Darkness, Bernadette. Freely gave herself. What the hell can there be to misunderstand about that?" Nova snapped.

Thunder rumbled so loudly, that it seemed to come from beneath our feet. Bernadette's eyes widened and flickered to the mirror. "You mustn't upset her, Nova."

"What are you—?" Nova began, and then her eyes widened as she followed Bernadette's glance to the mirror. "What have you done?" she whispered.

"I only wanted to speak with her," Bernadette cried, one hand reached out in supplication, as though one of us might drop the understanding she craved right into her palm, like a stone. "She has been reduced to a villain in our stories, you see. A featureless thing, tossed by the sea for too long, and washed up upon the sand, unrecognizable. I knew there must be more to her than that. I wanted her story. I decided to ask her for it. And so one night, I came alone to the clifftop where she died, and cast a circle."

Nova groaned. Eva and Zale stood motionless, spellbound by Bernadette's story. I could hear them on either side of me, breathing evenly, like sleep-walkers.

"I reached out to the spirits of our mothers and grandmothers in search of her. I urged them to bring her to me, so that I could speak with her. They... did not relinquish her easily. I suppose I ought to have known then. But I was too curious, too sure that we were connected, that I was the only one who would understand."

"You should have left her to rot in the spirit realm," Nova growled. "If it weren't for her... if she hadn't..." she glanced uncomfortably at me, but I understood. The Claires had always been in the shadow of the Vespers, a shadow made larger by the glaring betrayal of Sarah Claire. It was the reason Nova had let Bernadette carry on, the reason Bernadette began all of this in the first place: Claire witches had always been made to feel inferior because of Sarah's actions. They carried her shame.

"I thought I could learn the truth! To free her—and us—from the burden of that night so many years ago," Bernadette said tearfully.

"Yeah, and how's that going for you, huh, Bernadette?" Nova sneered.

Bernadette flinched, as though she'd been slapped. Eva reached out and placed a hand on Nova's forearm. They caught each other's eye, and Nova took a deep breath, forcing herself to calm down.

"I'm sorry, Bernadette," she said. "I shouldn't... what happened, when you spoke to her?"

Bernadette's eyes took on a faraway look. "She whispered to me. At first, she thought I had come to scold her, but I was able to convince her I had not. I told her I knew what it was to be misunderstood, that she could tell me the truth, and I could clear her name. But she... she did not want to talk of herself. She wanted to know about me." She smiled wistfully. "She wanted to hear about my visions, what I had seen. I told her about my paintings, and the visions I'd had that inspired them. She didn't scoff or demean them. And she understood that I couldn't explain them." Bernadette shook her head a little, and looked at Nova again, locking eyes in an accusatory way. "No one ever treated me that way—like they understood."

Nova bit at her lip but stayed silent. Even in the short time I'd been in Sedgwick Cove, I'd witnessed the way Bernadette had been treated, especially by her own family. It was clear no one took her very seriously, and that they all thought she was too fragile and too confused to be much of a threat—or an asset—to anyone.

An oracle, the poor soul. What mind could withstand such a burden, Phoebe had lamented aloud, that day in the gallery. The day I'd first seen Bernadette. And the day I'd first seen one of her paintings.

And one of her prophecies.

"I promised to come back. I promised to speak with her again," Bernadette went on, interrupting my thoughts. "And I would have! It wasn't a lie. But she didn't want me to go. She didn't believe that I would come back. But a dangerous storm was gathering over the ocean, and I hurried to close out the circle as the first of the rain fell." She shook her head, and her voice fell to a whisper. "It all happened so fast. I tried to close it properly, but the wind whipped everything around, toppling the candles, scattering the salt. And somehow, in all the confusion... Sarah slipped through."

"Slipped through?" I repeated, uncomprehending.

"She didn't close the door successfully. Sarah remained on this side of the veil," Eva muttered, her eyes still fixed on Bernadette in fascinated horror.

"She whispered to me," Bernadette said, fear illuminating like torches behind her eyes. "While I slept, while I was awake. Sometimes, in the very corner of my eye, I could see her beside me, but when I would turn... nothing at all. I would fall asleep to her whispers and wake up standing in the hallway, in front of one of my paintings. She was trying to ask me something... or tell me something, but I couldn't hear her. Night after night, I woke up staring at those paintings, without having any idea why. I tried to open another circle, even went back to the clifftop to do it; but she hid from me, clung to the shadows of me, afraid that if she showed herself, I would slam the door again and leave her on the other side of it. I needed a better way to communicate with her. I needed a conductor."

Bernadette's eyes flickered to the mirror, and we all followed her gaze. For the briefest of moments, I thought I saw movement in the mirror, like a shadow, but it was gone again before I could be sure of it.

"Conductors are dangerous, Bernadette," Nova said, unable to keep the impatience out of her voice. "Everyone knows that. You don't mess with the integrity of the veil, it's like... witchcraft 101."

"Fear is simply the name we give to things we do not understand," Bernadette said, her eyes taking on that glazed, faraway look again. "We would rather fear something than acknowledge and embrace our own insignificance and ignorance. When we humble ourselves, then we truly see."

"How very Zen of you," Nova murmured, sarcasm in full effect, though I could feel the tremble in her legs where they pressed against mine.

"So, what happened then, Bernadette? How did you find a conductor?" I asked, endeavoring to keep my voice politely interested, even as I glanced around for a weapon or object that might be within reach.

"I tried other Claire family heirlooms, but I still couldn't connect clearly enough with Sarah," Bernadette said. "I knew what I needed—something of hers. But the only known relic of the Lost Second Daughter was in the museum at the Historical Society. And so, I had to break in."

"I heard about that," I said, another piece of the puzzle falling into place. "That first day, at the gallery. Ostara mentioned the break-in, and the mirror."

Bernadette nodded. "Sometimes I wondered if she knew. I thought someone must surely sense Sarah in the house, attached to me. But no one ever said a word." Her voice hitched and shuddered. "No one saw the way she was consuming me, using me up. No one."

"So you had the conductor," Eva prompted suddenly, her voice higher than usual in her fear. "What happened then?"

Bernadette looked up at Eva, as if almost surprised to find her standing there, and took up the thread of her story once again. "It took me ages, but I found the spell that would bind Sarah to the mirror. Once I had done that, we could communicate at last. It was very tiring at first," Bernadette said, her face taking on a hollow sort of expression that suggested something a good deal worse than 'tiring'. "We had to deepen our connection over time, but soon the whispers were clear. I could see her face in the contours of mine. And finally, I could understand her heart." Her eyes filled with tears. "Such a heart," she murmured through trembling lips. "And that was when she told me."

We all waited in utter stillness for her to go on, but she seemed lost in a fearful reverie; and so it was several seconds before Eva nudged Nova, and Nova cleared her throat and asked, "What did she tell you, Bernadette?"

"She told me about my paintings. You see, she'd understood them even when I had not, for she had seen the same thing in her own visions. She explained that a First Daughter would be taken and offered up to the Darkness. The paintings were not just prophesies, but instructions. We were all bound together now: Sarah, the Darkness, and I. We were all too intertwined, separate beings and yet dependent on each other—conjoined with a single beating heart."

"Conjoined? More like a parasite, leeching off you and your magic!" Nova cried. "You expect me to believe you'd have done all of this if Sarah hadn't been controlling you?"

"Not controlling! Illuminating! This was always meant to be. I just didn't know what it all meant. But Sarah knew. It was the Darkness's will, waiting to be done."

"And you think you were meant to do it?" Nova cried out, and although I couldn't see her eyes, I could hear tears in her voice. "What if you were only meant to discover it? To warn others? What if you were meant to save us from the Darkness again, rather than feed us to it? Have you ever stopped to think of that?"

Bernadette had thought of it. I could see it in the twitching muscle below her eye, and in the set of her jaw. "No. This was foretold. I would serve him. I was... weak, as she was."

"No, you were gullible! When have you ever been drawn to the Darkness before?"

"I was drawn to Sarah's story, and she was the Lost Second Daughter! Don't you see? The weakness in me was drawn to that weakness in her!"

"Bernadette, that's not true!" Nova cried. "Are you even listening to yourself? Your pity and compassion is what drew you to Sarah. You thought she must be misunderstood, like you. It was empathy, don't you see? For someone you'd never even met. You wanted to give her redemption, not join in her disgrace. But she took that pity and she twisted it, used it to her own advantage. She made you into the tool she needed to—what the hell even are you doing? Why have you done all of this?"

Bernadette's confusion seemed to concentrate, to solidify itself into certainty at Nova's last question. Perhaps she didn't fully understand how we had gotten here, but she understood fully the reason. "We are restoring the balance," she said, with a placid little nod of her head.

"What balance?" I asked, stealing another glance at my mother. "I'm sorry, but we don't know what you're talking about."

"It's like an eye for an eye," Bernadette said, with all the patience of a school teacher trying to explain a complex concept to students who were barely paying attention. "When the Darkness rose, a Second Daughter was lost in the struggle. It's only fair now, that in the second rising, a First Daughter should rectify this loss."

"Meaning?" I asked.

"Meaning that your mother will provide the vessel for Sarah to return. In Sarah, the Darkness has the servant he had always searched for. He was robbed of her all those years ago. Today, at last, she shall be restored to him, a Second Daughter in the body of a First Daughter, binding both covens to him for all time." Bernadette sighed contentedly, for all the world as though someone had just handed her a cup of tea after a long day. She had told her story. She had arrived at last at the end of the confession, and the weight had been lifted from her. I stared at her almost-euphoric expression—the relief, the sheer gratitude for having excised it all from her breast.

"So you're... you're saying that Sarah is going to... to what, possess my mother?" I asked, the words hollow.

"She will replace her. Your mother's spirit will pass on," Bernadette said mechanically.

"Like hell she will!" I cried.

"Absolutely not!" yelled Zale.

Nova flung out an arm, and we were startled into silence behind her. "You know we can't just stand by and watch that happen, Bernadette," Nova said, trying to sound very calm and logical. "Surely you understand that?"

Bernadette's expression crumpled. Nova went on.

"You're going to have to stop us from trying to help her. You've already threatened to poison us. Is this what you want? Is this really who you are, someone who sacrifices others to the Darkness against their will? Who would kill a bunch of kids, including a member of your own family, to make it happen?"

Bernadette's whole body trembled as she listened to these words. I watched with almost reckless hope as doubt and fear and sadness chased each other across her features. "I... I don't... want to hurt anyone... I..."

"That's right," Nova said, soothingly now. "Of course you don't. That's not who you are, Bernadette. Don't forget who you are."

"I..." Bernadette's voice died on a sudden gasping intake of breath. She flung her hands up over her ears, as though trying to block out a sound none of us could hear. "I didn't... please don't be angry... I..." and then she flew to the mirror on the wall, pressing her face right to the glass, tears running over the apples of her hollowed cheeks as she sobbed. "No, it's not true... I'm sorry... I... maybe we could do it without hurting anyone? Maybe there's a way to..."

But then she stopped speaking. Her features in the mirror warped and twisted strangely, and though I could hear nothing, a bitter coldness blew through the room like an arctic wind, stealing a gasp right off my lips, and causing the four of us to pull together even more tightly. I threw a terrified glance at the candle still burning fretfully at my mother's feet. It had not gone out. Yet.

Bernadette, meanwhile, was in the thrall of the mirror—and of Sarah. Hers was the face that was transforming Bernadette's reflection, here narrowing an eye, here widening a cheekbone, there stretching one side of the mouth, until Bernadette was nothing more than one of her own paintings under a warped and cruel brush, making and remaking her features with every stroke, until I could hardly stand to watch any longer. The mouth of the reflection moved in a litany of silent persuasion that no one but Bernadette could hear. Nova was frozen in front of me, her mouth hanging open in silent horror. Thank God Eva had her shit together enough to realize this might be our only chance to say anything without being overheard.

"We're going to have to find a way to break that circle," she whispered. "Anyone have any ideas?"

"I know you're not asking me." I muttered helplessly. I could have screamed with frustration at my own uselessness.

"I don't know what half of these sigils are," Zale murmured back. "If we could get through the circle, we could protect your mom with a binding or something, but..."

"Yeah," Eva murmured, and I could practically hear her wheels turning. "We could... could we bind her to *herself*, I wonder?"

"Would that work?" Zale hissed.

Eva shook her head minutely. "We're in uncharted territory here, MacDowell. If the Darkness itself is behind all this, we're probably screwed no matter what we try, so we might as well do something."

"Please tell me someone has a plan, because I'm not sure how much longer I can spin this out, and I don't think Sarah's going to let her listen to us," Nova whispered over her shoulder. We all looked over at Bernadette, who was now pleading tearfully with the reflection that was both hers and Sarah's at the same time.

Under cover of her sobbing, Eva leaned forward and whispered into Nova's ear. I caught the words "binding" and "mom" and something that sounded an awful lot like "last resort."

"Will that work?" Nova muttered.

"No idea."

"Awesome."

At that very moment, Bernadette let out a howl of misery as she stumbled back from the mirror. The heel of one foot made contact with the perimeter of the circle, and I heard a distinct sizzling sound before she howled again, stumbling back toward the wall. She hit the stone hard, all the breath whooshing out of her; and then she slid down the wall, still sobbing, clutching at her foot. I saw that the back of her ivory ballet flat had been burned clean away, and that the skin on the back of her heel was blistered and raw. She couldn't cross her own circle, I'd realized. Something about the spell was keeping her out. I wondered if she'd even been aware of it until that moment, for her face was eloquent with betrayal.

Under cover of all this chaos, Zale had begun surreptitiously casting the circle. I wondered how that was even possible, until my eye fell on the curve of the outer wall and I realized: we were in a circle already—the lighthouse itself. I watched his hand shoot out behind him, scattering a stealthy handful of salt on the floorboards, and he murmured under his breath.

"Wren," Eva whispered.

"Yeah?"

"Do you still have that bottle Xiomara gave you?"

I fumbled with my back pocket and drew out the tiny bottle, keeping it hidden in my fist. "How did you know about that?"

"She's been worried about you since you got here. I saw her preparing it for you. Do you have it?"

"Yeah."

"Good. When I say so, use it."

"Use it how? What am I supposed to do with it?"

"Drink it. I... think it should protect you."

"Protect me from what?"

"Bernadette can't get into that circle. But you can. Drink that—not all of it, save some for your mom—and step into the circle when we distract her. Once you're in there, give the rest to your mom, so you can both step back out safely."

"What are you going to do?"

"We're going to try to distract Bernadette and Sarah."

"But how... and what if it doesn't work?"

"Let us worry about that. You have to try to get your mom out of there. We're running out of time."

I looked down at the guttering candle, little more than a pool of wax at this point. She was right. It was the only chance we had.

"It's all too late now!" Bernadette's voice shouted suddenly, and my head snapped back around to look at her. She hadn't noticed our near-silent scheming—she was looking down at her own hands with confusion, as though she had suddenly noticed that a stranger's hands had been sewn to her wrists.

"It's not too late," Nova whimpered. "You don't have to go through with this."

"Oh, yes, I do," Bernadette said, nodding her head violently. "It was set into motion by hands other than mine, and I am powerless to stop it." She looked up at Nova with a sad smile. "I belong to Sarah. To the Darkness. I chose."

"You can change your mind," Nova pleaded.

Bernadette laughed, a dark and twisted sound, and as she laughed something rippled over her face, and beneath it, for just a moment. A different face looked out at us, a face hundreds of years dead, a face wild with triumph. "I cannot change my mind. I do not want to change my mind. I could have turned back when I realized who we served, but I didn't. I didn't."

"So what are you going to do, then?" Nova asked, her voice breaking. "Kill your cousin? Kill all of us? And then what? How do you propose to get away with it? Or did Sarah and the Darkness forget that tiny detail? That you'll be the one taking the blame?"

I watched with fascination as the fear kindled in her eyes was washed away, like a footprint in the sand under Sarah's power, as she poured her poisonous lies into Bernadette's head. Bernadette's voice and expression were calm as she replied. "They will look out for me."

Nova barked a dark, bitter laugh. "Yeah, because the Darkness has a reputation for loyalty and mercy. I'm sure that's gonna work out just great for you."

Behind me, I heard the whispered words from Eva, who was completing the spell. "With these elements together under spirit, I cast a circle of protection above, below, and within."

The whole lighthouse seemed to shake on its foundation, a strange light suffusing the stones where the walls met the floor. At the same moment, the inner circle, the one Bernadette had cast, began to glow red, strange sparks emanating from its perimeter, and a foul wind blew out from it. It smelled of smoke and sulfur, and something sweetish and rotting that turned my stomach.

"What the—" Zale muttered.

"Is that...bad?" I whispered.

"I have no idea," Eva said.

"What have you done?" Bernadette shrieked. Whatever was happening, she hadn't expected it. Was Zale's protective circle working?

Through the haze, I saw my mother stir, trying to lift her head before letting it droop again onto her chest, and it was all I could do not to leap through the circle and burn myself to a crisp to get to her.

"Wren, drink it now!" Eva whispered.

The air around us shimmered with a heat haze, and suddenly I could see another figure within that inner circle—a figure I knew, one that was both familiar and terrifying. The Gray Man reached out and beckoned to me, inviting me in. No one else seemed to have noticed him—perhaps I was the only one who could see him. I pulled the tiny stopper from the bottle, and drained half of the contents.

"I'm ready," I whispered, but whether the words were meant for Eva or the Gray Man, I couldn't have said.

"Now!" Eva shouted.

Utter chaos broke out. Zale ran for the mirror, plucking it from the hook and smashing it on the ground. Bernadette screamed, dropping her knife in her desperation to get to the mirror. Nova dashed forward and kicked the blade clear across the room, while Eva dove at Bernadette, trying to wrestle the ring of keys away from her.

And as all of this unfolded around me, I closed my eyes, held my breath, and stepped over the circle's border.

22

First, there was nothing but searing pain as the heat of the spell burned over me; but though I felt like my flesh must surely be charred away, a quick, incredulous examination revealed that I was completely unharmed. Xiomara's elixir of rue had worked—the crossing into the circle had been painful, but the ferocity of the magic had left no mark on me that I could see.

The next thing I noticed, even as I blinked the tears of pain from my eyes, was the strange, muffled silence. A second ago, everything had been chaos—my friends shouting, Bernadette screaming, the magic sparking and exploding everywhere, like it would take the very lighthouse down to rubble, but now: nothing. If I concentrated, I thought I could hear the continued sounds of the confrontation, as though from deep underwater.

Finally, I was able to look around me. My first, fleeting impression was that I had been trapped in some kind of monstrous snow globe. Ash fell gently around me, and smoke swirled in strange, unnatural patterns. The floor beneath my feet was cracked and hot. I could see almost nothing outside of the boundary of the circle, but for shifting shadows and flashes of dull light. It was as though a curtain had come down between me and the rest of the room.

"Mom."

She was there, still tied to the ladder, which was smoldering like hot coals behind her. I stumbled forward, almost knocking into her, and pressed my hands to her face, swallowing a sob.

"Mom?"

She groaned and lifted her face, squinting out of bleary, bloodshot eyes. "Wren?"

"Yes, it's me," I replied, in a cracked voice.

"You weren't supposed to come. I didn't want you to come," she murmured, frowning at me for all the world like she would have liked nothing better than to ground me, if she could just keep her eyes open.

I actually laughed, one wild sob of laughter that bubbled up out of me. "Well, it's too late for that. I'm here, and everything's going to be fine." The lie slipped out easily, an automatic impulse born of the desire to wipe the worry from her face. My mom was still trying to talk, despite the way her words slurred together.

"It's Bernadette—"

"I know."

"I don't know how... there's a mirror... Sarah Claire..."

"I know all that, Mom. It's okay. I'm gonna untie you, okay? Just try to hold still."

It was an almost ludicrous request, because she could barely stay conscious, let alone move; but she stopped trying to speak, and let me work at the knots that bound her to the ladder.

At last the scraps of fabric and rope fell away, and my mom sagged against me, unable to bear her own weight. I staggered and fell against the ladder, which made an ominous cracking noise, and hurried to shift my mom's arm more securely around my neck. I looked down at the candle, now little more than a pool of wax cradling a tiny, flickering flame. I was nearly out of time.

With shaking fingers, I uncorked the bottle of the rue elixir and put it to my mom's chapped lips. "You have to drink this."

She obeyed me like a small child, tilting her head back while I tipped all the remaining liquid into her mouth. She swallowed it, spluttering a little, and I tossed the little bottle aside. I had no idea if the rue would still work for me— maybe it could only protect me once from that kind of magic—but I felt confident that my mom, at least, might make it back through the barrier okay. I began edging her toward it, step by shuffling step, staggering under her weight as she sagged against me. But we'd only made it a few steps when it began.

The air filled with that familiar sound, the sound of soil shifting and insect parts buzzing and sawing. The strange scent of rotting and soil and the tang of hot metal filled my nostrils, even as panic swelled in my chest. He was coming.

I heaved more quickly, dragging my mom's feet against the floor with a grunt of desperate effort. Around our feet, insects were forcing their way up through the floorboards by the dozens—millipedes and spiders and ants and worms—all scuttling and curling into a seething mass. I kicked them violently out of my path, with a strangled cry of horror. They were trying to flee the circle, blindly crawling over each other to reach the edge, only to ignite like tiny firecrackers as they made contact with it. I watched a millipede crumble to ash in a frozen moment of horrified fascination; but then my mom groaned again, and I snapped out of it, dragging her a few more inches. We were almost there. A few more steps... we were almost there...

And then the sound shifted, warping on the air into a voice. A voice I dreaded because I knew it like I knew my own name.

"There's my Little Bird."

Terror boiled like lava under my skin. I knew what I would see if I turned around, knew exactly—and yet every impulse, every primitive instinct for self-preservation, was screaming at me to flee like the insects. Even if I went up like dry kindling, it would be better—kinder—than what awaited me in the call of that voice. I also knew that he wouldn't simply let me leave. I would have to face him, my childhood nightmare made manifest.

What choice did I have? What choice had I *ever* had? I turned.

The Gray Man loomed before me, faceless and menacing. He was tall—even taller than I remembered, with strangely long arms and too-large hands. His body curved with an almost serpent-like smoothness, and in the gray smoky nothingness that made him up, there was a writhing, a pulsing, as though a million smaller things seethed beneath his surface, desperate to break away from the whole. And around it all, Darkness itself roiled like a thundercloud held captive.

Perhaps it sounds absolutely crazy to say it, but something in me breathed a sigh of relief. All these years, I had convinced myself that the Gray Man was a figment of my imagination. There was something comforting, even as I stared down a waking nightmare, that I hadn't invented it all, dredged it up from a child's overactive imagination. My imaginary friend wasn't imaginary at all, though he was most definitely not a friend.

His head tilted to one side, curious. And then, though he had no discernible features, he smiled—the shape of his face contorting monstrously to suggest the expression even without the presence of a mouth. I swayed where I stood, wanting to vomit, to run, to strike out with magic I didn't even think I possessed. But I didn't—or couldn't. I just stood there, my mother's weight pinning me in place on shaking legs.

"I know you," I told him finally, feeling a fleeting flash of pride that my voice was not shaking, even if the rest of me was.

"Indeed, you do, Little Bird. You remember me, then?" the Gray Man asked. The words dropped into my head like intrusive thoughts, and I wanted to claw them out of my brain. They didn't belong there.

"I... I know who you are," I told him, almost defiantly.

"Do you? Tell me."

"Y-you're the thing they all talk about. The Darkness."

The Gray Man laughed, a grating screech of wings and clicking pincers. "I am not what they talk about. I am what they fear to talk about. I am the unspoken word, the omitted terror, the whispered suggestion. If they really knew me, they would never dare to conjure a thought of me."

"But... what are you?" I asked, the question bursting from my lips with childish impatience.

"I am unknowable, Little Bird. I am older than the rocks and deeper than the sea. I have always been and I will always be. My name is lost to the ages, and so they call me the Darkness. They fear me, because they know that I could turn their hearts to me with a whisper. I bend all to my will and gorge myself on their despair."

A wave of terror broke over me, and it was all I could do to stay on my feet. Perhaps my mother felt me stagger because she let slip a soft moan. The sound steadied me again. *Don't forget why you're here,* I told myself.

"You aren't as powerful as you think you are," I told him. "The Vesper witches bound the deep magic of this place from you. They defeated you. That's why you're doing all of this. That's why you want my mother. You want to break the Covenant of the Three, so you can have this place again."

The Gray Man laughed again. "There is no defeating me, Little Bird. The tide of power may have turned in their favor for a time, but time means nothing to a creature like me. What is a day, a year, a millennium to one such as I, a thing eternal and unchanging?"

"Time might not matter, but this place does," I said. "If you're so powerful, why stay here? You could go anywhere, do anything. But you don't." A thought popped into my head, and I knew it was true before it fell from my lips. I spoke it as a revelation. "You need this place. You're tied to it."

The Gray Man stood still and silent in the moments after I spoke, and I felt his anger on the air like a sour taste on my tongue, but it did not terrify me like it ought to have done. Perhaps I'd already reached the pinnacle of terror—perhaps it was impossible to be any more scared than I was already—there was something perversely comforting in that thought, and I clung to that comfort as I went on.

"The Covenant of the Three bound you here. You can't leave, but you can't access the deep magic either. You're trapped. That's why you want my mother. She's the third Vesper witch. She's the one standing in your way."

"Ah, but that's where you're wrong. I do not want your mother at all."

This pulled me up short. "What do you mean, you don't want her? You told Bernadette to kidnap her. You were seconds away from putting Sarah's ghost into her body."

"I see. Little Bird does not yet understand. Would you like me to explain?"

No, I want you to go straight to the depths of hell where you undoubtedly came from, and rot there, I thought savagely. Aloud, I said, "I'd rather leave."

"Oh, but you can't leave. You've only just returned. I've waited entirely too long for this."

I stamped my foot in frustration, and my mother mumbled incoherently on my shoulder. "You don't make sense. You took my mother. Now you don't want her. So I'm taking her with me."

"You misunderstand me. I did not take your mother because I wanted her. I took her because I needed her. I needed bait, to lure you here."

I shook my head. "That doesn't make any sense. My mother is the third Vesper witch. If she renews the Covenant, you spend another generation bound here. I don't have anything to do with it."

"Oh, my sweet Little Bird. You have everything to do with it."

"I'm not your Little Bird! Stop calling me that!"

"But you are mine. You have been for a long time. Don't you remember? You already know me."

I looked at the Gray Man, and he gazed eyelessly back, waiting.

"I know you tried to take me into the sea when I was just a child. I know

Asteria used her magic to protect me from you all these years. What I don't know, is why. Tell me," I finally said.

"I can no longer access the deep magic here, but I can listen to it," the Gray Man said. He took a step toward me, and I dragged my mother a step closer to the perimeter, away from him. "I listen to its song, a song that ebbs and flows like the tide, but in familiar patterns. I listened for many hundreds of years, searching for a deviation that might present me an opportunity. I was patient... so very patient. And then I heard it. A counterpoint—a deep and powerful new melody in the song. It spoke of great power. I gathered what strength I had, took this form, and followed the song to a garden behind a cottage, where a small girl played with a cat in the flowerbeds."

I was shaking my head, like I could erase everything he was saying with the simple motion. He ignored it.

"I stood outside the gate and watched her. The song grew stronger. It rose up under her, wrapped around her like a blanket, followed her steps like a familiar. She was the key, the song whispered. If I could command her, I could escape the cage in which I had been imprisoned."

He took another step. I could not move away, or perhaps I didn't want to; I was too caught up in what he was saying, a fly in a web.

"I could see that the child was, for the moment, unprotected. The door to the house was open—she had, through machinations of her own, engineered her temporary escape into the garden. The chance was too good to miss. I took it. Had I my full power, I could have consumed her and her power in less than an instant, but in this form, all I could do was coax her. I approached the gate and called to her."

Was I simply picturing the scene as he spoke, or did I remember it? I couldn't be sure, but I was mesmerized just the same. The Gray Man held out a hand, and I could feel the magnetic pull of it, the inherent temptation of the invitation.

"She—or should I say, *you*—came so willingly. No trace of fear, no hesitation. It was truly too easy. I did not lie to you, to convince you to accompany me. I did not have to. I whispered to you of your power, of the great things we could do with it together, and you whispered back, alight with possibility."

"I was a child," I finally managed to choke out. "Practically still a baby. I had no power then, only the potential for it, a potential I never reached, by the way. I've never successfully cast a spell on my own."

"Children have much more knowledge of themselves and their potential than their elders do. You doubt and scoff now, but that is the effect of the world upon you. Once you whispered of your effect on the world. Once you knew your own power."

I shook my head. "This is wrong. This is all wrong."

"That day, you knew better. You came with me to the shore, hand in hand, with a single purpose. We would walk into the water together and we would emerge again as one."

My stomach roiled at every twisted implication of his words. For a moment, I thought I might be sick, but then I barked out a hysterical laugh. "And then what? You and the super-charged toddler would rule the world? I didn't realize one of the side effects of binding you here was insanity."

My snark and skepticism did not even seem to register, as he plowed relentlessly on. "We would have succeeded were it not for your grandmother. Not only did she snatch you from the maw of the ocean, but she placed upon you a powerful spell of protection. I could not touch you then... could not find you."

And it was my mother's words that echoed through my memory now: *When I came back, she had you in your own protective circle. You were soaking wet and smelled of the sea, and you were sound asleep. She wouldn't tell me what happened, only that you were safe now.*

"The protection would last as long as the witch who cast the spell lived. And then, your grandmother knew, you would be on your own."

I didn't want to believe him, but everything he was saying made terrible sense. Still, I shook my head. "No," I whispered. "No."

"You do not have to take my word for it—"

"Like I'd take your word about anything—"

"—because I am offering you the same choice tonight."

The words buzzed around inside my head like a horde of burrowing insects. I swallowed, my mouth and throat suddenly desert dry.

"What do you mean?" The words were less than a whisper, but the Gray Man heard them nonetheless. I don't even think I needed to speak aloud.

"I am offering you a choice. A trade if you will. I will release your mother. You will remain here with me."

Where my heart had been pounding wildly a moment before, there seemed to be nothing but a cavernous emptiness inside my chest. "You're lying," I whispered. "If you let my mother go, the Covenant of the Three will be renewed. There will still be three Vesper witches in Sedgwick Cove. You will still be bound."

The Gray Man's face stretched into that warped suggestion of a smile again. "But I will have you, Little Bird: you are the one weapon I need to break that Covenant. With your power in my service, the Covenant will crumble regardless."

"No, Sarah is the Daughter who tried to help you rise. She's the one you want—"

"She is nothing. A lingering wraith of the veil. She has served her purpose, and now she will drift back into the obscurity she came from."

I could have laughed. Sarah had put her trust in the Darkness, and Bernadette had put her trust in Sarah. And they'd both been used—betrayed —as anyone but they could have predicted. Sarah would not rise again to serve her master. Her service was over, and he would not reward her for it, especially now that he had what he wanted.

Which was... me? My head was spinning, my heart pounding. I couldn't believe it, and yet all the details kept falling into place, like missing pieces of a puzzle—each one fitting perfectly to plug the gaping holes in my life. All but one: this great power he spoke of—how could that possibly be? I knew nothing of witchcraft. I'd never cast a single spell, and everything I'd tried to help my friends with, I'd only bungled and stumbled my way through. But maybe it didn't matter because what choice did I have? If I refused, my mother would die. Sarah would take her over, and the Covenant of the Three would be broken. Sedgwick Cove would fall to the Darkness, and it would be all my fault. If I went with him... well, I couldn't be entirely sure what would happen to me; but at least my mother would be safe, and Sedgwick Cove, too, because whatever he said, the idea of me having some great hidden power was the one piece that didn't fit.

It wasn't true. It couldn't be. Every moment of my mediocre existence flew in the face of it.

My decision was made. I only had one question, and it fell from my lips in despairing tones. "How did you know I would come?"

"Mortals are slaves to the weakness of love—controlled by it like puppets on strings. What could be more predictable?"

"Love is not weakness," I whispered.

He did not answer, his blank face merely tilted slightly, waiting.

I looked down at my mother's soot-streaked face. I planted a tremulous kiss on her forehead. Then I turned back to him. "Let her out," I said.

He inclined his head, and I felt the intense heat of the circle cool slightly. Trusting this meant she would be safe to pass through it, I swallowed a sob and, with a grunt of effort, heaved my mother's weight away from me and right through the barrier. It swallowed her like a stone dropped into deep water. If I squinted, I thought I could see the shape of her, a dark heap on the ground just on the outside of our strange and silent cocoon. I turned back to the Gray Man.

"I'm ready," I said. It was a lie, but it didn't matter.

He held out a hand to me, and though every cell of my being screamed against it, I reached out and took it.

23

Everything went instantly, blindingly dark, like the world was an eye that had blinked. Then the moment was over, and we stood on the windswept beach once more, hand in hand at the edge of the water in the dark, my nightmare come true.

No, not a nightmare. A memory all along.

A storm gathered out on the horizon, a menacing bank of clouds that twisted like a living mass in the sky. As I stared at it, lightning forked through it to strike the surface of the water. A gust of wind whipped my hair around my face. I breathed it in, savoring the tang of salt in my nose.

I turned my head and looked toward the lighthouse. Lights shone from the windows, but it was impossible to tell what might be happening inside. Had my friends realized I was gone? Was my mother okay? I had to tell myself that they would take care of her. They would go for help. It would be okay because it had to be. Because otherwise, I would never be able to go through with this.

Steeling myself, I turned my head to the other side, where I knew he was standing beside me. There he was, his face closer to mine than it had ever appeared in my dreams. I no longer had to crane my neck to gaze up at him. He turned as well, the blank gray emptiness of his face nonetheless giving the impression of an intense stare.

"What happens now?" I asked, though I knew at least part of the answer, because I'd been here before—only this time there was no Asteria to save me.

"You must walk with me into the sea. The sea guided the Vesper witches to these shores. You must relinquish your place here by offering yourself to the sea."

I laughed bitterly, though nothing could have been less funny. "You expect me to just... let myself drown?"

"Certainly not. What use would you be to me dead?"

"Look, I'm not sure what mystical thing you think is going to happen if I just... walk out into the damn ocean, but I promise you it's not going to end well for me."

"Oh it will not be an ending, but a beginning. We will walk into the sea as two separate beings, but we shall emerge as two halves of the same whole. My eternal state, your magic, mixed together by the sea and joining us with immeasurable power."

I simply stared at him, too horrified and fascinated to speak. For one fleeting instant, I saw it: the flash of the image in my mind. The Gray Man, taller, more terrible, smoke rolling off him like mist off the water, and me beside him: beautiful and terrifying, my hair streaming behind me, and dark power glowing in my eyes, as ancient and ungovernable as the sea crashing behind me.

And then the image shattered, and I was just myself again, shivering in the needling, misty rain that had begun to fall on us.

"It is our destiny," the Gray Man said, as though he had seen exactly what I had just seen. And then, without another word, we began to walk forward.

I don't know how I put one foot in front of the other. I hadn't consciously decided to move forward. Maybe I had no choice. Maybe this was as inevitable as the changing of the tides, a foregone conclusion from the moment he saw me, a toddler chasing a cat in a garden. We had come full circle.

Still, a part of me was fighting it, the very human part, who was still sure I would drown, who was sure I had no power at all, and that I was sacrificing myself for nothing.

No, not for nothing, another voice inside me whispered. For my mother. For my family. For the rest of the people in this place that had always been my home, even if I hadn't known it until a few days ago. Perhaps it was this that propelled me forward, as the bitterly cold waves broke over my shins, soaking my jeans, casting salty spray up into my face.

My heart was pounding like it would break through my ribcage. My breath came in short, sharp, panicked gasps. Tears gathered in my eyes, spilling over to join the salt already on my cheeks. And yet, no part of me was fighting to turn around, only to plunge inexorably forward to meet... whatever might happen. The water lapped at my chest now, rolling with a steady rhythm like it would rock me to sleep. I closed my eyes, succumbing to it.

Let it be like falling asleep and slipping into a dream. Please.

And then it began to happen.

A tingling sensation began beneath my ribs, and in the tips of my fingers. At first I thought it must be the numbing cold, but it was not. This tingling was warm and deep, like a promise. The Gray Man's hand tightened around mine... perhaps he could feel it, too.

And then it was as though something broke open inside of me. It wasn't exactly painful, but I had to brace myself against it. Something was waking up, filling me up, probing at my boundaries, urging me to surrender to it. *Was this it?* I thought. *Was this what death felt like?*

No, it was too bright. Too alive. It sang in my bones and seared beneath my skin. I realized it just as the water closed over my head.

This was what magic felt like.

Something inside me was singing for joy. It was true. There was magic in me, a magic I could barely understand, much less control; and yet it was mine, fully and completely. In the hum of it was a song older than the world, deeper than this ocean. And powerful... so powerful that it threatened to steal the last reserve of air from my lungs.

It was true. I was powerful. How could I ever have doubted it? But the wonder twisted instantly to fear. This power would belong to him before I could even learn to wield it. I would be his tool, just as he had said, and he would use me to destroy everything I tried to save. My anger screamed inside me.

You idiot, Wren. It's all been for nothing. He was right all along, and you played right into his hands.

And the magic inside me sang again, louder this time, and I heard the truth it was singing to me:

If this magic is powerful enough to kill for, it is powerful enough to save you. He wants it. Do not give it to him. He thinks you cannot fight back. So... fight.

Fight.

Everything stopped. The ocean around me went unnaturally still. My lungs, burning for air, calmed. The Gray Man tried to keep walking forward—I felt his confusion when he found he could no longer pull me along, his spell over me broken. Through my eyelids, a brightness began to penetrate the dark. I opened my eyes.

The water around me was suffused with golden light. I looked down to find the source of it—*me.* As I watched, it spread through my chest, filled my torso, crept down my arms and legs. As it surged through my hands the Gray Man let go with a muffled cry of fury. The magic sang in every particle of me, sustaining me, directing me.

What do I do? I implored the magic.

Call them to your aid. The elements. Call them to you.

And so, as the magic sang in my bones, filling me and sustaining me, I called the elements for the very first time, starting with the one I needed most.

Element of air, I call on you. Come to me, now. Sustain me.

With a roaring force, air came to my aid, blasting down into the water from above, whipping it into a frenzy around me, creating a whirlpool that sucked the water into great spinning walls around me. Suddenly, I was standing, dripping wet, my feet half-buried in sand, a salty breeze whipping my hair and filling my nose and mouth as I sucked in great lungfuls.

The Gray Man stood beside me, frozen in fury, unable to touch me as the magic rose like smoke from my skin, his face split by a black gaping hole that trembled with a silent scream. Or perhaps it wasn't silent at all—perhaps the magic's song was simply drowning it out. Able to use my voice now, a called out to the next element that could aid me.

"Element of water, I call on you. You brought the Vesper witches to this place once before. Please, help me home again."

With a surging force, the ocean answered my call. The walls of the whirlpool collapsed at once around me, but crashing over me, they bore me up on the crest of a great wave. I screamed in terror, but the wave did not batter or pummel me. It carried me, borne on its back, toward the shore again. It gave a heave and I tumbled onto the sand in a wet, shivering heap. For a moment, I simply gasped, trying to regain my breath. I stared around me, but the Gray

Man was nowhere to be seen. Hope surged in my breast—could he truly be gone?

The hope receded like the tide as my eyes found the ocean again and watched with wild dread as the Gray Man emerged from the water—his figure less human now than it had been, grotesquely stretched and distorted, limbs curved and wicked, neck elongated, and black eyes burning like pits of fire in his face.

It wasn't enough. I couldn't escape him.

Call, the magic sang to me. *Call for help and help will come.*

I staggered to my feet, facing the Gray Man as he marched inexorably forward, dark power drifting in his wake like smoke. I summoned every last bit of courage in me and called again, my voice brittle but not broken.

"I call on the element of earth. Please, help me."

At once the ground beneath my feet began to tremble. Behind me, chunks of rock shook loose from the cliff face and crashed to the sand, but I could not turn to look. My eyes were fixed on the Gray Man where he now stood on the shore, free of the ocean's clutches, and bearing down upon me with a fury that I could taste on the air. As I watched, the earth beneath him began to undulate like the waves behind him. Almost against his will, he dragged his eyes from me, and looked down just in time for a great gaping chasm to open in the sand beneath his feet. Great walls of sand rose up on every side, and poured into the yawning rift, carrying the Gray Man with it, like the tide. He vanished as the chasm filled with sand again, as though it had never been.

My legs suddenly seemed to liquefy, and I sank to the ground, shaking. But even as I put my hands to the sand, I could feel the Gray Man there, his fury and his power vibrating in the sand. I had not stopped him—this was not over.

I felt so drained, so utterly empty, the magic still singing faintly in my fingertips as I raised my eyes to the sky. "I call on the element of fire. Come to my aid. Help me finish this, please."

I heard the rumble of thunder, and lightning began to glow in the clouds over the sea. A forked bolt of lightning split the sky, striking at the base of the lighthouse. Then a second bolt closer, near the cliff, and charging the air with the tang of electricity.

The chasm in front of me was opening again—the Gray Man was fighting his way free. I felt his monstrous power rising up, splitting and cracking along the fault I had only just closed. I watched in terror as first one elongated hand appeared over its edge, and then another. His nightmare of a face hovered just above the edge. The eyes locked on mine, and the face split into a leer.

"You are mine, Little Bird." His words filled my head, fed on my fear.

The chasm widened and spread, cracking along the sand toward me—the earth would surely swallow me, too. A deafening clap of thunder boomed, just as one more bolt of lightning shattered the roiling gray of the stormy sky.

This time, the lightning found its mark. It struck the Gray Man where he stood, igniting him like an explosive. The smell of sulfur and charged air blasted outward, even as the sand rose up around him in strange, jagged formations. He writhed and screamed, contorted and burned where he stood.

This was the moment. I had to finish it. And I couldn't do it alone, whatever the power I possessed. I needed the First Daughters.

"Spirit," I whispered. "I call on you. On the Vesper witches that came before me, I call on you. Help me. Help me to bind him in this place."

I tugged Asteria's charm from my neck and it came loose. With shaking fingers, I tugged out the folded drawing of the Gray Man, and the ribbon that Asteria had wound around it thirteen years ago. The words found their way to my tongue, as though I'd always known them, and I repeated them over and over again, as I wound the ribbon around the paper.

"I bind you from doing harm," I whispered. "I bind you to this place."

All at once, the wind rose up around me: a warm, soft wind made not of air, but of voices—a chorus of spirits, gathered around me, echoing my words, and speaking others besides—incantations I could not fathom, charms lost to the ages; but I could feel them deepening the magic around me, and within me. The ribbon under my fingers grew hot to the touch, the paper smoking and sparking; but I didn't stop winding it around and around, the words of the binding spilling from my lips on the current of the magic that was pouring forth, dragged up by sheer force of will, because it was working—I could see it.

All around the Gray Man, fire and molten sand was shifting and twisting, wrapping his flailing limbs, encasing the dark furious storm of him. Now I could hear other voices, not just the ones on the air, but voices beside me, behind me—real voices cracked with fear and thick with tears, stumbling and stammering over the words of the binding, lending their strength and their magic to the spell. The Gray Man reached forward with one last, desperate lunge, elongated fingers clawing the air between us as, in one final burst of red heat, the molten sand closed up around him. A clap of thunder released a torrent of rain upon us, sending up a hissing cloud of steam that swallowed the Gray Man from view. When it cleared at last, the Gray Man still reached for me beneath a blackened shell of molten glass.

I gaped at him, mesmerized by the long, outstretched fingers that still beckoned to me. Could it really be over? Had it worked? I took one staggering step forward, and felt a hand grab my wrist.

"Wren, no! Don't go any closer!"

I turned, my head spinning, to see Eva standing there just behind me, her cheeks glazed with tears, and her eyes wide. Behind her, Eva and Zale were there, Zale with my mom slung over his shoulders in a fireman's carry. And behind them, hurrying across the sand toward us, Rhi and Persi, their faces starkly white.

"Wren! Goddess above, what has happened here?" Persi cried.

Rhi was downright hysterical. "Is... is that Kerridwen? Oh, Kerri, oh no, she's not... is she...?"

"She's alive," Zale said, his voice hoarse and trembling. His wide eyes were fixed on what remained of the Gray Man, his expression equal parts fascination and horror.

I felt my grip on consciousness weakening. "How did you know where to find us?" I managed to ask, my words slurring together.

"We saw the light from the lighthouse, and we knew something must be wrong. We ran straight here and we... we saw..."

"Never mind what we saw," Persi said quickly. "Or how the hell it was possible. Rhi, we have to gather the Conclave. We don't have a moment to lose."

"Why—" I tried to ask, but my voice trailed away. I was tired. So, so tired.

"Wren?" Eva reached for me, her voice full of worry.

I tried to tell her I was okay, but I couldn't, because the darkness closed over me at last, like the water, like the lightning sand, and I knew no more.

24

I dreamed of the Gray Man again.

He stood upon the beach, like a statue beneath his shell of molten lightning sand, and I stood facing him, his fingers reaching for me. I wore a white sundress, like the one I'd worn that night so many years ago, but I wasn't three-year-old me anymore. I wasn't even sure I was me at all—the hair that whipped past my face was at once brown and frizzy, like my own, now silvery blonde, now red curls twisting in the air like banners.

I was me. But I was them, too: the Vesper witches who had come before me, and the ones yet to come. And the Gray Man? He was the Darkness in one form... the form that could reach out and take a child's hand. But he, too, contained multitudes.

As I watched, the molten glass began to crack and splinter. Insects began to spill from the fissures and scurry up through the sand. The wind carried a hint of sulfur, and a whisper of a voice that was not a voice.

It's not over, Little Bird.

The glass exploded.

I woke with a start, sitting bolt upright, a cry on my lips.

I was in my bed at Lightkeep Cottage. Rosy, late afternoon sunlight filtered in through the gauzy white curtains. An indignant yowl told me that Freya resented my sudden and violent return to consciousness. She glared at me as she settled back down again, near my feet. I gathered her up, despite her wriggling, and buried my face in her fur. She tolerated it with a huff.

"Wren? Are you okay?"

I looked up to see my mother's anxious face peering around the doorframe. She had a shadow of a bruise on her left cheekbone, and a cut on her lip, but otherwise she looked fine. She was halfway across the room, expression anxious, before I could summon my voice.

"Mom! It's okay. Just a dream," I told her, in little more than a harsh croak.

She sat on the bed beside me and wrapped her arms around me, and we spent the next ten minutes in tearful, incoherent babbling: trying to ascertain if the other was okay, scolding, apologizing, and generally weeping all over each other.

When we'd finally calmed down, she sat, wiping tears and salt-stiffened strands of hair from my face, her breath still hitching occasionally, as she tried to keep the tears at bay.

"What happened on the beach... after I... how long have I been out?" I asked, the questions tumbling over each other, as my fuzzy brain tried to figure out what to ask first.

"You've been asleep for almost eighteen hours," she replied, still stroking my hair. "Rhi gave you a little something to keep the sleep restful, but she thought it might wear off soon. Are you sure you aren't hurt? I treated a few minor burns, but I couldn't ascertain any major injuries..." She bit her lip, fully in nurse mode.

"No, I... I really think I'm okay," I told her, trying to work my way back through the jumbled memories of the previous night. "But what about you? Are you—"

"Perfectly fine," she said firmly. "The effects of Bernadette's concoction were already wearing off by the time we got out of the lighthouse. And these were just from the struggle to get out." She gestured impatiently at the bruise and cut on her face.

There was a soft knock on the partly-open door, and Rhi's face appeared around it. "How's the patient?" she asked tremulously.

I summoned a smile, though it felt strange on my face. "I'm okay, thanks."

"Hungry?"

I wasn't sure if I was hungry or not, but I nodded anyway, and she entered the room with a tray heaped with food and a steaming cup of tea. She set i down on my lap. I picked up the cup of tea, more out of politeness than anything else, but the first sip felt like heaven, warming me through and clearing a little more of the fog from my head.

It was only then I noticed Persi was there, too, hovering in the doorway like she was afraid to come in. Her usually flawless makeup was smudged in shadows under her eyes, and her hair was piled in a messy bun on her head.

"So. You're alive then," she said stiffly.

"Looks like it," I said. "Sorry, it looks like you've still got an underage landlord."

She smirked. "I prefer it to the alternative."

I swallowed another mouthful of tea. "I suppose I should explain what—"

"Eva told us everything," my mom said, stepping in swiftly. "Well, everything she could. There were parts of it she couldn't explain... like what happened on the beach after you left the lighthouse. And of course, I already knew about Bernadette."

Persi made a soft growling noise in the back of her throat. "Sorry," she muttered when we all looked at her. "I just... I can't believe she fooled me like that."

"It sounds like she fooled a lot of people," Rhi said gently.

"And was fooled by them," Mom added. "Once Sarah had her in her grip, I'm not sure she had a choice anymore, but to do what she was told."

"She had a choice," I murmured. I felt three pairs of eyes on me. "She was manipulated, yeah, but she told us herself. At some point, she had to choose to serve the Darkness. And she did."

No one spoke for a moment. And then...

"And on the beach? After the lighthouse?" my mom urged.

I shook my head. "I was trying to save you... to save everyone. He wanted me. Well, not me... my magic. And I was so sure I didn't have any until..."

"Until you singlehandedly commanded the elements, and wielded them to defeat the Darkness?" Persi supplied dryly.

I managed a small smile. "Yeah. Something like that."

"Defeat is a strong word, I fear," Rhi said. I met her eye. Her face was pale and drawn. "The Darkness has been beaten back, certainly, but it is far from eradicated."

"We can worry about that another day, though, can't we?" my mom ground out between her teeth, giving Rhi a significant look.

Rhi's eyes widened, and she stammered, cheeks blushing. "Oh, right. Yes, of course, I didn't mean to... what you did was... was..."

"Remarkable," Mom finished, and I was stunned to see unmistakable pride gleaming in her eyes.

"I... I thought you'd be mad at me," I said.

"Mad at you? How could I ever be mad at you, my sweet, brave girl?" my mom asked, a glaze of tears clouding her eyes again. "If I'm mad at anyone, it's myself. I thought I could run from who we are. I knew it would catch up with us one day, and I did nothing to prepare you for it. When I think of what you must have gone through, I..."

"It's not your fault, Mom. You didn't know. Well, okay, you knew about the whole witchcraft thing, obviously, and yes, that would have been helpful; but Asteria never told you exactly what happened that night when I was little. If she had—"

"I would only have run further," Mom finished, looking sad. "I just... I couldn't bear to put you in danger, Wren. But by running from it, that's exactly what I did."

"I didn't help, though. I never told you about the Gray Man. I never told you about the dreams, or when I started seeing him again, here. So maybe, since we both screwed up, we can just forgive each other and let it go?" I suggested tentatively.

My mom's face broke into a watery smile. "I like that plan."

"And..." I thought back to every clueless, helpless moment I stumbled through until my magic spontaneously appeared. "...now that we know I've inherited the Vesper magic, I could really use some help figuring out exactly what the hell I'm doing."

Persi chuckled. "I don't know, kid. You looked like you were handling it just fine down on the beach."

"Of course, we'll help you," Rhi chimed in at once. "Your proper magic education starts today. Well, maybe tomorrow," she amended, as I stifled a huge yawn.

I smiled, but it slipped off my face almost at once as the worries began to creep back in. "What happened to Bernadette?" I asked, and though I tried not to, my eyes darted to Persi.

"She's alive," Mom said, her tone very careful.

I looked at her. "And?"

"And she's... well, we're not really sure. She's been brought back to the Manor, and the Conclave have used some very powerful enchantments to subdue her, but..."

"But?"

"But Sarah's still attached to her, somehow," Persi said, her face and voice almost expressionless. "They don't know if they'll ever be able to separate the two."

I tried to imagine the absolute horror of having another person—especially one as manipulative and dangerous as Sarah—twisted up in my body and mind forever, and shuddered. "So... what will happen to her?"

I was met with solemn faces and helpless shrugs. No one knew. Bernadette's fate was, as yet, a mystery.

"What about the Gray M—I mean, the Darkness?" I asked. "You said the Darkness isn't defeated but, to be honest, I think I knew that when we were still on the beach."

All three of the Vesper sisters' faces fell into serious lines. My mom cleared her throat. "We convened the Conclave while you were resting."

"And?" I asked eagerly when she didn't go on. "What did they say?"

"We... we will have to tread carefully. The glass formation from the beach was removed to a safe location and has been placed under as many protections as we could throw at it until it can be examined properly. It's unclear how much, if any, of the Darkness remains within it. But time and investigation will reveal that. For now, we just have to be patient... and very vigilant."

I bit my lip. I'd been hoping for a more concrete answer but, as I was beginning to learn, witchcraft was not a practice of concrete answers. Sometimes, it was a practice of no answers at all. Still, I tried for one more.

"And the Covenant?"

Rhi, Persi, and my mom exchanged a look. "We renew it tonight. As long as..."

"As long as...?" I prompted impatiently.

"Well," my mom swallowed hard, "I know you were willing to stay before all of this happened, but you might have changed your mind after... after going through such a traumatizing experience—"

Suddenly, I understood what she was hesitating about.

"Mom, it's okay. I want to stay."

"I was thinking maybe if we... wait, what?"

"Yes. I said yes."

My mom looked at me as though I'd gone temporarily insane. "Wren, I haven't even finished what I—"

"You're asking me if I still want to stay here. Permanently. The answer is yes."

My mom blinked. Persi laughed. Rhi sniffed tearfully.

"Are you... are you sure?" Mom asked.

"Yes! It's... I can't even explain it," I said, with a groan of frustration, "but from the moment we pulled up to this house, I felt... I was..."

"Home."

It was Rhi who said it, but I could practically see the word perched on my mother's lips.

"Yeah. This is where we're meant to be, Darkness or no Darkness," I said.

We all looked at each other—the four Vesper witches of Sedgwick Cove. And I knew in that moment that, whatever else we might do, and wherever else we might go, nothing within us would ever supplant that truth.

We were the First Daughters. And we were here to stay, whatever may come.

That night on the clifftop, a circle was drawn, and three Vesper witches stepped into it. They lit a fire under a cauldron, and added the elements that would spark very old magic in its belly. They spoke words of great power, words left for them by the kin who walked the shore so many years before them, tracing their very footsteps, the connection singing in their veins. And one by one, they drew a knife across their flesh, and sealed the Covenant with their blood.

The Covenant of the Three, renewed.

They weren't alone. The Conclave stood around them, the matriarchs of our magical community, overseeing the completion of this most crucial safeguard to our home, even as we all knew that it could not last. The Darkness had strengthened. He was not content to wait any longer, and we would need to be prepared to meet him in this place we called home and defend it from him.

And nearby, I sat and watched, too, perched on a rock with Zale, Nova, and

Eva beside me, all wrapped in the same, reverent silence until the circle was closed. No one outside of the Vesper witches and the Conclave had ever seen the Covenant renewed but, as Xiomara had said, we had earned the right to witness it with our own eyes.

"This renewal took a great deal more than three willing Vesper witches," she told us. "It took your sacrifice and your courage. You are as much a part of it as they are, and it is only right that you should be there, all of you."

The rest of the Conclave could not argue, even if they wanted to. They owed us too much, and they knew it. They also knew that the old traditions of keeping the Darkness at bay would need to be revisited, adapted, and changed; and that meant opening doors that had previously been closed. The Covenant was no longer a secret, and how to proceed in the days to come would be as much our generation's work, as theirs.

"Well, that's that. The Covenant of the Three, renewed," Eva sighed, as we watched the circle close. "It's not like how I thought it would be."

I turned to her. "What do you mean?"

She shrugged. "I thought I'd feel safer. Like it was all over. Instead I feel like..."

"Like this is the calm before the storm?" Zale suggested.

Eva smiled grimly. "Well put, MacDowell."

"I know what you mean," I said, watching the last remnants of smoke rise from the circle, as the flames under the cauldron were doused. "I want to be excited to learn magic and become a real witch, but all I can wonder is if I'll learn enough for the next time I have to face him."

"Yeah, because you sucked so badly at it this last time," Nova said, rolling her eyes. She caught my eye, though, and smirked just a little.

"That was seriously one of the sickest things I've ever seen," Zale agreed, nodding.

"Yeah, I don't think you need to worry about having enough magical ability," Eva said, laughing. "Although, you may need to worry about having too much."

I tried to return the laugh but could only manage a smile. "I didn't know what I was doing. I don't even think I was in control of it. It... it scared me."

Eva patted my shoulder. "Raw magic can be scary—ask any witch, they'll tell you. But knowledge and control will come. It's what we all have to learn. You'll be okay, Vesper."

I nodded, trying to believe her.

The adults started moving away from the clifftop, wending their way down toward the rocks, where we sat.

"Well, that's it, I guess," Nova sighed. "Another generation of Claires playing with fire and Vespers putting it out. What a legacy."

I turned to her. "That's not the legacy. Not anymore."

"Look, you don't have to be nice about—"

"One Claire made a mistake last night, that's true, but another Claire braved the Darkness itself to fix it. I couldn't have done any of this without you. As far as I'm concerned, there are no Second or First Daughters anymore. It doesn't matter who came first or whose blood protects this place. All that matters now is who stands and fights for it. And in that, the Claires and the Vespers stand together."

"Don't forget the MacDowells and the Marins, too!" Zale added.

Nova's face twisted as she tried to fight a smile and welling tears at the same time. She compromised by rolling her eyes instead. "That was like... *super* cheesy, Vesper."

I smiled. I couldn't tell if Nova and I were friends yet, but we were allies, at least. And that was a place to start.

The adults reached us then, and we said our goodbyes.

"It's done," Ostara said solemnly. "Now the more daunting task lies ahead. The Darkness wielded more power and influence than we thought possible, especially while bound. We are facing unknown dangers in the coming days."

"Oh for goddess's sake, Ostara, save the doom and gloom for tomorrow, at least," Lydian barked from her mobility scooter.

"Tonight's feat was not lightly accomplished," Xiomara added, nodding. "Let us honor it, and let it be enough."

Ostara paused before nodding, reluctantly. "Very well. For now."

We lingered a few minutes more under the stars, saying goodbyes.

"Are you sure you don't want to come hang out?" Eva asked. "Xiomara's going to cook."

I shook my head. "Thanks, but not tonight. I think I'm going to head home instead."

"Of course," Eva said. "We'll see you around."

"Yeah, you will," I said, and the thought made me feel lighter. "What do you guys do around here during vacation, anyway?"

"Oh, the usual," Eva said with a casual shrug. "Seances, summoning demons. Summer shit, you know." And with one last laugh, she turned with a wave, and followed the others back toward town.

Only Persi, Rhi, Mom, and I remained. Rhi had the cauldron clasped in her arms, wrapped in a quilt to protect her from the heat.

"I asked you if you had a cauldron, and you said no," I accused her.

"I didn't say no. I said it was in the closet next to my broomstick," Rhi said, winking. "And if you'd looked in the closet, that's exactly where you would have found it."

"Can we get going?" Persi asked. "The summer solstice is only a few days away, and I haven't even finished my outfit."

"What happens on the summer solstice?" I asked.

Persi grinned. "You'll see," she said, and she turned to head down the path, dark hair swinging.

I reached for my mom's hand. "Ready?" I asked.

"Ready," she said. A single word, heavy with meaning. But shared between us, the burden was lighter.

There was a light burning in the window of Lightkeep Cottage, guiding our steps like the lighthouse guides ships, toward the safety of the Cove.

We followed it home.

ABOUT THE AUTHOR

E.E. Holmes is a writer, teacher, and actor living in central Massachusetts with her husband, two children, and a small, but surprisingly loud, dog. When not writing, she enjoys performing, watching unhealthy amounts of British television, and reading with her children.

To learn more about E.E. Holmes and *The World of the Gateway*, please visit www.eeholmes.com

Printed in Great Britain
by Amazon

30561696R00155